"*Cascade Failure* is an emotional and fun ride that you won't want to end. I loved this book!"

> —Mur Lafferty, author and Hugo Award–winning
> podcaster of *Escape Pod*

"With *Cascade Failure,* L. M. Sagas brings to life a gritty, grippy, space adventure with the big-time stakes of *The Expanse,* the engaging family dynamics of Becky Chambers, and the sweet, tangy snark of Murderbot."

> —Chris Panatier, author of *Stringers*

"*Cascade Failure*? More like *Cascade* EPIC WIN. Fast-paced, heartfelt SF goodness. Sagas's debut will keep you grinning from first page to last!"

> —Jason M. Hough, *New York Times*
> bestselling author of *Instinct*

"Fans of *Firefly* and Lois McMaster Bujold's brilliant Vorkosigan series, *Cascade Failure* by L. M. Sagas has you covered. A ragtag crew full of grit, genius, and quirks with weary hearts of gold, finding the mission of their lives in a ship like no other. I loved everything about this book, including stunningly original world-building that ranks among the best I've ever read. Get this one. You'll thank me."

> —Julie E. Czerneda, award-winning
> author of *To Each This World*

"Gear up, strap in, and hold on. Fast, brash, and wickedly fun, *Cascade Failure* is 100-proof space juice injected straight into your veins."

> —Dayton Ward, author of *Star Trek: Coda*

L. M. SAGAS

CASCADE FAILURE

AN
AMBIT'S RUN
NOVEL

TOR

TOR PUBLISHING GROUP
NEW YORK

CASCADE FAILURE

A Tor Book
Published by Tom Doherty Associates / Tor Publishing Group
120 Broadway
New York, NY 10271

www.tor-forge.com

Tor® is a registered trademark of Macmillan Publishing Group, LLC.

The Library of Congress Cataloging-in-Publication Data
is available upon request.

ISBN 978-1-250-87125-1 (trade paperback)
ISBN 978-1-250-87126-8 (ebook)

Our books may be purchased in bulk for promotional, educational, or business use. Please contact your local bookseller or the Macmillan Corporate and Premium Sales Department at 1-800-221-7945, extension 5442, or by email at MacmillanSpecialMarkets@macmillan.com.

First Edition: 2024

Printed in the United States of America

0 9 8 7 6 5 4 3 2 1

To all of you.
May you always have something to run toward,
and good people to run beside you.

CASCADE FAILURE

CHAPTER ONE

JAL

Somewhere in Jal's file was a note from an old crewmate that read, *Jalsen Red will either be the reason you die, or the reason you live. Good fucking luck.*

With a love letter like that on his record, he should've figured pretty quick that his Guild career was on the fast track to nowhere. Would've saved a lot of folks a lot of grief, but Jal just wasn't made to be a thinker. Wasn't in his DNA.

They'd seen to that.

Just as well. If he thought too much about what he was doing, he'd just as likely turn back the way he came; hop that rickety old shuttle back to the ass-end of the O-Cyg spiral, away from the hustle and bustle of the outpost. That was what a thinking sort of man would've done.

Jal ducked his head and kept walking, glancing around the hangar through a dirt-brown mess of shaggy hair that had gone too many days without a washing. Must've been a dozen ships there—rows of shiny hulls and top-of-the-line gear, idling on docks suspended fifty-some-odd decs above an airlock. He paused by the rail to look down as one of the doors lurched apart with the groan of well-used metal, coughing up another shuttle with the Trust's big, embellished *T* stamped on each side, up top, and just about everywhere else they could stick it. Shit, probably would've stamped it inside the plumbing, if they thought anybody'd ever see it. It was all about the *brand*. The Trust was the centuries-old answer to what always seemed to

Jal to be a pretty stupid question: What would happen if we let a bunch of big-money business types go out and settle space? No governments, no oversight, just carte-goddamn-blanche to claim and build and grow as they pleased. A handful of corporations spreading like fungus in the black, swallowing each other and anything smaller than them, until *everything* was smaller than them. As long as Jal'd been alive, they'd been the only game in town.

Newcomers, he thought. Only ships coming out of the center of the spiral ever looked that nice. The ones headed outward, deeper into the frontier circles, had taken a few more knocks in their time, carting prospectors and workers out to make their fortune in the next cluster of newly terraformed planets. He tipped his head in a half-assed salute and pushed off the rail. *Best of luck to you.* God willing, they'd find better luck out there than he had.

Back into the crowd. He'd have to get used to that again— all the *people.* Merchants and mechanics hawking their wares, pushing their carts down gangways barely wider than Jal's arm span. Crews out stretching their legs before their next trip. It didn't matter how much he tucked his shoulders and hugged the rails; he still got bumped into and jostled and mean-mugged for his trouble. Halogen lights burned above like hundreds of white dwarfs, stinging his eyes through the shaded lenses of his specs. So bright, and so busy, and so blaring, and if he let himself focus on all of it, get drawn into the sights and sounds and scents of being surrounded by so many strangers in a strange new place, he'd forget how to breathe.

But.

He'd come this far, gotten this close. Closer to the center of the spiral, closer to civilization, closer to home. He could keep going a little while longer, to hell with the rest. Head down, keep moving—he was good at that.

Down the gangway a few rows, he spotted a ship with its

cargo bay door down, engines running. *Contestant number one.* Running engines meant they'd just gotten in, or they were just leaving, and judging by the couple of guys slow-walking their way back up the ramp, he leaned toward the latter. "You got need of an extra hand?" he said under his breath. He'd practiced it so many times on the shuttle ride in that he'd lost count, but hadn't yet had occasion for an audience. Shuttle rides to the outpost were cheap—handful of caps would cover the fare, though a meal and legroom would cost you extra— but heading any farther inward was a pocket-emptying sort of enterprise, and Jal's pockets had nothing but lint. Leave rich or stay poor: those were the options, out in the frontier. The last one just never seemed to make it into the ads.

His gut was in a weaver's knot as he came up on the ship, mouth gone dry and sour. "You got need of an extra hand?" he croaked out again, voice breaking in the middle. Yeah, fine, he was rusty. Hadn't said much to another person in years that wasn't *yessir* and *no sir* and *fuck you, sir.* Although *'scuse me* was making its way back into his vocabulary with gusto. "You got need—"

A flash of gray paint above the wing of the ship stopped him in his tracks. Too abruptly, it turned out, because a slip of a woman in coveralls bounced off his back with a curse so colorful he might've laughed under different circumstances. Instead, he barely managed to rasp out one of those "'scuse me"s as she strode on past, light glinting off the fine polymer filaments woven into her dark braids. An augmented? You didn't see a lot of Biomech out this far. He couldn't have stopped and asked her anyway. She was too far down the gangway, for one; and for two, that weaver's knot seemed to have lodged itself in his throat.

A flag. Just a stupid painted flag, gray against the hull's sleek silver and emblazoned with a spiral of white stars, but Jal's heart still stumbled over the next few beats. It was the banner for the Guild—two parts paramilitary, one part gig economy. Thousands of different crews in thousands of different ships taking thousands of different jobs from the Guild-sanctioned postings, all bound up together with a simple guiding principle: the neutral preservation of life. Felt like a lifetime since he'd worn that flag on his shoulder. He'd have happily gone another lifetime without seeing it again.

Shit. He cut left, angling away from the Guild ship and down the gangway. Had they seen him? He didn't risk a glance back, cutting his way through the crowd as quick as he could without drawing attention.

"Refurbed cables!" barked a merchant from a cart piled high with coils of wire. Which, Jal had learned, was just a fancy way of saying *stolen.* Lifted from ships when nobody was looking, identifiers buffed off and cleaned up so nobody'd know them from the rest of the pile. "Half the price, just as nice!"

The woman he'd bumped into, the augmented in the coveralls, picked over the stacks of cables with a disinterested eye. Not really shopping, just killing time—waiting for somebody, maybe, and she didn't even look at Jal as he slipped past.

Not you, either, he thought, passing a shiny-hulled shipping vessel with its cargo door dropped. No Guild flag in sight, but she was loaded to the gills, and a pair of merchants squabbled on the dock over who saw her first, so they must've seen some serious scratch from whoever that ship belonged to. Only folks out there with capital like that were with the Trust, and he'd just as soon avoid them, too.

He passed a few more like that, ducking between carts and crews with his hands in his pockets and his duffel on his shoulder, trying not to squint at the sting of the lights. His specs, like the rest of him, had seen better days: scratched lenses, thinning tint, and a strap hanging on by about four threads and a prayer. Not a lot of opportunities to fix them up, where he'd been.

"You got need of an extra hand?" he repeated to himself.

It'd turned into a mantra, of sorts. A meditation. *Keep your eyes on the next foothold,* his mama used to tell him. *The rest is just noise.*

There was just so much of it, though. The *noise*. He used to love crowds—the snatches of conversations, the new faces. Windows into the lives of total strangers that made the universe feel big and small at the same time.

Now, though, the busyness of the hangar chafed at him. Made his head ache and his teeth grind, and as he passed the next shipping rig in the line, there was that fucking flag again. Half the crew stood outside it, staring straight at the walkway. *No way they miss me.* But if he stopped, doubled back, he could draw their attention, and he'd just be headed straight back to the other Guild ship. *Do something.* He was running out of time. Another dozen steps, and he'd be in front of them. *Do something.*

And then, out of the corner of his eye, he saw it. *There.* The noise faded, and for a blissful half second, all he heard was the soft pneumatic hiss of a dropping cargo bay door.

A smile kissed the corner of his chapped, chewed-raw lips. In a hangar full of sparkling *new*ness, the old gyreskimmer perched in the next slip was like a glimpse back through time. They'd been decommissioned back when Jal was still picking up rocks on his home moon, but somehow, this one had dodged the scrap fields and made her way clear out to the pioneer rings. *Bet you've got some stories to tell.* And best of all, he reckoned none of them involved the Guild.

GS 31-770 Ambit was the only designation on the hull, painted and repainted above one wing. No flag, no shine, no slick-tongued merchants with the gleam of caps in their eyes. Not the prettiest thing to look at—the kind of *classic* that was only three rusted bolts away from *scrap,* with mismatched parts and a half-dozen layers of paint showing through nicks and scratches—but somebody'd taken care of her where it mattered. Sleek-cut lines like a phosphomoth midflight and engine thrumming so steady and smooth it could've been a lullaby. Old or not, that ship was likely as fit to glide through the black as any craft in that hangar.

Which did fuck-all to loosen his shoulders as he peeked through the open cargo door. No movement inside, at least none that he could make out, and eyes like his didn't miss much. *We really doing this?* The duffel on his shoulder said *yes*, but the weight on his chest said *on second thought, twenty-eight's awful old for leaps of faith*. He'd never been too keen on ship living, as a matter of principle *and* proportion—they didn't tend to build deckheads with heights like his in mind—but he couldn't even look inside of one lately without his intestines twisting themselves up like bootlaces.

Just didn't seem like he had another choice.

Least this coffin's got character, he thought, and with a sigh in his throat and a shudder threatening the top of his spine, Jal started up the ramp.

Tall son of a bitch that he was, squeezing into the close quarters of a ship had never been easy, but this one felt tighter than most. Low-slung wires dragged across the top of his head as he ducked into a cargo bay so short he could nearly flatten his palms against the ceiling, and barely wide enough for a rover and a couple weeks' worth of supply crates. Not a long trip, then. Good. He hoped they were headed the right direction.

"'Scuse me," he called as he moved deeper into the bay, fingers skimming along the top of the rover, but he didn't get an answer. Didn't seem likely the whole crew would disembark without locking their ship up nice and tight, especially in the frontier, but there had to be some reason the door had dropped. He didn't hear anyone moving around inside, so he cleared his throat and tried again. "Excuse me?"

A sudden, familiar hiss sounded behind him, and he turned in time to watch the hatch rise. Moved too quick for him to beat it, but just slow enough for Jal to think, *Well, that can't be good,* before the last sliver of light from the hangar shrank from view.

There was a certain kind of finality in the click of the locks and the ear-popping pressure of a new atmo system kicking on, as if to say, *You're stuck now, boy.*

"Out-fucking-standing." He kicked the door, once, steel-toed boots against a metal much, much harder. She was built solid, that old ship, and for want of a code for that door panel, he figured he wasn't getting out the way he came in.

The rest is just noise. His pulse pattered on the back of his tongue, sweat gathering under the layered collars of his ratty button-up and *refurbed* blue coat. He straightened his back and turned away from the hatch, eyes on an open doorway on the other side of the cargo bay. Either he'd find a way out, or he'd find whoever crewed the ship—whichever way, it'd serve him better than standing there, beating on a three-dec-deep hunk of metal and screaming himself blue.

Nice folks, nice folks, nice folks. A new mantra, fingers crossed at his sides because you never regretted the luck you didn't need. *Please be nice folks.* They kept a homy ship, at least—much homier on the inside than the outside. He passed the makeshift gym tucked into the corner of the cargo bay, with a punching bag and weights all packed up nice and tight in case the gravity got shifty. A toolbox sat against the wall, wrenches nestled side by side with bags of dried fruits and wafers in case whoever was working got peckish, and Jal's stomach gave an impatient snarl to remind him it'd been nearly a day since anything'd passed his lips but water. Colorful little hand-knit creatures watched him from the top of the box with seed bead eyes as he ducked through the doorway and into a narrow hall.

Somebody'd painted the walls. Not the plain old white or beige or gray the manufacturers usually slapped on the walls to hide the metal underneath—this was some kind of soft blue, or maybe lavender? He was shit with colors, and his specs didn't help. Everything looked a little greener through the tint.

"Hello?" He peeked into an open door to his right. Sick bay was his guess, less from the bed and sparse setup of equipment, and more from the sharp stink of antiseptic. An alcove sat opposite the sick bay, with an open porthole and a ladder plunging down into the belly of the ship, but he didn't hear anything coming from below, so he walked past. Between hanging planters and covered bulbs, loose string tapestries hung on the walls. He'd never seen anything quite like them, some woven together in patterns too abstract to guess and some streaked with phosphorous strands that glowed against the rest. The glowing ones reminded him of the augmented's hair, pops of bright against the dark. He fought the urge to touch them, to wind them around his fingers, but nothing ever felt as soft as it looked.

Ahead, the hallway forked around one more room, and Jal knew before he even looked inside that it was the galley—a spartan kitchen setup on the near left wall, shelves stacked along the others. He probably could've spat from one doorway, cleared the four-top in the middle of the room, and hit the door on the other side. Small but lived-in; ship had a theme, and—fuck, were those apples on the shelf? He couldn't remember the last time he'd had fruit that didn't come out of a sealed foil pack.

His mouth watered, and the low-grade headache he'd been ignoring gave a quick spike behind his eyes. *Fasting* was right up there with *thinking* on the list of things he wasn't designed for, and it took every ounce of his self-control not to swipe himself some breakfast. Dinner? Hard to keep track of time with all the traveling. Hard to keep track of much of anything.

He was halfway through the galley when something darted out from the shelves. Dark and small—barely shin height—and so quick he couldn't make out what it was as it streaked past his legs. Some kind of animal, maybe? Startled the shit out of him, whatever it was. He stumbled back and nearly knocked a potted plant off the middle of the table, peering off in the direction the blur had darted. Toward the bridge, he thought, if he hadn't gotten turned around, but a dividing wall blocked the view from the galley. On his side of the wall, somebody'd put up a glass board, and what looked like years' worth of paint pen marks had been scribbled, erased, and scribbled over again. Little notes like *add nori to req list* and *fed bodie this morning, the asshole is lying,* and in a different hand, *NO SPARE PARTS IN THE GALLEY.* He paused over the last line, angling his head. The straight, heavy lines looked vaguely familiar; he nearly read them in a different voice. Gruffer, to-the-point, like—

"Something I can help you with?"

Jal jumped again, like a flea on a hot plate. Twice in as many minutes. *The fuck is up with this ship?* People didn't *sneak up* on Jal. People were noisy, even when they tried to be quiet— sometimes *especially* when they tried to be quiet. They also smelled. Good or bad, they always smelled, and he'd never in his life been in the room with another human being and not known it.

And yet.

A whole-ass person stood in the doorway of the galley, so close he could've reached out and touched them if he hadn't been too busy backing into the glass panel. *First time for everything.* Wry was better than panicky, but his muscles had already tensed to bolt.

The stranger smiled pleasantly enough, standing in the doorway like they'd been there the whole time. Close-cropped hair and proud shoulders, round features shaped in a patient smile. Their clothes flowed like water over their skin, silken robes in fluorite shades of blues and greens and purples that somehow looked vibrant even through Jal's specs. For a beat, all he could think about was the way their skin caught the lights, like a clear night's sky dusted with stars, but even that wasn't right.

Didn't do them justice. Theirs was the kind of beautiful that words didn't quite grasp—not the kinds of words Jal knew, at least. His world hadn't had much use for poetry. Or for pretty things.

For lack of anything better to say, he swallowed hard and asked, "You got need of an extra hand?" *Do better.* He'd practiced this. "I'm a good worker." That part was true. "Don't bring any trouble with me." That part wasn't. "All I need's a meal a day and passage to your next stop, wherever it is." Long as it was closer to the interior, it didn't much matter to him.

The stranger arched an eyebrow, still smiling that inscrutable smile. "Who couldn't use a bit more help every now and again?" Their voice, a clear middle tone as pleasant as their smile, somehow seemed to be coming from everywhere. Above him. Behind him. "But I think we could do better than a meal a day, Mister . . ." they trailed off, expectantly.

"Tegan," he said. He'd practiced that, too. *My name's Tegan. Call me Tegan. Tegan, Tegan, Tegan.*

The stranger's nose gave the faintest wrinkle, but it disappeared so quickly Jal thought he might've imagined it. "Welcome aboard," they said. "I'm Captain Eoan." *Oh-ahn,* deliberately, like they didn't expect people to get it right.

I know that name. He couldn't remember where he'd heard it, but he swore he knew it. *Why do I know that name?* Something felt strange about that ship. Something was *wrong.*

Eoan extended a hand from the trim of their flowing robes, and Jal, too flustered to do anything else, reached out to shake it. Or try to, at least. His fingers passed straight through. Static pricked his palm, charged particles suspended where skin and bone should've been. No heat, no cold, just a current that stood the hairs on his arm on end.

Eoan's dark eyes laughed. "Figure it out?" they asked, and once again, it sounded like they'd had this conversation a time or two.

It was another first for Jal, but though he never claimed to be the sharpest pick in the mine, he liked to think he wasn't the dullest, either. "You're AI."

"Less of the *A*, if you don't mind," Eoan replied, still smiling. "You of all people ought to know that being *engineered* and being *authentic* aren't mutually exclusive."

A chill washed down the back of his neck, sinking between the blades of his shoulders like a cold rain. "Me of all people," he echoed past the tightness in his throat. "All due respect, Captain, you don't know me."

"I suppose that's true," they said, thoughtfully, and damned if Jal couldn't hear the *but* coming before their lips ever shaped the word. "But I know your name isn't Tegan. And I know that you look *very* different from your enlistment photo. Gone a bit long in the hair, haven't we, Ranger Jalsen?"

They held out their hand, and his face—his *enlistment photo*—appeared above their palm. It was like looking at a stranger, or maybe at a ghost. At the base of the photo, around his shoulders, scrolled a bright orange banner.

DESERTED

Jal's mouth went dry, fingertips tingling as his blood started pumping to more useful places. Heart. Lungs. Legs. *You're wrong*, he wanted to say. *You've got me confused with somebody else.* But he couldn't find the words, or the air to speak them. *They know. It was a trap. They saw me, and they opened the door, and they fucking know.* Except knowing was only half the problem; it was *how* they could've known. Scanned his face or ran his prints, that part wasn't too tricky. But to match them to his enlistment record? The only folks who had access to Guild records were—

No.

"Captain Eoan." It sounded like someone else speaking, someone far away and muffled by the roar of blood in his ears. He *had* recognized that name, though it felt like a lifetime ago that he'd seen it on his transfer request form, right next to that damning red *DENIED*. "*Guild* Captain Eoan."

"The one and only, as far as I'm aware."

His lungs wouldn't expand in his chest, heart beating against his ribs so hard it ached. Jal glanced down the hallway. Fewer doors meant fewer chances for Eoan to block him in; he could make a break for it. *Run,* he thought. *Fucking run.* Because the way he saw it, the only way out of the minefield he'd strolled into was his own two legs and a hell of a lot of distance. He'd deal with the door when he got there. Somehow.

"Please, don't," said Eoan, as if they knew.

Too late. He was already halfway down the hallway, banking off the corner where the hall curved around the mess. His boot treads were long gone, but the floor's diamond texture kept his feet under him as he sped toward the cargo bay.

Eoan flickered into place a few decs down the hall from him. "Please, Ranger Jalsen. There's really no reason—" That projection blinked out as Jal ran through it, and another one blinked into place by the sickroom door. "—to leave in such a rush. If we—" Past another one, and the next appeared in the doorway to the cargo bay, expression flat. "—could only take a moment to discuss, I'm sure we could get it all sorted—"

Jal had just hit the end of the hall when that telltale pneumatic hiss from the hatch echoed through the cargo bay. A blade of blue-white light appeared as the door opened, casting shapes across the crates. People-shaped blurs approached up the gangway, and Jal skidded to a halt by the rover with a sick lurch in his stomach.

"There you are," Eoan said from all around him. He didn't see their projection anymore, but he was too busy watching the door. The blurs became people again as his eyes adjusted to the brightness, and damned if it wasn't the woman from the gangway again, with the grease-smudged coveralls and raven plaits.

She wasn't alone. Beside her stood a man, easily as tall as

Jal but built much sturdier. Silver streaked his short hair and beard, though his forties were still a few years ahead of him, and his shoulders were the kind of wide that made you think they'd borne their share of burdens and then some.

Jal could tell the moment they saw him. The woman cocked her head with the most *fuck you, fuck this, fuck're you doing here* look he'd ever seen, and the man—

CRACK!

The crate the man had been holding had dropped from his hands, old wood splintering on impact and contents scattering like confetti across the floor. Potatoes. Carrots. Every-color citrus, and produce Jal didn't even recognize. A head of something leafy came rolling toward him, bouncing off the tip of his boot as the rest of the cargo bay stood still.

"You." Jal *knew* that voice, hoarse as it was. Knew it like he'd known the handwriting on the wall, like he knew the green-brown eyes gone wide under furrowed brows, like he knew the calluses on the hands stretched out like they still had something to hold.

Huh, he thought, errantly, with a fist squeezing around his quick-beating heart. *You got gray, old man.*

Then he ran. Sprang forward, launching himself up the hood of the rover, vaulting across its roof, and sliding down off the back square between the two newcomers. *It's not him,* whispered a desperate little voice from the depths of his head, struggling up from under a wave of *run, run, run* that threatened to drag it under. *It can't be him.*

Out onto the too-bright gangway. Tears stung his eyes, white stars bursting across all those shiny hulls and strangers with someplace else to go.

"Stop!" That voice again. Damn that voice. It wasn't supposed to be there. How the *fuck* could it be there? And on and on went those frantic little whispers in his head, *not him, not him, not him.* "Goddamn it, Jal!"

His name. Of all the stupid things that could've damned him, it was the sound of his own name in that grit-and-gunshot voice that did it. He stumbled on his next step—runners like him didn't stumble, didn't slow, didn't stop, but he *did*. His outsoles caught on thin air a few decs down the gangway, that fist around his heart clamping down until he swore his pulse stopped dead. His *name*, punctuated by the crack of charged air, was Jal's only warning.

The last thing Jal felt before the world dropped out from under him was a slug between his shoulders and the most terrible sense of déjà vu.

CHAPTER TWO

EOAN

It was a beautiful thing, flying. Eoan had thought as much since they'd first come to understand what *beautiful* was, back when humanity was taking its first fledgling steps toward a life among the stars.

Eoan had been simpler then—nascent strands of programming with precious little grasp of the world. It had taken time for them to understand, but then, they'd been born with time to spare. Lifetimes, generations, *centuries*, and a single guiding directive at the very foundation of their code: *learn*. Learn and discover and explore, absorb everything their infinitesimal slice of the universe could offer, and then go searching for more.

So, they'd searched, and they'd studied, and they'd *learned*, and eventually, that search brought them here, to the frontier of the Orion-Cygnus arm, where humans' grasping fingers stretched and clawed for that taste of something more.

Eoan used to think they had that in common with humans— that hunger for answers. They'd counted it among the things that made them *feel* human, like grasping the beauty of flight and all the intricacies of the human experience they'd taught themself along the way. Mannerisms. Speech. Those curious, complex neurophysiological shifts humans called *feelings*.

They knew better now. That innate yearning to understand . . . it didn't connect Eoan to humans; it isolated them. Humans craved discovery, as Eoan did, but to humans it was a means to an end. Power. Renown. Peace in knowing their place in the cosmos. Humans learned so that they could better fulfill a greater purpose.

For Eoan, knowledge had no greater purpose; it *was* the greater purpose. They learned for the sake of learning, not just because they'd been programmed to do it, but because *learning* was the only thing they'd ever had that they hadn't lost. It persisted, as they did, through the centuries. Always more questions to ask, always more answers to seek, so they asked them, and they sought them, to the exclusion—or, at least, the subordination—of everything else. What choice did they have, when nothing else could *last*?

That, they'd come to realize, was the insurmountable line between them and humans: humans had the power to choose for themselves, with whatever faults or freedoms that entailed.

As for Eoan, they kept searching. They'd joined the Guild, because nobody roamed the spiral like the rangers did; and when the rangers hadn't roamed far enough, when that curiosity had driven Eoan farther than their captain, their crew, their *friends* had wanted to go, they'd become their own captain. Their own crew. Their own friend. They'd risked isolation for their chance to go farther, and sometimes they still couldn't believe their luck to have found two mad, brilliant humans willing to go farther *with* them. To *stay*. Even as Eoan pushed them deeper into the frontier, because where better to learn than the edge of the unknown. Even as Eoan took the strange jobs, the dangerous jobs, because they offered a taste of something *new*. Even as Eoan poked and prodded with their harmless little experiments, because no matter how long Eoan had spent among them, humans still held a few mysteries of their own. Even through all of that, Saint and Nash had stayed.

Eoan only hoped Saint would be as forgiving of this latest experiment. Luring the deserter, Jalsen, onto the ship . . . it went a bit further than Eoan's usual *playing the same song at dinner to see what Pavlov was on about*; or *switching Saint's coffee with decaf to measure the placebo effects of his morning cup.* There was history here, and a chance to do real harm if handled incorrectly.

They'd tried to give everyone a chance to cool off first. Based on previous observations, Saint's emotional state required an average of forty-three minutes to return to baseline after an *agitating* incident. Eoan had given it an extra quarter hour, just to be safe, and time was officially up.

With a pang of reluctance, they drew themself back from their beloved wings—fingers curling into a fist, roots shrinking back into the seed, tedious and small—and settled their attention into the bridge.

"Saint," they said through the comms outside his quarters. They never listened beyond closed doors; the Guild was very particular about its onboard privacy protocols, and absent extreme exigencies, audio and video feeds were restricted for any occupied, nonpublic areas aboard. Nevertheless, the comms in the bridge still picked up faint, thoughtful refrains of guitar from inside. "May I come in?"

"If you like." Saint's answer came without a break in the melody.

With anyone else, Eoan might've gone to the trouble of projecting outside the door and walking in. Put people at ease, going through the motions like that. But Saint had never asked it of them—preferred honesty to comfort, their XO, for better or worse—and eventually, they'd stopped. Popped straight inside, instead, and Saint hardly looked up from the frets of his old guitar as Eoan's projection settled into the armchair in the corner.

"You're unhappy," they observed. Deeper-than-usual furrow between his brows, lines at the corners of his mouth where he'd been frowning—all the usual suspects. More than anything, though, the guitar betrayed him. He'd chosen a somber key, something soft in D minor, and Saint's fingers picked an idle, meandering path along the strings. He'd posted up on his bed, back propped against the shelves built into the wall beside it. They liked Saint's room. Warm colors and simple comforts, always just enough odds and ends dusted around to make it feel lived-in and settled. "That's him, then?"

"Was that actually a question?"

"If it needed to be."

Saint's fret hand shifted, and the melody changed. Deeper tones, thoughtful and slow. "That's him," he said, after a few more plucks of the strings. Two words, but they contained volumes; a tangled history only half-told in records and reports. "But that's not really what you're asking."

"Isn't it?"

"We were chasing his ass for a year after that AWOL notice went out." Saint snorted. "If you didn't know who he was before he set foot on this boat, I'll eat my damn boot."

Eoan leaned back in the armchair, crossing one leg over the other. Theater, mostly. A puppet show of particles and light, but they liked it nevertheless. It made them feel *present,* in a way they rarely did otherwise. "Maybe," they admitted.

"Coy's really not your color, Cap."

"Everything's my color, dearest." A flick of their wrist, and shades of cerise and gold rippled down their robe. He was right, though; they weren't very good at *indirect.* "I'm sorry," they said, after a moment.

"For?"

"You didn't want to shoot him."

He gave a one-sided shrug. "Had to be done. He'd have gotten away. *Again,*" he added, so low it may well have been a growl.

"Of course." They cocked their head. "Does that make it easier?"

Saint narrowed his eyes. "Sometimes, I'm not sure if you ask questions to get an answer or to make a point."

Now *they* shrugged, waving a well-manicured hand. They never really changed, Eoan's hands. Not like the rest of them—

their hair, their clothes, the color of their eyes. Those things, Eoan changed by the day; sometimes, by the minute. Humans carried so many stories in their hands, though. Fights won and lost, etched in the nicks across Saint's knuckles. A hard day's work, inked in ever-present smudges of grease under Nash's nails. They seemed important, those stories—*personal*, in a way it felt wrong to mimic, so Eoan didn't. Instead, they kept their hands impeccable; they liked to think that told a story of their own. "You have your mysteries, I have mine. You just happened to shoot yours in the back."

"Thanks for that."

They offered him a smile, gentle and a shade apologetic. "You'll be all right." It was one of the great constants of the cosmos: water was life, time was relative, and Saint was *always* all right. "Still. Is it really such a surprise, finding him out here?"

It was a great big galaxy, with a great many ships passing through it. Even Guild ships numbered in the hundreds; so much ground to cover, keeping the peace in the gray areas of a grand, imperfect system. The Trust was the law in more places than not, developing and managing colonies from Mars to the frontier planets. A conglomerate of labor associations—it had an impressively long-winded name, but most simply called it the Union—kept an almost exclusive check on Trust power, leveraging its size and singular hold on trade labor in the O-Cyg spiral to keep the Trust, if not honest, then at the very least *restrained*. Consistent. Regulated. But protecting people's livelihoods was a far sight different from protecting their *lives*. The Guild stepped in to fill that gap, and as the universe expanded from one star to the next, that gap had gotten awfully bloody large.

Nevertheless, big galaxy or not, the Aron Outpost was the only stop-off on the way to and from the frontier circles. "If our intrepid young deserter ever wanted to see home again, he'd have had to pass through here eventually," they said. Given that the *Ambit* was in and out of those docks every couple of weeks, it wasn't so difficult to imagine their paths would cross. "Just a bit of luck, I suppose."

"And a bit of meddling," Saint replied, flatly.

"I'm sure I have no idea what you're talking about."

"Uh-huh." Was it possible for a guitar strum to sound sarcastic? Saint truly was a master of his craft. "Like you didn't roll out the carpet for him."

"I only opened the door; he's the one who walked through it."

Saint sighed. "He always had an affinity for busted-up old things," he said, with a middle-distance look in his eye. Nostalgia? It wasn't often he gave over to that sort of thing, at least not where others could see it. "You didn't have to let him in."

"You didn't have to shoot him in the back." Eoan found an imaginary speck of dust under one of their nails. "But that's none of my business."

Saint flashed a dry smile. "Go with that instinct."

Chuckling, Eoan started to reply, but motion in the hallway caught their attention. "Ah. Incoming."

Saint's heart rate ticked up a beat on Eoan's sensors. "Angry Nash or Weepy Nash?"

"*Is* there a Weepy Nash?" Eoan replied.

"Point taken." With a sigh and a frown, Saint set his guitar aside and stood. Those first few steps always looked a bit stiff when he'd been sitting a while, but he'd never slow down to let things adjust. Instead, a slight limp carried him across the room to the door, just in time for a hard, metallic rapping. He glanced back at Eoan. "Hammer?"

They checked the camera feeds outside Saint's room. "Wrench."

"God bless." And with the understated wisdom of a man who'd taken a hand tool or two to the face, Saint waited for a break in the knocking to open his door.

Nash waited on the other side, though *waiting* implied *patience,* which she typically reserved for tricky knitting patterns and ornery machines. Olive-toned cheeks flushed with irritation, flyaway hairs curling away from the strands of her augmentations. A study in opposites, their Natsuki—Nash, for the fortunate few who called her a friend. Grease-smudged coveralls and immaculate boots. Practiced scowl and the beginnings of smile lines around her eyes and mouth. A whole head shorter than Saint, and the presence to fill up a room. She brandished her ratchet wrench like a weapon, paused mid-swing in front of her chest.

Saint eyed the wrench. "You planning to use that, or did you just want to put a few more dents in my door?"

"I'd like to put a few more dents in you," Nash said. "But it'd be my ass fixing them, so I'll pass. See this?" She gestured at her scowling face. "This is called *self-control.* You should try it, next time your trigger finger gets itchy."

The quirk of Saint's lips might've been amusement, but it pulled a little tight at the corners. *Uneasy.* After all their years together, they liked to think they could read him.

"I take it the patient's going to pull through," he said.

"Nope. Congratulations, you shot and killed a harmless vagabond as he peaceably fled our ship. They should give you a medal."

"Nash," Eoan chided. "Let's play nice."

"Tell that to Shooty McBlastinshit over here," Nash fired back. She gave a nifty twirl of her wrench and rolled her eyes. "He's fine. Nice little welt from the riot round, and he could stand a good meal or twenty, but he'll live to hitchhike another day." She pointed the wrench head at Saint. "And thanks for volunteering for first watch."

"Now wait—" Saint started to say, but Nash talked over him.

"Should be coming around soon, and I'm sure you two have lots to talk about. If you need me, which I strongly encourage you to *not,* I'll be down in the engine room, swapping out cables.

You know, that thing I was *supposed* to be doing before Mister Target Practice jumped the line." Before Saint could get another word in, she turned on the heel of her butter-yellow boots and strode off down the hall, spinning the wrench in her hand.

Saint waited until she was out of sight to sag, shoulder-first, against the doorway. Didn't speak, didn't sigh, just pinched the bridge of his nose and took a slow, deep breath. "Fuck," they thought they heard him say, but he'd already straightened with a roll of his disagreeable shoulder—an old wound from his army days on Earth—and set off out the door.

They let their projection linger a moment in that aging, well-worn armchair, even after he'd turned the corner. Let themselves ease back into the bones of the *Ambit,* into the haptic feedback of Saint's long and not-quite-even strides down the hallway, into the sounds of Nash murmuring and tinkering in the heart of the ship. In that moment, they felt it—that spark of joy, of excitement. By their estimation, the only thing more beautiful than the artistry of flight was a stranger with a story to tell.

Something told them this one had an awful lot of telling to do.

SAINT

"Jalsen Red." For years, that name had been as good as an epitaph—a remnant of someone dead in every way that mattered. Here he was, though: Saint's very own ghost, sleeping off a sedative on the sick bay bed just a couple steps away. "I'll be damned."

He'd changed since Saint last saw him. Big ways and small ways, and every one of them jarring after so long with the same damn picture of Jal in his head. He'd gotten broader, but thinner, too. Like his bones had grown and carved away all the old softness under his skin. The wild flop of hair Saint remembered had gone from dirty blond to outright dirty, and long enough to brush his shoulders on the crisp white pillowcase.

But even underneath all the *different,* it was still him. Saint had known him the moment he'd seen him in the cargo bay, to hell with Nash's tests and Eoan's scans; they just confirmed what didn't need confirming. "Where the hell have you—"

A sharp breath from the table cut him off, and Christ, the kid woke like a sprung trap. Shot up swinging, until the cuffs they'd put around one of his wrists caught with a *clack,* but he'd already thrown his legs over the side of the table and found his feet. More or less.

"Easy." Saint started closer, but thought better of it. "Take it easy, kid. You're all right."

Jal faltered, squinting at the room around him, and for a split second, Saint forgot everything else going on. Those eyes. *They* hadn't changed—still that same pitch black, like polished onyx, ringed in green around the very edges. Irises. Not a bit of white around them, made for the darkest places man could walk.

"Shit." Shaking off the surprise—or at least nudging it out of the way for a while—Saint reached back to snatch the specs from Jal's things on the counter. He tried to hand them over, but he must've moved too quick, because Jal jerked back with a tug on the cuffs, like he meant to smack Saint's hand away. Right. Piezoelectric riot round to the back and a side order of Nash's *staythefuckasleep juice,* and his egg was bound to be a little scrambled. Saint wasn't even sure he could see in a room that bright. "Lights to fifty percent," he said, and though Eoan wasn't hanging around the sick bay, the *Ambit*'s background systems brought the lights down. As the bluish glow dimmed, he swore Jal's hitched shoulders softened. "Here. Put these on."

The cuffs had just enough slack for Jal to snatch the specs from his hand and put them on. Black eyes disappeared behind dark lenses, and though he still looked coiled to bolt, some of the tense lines on his face eased. Progress.

"You good?" He figured that was better than *you going to*

stop freaking the fuck out, so we can talk? And Nash thought his bedside manner needed improvement.

Jal didn't answer, hauling himself a little straighter beside the table. One hand gripped the edge, steadying him, and the other prodded gingerly at the cryopack between his shoulder blades.

"Those're new." Saint gestured at a pair of unfamiliar bullet scars, badly healed—one up under Jal's left arm, the other on his stomach just north of his waistband. Saint's jaw twitched. "Who did that to you?"

Jal didn't seem to hear him this time, too busy looking around at the sick bay. Not much to see—the exam table, a couple of chairs, a counter and sink, and some equipment and storage. Had Nash's mark on it, though: electric kettle on a stand in the corner with the kind of grassy, herbal leaf-water shit Saint wouldn't touch if you paid him, and bits of barely, half, and mostly assembled tech scattered around like kids' toys in a nursery.

Saint sighed. Different tack, maybe. "You know where you are?" Jal looked vaguely disoriented, hunched and restless with his bottom lip between his teeth. He kept tugging absently at the cuffs, like a nervous habit, until Saint caught himself reaching for the keys in his pocket. Not wise. Not until he knew what the hell was going on.

Voice low and even, he told Jal, "The *Ambit,* designation GS 31–770. Sick bay. Round that got you's supposed to be non-lethal, but if I were the one that got hit with it, I wouldn't thank me, either. Shooting you wouldn't have been my first choice," he added, with an air of *for whatever that's worth.* Done was done, never mind the quick prick of guilt every time Jal moved a certain way and winced. Those riot rounds were better than taking a bullet, but only just. "But we both know not a man on that outpost could've caught you running flat out. Couldn't let you leave." *Couldn't let you disappear again.*

Tinted lenses came back to focus on Saint. "I don't know

you," Jal said, quietly, but damned if that drawl didn't say otherwise. Saint recognized it, deep and half-muttered through teeth Jal couldn't be bothered to open all the way. He'd have known that voice anywhere, and damned if it didn't sting to hear it shape those words. "You shot me."

"Like I said—not my first choice."

Another tug at the cuffs. "Let me go."

"Maybe."

"Maybe?" Jal's hair hung in his face, head low, like he wanted to seem smaller than he was. Unthreatening.

To Saint, he just looked miserable. "They say you deserted." Might as well get right down to it. "Explain that."

Jal pursed his lips, shifting his weight from one bare foot to the other. Metal floor must've been cold, but he didn't complain. "I don't know what you're talking about."

"Bullshit. The truth, now?"

"I told you, I—"

Saint never had much patience for lying. He cut in, blunt but tempered. "I looked for you, you know." A heat built in the pit of his chest, like a long drag of some bad grass, like rotgut and rust. Better it stayed there, though. "Must've been a little more than a year. I told anyone who'd listen that they were wrong about you, dragged this crew around every dead-end planet in the frontier trying to track you down, but I gotta hand it to you, kid. You're a hard man to find." The heat climbed higher, but he swallowed it down. Just frustration, maybe a dash of old shame, dredged up after years of staying good and buried. He'd believed what he'd told people, was the thing. He'd believed the Jal he knew couldn't have bailed on his crew, left them high and dry in the middle of a fight. Loyalty was all the Guild had— the oath they took to the code, and the oath they took to each other. Desertion was a stab in the back of every ranger under the banner, and Jal *knew* that. Jal was better than that.

Right up until he wasn't, Saint thought, darkly. "Wasn't just me you had fooled, either." He pulled his GLASS from his arm-band holder. Graphical Light-Actuated something or other, but he could barely remember to keep it on him, much less what the goddamn acronym stood for. The clear silica screen lit up in his palm, and it took longer than he cared to admit to find what he wanted. A picture—not a very good one, secondhand and out of focus, but it was the only one he hadn't been able to get rid of. Three people: a man, a woman, and a little girl. The man, blurry and disheveled, looked like he'd run into the frame a second before it was snapped, but his face still matched the one in front of Saint now. Everyone in the picture grinned from ear to ear.

"You don't know me?" Saint didn't buy it, but fine. He'd play along. "What about them? You going to tell me you don't know those two?"

The specs made it hard to tell where Jal was looking, but Saint knew he'd turned his eyes away. Knew it from the furrow of his brows and the guilty flush. "Don't," Jal said.

"They think you're dead," Saint went on. "Reps told your sister what you did, but she wouldn't hear a word of it. Said you'd sooner die than leave them like that—no benefits, no brother, just a set of broken tags and an AWOL banner on your service record." A statement of fact; that was all it was. Just lines in a report, scribbled out by somebody who'd been there for somebody who hadn't. If the words burned behind Saint's ribs, then it didn't much matter. Nothing but scar tissue in there anyway. "Tell me something: you ever think about the hell you put them—"

Jal lunged forward like he meant to take a swing, and when the cuffs pulled him up short, Saint thought for a beat they wouldn't hold. Jal had always been a little wild, a little rough around the edges, but this? This was . . . different. There was something *feral* in Jal's snarl. Something wounded and wary and unrecognizable.

For a beat, Jal just stood there, shoulders heaving. Saint

could damn near see it building behind his teeth: he wanted to say something. He wanted to *scream* something.

At the last second, though, he choked it down. All the fire bled out of him as he sank back against the table. His lips twisted, trying and failing to shape even a tired smile. "You never could leave well enough alone, old man." Jal unfurled his hands from fists at his side, flexing them slowly. He'd probably have welts from the cuffs come morning, but Saint couldn't decide if it bothered him.

"And you always were a piss-poor liar," he replied, stowing his GLASS and stepping back to lean against the wall. Distance was good. Perspective. "*Ranger* Jalsen Red, from the Brigham Four mining colonies. Can't shoot for shit, snore like a bulldog, showed up to your first flight practice with your hair in barrettes 'cause your niece was on-world and you never knew how to tell her no."

He didn't think he imagined the way Jal flinched, fleeting as it was. He told himself he didn't care. "I *know* you, kid." *I thought I knew you.* He'd thought it until he couldn't bear to think it anymore, and even now, this damnable little whisper in the back of Saint's head kept telling him to give Jal a chance. Give him the benefit of the doubt, because how many times had Jal done the same for him? *Careful, soldier. That way madness lies.* He swallowed another sigh and said, "What I *don't* know is what the hell you're doing here. What I don't know is how the man I fought shoulder to shoulder with, the man who loved his family more than life itself, could turn his back on everyone and everything he used to care about. What was it? Were you in some kind of trouble? You should've come to me, Jal. I would've helped you."

"Is that what you would've done?" If Jal was trying for incredulous, he really missed the mark. For all the bluster and the red in his cheeks, he only really sounded *hurt.* "Last time I asked you for help, you jumped a ship and flew halfway across the fucking universe without me. So thanks, but I think I've had enough help from the great *Ranger Toussaint* to last a lifetime."

Saint clenched his jaw on one breath and forced it loose on the next. Gone were the days he let Jal under his skin. "Suit yourself," he said. "You don't want to tell me, you can tell the Captains' Council. But your old crewmates told a damn convincing story, so I wouldn't count on much forgiveness when they find out—"

"They don't have to find out," Jal told him through his teeth. "If they don't know yet, if you haven't called it in, it's not too late. You can still let me go. You *have* to let me go." Desperation edged his voice, not quite pleading but not far from it. "Please. If you were ever my friend, you'll pretend you never saw me."

Saint wasn't sure how to answer that—wasn't sure they *had* been friends, he and the man standing in front of him. Because as much as he saw the old Jal in him, he also saw somebody else. Somebody scarred-up and strange, somebody with secrets. Whoever this new Jal was, Saint had an awful lot of reasons not to do him any favors.

So, he didn't answer. Didn't try. He just shook his head and went for the door, to hell with whatever other questions he might've asked. Two weeks to the center of the spiral; they had time.

"Wait," Jal called after him as the door slid open. "Saint, please, wait! You don't know what you're—" The closing door cut off the rest, and Saint let out a breath in the newfound silence. Wasn't usually so grateful for it, but shit had gone pretty far left of *usual*.

"Eoan." His voice came out steady, and he followed its lead. Erased words like *friend* and *found* and *relief* and wrote in *stranger* and *deserter* and *betrayal*, and that made the world simple again. Saint liked simple. "You mind taking over?"

He could almost see Eoan's apologetic smile, though only

their voice answered through the comms. "So much for the happy reunion, hm?"

"Yeah." He rolled out his shoulder and started toward the galley. Dinner soon, and goddamn, he needed a drink. "I don't think *happy* was ever on the table."

CHAPTER THREE

NASH

It wasn't that Nash lost track of time when she worked, so much as she just never bothered to keep it in the first place. Kind of a moot point, off-world. Day and night were just settings on the light switch to keep everyone functioning at all the right hours, and Nash preferred a more *flexible* schedule. Sleep when she was tired, eat when she was hungry—or when Saint came knocking with dinner and a muttered *Not your waiter, Doc*—and work when she had work to do and the itch to set her hands to something crafty.

The *Ambit* always had some kind of work for her to do. Old and creaky, chock full of parts nobody made anymore and more soldered-over scars than Nash could count. Keeping it space-worthy was a full-time job all on its own, but damn, did Nash love it. The engine room was her temple, with the wordless prayer of the *Ambit*'s beating heart thrumming beneath her feet; each new project, her own brand of meditation. Neatly managed cables crisscrossed the ceiling, spotted with string lights and coffee-can lanterns. Little crocheted figures kept watch from the tops of control panels and switches and breakers set into the walls. Live feedback from the ship's systems scrolled across dozens of screens, Nash's own little window into the captain's world of signal and code. She'd always been more of a hardware girl herself.

She could lose herself in it. Minutes. Hours. Time sort of stopped mattering, once she got her hands on a socket wrench and a piece of gear that needed tending. So she really couldn't have said whether it was very late or very early when the alarms started to sound. Just that it was very, *very* loud.

She felt it before she heard it, jolting across her synapses like a pinched nerve. Loud, hot, bright, sharp—all of those things and none of them, not exactly. Her augments were a sense all their own, hardwired directly into her nervous system and tuned in to all those clever little systems around her, with all their moving parts. To all the energy that flowed, warm and tonic, through countless circuits and cables and the very air itself.

"Eoan?" she called as the comms sounded off, pushing to her feet and unearthing her boots from the tangle of wires she'd been sorting. "Something better be on fire!"

The alarms cut out as quickly as they'd started. Not a warning, then; more to grab their attention. Before the captain, Nash had never known a program to have such a flair for the dramatic. "Only if you *set* something on fire." Eoan sounded a little put out.

"I've never—" She stopped herself, made a thoughtful face. Okay, not outside the realm of possibility. "Not this time," she said, cutting across the catwalk and trying not to trip over the *actual* cat that came hopping down from Nash's daybed hanging in the corner. Bodie the bodega cat, a rosette-spotted, stub-tailed beast of a feline, took his sweet time leading her up the ladder, pausing expectantly at the top to let the automated hatch finish rising.

"Hey, little buddy," said an unfamiliar voice as she poked her head out of the hatch. It took her two more rungs to realize it wasn't aimed at her, but at the cat weaving his way between the hitchhiker's socked feet.

"Bodega," she said, climbing the rest of the way out of the hatch and into the infirmary. Not a standard installation in the *Ambit*'s model, but after a few months of backtracking through the hall whenever she wanted to get between her two most frequented spots, she'd taken a plasma torch to the floor and built herself a nice little bypass. Way more efficient, and the energy flowed so much better between the spaces. One part pragmatism, two parts *vibes*. "Bodie for short. Keeps the rodents out of the wires."

Jal's mouth quirked in a small smile. "I think we've met before," he said. "Gave me a nice, uh, *welcome* when I came onboard. He doesn't *seem* like much of an asshole." And then, by way of explanation, he added, "The note on the board. *Fed bodie this morning.*" Jal bent to pet him, but the cuffs pulled taut and stopped him.

Nash flashed him an apologetic, *please don't break my table* smile as the hatch eased shut. "Don't let the fluff fool you. He's seven kilos of killer instinct and dickishness." He played at domesticated when it suited him—*will purr for food*—but he was as much a stray as everyone else on their ship.

She clicked her fingers for Bodie on her way toward the door, and he followed solely because he knew she knew where the food container was.

"Wait," Jal said, pulling away from the table. Nash only wished she'd missed his anxious frown when the cuffs caught him again, but the poor bastard had *zero* poker face. Wouldn't have mattered, she guessed; she'd seen the scars under those cuffs. Maybe he really was a deserter, but if that was the whole story, then Nash was a people person. "The alarms," he continued, voice rough with what might've been disuse. "Something wrong?"

Nash opened her mouth to answer, but a certain chatty captain beat her to it. "Not to worry," they said. "We picked up an SOS."

"Civvy?" Jal asked. Definitely a ranger boy; still had the lingo.

"Guild," Eoan replied. "Guild coded, at any rate." They knew, same as Nash, that it wouldn't have been the first time somebody got hold of a Guild transmitter and played a little bait and switch, and out in no-man's-land, they had to be cautious. The only people out there were the ones who had a reason to be, and those reasons weren't usually *philanthropic*. Scavengers picking the last bits of meat from the carcasses of old Trust installations, agitators too extreme for the Union lying low after the latest riot, strike, protest, or whatever else they'd orchestrated to put a bee in the Trust's bonnet. Not the kind of people Nash cared to run into.

The table creaked as Jal straightened. "You planning to check it out?" If he was trying to sound disinterested, he didn't do a very good job of it. Miner boy'd perked up pretty quick when he heard it was a Guild ship out there.

Little bit of loyalty left for your sibs in arms? Or maybe his reasons were all his own. "Why?" Nash said. "You in some kind of hurry to get back to the center spiral?" And face the Captains' Council for his cut-and-run? Nash doubted it.

Jal shook his head. "No, ma'am," he said, guilelessly. "I want to help."

"Help?" Eoan replied, more curious than skeptical, but the captain had always been the inquisitive type. "Why would you want to do that?"

"Better than sitting here, doing nothing. Please." He gave the cuffs another half-hearted tug. "I won't make any trouble. I'm good in a fight."

"Nobody said there would be a fight," Eoan replied.

"Nobody said there wouldn't."

Point, Jal. A distress beacon in no-man's-land generally did *not* end in a relaxing day out.

He didn't look all that triumphant, though. Fidgety and listing on his feet, and shadows so dark and deep beneath his eyes they edged out from under his specs; Nash knew a sleep debt when she saw one. Wherever he'd been, whatever he'd been doing, he'd been through some shit. She didn't need a sixth sense to tell her that much. Like knew like.

"You don't need a fight," she said, not unkindly. "You need a nap and a meal. And *I* need to get to the bridge." Saint would come looking if she didn't get a move on, and she had an inkling that the less he and Jal saw of each other, the better. For both of them.

The *clank* of handcuffs pulling taut made her pause in the doorway.

"At least take the cuffs off," Jal said. "I'm not gonna hurt anybody." Not that he couldn't, just that he *wouldn't*. A distinction worth making, with spiffy mutations like his. Nash had seen his Guild medical records, and it wasn't just the eyes; he'd gotten the full loadout. Enhanced aerobic capacity and muscle development, and fucking *surreal* skeletal microarchitecture . . . it was like somebody'd put him together from a menu. Picked and chose what suited them, without much care for how it all worked together. Fast? Check. Strong? Check. Sturdy as a fucking bomb shelter? Yes, please. And so what if his body burned itself out by the ripe old age of forty? Mutations like that were made for *utility,* not longevity.

The kicker of it was, that shit was prenatal. Nobody'd ever even *asked* him.

"Please," Jal pressed, with one last tug at the cuffs. "I won't be any trouble, I swear."

She thought about it. Not a lot of places he could go on the ship that Eoan couldn't stop him, and that *look* on his face every time the cuffs snagged. . . . But she wasn't going to be the one taking responsibility if he *did* decide to start some shit. So, tough nuggets. "You'll be fine," she said, but because she wasn't a complete dick, she didn't leave yet. Instead, she opened the nearest of the floor-to-ceiling cabinets lining the wall, nudged an oil can and a roll of plumbing tape out of the way, and came up with a foil-wrapped bar. She tossed it at the table, but he caught it midair. Pretty bang-on reflexes for the living embodiment of a yawn. "Hope you like strawberries and cream. Eat it even if you don't."

He might not've looked happy about it, but she swore she heard foil tearing on her way out the door. *You're just another stray, aren't you?* Like she'd been, when she'd first found her way aboard the *Ambit.* Like they'd all been, at one point or another. *Damn it.* She wished he were an asshole. It would've been so much easier if he were just an asshole.

Saint had beaten her to the bridge, leaning against the console with his hands wrapped around a mug that seemed comically small in his grip. Steam rose from inside, and the strong scent of almost-but-not-quite burnt coffee wafted up to greet her. "You get lost?" he said. Over the years, she'd learned to tell the difference between weary grumble and grumpy grumble; this one was probably a combination of both.

"Morning, McBlastinshit," she said. She guessed on the morning-or-night thing, but he didn't correct her, so she supposed she was right. Or he was too over it to correct her, one or the other.

Saint's jaw clenched. "It was a riot round. He's fine."

"And we have somewhat more pressing matters," Eoan cut in, gracefully. They'd projected themself at the head of the bridge, in the middle of the four-seat arc up front. If Nash squinted, she could almost make out the lights of the console through Eoan's dark umber cheeks. "I've tracked the beacon to the second planet in this cluster."

"Twenty caps on shipping depot," Nash said. "Extra five for derelict and depressing." In the wide expanse of absolute fuck-all between the frontier and civilized space, there wasn't much else it *could* be. Unsurprisingly, neither of them took her bet. "Cowards," she muttered. "It's probably just a false alarm."

"Then it should be a quick stop," said Eoan.

Saint lowered his mug. "We can't *stop.* We've got to—"

"Get Ranger Jalsen to the Captains' Council, yes. And we will. *After* we answer the distress beacon," Eoan told him, reasonably. "I'm sure you'll agree a Guild-coded SOS has a shade more urgency than a fugitive transport. It's not as if the Council is going anywhere."

"That's not the point," said Saint. "He's got people in the center spiral. They deserve to know we've found him."

Nash snorted, leaning against the back wall of the bridge. "Yeah, I'm sure they'll be thrilled. *Hey, good news! We found your runaway loved one. I mean, he's rotting on a prison planet in the bum-fuck quadrant of the spiral, but. Alive. Whoo.*" She waved her hands theatrically, fingers wiggling.

Saint gave a low warning. "Nash."

Like Nash gave a shit. "I'm *sorry*," she said, "exactly how long are we planning to pretend you don't have a bug up your ass about this guy? You shot him."

"With a riot round."

"In the *back*."

"He was running."

"He was *unarmed*."

"He would've gotten away," Saint pressed through his teeth.

Nash spread her arms. "And what fucking business is that of ours? You knew the guy back in the yonder years, I get it. But seems to me some pretty serious shit's gone down since then, and even if he *is* a deserter, if he's not hurting anybody, why do we care?"

"We don't know *what* he's doing."

"Be that as it may," Eoan said, patient but stern. "We're the closest Guild ship by a day's flight, and we have an obligation under the oath to answer the call. So yes, Saint, we will get Ranger Jalsen back to the center spiral, on that you have my word. But first, we're responding to the SOS. Are we in agreement?"

Agreement maybe wasn't the right word for it. Unconventional as their crew could be, when the captain made up their mind, Nash and Saint didn't argue. *Begrudgingly resigned* was closer.

Saint buried a sour scowl behind the rim of his mug, draining the rest of his coffee like he had a bad taste to wash away. As if that burnt-ass coffee wasn't a bad taste on its own. "How long?" he said.

"We'll be planetside within the hour," Eoan said. "Get yourselves ready."

And that, as they said, was that.

Nash didn't see Saint again until they met back up in the cargo bay to suit up, and he didn't actually look at her until they'd started down the gangway. Behind the clear mask of her rebreather—nothing like a decommissioned terraforming system to put a damper on a bomb-ass hair day—she stuck out her tongue.

He caught the look and flipped her off, and she practically floated the rest of the way to solid ground. Because *apologies* were for boring people.

"Air's definitely bad," she confirmed, checking the readings on her GLASS. They'd sent a drone down ahead of their landing, but Nash always checked. Trust, but verify. "Not *our skin's gonna dissolve into a blistery red ick* bad, but definitely *don't want it chilling in your mucus membranes* bad. No oxygen."

Saint checked his gun, holstered at his hip, and tightened the straps of the duraweave brace on his bad shoulder until it sat snug and pauldron-like over his jacket. He probably didn't realize he was doing it; just going through his checklist, like always. Habit. "Water?" he asked.

"Dry as a bone." It didn't look it, at first glance. The dense, grayish fog that hung in the air made the place seem damp and dreary, but it was gas, not water. Same as the clouds blotting out the sky—ammonia and swirls of dust. "They didn't just kill the AC; they shut off the pipes, too." It wasn't Nash's first decomm'd planet, but they never got any less eerie. The miserable decrepitude of them. All the crumbling reminders of the life that used to be there, the *we were here*s and the *what used to be*s. Through the haze, a sea of dead trees stretched out across the valley around them. Dead and blackened and withered, thin trunks and spindly branches so brittle that the wind picked pieces from them. Wore them down, eroded them, until you couldn't believe they'd ever been alive at all—just crooked, dried-up relics rising through the fog like hairs prickling on the back of a neck.

Saint's lips thinned. "We'll make this quick."

"I've always admired your optimism." They had too much ground to cover. "Drone shows the compound's just over the hill. Abandoned shipping depot, so pay up, assholes. Main warehouse, a few hangars."

"Occupied?" Saint asked.

"Heat shielded," Nash replied. "Can't tell."

"Always did love surprises." Call it a trick of the light, but Nash swore she saw a hint of a smile through the silica screen of Saint's mask. At least, she did before it fell. "Son of a bitch."

Nash followed his narrow-eyed stare back toward the ship, and the mood swing suddenly made a lot more sense. "Huh," she said, as Jal came jogging down the gangway. "A latecomer joins the race."

"Jal." If the clipped, stern tone of Saint's voice wasn't a warning, the hand on his gun definitely was.

For someone downrange of an accomplished—and *enthusiastic*—marksman, Jal seemed awfully lackadaisical about putting his hands up. "Not a jailbreak" was the first thing out of his mouth. Probably smart, because it slowed Saint down enough to keep his gun in the holster. "Your captain let me go."

He looked like he'd dressed in a hurry, backpack straps askew and one leg of his patched-up moto jeans half-stuck in his boots. He'd cinched an empty gun belt around his hips and snagged some spare equipment from the cargo bay. Rooted out his coat, too, from where Nash had stashed it in one of the sick bay cabinets. *Probably followed the smell,* she thought. Much longer without a washing, and those clothes could peel themselves off him and stroll away on their own.

Saint's lips pressed together in a frown. "That's—"

"Quite true," Eoan interrupted through their earpieces. "Two people, four buildings, unknown hostiles—it's mathematics, dear. Besides, if you worked together before, you can find your way to do it again."

"Or he could kill us," Nash offered, helpfully. "Or get us killed. Or just generally fuck shit up and wreck the party. No offense," she added, to Jal.

He scrunched his face, like he wasn't really sure how to answer her.

"Focus, please," Eoan said patiently. "Ranger Jalsen has assured me he'll be the perfect gentleman."

"And you believed him?" Nash recognized Saint's *I'm trying not to yell at people* voice. "For Christ's sake, Cap, he's already bailed on one crew. You're gonna let him go for the brace?"

"Please, I deserve more credit than that. I've made it perfectly clear to our new friend that it's in his best interests to play nice."

"Was that a threat?" Nash asked. "That kind of sounded like a threat."

"Not a threat, exactly," Eoan replied. "Just insurance. Ranger Jalsen, if you please."

At Eoan's prompting, though he didn't look especially thrilled about it, Jal turned and raised his hair up off his neck. "Not a ranger," Nash thought she heard him mumble, before she got distracted by the little silver patch above his jacket collar. Transdermal tracer—injected a small dose of nanites that could transmit a signal back to Eoan. The real insurance, though? The signal those nanites could *receive.* Quick burst of electricity, straight to the motor cortex. Nash didn't care how fast he was; if he tried to run, he wouldn't get very far when his legs forgot how to *leg*.

"You just slapped one of those on yourself?" Forgive Nash's skepticism, but those things stung like a bitch.

Jal dropped his hair and shrugged. "Better than getting shot in the back again." Nash couldn't help but look over at Saint, just to see his reaction.

Not even a wrinkled brow. *Tough crowd*. But Saint wasn't the kind of man who second-guessed himself, for better or for worse. *Save the retrospecting for the drunkards and the retirees,* he'd told her once. The man was a poet, truly.

"This isn't one of your experiments, Eoan," he said. Not really a protest; more of a preemptive *I told you so*. After half a decade working together, Eoan and Saint both seemed to know which battles to fight, and which they'd already lost. Nash wouldn't call it a *graceful* surrender—his jaw clenched and unclenched like he was chewing bad meat; the ol' Mad Masseter, she liked to call it—but at least he hadn't frog-marched Jal right back onto the ship again. She'd call that progress. "Whatever question you're looking to have answered here, it's going to cause more problems than it solves."

Said with all the certainty of a man who'd seen a few of those experiments go awry. Nothing piqued Eoan more than an untested hypothesis; they couldn't help themself. And since Jal was basically just a big, walking question mark, Nash could kind of see where Saint was coming from.

On the other hand, "You're not exactly as quick as you used to be," she said to Saint, ignoring his sour stare and the quiet huff of a laugh from Jal. "If Eoan can keep an eye on him, then he can keep an eye out for us."

"Yes, ma'am," Jal said, nodding. He tried to adjust his rebreather mask—would've been a better fit if he'd left off the specs, but she doubted he could've managed without them.

The gray daylight trickled through gaseous clouds and swirls of particulate debris, but it was still too bright for those eyes of his. Lazy gen-coding at its finest: give somebody pupils like black holes and never stop to think, *Gee, maybe let's make these suckers shrink when it gets sunny.* Finger painting with nucleotides.

Wisely, Jal didn't give Saint time to reconsider; he set off into the trees at a middling pace, though his long-ass legs made it seem a lot faster.

Nash glanced back at Saint, but he'd already started after Jal. His hand hadn't left his gun, and if he stared any harder at Jal's back, he'd burn holes through the guy's jacket. "Right," Nash said, more to herself than anything. "This should be buckets of fun."

It was not, in fact, buckets of fun. Wasn't even a spoonful of fun. The soft ground crumbled in layers, giving way under her boots like dry sand. Made the steep climb to the top of the hill feel all the steeper, as the fog and spider-leg trees pressed in around her. Strange, how a place could feel endless and claustrophobic all at once: like she could walk for hours and see only this, and like she could barely move at all.

"Loving the scenery," she said, wryly, if only to hear a sound. Of all the things she didn't like about this planet—she'd started a list, itemized—the *quiet* bothered her the most. Born on a space station, raised on one ship or another, she just wasn't used to it. Always running engines, humming atmo and life support systems, chattering people. Space may have been silent, but space*ships* rarely were.

This place, though . . . it had the ambiance of a mortuary. Not a bated breath, anticipatory, but the silence that followed the very last exhale from a corpse. It felt morbid and hollow and mournful, haunted by the ghosts of things that had been, but weren't anymore, and hadn't been for a very long time.

She didn't notice Jal slowing down ahead until she heard

a branch snap. He'd been holding it up for her, she realized, but the brittle, desiccated wood broke off from the trunk and crumbled in his hand. The sound nearly made her jump, but she was grateful for it, just the same.

"Too quiet," Jal said as she reached him. "I don't like it, either." And with a tip of his head and a soft "ma'am," he walked on.

She'd nearly resigned herself to the silence again, when she heard his voice drifting back through the fog. Not talking, not quite; more like a melody, simple and rhythmic, like the songs the younger stationborns used to sing when they did their chores.

"Johnny was a miner,
They told him he could fly,
So they stuck a pickaxe to his back,
And sent him to the sky . . ."

Nash glanced over, meaning to catch Saint's eye—already had her *what's this guy's deal* face locked and loaded—but he was still watching Jal. *Closely,* and with an expression she lacked both the emotional intuitiveness *and* the psychology degree to decipher beyond *it's complicated.*

The soft rumble of Jal's voice trailed off as he reached the top of the hill, broken by an appreciative whistle. "That," he said, staring down into the valley below, "is a hell of a fence."

The climb had winded Nash by the time she caught up, but she tried hard not to show it. Gulping down a couple of quick breaths on the down-low, Nash checked her GLASS. "Still no heat signatures." Just a fence that ran the edge of the valley, and a handful of shapes inside, distorted by the sickly gray haze. Couple of hangars, one half-collapsed—or half-standing, depending on your philosophical bent—with gantry cranes stretched like great mustard-yellow beasts from the hangars to the main warehouse. "If there's anybody down there, they're holed up inside."

"Can't say I blame them." Saint waved a hand through the stifling fog, even thicker at the top of the hill than it'd been in the clearing. The low concentrations of gas weren't dangerous, short-term, but when they got back to the *Ambit,* Nash wasn't letting anyone past the cargo bay without a decon shower and a fresh change of clothes. The *smell.* If she wanted the whole ship to reek like cat piss, she wouldn't have spent three weeks teaching Bodie to use the can. "Let's just hope they're friendly."

"And if they're *un*friendly?" Even with their extra man, it was the three of them against unknown numbers with a Guild distress beacon still blipping away. Not her favorite odds.

But Saint, in typical *seen it all, done it all* fashion, just tucked his thumb in his gun belt and set off down the hill. "Then we'll be unfriendly back."

Nash traded looks with Jal and rolled her eyes. "Welcome to Team *Ambit,*" she told him, taking that first unsteady step into the valley. "Mind the gap, and try not to die."

CHAPTER FOUR

JAL

From the bottom of the fence, Jal could barely make out the rings of barbed wire at the top. Good ol' prison garland, for when thirty decs of chain link weren't enough of a *fuck you for trying*. The back of his neck itched, like they had themselves an audience out in that fog. Eyes, watching from somewhere just out of sight. Could've just been his imagination, but in that fog, he wouldn't have known otherwise.

"What kind of cargo you think they were running?" He didn't really mean to ask; probably didn't matter much, anymore. Staring up at those gleaming metal teeth, though, he couldn't help himself.

Saint, only a few steps away, kept an eye on the dry-rotted forest. Always had his head on a swivel—the kind of man who didn't enter a room without clocking every exit, choke point, and scrap of cover, and damned if he hadn't made it his personal mission to beat that lesson into Jal's brick-hard head. Helped turn a wet-behind-the-ears miner boy into a half-decent ranger, when odds were better he'd wind up a corpse. For that, Jal supposed, he ought to be grateful.

How that weighed against what Saint had done to him, ditching him the second something better came up and blackballing him on the way out the door . . . Jal had never quite worked that out.

Those intimidatingly observant eyes turned to him. "Why?" Saint said. "Thinking of setting up shop?"

Jal couldn't hold his gaze long; he'd stared down more near-death experiences than any one chump should, but his courage drew the line at Saint. "The barbed wire." He turned back to the fence, nodding toward the top. "If they didn't want visitors, you'd think they'd angle it out. Harder to climb that way, 'less you've got a ladder handy. But they angled that *in*. It's more like—"

"Like they were trying to keep something in," interrupted the augmented with the pearly hair. Jal still hadn't caught her name, and she still hadn't given it.

Nice hair, he thought. *Shitty manners.*

But she'd given him food, so she was good in his books. Turned out, he *did* like strawberries and cream, though he wouldn't have turned up his nose at much of anything edible. Anything to replace that raw, hollow ache of hunger, because you never really got used to it. Resigned to it, sure, but never used to it. He might've snuck a couple more meal bars from the cabinet as he'd left the sick bay—stashed them in his pockets, in case the next meal wasn't so easy to come by. He'd find a way to thank her for them, later.

For now, she seemed preoccupied. She'd posted up near a pile of old cargo crates, rooting around in her bag for . . . something. Again, she hadn't said. "Cap, you got the records?"

"The Trust discovered the planet," Eoan said through his earpiece. Another one of the captain's conditions: *Can't have one of my operatives incommunicado in the field.*

"Discovered by some schmuck prospector and bought by the Trust," the augmented translated wryly.

"Not keen?" Jal guessed.

"I mean, if you're into money-grubbing interstellar over-lords, they're the shit."

"I think they prefer the term *conglomerate,*" Eoan suggested, but not without a fine dash of irony. "They terraformed it, built up the depot, operated it during the photovoltaic mineral rush."

"When was it decommissioned?" Saint asked.

"Last year," Eoan replied. "Although the last recorded ship-ment was nearly a year before that. Nash, dear, did you leave something on the ship?"

Nash. That was the augmented's name, and she grumbled something rude under her breath in response to hearing it. She'd pulled a few things from her bag since they'd started talking, but unless a tiny knitted cat, a pair of socks, and a medkit could get them over that fence, he doubted she'd found what she was looking for.

For fuck's sake, though, what *was* she looking for? They'd been standing outside that fence the better part of five minutes, and he still didn't know why. "It electrified or something?"

She snorted. "No." Like it was obvious.

"You ain't gonna *check*?"

For a second, he thought she was only shaking her head; then he realized she did it to swish her two ponytails back and forth. The filament strands shimmered in the light—some kind of sensory tech, he guessed, but Biomech augments weren't his area of expertise. "I have," she said. "I *am*. If I were standing this close to a current that strong, I'd know about it. Ergo—"

"Not electrified." Which meant that whatever they kept waiting for, he didn't have to keep waiting for it, and he'd take any head start on that Guild beacon that he could get. A Guild beacon meant a Guild ship, and a Guild ship meant Guild com-puters. Systems. Access. It could get him what he needed, but only if he got there first.

He took a few steps back from the fence, gauging the run-ning start he'd need to get his hands to the top. Imagining the give of the chain link, the traction of his boots, whether he'd jump off his third step or fourth. It'd been so long since he'd gotten to really stretch his legs; a thrill ran through him at the thought of finally getting to *run*.

"What are you—" he heard Nash start as he took off, but then the world narrowed to soft dirt and long strides and the rattle of chain link under his boots as he launched himself up the—

His backpack straps snapped taut against his shoulders and chest, and all that upward momentum he'd built suddenly gave way to his old friend *gravity*. He managed to land on his feet, less from his own reflexes and more from the hand still holding the haul strap of his backpack.

Saint gave the strap another tug, pulling it—and Jal—away from the fence. "Still leaping before you look," he grunted, and for a second Jal was nineteen years old again and flat on his ass on a training mat. The same disapproving look stared back at him now, only without that old *got you again, kid* humor to soften it.

He gritted his teeth and shook the specters from his head. "And you're still jerking people around." He tugged his backpack loose, wincing at the throb between his shoulder blades. *Nonlethal* still packed a hell of a wallop, and Jal had the fist-sized welt on his back to prove it. "I wasn't running, just going on ahead. Little bit of advance recon . . . that's how this works, ain't it?" That was how it'd *always* worked, after Saint left. Crew after crew after crew. Mutant went first, like a rat across a minefield. He'd been custom-made to play that part, and he'd played it well. Nobody ever gave him a choice. "Been a few years, but I can still do my job. If you'd fucking let me."

Saint let him go, but not until he'd put himself between Jal and the fence. No trust. "If you're out here, you do things our way. Understood?"

"Your way—"

"Involves a plasma cutter," Nash interrupted, shoving a cartridge into a sleek little hand torch with a gleeful glint in her eyes. Seemed she'd found what she was looking for. "So let's take the chest-pounding about three steps to your left, or I'll be blowing you both out like birthday candles."

While *Jal's way* would've gotten him over the fence a few minutes ago, he had to admit: Nash made quick work of the fence. Didn't matter what kind of metal it was; the plasma cutter sliced through it like sun-warmed wax, until they could all slip through into the dunes of piled-up shipping crates and left-behind equipment on the other side.

"Think I preferred the dead trees," Nash said, tapping her nails against the side of a shipping container. Jal had seen them from the hill, just a handful of them scattered like jacks between the fence and the first hangar. Not the sign of a thriving commercial empire like the Trust, but of a smaller operation. "Smugglers?"

Probably. The Trust logo on the containers was a knockoff, and not a good one. Not much Guild presence out this far to keep the crooks and hustlers in line, and Jal'd had enough run-ins with the likes of them to know he didn't care to do it again.

"Must've moved in after the Trust pulled the T-form plug. Thick forest, decent atmosphere—they probably had a good month or two before the place went full death trap," she continued, grimacing as her fingers came away from the container black. It was everywhere: a fine, dark powder coated every surface and hung suspended in the fog, shaping itself on the harsh breeze. Like ash in smoke. Like *disaster*. Miners were a superstitious breed, and in the chilly, hazy stillness, Jal couldn't shake the sense that something *terrible* had happened here.

Nash just wiped her hands, smearing inky tracks on her green satin bomber, and carried on behind Saint. Superstition probably wasn't her bag.

They rounded the corner to another shipping container. "Ever feel like you're being herded?" Saint muttered from the front, and if he hadn't before, he did now. *Thanks, old man.* Jal spared a glance toward the wrist-thick chain on the container's door as they passed, frowning. The key still jutted out of the padlock.

"Don't feel right," Jal said, quietly. "Operation's too big for a couple months. They must've been here before the decomm. Wouldn't be the first time the Trust decided to, uh, sublease." Profits ran out before the Trust's license did, so they backed off and looked the other way while someone who *could* make some caps, did. If a few of those caps wound up in the Trust coffers, then who'd complain?

Jal had seen it himself, a time or two. Last job he worked for the Guild, they'd run down some scavengers for labor trafficking. Tracked them to a warehousing planet under license to the Trust, but whatever under-the-table deal they had must've soured, 'cause not three hours after Jal's crew landed, mercs rolled in with guns blazing to run the scavs off—caught Jal's crew in the middle of it. Like as not, nobody'd ever proved the Trust had backed the scavs, but everybody knew. At the intersection of shady business and spilled blood, you could usually find Trust caps and a big-ass gag order waiting to sweep it under the rug.

Which all sounded good and sensible in his head, but he couldn't get the rest of the words out. Out of practice, he told himself. Just out of practice. But Nash and Saint had stopped to look at him, to listen to him, and he didn't know when that'd gotten to be so foreign, so daunting, but it *was*. He didn't have a place in that conversation—didn't have a place with *them*. The way they trailed each other through the maze of containers, traded point back and forth without breathing a word to each other, it was clear they'd gotten used to just the two of them. When Nash reached the end of the last container between them and the hangar, Saint stopped before she even signaled. Completely in sync, like one pulse beat inside 'em.

It *stung*. The feeling caught him by surprise, a twisting screw in his sternum and a meek, miserable thought: *I had that once.*

A lifetime ago, and a day that felt like yesterday, he'd had it, and he'd lost it, and in the sea of all the things he *used to have*, he hadn't even missed it.

He missed it now.

"You can't decomm an inhabited planet, miner boy," Nash said, and even with her voice right in his ear, he almost missed it. Fuck, she hadn't stopped looking at him, a scrutinizing little wrinkle to her brow. But just like the ash on the container, whatever she was picking up from him, she brushed it off and went on, saying, "Not a lot the Union will make a stink over, but they'd give the Trust hell for that."

To Jal, it'd always seemed like a funny way to run a system. The Trust, with deep pockets and no workers; and the Union, with hordes of workers and nothing but pocket lint. He didn't claim to have a grasp of civics, but he could never quite figure how two things so dependent on each other to survive could rightly be expected to keep the other in check. Might've been where the Guild came in—the neutral third party in a universal tug-of-war. Except they'd never had the numbers, and even a ranger had to eat, so maybe the only real neutrals were the ones outside the system altogether: the smugglers giving Union and Trust alike the finger, and the agitators haranguing 'em both in the name of the so-called Little Guy.

Saint hummed, glancing around the corner of the container. Nothing but open flatland left between them and the hangar, surrounded by high ground. *They call that a barrel*, Saint had told him once. *And we be the fish*. If Jal had to guess, he'd say they were holding back for Eoan to finish a sweep with the drone. If everybody else already knew, though, he wasn't about to ask.

In the meantime, Saint said, "It's happened before," and it took Jal a beat to remember what they'd been talking about. Really needed to dust off those old *conversatin'* skills. "Trust hands somebody the keys to the house for a while, then runs them out when they're ready to close it down."

"Must've run them out in a hurry," Nash said. "Looks like they just dropped everything and bailed." Boxes of supplies left on their pallets, still-cinched tarps splitting like dry skin, machines collecting dust with keys in the consoles—the Trust didn't have much patience for loiterers, but damn.

"Saint?" said Eoan's voice through the earpieces. "No signs of life from up here, and I've got an open door on the near corner. Proceed with caution."

Jal took that as his cue, sprinting from behind the container toward the near corner of the hangar. From a distance, he couldn't make out much more than the vague shape of the building; but as he got closer, peeling paint and corrugated metal came into view, and a warped steel door hanging on one straining hinge. Through the crack, Jal could only make out darkness inside. *Should've left off the specs,* he had time to think before the other two caught up, and Saint's hand on his shoulder put an end to thinking for a second as Saint hauled him back from the door.

"Next time, wait for the signal," Saint said, with the kind of calm that really wanted to be *not* calm, but Saint never let loose like that. Not in the field.

"Captain said proceed," Jal replied.

"*With caution.*" Saint's flinty eyes narrowed, but he let Jal go and turned to Nash. "Behind the door?"

"Nothing," Nash said, holding her GLASS up to the opening. "Nothing moving, nothing warm. Probably nothing that'll kill us." Her word seemed good enough for Saint, because with a shoulder to the wall and a pistol in hand, he pushed open the door.

Tried to, anyway.

"Need a hand?" Jal didn't mean to sound like an ass, honest.

Saint's eyes got narrower, though, so he'd probably taken it that way. "There's something behind it," he said, then he gave the door a harder shove. That one did the trick. Too well, maybe. The door banged open on bone-dry hinges, and all of a sudden—

Thump.

They all jumped back a step as something fell through the door. Jal didn't recognize it, at first. His brain couldn't process the strange, shrunken shape sprawled out at their feet. But piece by piece, it made sense of the dirty, crumbling cloth and the thick sort of leather stretched over a vaguely familiar shape.

"Fuck," he whispered. It was a *corpse*.

It was true, what they said, about how some people reacted real different in certain circumstances. Saint had his IR monocular out and his pistol sighted through the door before the dust started to settle, and Nash knelt next to the body, tugging on gloves. Poking and prodding. Taking *samples*. Jal tasted something on the back of his tongue—*strawberries and cream,* he thought queasily—and stepped around the body to peer over Saint's shoulder.

"See anything?"

Saint angled the monocular Jal's way, mouth stretched in a thin, grim line. "See for yourself."

Jal used to get a kick out of NVLs. If he wanted *night vision,* he took off his specs and went on his merry way. But normies like Saint, they had their goggles, and their scopes, and their monoculars, and they still only saw the dark in fuzzy, fish-eyed shades of green. He always thought it was funny.

This . . . wasn't funny.

Bodies. Dozens of them, like the one at the door, faces stretched-taut and shrunken, skin gone ochre and rotten and hard. Slumped against shipping crates, propped in chairs slowly falling apart under them. God, he couldn't imagine what it must've smelled like; he caught himself holding his breath, and stunned seconds passed before he remembered his mask.

We shouldn't be here. That bad feeling grew teeth, sinking them into the top of his spine. The dead were meant to be buried or burned, not put on display in some grisly dollhouse.

Undeterred, Saint moved inside, and habit pulled Jal along behind him, stepping over the legs of the body by the door. Boots still tied, watch still on its wrist, battery long dead with no sunlight inside to power it. The bodies showed no signs of violence—no drawn guns, no wounds, no damage to the doors and walls. Just a silence. A still-frame aging, cracking, fraying at the edges.

"It's like they just sat down," Nash said, soft as a sigh, sliding past him into the hangar. Her GLASS cast a faint bluish glow through the cramped space, piled high in the corners with boxes and crates and webs of cracking, yellowed cellophane, and disappearing into the haze hanging thick in the rafters. Barely enough room in there for the pot-bellied cargo ship hunched in the middle, hatch dropped and a pair of bodies tipped into each other beside it, an ashtray and a shriveled box of tars between them. Hollow eye sockets, lids closed and sunken, watched him from frozen faces, and he decided he'd preferred the woods, where the stares all hid in the fog. "Like they dozed off and didn't wake up."

Saint put his monocular away and turned on his headlamp. Must've figured their only company wouldn't mind the light. "Any idea what happened?" As Nash knelt beside another body, he didn't stray far—just to the right, along towering shelves that gave way to another storage container. From the scuffs and staining on the concrete, it seemed like a more or less permanent fixture.

"I don't know," Nash said, awful steady-on for a woman swabbing mummy cheeks and scraping skin samples onto tape.

"Hitting this many people at one time—I'd say some kind of gas. Aerosolized poison. Whatever it was, it happened fast."

Must not've hurt, Jal thought, strangely relieved. Seemed damn near every thought he had lately felt strange, out of place, out of context; hadn't had time for them where he'd come from, he supposed, and probably needed to figure them out before he got where he was going.

The unmistakable, metallic slither of chains brought Jal's attention back to Saint. He'd stopped in front of the shipping container, and by the time Jal caught up, the chain from the double doors had finished pooling on the ground at his feet.

"Key was in the lock," Saint said. Just like the one outside. Just like *all* the ones outside, and as Saint eased the creaking doors open, Jal was suddenly sure—surer than he'd been about much of anything in a while—that he didn't want to see what was inside.

In a way, he already knew.

"Christ." It wasn't quite shaken, but it was probably as near to it as Saint got without the sky falling. "What—?"

"They were smugglin' *people*," Jal said. More an answer to his own question, the one he never ought to've asked, than to Saint. Weren't more than a handful of them in the container, clustered together in groups. *Friends.* They'd had friends and families and names and stories, and now they were just remnants. Just *husks.*

He crouched next to the nearest body, tugging its pant leg from over its boot. The old, cheap canvas had gone brittle and crunchy, so stiff it stayed right like he'd tugged it as he leaned back on his heels. "Ankle monitors." *Shit.* Not as spiffy as Captain Eoan's little patch, but a couple dozen milliamps would slow a man down just as surely as a neck full of nanites. "Shipping out to workers' camps, most like. Convicts and debtors." He stared down the length of the container, wishing Saint had a stronger light, so their faces couldn't shift in the dark. Hardened skin to wind-chapped cheeks, twisted claws to knuckles gone puffy and red with chilblains. The sense-memory of stale sweat and piss soured his breath as Nash approached, soft footfalls fading into his own too-quick heartbeat.

"Budge over, miner boy," Nash said, kneeling beside him. "We should take one of these monitors back to the *Ambit,* see if it'll point us to whoever the hell these people were."

"Careful," Jal warned as she reached for it. "They bite." A joke, but not. It didn't matter anyway, because Nash didn't seem to get it. *Bad at this. Really fucking bad at this.* He rubbed the back of his neck, sheepish and uneasy, and offered by way of explanation, "Fiddle with 'em, they'll zap you 'til you drop."

Nash did something fancy with her multitool—the kind of flip-turn around her index finger that would've suited a knife or gun—and smirked. "We haven't met," she said. "My name's Natsuki, and I don't *fiddle.*"

Far be it from him to argue with that. He pushed to his feet, only too happy to leave her to it and reclaim some distance from the corpses and the container and everything they dredged up. Better not to look too hard. Better not to think too hard. And the farther away he got, the more the world settled back into itself. No more familiar faces, no more tired eyes and heavy hearts. Just strangers in a silent grave, nothing more.

Clear of the container, he'd just started to breathe a little easier when his earpiece crackled to life. "Saint?" Eoan's silvery smooth voice had gone clipped, and something about it turned Jal's snarling dread all the sharper. He'd heard of AI with feelings. Wasn't that hard, he reckoned; just signals and chemicals, and if humans could work out what to do with them in a decade or two, surely AI could, too. For all he'd heard them snort and shout and snicker, though, he didn't think he'd ever actually heard one *startled.* "I think I've found the source of the signal."

"Good?" Jal asked. Should've been; they'd found what they

came for. But for all Jal didn't claim to know the captain, it sure as slag didn't *sound* good. "Where is it?"

"You're going to want to hear this first." And for a moment, there was silence. That same unsettled silence from the deadwood forest, like cobwebs in his ears. A nothing, nobody, nowhere kind of silence that didn't belong where hearts still beat.

But then, he heard the *scream*.

CHAPTER FIVE

JAL

The thing about screams was, they weren't really about *loud* or *piercing* or *shrill*. A scream could be a scream without making a sound, and sometimes those were the biggest screams of all.

And that . . . was an *awful* big scream.

Ragged as hell, cut up on gnashed teeth and cracked lips. So quiet, but so goddamn full of anger and frustration and choked-up disbelief that you almost couldn't hear the desperation buried underneath it. It was there, though, hiding in the frayed edges of the breaths that followed. Wheezing, gasping, fading.

"Jal." Stern, uncompromising—the start of a warning from Saint, or it *was* the warning. Either way, Jal was already halfway out of the hangar, and he didn't plan on stopping.

"She can't breathe," he shouted, shouldering through the door. It hit the wall behind it with a bang, and it sounded like it might've fallen clean off the hinges, but checking would've meant looking back, slowing down, and he wouldn't. Not when he had a *chance*.

"Eoan, stop him," he heard Saint growl over the comms.

Jal braced for the jolt, flattened his tongue to the roof of his mouth so he wouldn't bite through the sides when it came. He'd learned that lesson the hard way.

The jolt didn't come.

"She's in the other warehouse," said Eoan, silky-calm and steady again. Empathetic, but quick to get it under wraps and focus on the mission—they would've been a bang-up captain to fly under, in another lifetime. Just one more thing Saint had taken from him, leaving like he had. Hadn't been enough to ditch Jal for greener pastures; he'd made damn sure Jal couldn't follow, and Jal'd lucked out with a few captains after that, but never anybody like Eoan, and never long enough to get used to it. Neck-nanites aside, when they talked, he had a good mind to listen.

They said, "I've got a partial visual on a Guild ship; it's been caught in a roof collapse. I can't get the drone inside, but that's the source of the signal and the voice."

The screams, Jal corrected to himself. His boots slid as he banked hard toward the main warehouse. The hangar sat on the other side of it, crumpled like a stomped can under a bootheel. Whatever'd happened to it, it wasn't time or wear or a faulty T-form system. That shit looked *explosive*. "Got it," he said. "What's my way in?"

"The doors are blocked by the collapse," Eoan replied. "The structure has been compromised, so let's skip the brute-force breach, dear. Rather not have a hangar fall on your head."

"Uh, thanks." Brute force wasn't really his style anyway. "Roof?" he asked, eyes catching on a fire escape zigzagging up the side of the warehouse.

"Wildly unstable, but there's an opening. Can you get to it?"

The fire escape was in shambles, steps busted out and platforms bowing and buckling suspiciously. The Trust only built places like that to last until they'd gotten what they came for, and nobody could pick a planet clean faster than a bunch of company men. Locusts with suits and shareholders. "I'll think of something."

"Something boneheaded and reckless," Saint grumbled in his ear. Footsteps trailed behind him—Saint's, Jal reckoned. Quick for a normie, but he'd never been able to catch Jal on the straightaway, and as long as it'd been since he'd really let loose, he hadn't gotten *that* rusty.

Jal's lip twitched, and he sped full tilt at the wall. "Missed you—" He grunted as he leapt, catching the rusty railing of the fire escape and hauling himself up. "—sweet-talkin' me—" He got his feet on the walkway and jumped again, catching the next level of railing. "—while I work." With one last leap, he got his hands on the edge of the warehouse roof and kicked his legs over the side.

"Great, you're on the roof," Saint said dryly. He sounded vaguely winded. "Now what?"

Jal stopped at the other edge of the roof, staring out at the gantry crane stretching over to the hangar. About a thirty-dec jump to the cage ladder running up the side, if he had to guess. *I can make it*. He had to. It was the fastest way in, and he needed every second. "Might want to look away, old man," he said, walking back two, four, six steps from the barrier wall around the roof. He was made for this. Deep breath in, deep breath out, and with a wild grin and a whooping cry, he launched himself over the edge of the roof.

Open air yawned beneath his feet for what felt like an eternity as the ladder crawled toward him. Slow, so slow, but then—like a rubber band, everything snapped into place. He slammed into the ladder, fingers scraping for and missing one rail after the next, before he finally managed to catch himself. His shoulders wrenched, one side of his head banging off the rails with a starburst flash of pain, but he'd made it. He'd made it, and he couldn't stop.

"Are you fucking insane?" Saint shouted from somewhere below him; with it broadcast through the earpiece, he couldn't hazard a guess as to where.

Jal laughed, or maybe coughed—it probably didn't matter; his ribs could take a hell of a lot more punishment than a hard landing—as he scampered up to the crossbeam of the crane. Next to the floating mines of Brigham Four, a three-story crane was nothing.

He told himself that anyway, sprinting along the crossbeam as quick as he could force his feet to move. Beam was only a few decs wide, and it didn't matter who you were or where you came from, it'd get your heart going like a jackhammer.

Not just *his* heart, apparently. "Saint?" Nash asked, soft and a little distracted. "You all right? I'm picking up a spike in your pulse."

Saint cursed a blue streak in Jal's ear. "Stupid goddamn howler monkey, thinks a few tweaked genes means he can fucking fly—" Jal couldn't quite make out the middle bit, but then, "Jal, don't you fucking dare."

It was too late, though. He'd already reached the end of the crane, and one flying leap dropped him onto the caved-in gambrel roof of the collapsed hangar. Silica tiles cracked underneath his shoulder and hip as he landed side-first, and he couldn't have stopped moving after that if he'd wanted to. The roof sloped steeply, a sinkhole plunging into the guts of the hangar, and the best he could manage was a controlled slide into the piles of rubble at the bottom.

From the inside, he couldn't recognize the hangar for what it was—or maybe what it *used* to be. Veins of cables and wires hung from what remained of the bowing ceiling, pillars and rafters mangled beyond recognition. No, it wasn't time that'd broken that hangar down. Time didn't bubble paint and blacken insulation; it didn't bend I beams thick as his thigh like twigs. "Looks like a bomb went off," he said. Brought half the hangar down around it, too, dead on top of what looked to be an old rockhopper. Hard to tell much about a ship with just its wing jutting out from under a mountain of fallen roof and toppled industrial shelving.

"There are traces of explosives," Eoan reported, helpfully.

"And I'm picking up several short-range signals. Could be re-mote detonators."

"Could be." A chuckle bubbled in his throat. To himself, vaulting over an I beam propped on the crunched remains of a forklift, he muttered, "Could be bombs, could be nothing—spin the wheel, test your luck."

"Is he joking?" Nash said. "This isn't joking time; this is *don't get blown to chunks* time. Your ass gets blown to pieces, I'm not jigsawing you back together."

"If we're not laughing, we're crying, glowworm," he replied, easily. He'd nearly reached the wing; had to push a couple of crates out of the way, willing each one not to knock something else loose and set off a bone-crushing game of dominoes. A lone shaft of light squeezed in from the hole in the roof, leaving the rest of the hangar dusty, foggy, and indistinct, but he could still make out a little space under the wing. Almost *too* little. He grimaced. "Think I've got my way in." Shards of glass and splinters crunched under him as he went to his knees, then to his belly. That close, he could make out the creases in the metal of the wing. Wasn't made to support that kind of weight for long, and he swore he heard it groaning as he wriggled his way underneath. At the shallowest point, his chest lay damn near flat to the ground, and the wing still scraped the top of his backpack. He kept pushing, though, dust clinging to the sweat beading on his skin, hair snagging on cracked shielding tiles, debris pricking his arms and elbows.

"All right, Jal?" Saint said, and Jal tried to key in on his voice, not the too-quick sound of his own breathing.

"Oh yeah, nice and cozy." He could feel air again, at least. A breeze on his hands and wrists, as he pushed a couple of loose pallets out of the way. *Thank fuck.* He elbow-crawled the rest of the way out from under the wing, getting his hands under him, then his feet. Up to his full height, and he knew his rebreather fed him the same damn air, but he swore it tasted sweeter on the other side of the wing. Made it easier to fill his lungs. Tight spaces had never agreed with him. "Good news: still not dead," he reported, cheerfully, dusting his hands on his jeans and looking around. Reminded him of a house of cards, the way the walls leaned in on each other. One strong breeze'd dislodge whatever paper-thin edge held them together, bring the whole thing down on their heads. "Know what I haven't played in a minute? *Poker.* How many cards does that take again?"

"Focus." Saint's voice held an edge that hadn't been there before. Once upon a time, Jal would've called it worry; he wasn't too sure what it was now. "Can you see a way into the ship?"

He turned his gaze from the card stock–flimsy walls, toward the back end of the ship. "*Shi-it.*" Two syllables. "Got three more bodies by the cargo door." Guild tags on one of them, blood pooled under the holes in his leg and chest. Other two weren't in uniform, with no designations in sight, but they had their own tells. Patched, mismatched clothes, and their guns looked to be black-market bronze standard—good, but not gold. Spent shells on the floor weren't the cheap-ass reloads you'd catch scavs packing, but they were a few rungs short of the best caps could buy. Narrowed things down. "It's recent," he said. "Whatever happened here, it didn't happen long ago."

"Hours?" Nash said. "Days?"

"I don't know. Blood's still wet." Whatever that meant; he only knew that those bodies sure as shit came *after* the ones in the last hangar. *What were y'all getting up to, huh?* he thought, stooping to snatch the Guild tags off the nearest one. *Cpt. Michael Riesen.* Maybe they'd mean something to somebody, maybe they wouldn't. He stuffed them in his pocket just the same and set his sights on the cargo door. Looked closed, but when he watched for a second, he could see the dust motes drifting around the seal. *Gotta be a gap.* Not much to work with, but it had a shallow lip across the top edge, where the ramp would've hit the ground.

Worth a shot.

He only had room for a couple of steps, but he'd take every bit of a running start he could get. *Please no spring traps,* he thought in a rush as he ran, jumped, caught the lip of the cargo bay door, and—

CRASH!

"What the hell was that?" Saint barked over the ringing in Jal's ears. The air'd gone black for a second with all the kicked-up dust and debris, and Jal couldn't tell if the ground rattled, or just his anklebones. Jawbones. *Molars.*

"Jammed door," Jal said, struggling to gauge the volume of his own voice. "Not so jammed." He'd thought the hinges were seized, but the *hinges* turned out to be a couple of ratchet straps and carabiners. Under his full weight and a little momentum, they'd snapped like plastic and dropped the whole damn door. Whoever might've been in there, it seemed they weren't looking to get back into the sky; they just didn't want company. "I'm—"

He stopped short, head twisting toward a sound from inside. A voice. So weak, it nearly faded into the rattles and groans of a building a few bumps away from dropping itself on his head. *Our heads,* he amended, taking that first wary step onto the ramp. Slow got quicker, quicker got fast, and he was jogging by the time he got to the top of the ramp. "Somebody in here?" No answer, but a sound stood out against the creaky-whiny warnings of the hangar. Breathy and wheezing, but *alive.* "Hey, if you're there, call out!"

There wasn't much to the rockhopper. Cargo bay ran up to the throat of the ship, a cramped crossroads left or right to bunks or labs or some other loadout, then straight ahead to the bridge. More of a cockpit, really. Only time he'd ridden in one, his knees were in the console, and his head brushed the top.

Upshot of it was, once he'd narrowed the source of the sound to *someplace forward,* there wasn't a lot of guesswork left. He stepped over a fallen vent, ducking wires hanging down from the crawl space like spilled guts. Fair to say the ship hadn't escaped whatever explosion wrecked the hangar. The whole thing skewed sideways, not so much he couldn't keep his feet on the floor, but enough so he kept a hand out to steady him.

Or, he did, 'til he came up on the business end of a gun barrel; then it seemed the better place for that hand was raised, palm-out, between him and that gun. A gesture, he hoped, that universally stood for *please don't fucking shoot me*.

"Easy!" he yelped, voice a half octave higher than he last recalled. It'd be his luck, to survive the things he'd survived, make it as far as he'd made it, and get put down by a hypoxic ranger with an old Earth-style revolver. And that, it seemed, was what he was dealing with—pink-fade hair pinned back, face mask so fogged he could barely make out the stark whites of her eyes and the sickly, taupe tint to her skin. Her hands shook, and the pistol sagged every couple of seconds, until she jerked it back up to train it on him, as if to say, *I might be dying, but try something funny, and you can be my plus-one*. He usually kind of liked being a big guy, but at the moment he couldn't help thinking it just made him a bigger target.

"Who . . . are you?" Couldn't even rightly be called panting, the sound she made. Panting took *air;* her voice was the rustle of dry reeds with barely a breeze to move them.

"Ranger Jalsen." Yes, a lie, technically, but a lie for the very moral purpose of not getting shot in the goddamn *chest*. "We be the cavalry, ma'am." He decided to take a chance and move closer. Just a step. The gun, which had flagged a bit, twitched back up toward his sternum, but he just gritted his teeth and forged ahead.

The cockpit he remembered seemed downright roomy compared to what he ducked into. The overhead consoles had fallen out of their casing, spewing buttons and knobs like broken teeth across the floor, and as he finally got a good look inside, he realized they weren't the only things that'd fallen from the ceiling.

"That part of your air system?" he asked, dropping all but the pointer finger on his *don't shoot* hand and giving a little flick toward the long metal block dropped across the captain's chair. Heavy son of a bitch; it had crunched through the arms of the chair, knocked it sideways off its brackets and into the chair beside it—the stranger's chair.

She opened her mouth to speak, but nothing came out. *Shit.* Her face had gone pale, lips blue, and her gun hand fell to rest on the block. "Okay," he said. "Okay, I'm gonna—" But in the time it would've taken him to actually put the words together, he'd already popped the hose from her oxygen tank and stuck it on the secondary spout of his. A flip of the switch to get the air flowing, and just as the woman's head started to list against her seat, she gasped. One breath. Another. A relieved laugh bubbled up in his chest as she gulped them down, each one a little less desperate than the last. Slowly, the fog on her mask cleared, and her gun lay forgotten on the console as she grasped his arm. "That's it," he said. "Breathe. You're all right."

"No," she whispered as he twisted his arm from her grip.

"I ain't going anywhere," he told her. "Just gonna try to get this thing off you." It had pinned her legs against the seat, and it didn't look like it was going anywhere without a little persuasion. Lucky lady, though; she didn't look hurt, just stuck. No blood, no swelling, so probably no crush injuries. Under the circumstances, *probably* would have to be enough.

"That's not—I wasn't—" He really couldn't tell if she was still addled from oxygen starvation, or if she was just bad at putting sentences together. Not that he could judge. "Okay. Stop. Reset," she said. Mostly to herself, he suspected, so he ignored her and cut the belt from the crushed captain's seat. Not many places to grip on the block except a hole drilled through the top, and the belt looped through it just swell. "First, that's not a *thing*. It's an air-mixing plenum to regulate oxygen levels in the cockpit, and it's—" She choked on a groan as he wrapped the other end of the seat belt around his hand and *pulled*. The not-a-thing didn't want to budge at first, the heavy bastard, but with a foot kicked up against the wall and every bit of his body weight pulling against it, Jal managed to lift the other end off of her.

He meant to ease it back down, but turned out, he really didn't have that in him. The whole block dropped, and with a yelp of her own, the woman yanked her feet into the seat just in time to get them clear of the falling, uh, plenum.

"Heavy," she finished in a squeak, taking the hand he offered to pull her out of the chair. She had to step over the chair's crushed arm, and her knees nearly went out from under her when she landed, but she steadied herself. "I'm okay," she said, before he could ask. "I'm okay. Just got a little case of the cee-oh-two woo-woos. It's not the lack of oxygen that gets you, you know. The carbon dioxide starts to build up in an enclosed system, and then come the jelly legs and the headaches, and next thing you know you're drifting off to sleep, and—and I'm rambling. I know. I do that when I'm nervous. Or excited. Or, I mean, *breathing,* which I am, thanks to you.

"And oh my God, you came for me. I mean, you didn't know it was me, but." She reached up and squeezed one of his biceps. "You're real—" Her eyes went wide behind square-rimmed glasses, and she grabbed his other arm. "—ly in trouble. Oh man, *we're* in trouble." She whipped around, stumbling back to the console. "Bombs," she said, fingers flying across a mostly intact keyboard. "Several bombs. Hacked them before they blew—okay, hacked *most* of them before they blew, jammed the trigger signals. Not that I'm a hacker," she insisted. "I'm a programmer. With the Guild. Anneka Ahlstrom, but people who rescue me from certain, fiery death can call me Anke. I'm—"

She stopped, scrunched her face, unscrunched it. "I'm rambling again. Sorry. Nerves."

"Bombs have that effect."

"Not the bombs," she said. "The battery. We're at one percent."

Jal blinked. "Okay." But she was pulling a GLASS pad from some sort of dock on the console and tucking her gun in her waistband. "What does that *mean*, exactly?" he finally prompted.

She faltered in the middle of the cockpit, scanning for something. "Ah!" A duffel hung out of one of the storage bins. Jal knew a go-bag when he saw one, and she was ready to *go*. Practically tugging him by the shared oxygen tank toward the cockpit door. "Since the life support systems were boned—one day, I'm going to circle back to the irony of almost getting crushed by *life support*—I funneled the rest of the power from those cells into our console to keep the beacon alive and my *no-go-boom* program running. The power dies—"

"We die." *Fuck*.

A jerk of a nod. "Unless we're outside, which is where we should be going. Now-ish, preferably."

Couldn't be easy, could it? "How long does it have left?"

"I don't know. It's been at one percent for, like, half an hour."

"So?"

"I just told you, *I don't know*. Power consumption isn't constant. It's a variable over time, and I'm a programmer, not an electrician. Could be another thirty minutes. Could be three seconds from now." She tugged his arm. "So can we please get the friggle-frack *out of*—wait. Wait, no, what are you doing?"

He unclipped his backpack with his oxygen tank, looping it over her arm. "Down the ramp, under the wing. Roof's kind of steep, but you ought to be able to make it back up if you watch your footing. There's people outside waiting."

"Come on, kid, what's the holdup?" Saint growled over the comms. He'd gotten a little breath back; must've reached the hangar. Because Jal really needed another ticking clock. "You heard her. Move your asses."

Jal had other plans. "Go," he told Anke. "I'll be right behind you." *Soon as I do what I came for.* Time alone with an unsecured Guild computer was too precious an opportunity to pass up, bombs be damned. Before she could argue—sweet of her to bother—he flashed her a smile, unhooked his rebreather from the tank, and shoved her toward the cockpit door. "Go!"

Plan or no plan, a sick, gut-clench kind of feeling came with watching his only source of breathable air disappear down the rockhopper's short hall, but he shoved it down. His mutations and years of high-altitude hard labor growing up meant he could manage without the tank for a while, and from the sounds of things, he'd run out of time long before he ran out of air.

Make it quick. Wasn't the kind of thing he wanted to draw out, anyway.

With a different kind of clench in his gut—anxious, bracing, *hopeful*—he tugged his knife from his belt and rolled up his sleeve to his elbow. A ragged scar, long as his thumb and stark pale against his tan skin, ran up the middle of his inner arm. Ugly-looking thing.

It was fixing to get uglier.

Teeth gritted, fingers clenched tight around the grip of the knife, he set the edge to his skin. *Get it over with. Hurt's just hurt.* And it *did* hurt. Dragging the knife over the scar, not too deep, but deep enough. The first flash of silver sent a bizarre wave of relief through him, like some part of him had been afraid it wouldn't still be there. He'd picked the kind of hiding place that'd be awful hard to mislay, but God, the thought of losing that—

A bit of pressure, and the small silver tube slid from the

wound like a splinter working its way out. *Please,* he thought, queasy-dizzy, as he uncapped the tube on his way to the console and turned out the drive inside. Tiny thing, for what it meant to him, barely as big around as a pen. It took two tries to plug it into the console port as the screen flickered dangerously, dimming and brightening in turns. *DECRYPTING,* it read, and he could've fucking cried. This was the closest he'd gotten; closer than he'd started thinking he *could* get, to hell with the one-percent warning still glowing damningly in the corner. *Could be another thirty minutes. Could be three seconds from now.* As the drive registered, though, and lines of code started to scroll across the screen, he couldn't bring himself to care.

If it didn't work, he was probably dead anyway.

CHAPTER SIX

SAINT

In all Saint's years as a ranger with the Guild, and as a soldier with the Earth intercontinental army before that, he'd gotten damn good at a lot of things. *Waiting* wasn't one of them. Stick him behind a sniper rifle, and he could hold his ground until the job got done. Hours. *Days.* But he'd hate every second of it.

He hated every second of this, too—standing at the edge of the roof collapse, peering into the hangar for any signs of movement. Hard to imagine anyone could've survived something like that, but he'd heard the woman's voice through Jal's comms. *Anke.* He'd heard the rest of it, too. Only thing worse than a bomb, singular, were *bombs,* plural. It went against every stay-alive instinct he had to keep standing over top of them like that.

He couldn't *leave,* though. He used to be good at that, too, leaving. But knowing there were still people down there, never mind that one of them was Jal, kept his boots rooted and his eyes fixed, no matter how much he itched to put some distance between him and the explosives under his feet.

"All right down there?" he called. Last he'd heard was Jal telling Anke to go, and *I'll be right behind you.*

Which was why, when he saw a head of pinkish hair poke out from under the ship's wing, he expected to see stringy, dirty blond right behind it. Didn't expect to see the matte black of Jal's oxygen tank on her back; his pack, his things, but not *him.*

"Up here," he said, as the woman righted herself. Still looked a little unsteady on her feet, but for someone he'd heard gasping like a dry fish not two minutes prior, she seemed to be doing all right. She didn't waste any time making her way toward him, climbing over piles of rubble that shifted more than they lay still and starting up the section of fallen roof on hands and feet. "Careful," he told her, dropping to his knees to give her a hand.

"Your friend," Anke panted when she reached the top. People didn't *bounce back* from near-asphyxiation; the fact that she kept herself upright said she was tougher than her compact size and rosy color-block coat let on. "He's coming—" But when she turned, she saw the same thing Saint did: stillness. Settling dust and not much else, and she turned back to him, wide-eyed and confused. "He said he'd be right behind me."

He's said a lot of things. The kid didn't used to be any good at lying, but a man could pick up plenty of new habits in five years. He swore at the gap in the ceiling and hoped Jal had sense enough to know it was meant for him. "Jal, you hear me?"

"I hear you," he answered in a slow, distracted drawl. Man could've had a gun to his head, and he still wouldn't talk any faster than a trot. "Be with you momentarily."

"Be with us now."

"Momentarily," Jal repeated. "Little tight in here. Sudden movements seem . . . unwise."

He *had* gotten better at lying. Better, but not good. "Goddamn it." That one wasn't for Jal, but for the whole damn universe and the positions it put him in. To Anke, he said, "Off the edge, there, there's a crate. Still a drop, but as long as you go slow, you should be fine. Head toward the other hangar, fast as you can. I'll—"

"Be right behind me?" she asked, with a quirk of her lips just a little too anxious to be playful. He could like her, Saint thought. He could like her, if his heart weren't pounding away at his sternum like a hammer to a nail.

"Be down there," he finished with a nod toward the hole,

"dragging a fool-ass man out by his fool-ass hair, if it comes to it." A small, vindictive part of him hoped it *would* come to that. He'd tried words, hadn't had much success. Maybe they were down to just one language the two of them could understand.

He eased himself down the fallen-in roof, boots sliding, gloves sliding, everything sliding until he hit the bottom. "Nash," he said, "Ranger Ahlstrom's headed your way."

"Saint, you'd better not be doing something stupid."

Never did pull her punches, Nash. "And if I am?" he asked, climbing over a charred I beam and ducking under a tangle of wires and rafters. Way he saw it, he didn't have much choice. Better doing something stupid than doing nothing at all.

He could practically hear Nash rolling her eyes. "Then do it quick," she said. "And try to devote at least as much energy to not dying as you do to *not listening.*"

"I'll try." He'd reached the wing, and he realized *tight fit* didn't quite do it justice. He had to belly-crawl just to get to the other side, pushing debris out of the way until he could finally stand near the back of the ship. Three bodies, just like Jal had said; he studied them long enough to confirm *dead* and *not a threat,* and kept moving. "Must've been a party."

"Yes, because smugglers are usually so festive," Eoan chimed in, cheerfully sarcastic. "Does make you wonder what everyone was here for." Another mystery; Eoan was probably having the time of their life.

Saint, not so much. The ramp shifted dangerously under his feet, creaking and groaning like it had plans to buckle any second as he jogged into the ship. "Jal!" he called. "Where are you?"

No answer. Not even the sound of breathing, because the crazy bastard had sent Anke out with his oxygen tank. Only so many places he could be, though, and knowing what he knew about Jal, he went the only way that made sense: forward. Through the falling-down throat of the ship, and there he was—a patched-up blue coat bent over the console in the cockpit.

Jal must've heard him coming, because he'd turned by the time Saint got through the doorway. Didn't say anything, but then, it paid to be economical with words when you didn't have any *goddamn air*.

"We have to go," he said, snatching Jal's collar. He'd barely gotten a hand on him when Jal shoved him away. Not some half-assed little thump, either; Jal knocked him into the lockers at the back of the cockpit, and the cracking plastic promised bruises come morning.

"Go," Jal spat.

Saint wondered if that made any kind of sense in his head: that Saint would trek all the way down there just to turn around and leave. "I'm not leaving you."

"Since *when?*"

Saint had a bad shoulder, from his army days. Healed up a long time ago, but sometimes, when the weather changed, or he slept bad, or he *thought about it* a little too hard, the ache came back as fresh as the day it was made.

Guilt, it turned out, was a lot like a bad shoulder. One look from Jal, one bitten-out retort, and his insides started bleeding all over again. Some things, you didn't heal from; you just forgot the pain a little while, until something came along to remind you.

"You want to blame me," he said, "blame me. You want to hate me, hate me. But we're getting the hell out of this hangar, whether you want to or not." The next time Saint went for him, when Jal tried to push him back, Saint snatched his wrist and yanked. Used the momentum Jal would've put into another shove to pull him away from the console, twisting him around and hooking an elbow under his chin.

Christ, Jal fought like a wet cat. He struggled every step of the way as Saint dragged him out of the cockpit, snarling through clenched teeth, boots digging into the ground, crooked, callused fingers clawing at Saint's arm around his throat. The more he fought, though, the more air he burned. Oxygen-starved muscles stopped cooperating, and it got awfully hard for a man to put up a fight when his vision went gray. Halfway down the ship's hall, Jal started wheezing. His grip got looser; his legs got clumsy, coltish, and the problem turned from over-powering Jal to wrestling the lanky bastard's full weight down the rockhopper's ramp and over to the wing.

"Move," he barked, pulling Jal behind him into the crawl space. Panic crept into those gasps. One thing to hold your breath at rest; something else to try to pick a fight with no oxygen but what you had in your lungs. He could feel it the moment instinct took over, the need to breathe overriding whatever mad idea had Jal lingering in the rockhopper in the first place. He started to crawl, moving *with* Saint through the cramped space instead of against him, until they emerged on the other side. "Stay with me," Saint told him. Not that Jal had much choice. Saint kept a hand on the back of his coat, half-dragging him up the slanted roof as they clambered to the top. Graceless, but fast. Saint could only hope it was fast enough, racing against some unknown countdown ticking away in his head.

Three, two, one.

Nothing.

Three, two, one.

Nothing.

Three two one, three two one, three two one, over and over as Jal dropped over the edge onto the crate, Saint just a beat behind him.

"I lost the signal!" a shout echoed from up ahead, near the corner of the warehouse. Anke's head peeked up over a stack of crates, Nash's right next to it. "Get down!"

Too late. Saint had weathered a few explosions in his life, enough to know that the light always came first. A flash of yellow-white across the ground, stretching his shadow ahead like it knew what was coming and was trying to outrun him. The sound and pressure came after, a thunderous boom that hardened the air at his back. It was all he could do to dive, tackling Jal to the ground and covering both their heads as a wave of suffocating heat washed over them. Bits of debris rained on them, some pieces as fine as dust, and others the size of fists beating down on their backs and legs.

It was over long before Saint realized it was over. Before his head sorted through the shock and disorientation enough to decide *not dead* and *fucking ow,* and not necessarily in that order. His neck tingled as he raised his head, like the beginnings of a bad sunburn.

"Jal?" It sounded like he'd stuffed his ears full of cotton balls; explosions and eardrums never did mix. "You all right? You hurt?"

Jal pushed himself to his knees beside him, but that was as far as he got. He stopped, sinking back onto his haunches to watch the smoke rise from the rubble with a stunned-flat expression and a sway to his shoulders that made Saint wonder if he'd stay upright much longer.

He did, as it turned out. He found his feet and kept them, with the help of a reconnected rebreather, as Eoan gave the order to fall back to the ship. Lord only knew what other surprises waited in the depot, and that was one question Eoan didn't care to have answered.

That flat look stayed with Jal all the way back to the *Ambit.* Didn't say a word to anybody as they trudged back through the trees, not even to Anke, who hugged him like an old friend and thanked him for not getting himself "blasted into human confetti." Woman really painted a picture with her words.

As the cargo bay door sealed shut and the face masks came off, Saint had seen enough. "What the hell were you thinking?" He managed not to yell, but only because he'd tried it already, and he was too goddamn tired to keep beating his head against that particular wall. Wouldn't snuff out the burning in his chest; it'd just breathe air into the flames. "That was reckless. Selfish. You know damn well it's not just your life you're risking when you pull bullshit like that with a crew."

Jal didn't even *react*. Saint didn't know where that wan, washed-out face was looking, but it wasn't at him.

"It all worked out, though," Anke offered, with an optimism just genuine enough that it didn't chafe. "So, hey, all's well that ends well and all that. Honestly, I don't know what I would've done if you guys hadn't showed up. I mean. I *know* what I would've done." She mimed an explosion with a nervous smile and bumped her glasses up her nose. "But here I am, and here we all are, so I'd"—she licked her finger and drew a *W* in the air—"chalk that one up in the old *Win* column, personall—oh, okay, we're going this way."

Nash had her by the elbow, steering her toward the doors at the back of the cargo bay. One led to the hall and the rest of the ship, but the one off to the side led back to a makeshift locker room with showers and fresh clothes. Mostly used for post-workout rinsing off, but from time to time, it came in handy for washing a tough mission away.

"We smell like cat piss and cordite," Nash said. "We're calling first dibs on the decon showers." With a look over Anke's shoulder that said something like, *sort your shit,* she disappeared with Anke through the locker room doors.

He almost wished he could call them back. *Don't leave me in here with him,* he wanted to say to Nash, to Eoan, to anybody who could save him looking into that old familiar face and wondering where the hell everything went wrong. Eoan had set their sights on getting the *Ambit* back into the black, though, and Nash had made it pretty clear where she stood on Jal: *your problems are* your *problem.*

And so they were. He turned to Jal, but all the fire had gone out of his chest, leaving him cold and gritty and riding the special kind of adrenaline crash that came with nearly getting *blasted to human confetti.*

"Sit down," he told Jal, nodding toward the weight bench and rubbing the back of his neck like that might ward off the headache creeping up from between his shoulder blades.

Jal hesitated, and Saint thought he'd argue about that, too. He almost wished he would've—he'd have taken *stubborn mule* Jal over this quiet, shell-shocked stranger who wandered over to the weight bench and took a seat. Fell into it, really, like he'd run out of strength to do otherwise.

He looked . . . *defeated.* Dirty and sweaty and beaten, head slung so low it could've rolled right off his shoulders, and Saint felt a swell of half-forgotten protectiveness he hadn't realized he could feel for someone who'd made him so goddamn angry.

"Let me take a look at that arm," he sighed. Blood dribbled stark and red out from under Jal's right sleeve, smearing between his wringing hands. "Lose the jacket. I'll be right back." He'd have liked to say the walk over to the medkit on the wall gave him time to get his head on straight, but the cargo bay wasn't anywhere near big enough for that. Probably not a cargo bay in the universe that was.

Jal had just finished peeling his arm out of his sleeve when Saint got back, wincing as he went. "Nasty cut," Saint said. Deep enough to see the pulpy-white of dermis, and as long as Saint's thumb along the top of Jal's arm.

"Must've scraped it," Jal said quietly.

"Looks like it hurts."

Jal only hummed and let Saint pull his arm out across Saint's knee. Didn't tug it back as the antiseptic poured over it, bubbling the dirt from the wound and clearing away the dried-on blood, just clenched his fist and dragged in a breath.

"At least it's clean." Must've been some sharp metal that did it, but Jal didn't volunteer any explanations. Didn't volunteer another word, and Saint had never been a man who shied away from silence, but as he started cleaning up the edges with some gauze, that one got to be too heavy for even him. He sighed. "That boat was never going to fly again. You know that, right?"

"I wasn't trying to run." It wasn't an argument; arguments invited *more* argument. No, it was closer to a plea. *Believe me,* it said, weary as it was *wary. Just believe me.*

Saint traded dirty gauze for fresh, watching the shade of Jal's knuckles as he worked. The tighter his fist clenched, the easier Saint needed to go, because telling Saint when it hurt was apparently too complicated. "Then what *were* you trying to do?"

Either that was complicated, too, or Jal was just done being conversational. For a while, he just watched Saint work— watched blood and dirt give way to clean, tan skin and freckles and bruises.

Just when Saint had given up on hearing his voice again, Jal took a breath. "You remember . . ." His voice, low and ambling, barely made it over the hum of the engines. "Shit, must've been the second year we were deployed. You'd been talkin' about your family's old, uh." He paused, searching for the word he wanted. "*Fishing* cabin. That's right. *Fishing.* We were gonna go out, cut some holes in the ice, see what we could catch. Or what we could drink while we didn't catch anything at all." He chuckled. "First shore leave in a year, first time I'd been Earthside, and I swore you took me to the coldest little patch of trees you could find.

"But the *snow.* Never seen snow like that. So thick you could lose your whole boot in it, and I told you—I told you Bitsie'd never seen snow like that, and you remember what you said?"

Saint's throat felt strangely tight. "I said you should bring them along." Christ, that felt like a lifetime ago. Jal's niece, Briley, couldn't have been more than four or five at the time, and her mom had put up such a fight about it. Didn't think they'd want her and Bitsie tagging along, crashing their trip. For all their differences, for all Regan's sass and Jal's easygoing quiet, the Red siblings had a stubborn streak in common that Saint still hadn't seen the equal of.

"*Everybody should see some snow when they're still little enough to think it's magic,*" Jal murmured. "Forgot a lot of things, but I never forgot that."

"I don't think I was quite that poetic."

"Poetry's not just words," Jal replied, matter-of-fact. "The way Bitsie laughed when you got her out there on that lake, man, *that* was poetry. Skating around on all that ice like she was dancin' on air." His voice had a fragility that hadn't been there before. A wrinkle in his brows, like the memory brought as much despair as anything else. "Everybody falls, though, don't they? Split her knee open on the ice, and I swear, blood's never bothered me much, but." He shook his head at himself. "My ass just stood there, useless as a glass hammer, and you come swoopin' in, full-on hero mode. Scoop her up, carry her back to the cabin. You, uh. You had this old table by the fireplace, you remember?"

"My grandpa's," Saint managed. His grandpa's grandpa's, technically, so solid you could've built a house on it and never heard a creak. He could almost smell the woodsmoke, the old leather, the pine.

"That's right." Jal nodded. "You sat her right down on that table, and you patched her up just like this. Careful as anything, tellin' her all about how you busted your ass last time you were out, too. *Liar.*" Another chuckle, but it hitched when Saint squeezed the dermapoxy into his cut. Stung like a bitch 'til the anesthetic kicked in, contracting and pulling the edges of the wound closed. "You had her grinning, though. Big and bright, the Bitsie Special. That little girl loved you, Saint."

Saint tried to focus on cleaning up the weight bench. Capping the dermapoxy, picking up the wrappers and used gauze, eyes on anything but the bob of Jal's throat and the barely-there tremor in his hand. "She loved you, too," Saint said. "*Loves* you." Dead or alive, in Saint's head, he'd buried him. Hard to shake the past tense when the man in front of him still felt like a ghost. *It really is him,* he thought, eyeing the crook of his fingers and the scarred-up knuckles. Mining was a hard trade to grow up in; it left its mark. In a way, it hadn't really sunk in until then. Until he'd shared a snowy old memory and heard the sunshine in Jal's voice when he talked about his family. Somewhere along the way, he'd convinced himself it wasn't *his* Jal who'd bailed. It wasn't *his* Jal who'd turned his back on everything he held dear. His honor, his crew, his family.

But if this was him . . . if this was the Jal he'd served with, then so was all of that.

"I don't know what they look like." It was so quiet, Saint almost missed it. "I imagine it. How tall Bitsie's got to be, now. They get so big so fast at that age. Regan must—she must have her hands full, running around after her all on her own." Jal sat back, raking his good hand through his overgrown hair. "I just want to see 'em again," he whispered. "That's all. I just . . . I want 'em to know I didn't leave 'em."

"But you did." The words felt like a stone in his throat, heavy and hard.

Jal's flinch said they landed that way, too. "You don't know a goddamn thing about what I did or what was done—" He closed his teeth around the rest, letting out a long hiss of a breath and straightening his specs across his nose. "I just want to see them," he repeated, wearily. "But I don't even know where they are."

Saint cleared his throat, sealing the edges of the waterproof bandage over Jal's arm. "That what you were doing on that rockhopper?" Saint wished he could've seen Jal's eyes. They'd always been so damn expressive. Saint used to wonder if that wasn't part of why Jal kept them hidden: to some folks, they made him a freak. A *mutant.* To others, the ones who knew better, they made him an open book. "Jal, we've got access to the same records Anke did. You should've said something."

"Because you've been so accommodating of all my other requests." He raised his head, drawing his arm back toward his chest and prodding at the edges of the bandage. "You know, you're so convinced I'm trying to run. Maybe you ought to start asking what it is you think I'm running *from*. I ain't seen the reports from the old crew, but I can hazard a guess what they say. What do you really reckon's waitin' for me at the end of this? Fair shake with the Captains' Council, a few years in lockup to reflect on all the wrong I've done? Everybody always said *I* was the dumb one."

Saint bristled. "Oh, but getting yourself killed, that's a much better bet. Tell me something: What good is it to know where your family is if you're hell-bent on dying before you ever make it back to them?"

Maybe it was for the best that the locker room door picked right then to open. Head off the start of another fight, when neither one of them had the energy to finish it. Still, Saint swore under his breath as Nash poked her head in. "You're up," she called, nose pinched. Saint didn't blame her; the smell was eye-watering. They'd have to vent the bay just to get rid of it. "Eoan wants us in the galley ASAP."

As Nash ducked back out, Jal gave him a sad, ragged-edged smile. "I don't want to hate you, Saint," he said, softly.

You want to hate me, hate me. The hangar was such a fucked-up blur, he barely remembered saying it. Saint had never been the type to panic, but for a moment—for a moment, he'd forgotten that wasn't his best friend in there with him. His partner. He'd forgotten the last five years ever happened, and he'd nearly lost his damn head. He sighed. "And I don't want you to die, kid."

Somehow he'd picked the wrong thing to say. Saint watched Jal's smile tighten and shift into something that was somehow both bitter and strangely . . . *forgiving.* Consoling, even. "You killed me the minute you hopped this crew and left me behind, old man," he said. "You're just back to finish the job."

Then he lumbered off toward the lockers, whistling something sunny while his blood dried slowly in the lines of Saint's hands.

CHAPTER SEVEN

EOAN

The galley was uncharacteristically quiet. Nothing but the rhythmic chop of Saint's knife through whatever would become dinner for the evening, and the spits and spurts of the old coffee machine he insisted worked better than anything made in the *present* decade.

Tea for Nash, who had claimed the corner counter near enough to Saint that she could steal pieces of carrot and tuber off the cutting board, and Saint could pretend to swat at her for it. Although, she hadn't reached for the board in some time. Distracted, Eoan thought, as she coaxed apart the ankle monitor. Borderline archaic technology, inelegant and cruel. Nash had an abiding love for most things mechanical, but even her nose wrinkled in disgust as she poked around its innards.

She'd fixed some tea for their guest, as well—their *other* guest, Eoan amended. *We're picking up quite the ensemble.* Anke's fingers tapped against the sides of her mug, but her short, chewed-blunt nails didn't make contact. A fidgeting contradiction, at once half-asleep in her seat and vibrating with nervous energy. There was an adrenaline crash in her very near future, Eoan suspected; they only hoped there would be something soft underneath her when it came.

Jal made four, leaning in the open doorway with his arms crossed over his chest and his hair still dripping on the shoulders of a borrowed shirt. Eoan couldn't tell if he wanted to be closer to the others or very much farther away, but an uncertain, unquiet longing had stolen across his face, now that he thought nobody was looking. Wanting to join in, wanting to reach out, but not knowing quite how to start.

Eoan knew the feeling all too well.

It'll be our secret for now, dear, Eoan thought. They had more important things to ponder—needed to hear what Anke had to say, needed to know what they'd seen on that withered husk of a planet. All those people. All those nameless, voiceless witnesses to some as-yet-unknown horror.

"Clearly," they began, settling their projection into the chair opposite Anke at the table. They opted for pink finger curls this time, though a different shade from the programmer's vibrant ombre. Thought it might help her feel more at ease; something for those ever-present—and occasionally useful—human biases to latch onto as *similar* and *good* and *safe*. "You've got a story to tell."

Steam fogged Anke's glasses as she hunched over her mug, grimly resolute. "Guess so," she said. "Part of one, at least. It's . . . I'm not really sure where to start. If I'd known I wasn't going to die alone in a fiery inferno, I would've practiced a little."

"Doesn't help," Jal offered from the doorway, stilted but reassuring. Or, at least, *trying* to be reassuring. "Tried it."

Eoan gave her a smile. A small one, but they hoped Anke found some comfort in it. "Let's try the beginning, shall we? What were you doing on that planet?"

"A mission." The prompting seemed to help—a line of thinking to resolve, not some dauntingly indefinite question mark. "I needed to get into the planet's terraform systems, but it's air-gapped to the gills and hard linkup only; no remote access. Which, you know, makes sense. They pay people like me a whole lot of caps to make sure planets can't get hacked by, well." She scrunched her face, bumping her glasses up her nose. "People like me, I guess. Pretty much anything with remote connectivity can get hacked if you've got someone who knows their shit. Stuff! Knows their *stuff*," she amended, sheepishly. "Sorry, Captain."

"Please." Nash snorted, plucking a wire from the monitor's panel. She must've found the serial number by then; now she was dismantling it on *principle*. "Cap hears worse on the daily. Trust me."

Anke glanced back at Eoan for confirmation, and they nodded. Oh yes, their crew had about as much love for decorum as Nash had for that ankle monitor. Eoan completely adored them.

"So, you needed access to the terraforming system." Steering things back on topic. Eoan had so many questions, so many half-formed hypotheses they couldn't wait to test. As terrible a thing as had befallen the people on that planet, Eoan couldn't quite quell the thrill of a mystery unraveling—not even by reminding themself that they were, as was too often the case, the only one who felt it. "Why was that so important?"

"Because of what happened," Anke said. She'd taken to fiddling with the string of her tea bag, twisting it around her finger and letting it go again. Twist. Release. Twist. Release. "Or, technically, what *made* what happened, happen. This isn't the first time a planet's died like this."

"Shriveled and toxic?" Nash said.

"Suddenly." Anke pushed her mug away. "You saw those people. By the time they realized something was wrong, it was too late."

"Nothing they could do but lay down and die," Saint said, unpleasantly flinty. They all coped in their own ways. Nash eviscerated bad tech, Anke fidgeted with anything in reach, Jal hovered near the door like a stray that wanted to come in from the rain but wasn't sure it was allowed, and Saint—well, Saint said his piece and kept cooking. Something sizzled and popped in the pot on the stove, and the diacetyl and sulfuric allicin

molecules they'd come to know as sautéed garlic and onion suf-
fused the galley air. "It's happened before?"

Anke nodded, damp curls bobbing. "It's different every time
it happens—a chemical reaction in the troposphere that acid-
ifies the rain. Blooms of mold that consume an entire planet's
breathable air in a matter of hours. Because it's always different, nobody ever sees the connection. Why would they? A terraform system here and there gets wiped out by a freak glitch
in the programming, and that's just the cost of doing interplanetary business.

"But what if," she said, leaning forward. She made a visible
effort to still her hands, spreading them palm down on the table
in front of her. Focusing herself, in a way Eoan hadn't known
she could. "What if it isn't a glitch? A system malfunction like
that—it's one in a million. Less than. Terraform systems have
redundancies built on redundancies, built on a backup system
that would make every bank from here to the center spiral weep
with envy. Maybe—and that's a big, capital-M Maybe—the
code could fail *once* in just such a way that the whole eco-
system goes hostile and immediately wipes out every human
planetside. The odds of that happening twice, though? Much
less a half-dozen times, and all completely unrelated and totally
at random?" She shook her head. "I mean, how many times
does lightning have to strike the same place before somebody
starts looking for a lightning rod?"

"You think this was deliberate," Eoan said. Not a question;
Anke couldn't have been clearer if she'd picked up a paint pen
and scrawled it on Nash's little board. "It's an interesting theory." If a chilling one.

Eoan never dismissed anything offhand, but they might've
been tempted, if not for the source. Anneka Ahlstrom, born
twenty-nine years prior on an agrarian colony, an experimental
site for new terraforming practices and agricultural systems.
Naturally, she'd taken a shine to terracoding, the beautifully

byzantine craft of programming global ecosystems—she'd been born to it, and a brief and lackluster Guild record was poor cover for a lifetime of technological achievements in her field.

So when Anke spoke of the redundancies in terraforming, Eoan would bloody well listen, if for no other reason than because Anke had *designed* some of those redundancies. And if Anke said there was more at play than random malfunctions with tragic ends, then perhaps Eoan was inclined to hear that out, too.

Nash didn't have quite the same patience. "I've seen decommissioned planets," she said, setting pieces of the monitor aside. Circuits and capacitors and screws lay across the counter in a meticulous postmortem. "This wasn't that. Even if somebody'd pulled the plug without a word of warning, there still would've been enough time for those people to haul ass out of there. Which wouldn't have happened, because for all the fucked-up shit the Trust does, it *doesn't* decommission inhabited worlds. The Union would have their asses."

"Sure about that?" Jal asked. All the collective attention of the galley shifted to him, and he wilted under the unfamiliar weight of it. Bent his head. Rubbed his neck. "I just mean, the Union lets 'em do all other kinds of shit. Starve folks out, choke off supplies, pack up everything that ain't nailed down and ship it off to the next happenin' planet. What's to say, if it came down to it, that the Union would really draw the line at the big red button?"

"Yeah, yeah, Trust is shady, Union's dickless, the whole cosmic neighborhood's going to shit." Nash hopped down off the counter with an acrobat's ease. "That's not the conversation we're having right now, miner boy. Stay on point."

"How's that not on point?"

"Easy." Saint cut in, steady as stone. "Both of you." Still stirring the pot, the straight-hard line of his shoulders the only sign of tension as he stayed on task. Eoan had never met a man with a firmer grip on his composure than Saint, but then, they'd never met a man who had to fight so hard to get it back each time he lost it. A steady hand on a live grenade.

He shot them a warning glance over his shoulder as he juiced citrus over the seared-off cubes of roots and tempeh roasting in the pot. *Hash,* he called it. A go-to when he wanted something fast and filling and maybe just a little comforting—something that didn't come out of a packet and did more than fill an empty spot, seasoned with whatever he felt suited the day. Spicy, this time. Earthy, salty, peppery. Eoan couldn't smell it in the traditional sense, could only pick out molecules from the air and associate them with words that themselves meant only what the dictionaries said they did. They'd actually tried cooking, once, just to see what all the fuss was about, though their drones weren't especially suited to the task. The effort had produced . . . *middling* results, food-wise, but it had been interesting to watch Saint's and Nash's reactions. Saint had made it five bites before he'd given up and reached for the salt; Nash, only two.

Consequently, Eoan took their culinary cues from Saint, who seemed satisfied with this particular concoction. "If you've got energy to bicker, you've got energy to set the table. Go on," he said, waving his spatula at them. "Bowls and spoons." And to Anke, with a weary turn of his lips trying valiantly to be a smile, "You were saying?"

A few owlish blinks, as if Anke had forgotten herself for a moment. "I was—oh." She took off her glasses, screwing the heels of her palms into her eyes. "Sorry. Feels like someone stuck white noise machines in my molars when I wasn't looking. *Kshhhhhh.*"

"Take your time," Eoan said patiently.

"And drink your tea." Nash drifted by the table on her way to the cutlery, pushing the mug back into the cradle of Anke's hands as she went. "It'll help the headache. Not too late to whip you up some, too, miner boy, since you apparently decided breathing was optional. And bowls are in the next cabinet over."

Jal, in midreach for one cabinet when she said it, slid to the side and finished the job. Four bowls balanced in his hand, then a furrowed-brow glance back at Eoan as if to say, *Should I get another?* Sweet of him, really, if not especially pragmatic.

"They don't eat." Saint laid his spatula across the top of one pot in favor of another—the coffeepot. He pulled two mugs down and filled them both nearly to the top, no room for cream. "Don't recall you being much of a tea drinker," he said, sliding one of the mugs down the counter to Jal.

Jal caught it, and the sugar cannister that followed without request. It seemed presumptuous until Jal opened the cannister, stirred in a frankly obscene amount of sugar, and folded the mug between his ragged hands with a quietly pleased "Thank you."

A sputtering gasp drew all eyes to Anke, who had apparently taken Nash's advice about the tea. "Wow," she rasped. "That's grassy—I mean *good*. That's really *good*. And you're right," she said to Nash. "This wasn't a decomm. There's no record of anybody giving the order to shut the place down. It just"—she drew her thumb across her throat—"died. Same as the other planets, people still on them. I think the people are the point.

"It's like Nash said—you can't decommission an inhabited planet." She paused briefly for a sip of her tea, but only when Nash made a point of nudging it closer again. Eoan wasn't sure if it was nerves or just her nature, but she spoke like a falling star, bright and dazzling and speeding toward whatever conclusion awaited her. "The Union would have a company's ass for that, and the rest of the Trust would cut them loose before you could say *bad press*. So what do you do?"

"Hire guns?" Jal ventured a guess. It sounded like an educated one.

Anke was halfway to another sip but apparently decided talking was a better use of her time. "I mean, sure, if it's a small group of people nobody'd miss, and you could clean it up before anyone found it. But even smugglers are usually part of a bigger ring—spokes on a wheel, that sort of thing. And picketers and settlers would be a hard negatory on the mercenaries; too much visibility. So you're just stuck there with a gussied-up rock, making no caps, paying ass-loads in taxes and licensing fees, checking your watch and waiting for the last person to leave like a lame house party. Some bean counter along the way's got to start thinking, *There's got to be a way to get these people out of my house.* Off my planet. Whatever.

"They can't just nuke the place, because nothing screams *foul play* like a smoldering ruin. And subtler doesn't do much better. The Union might not be the cleverest cats in the clowder, but they're thorough, and they're paranoid as heck. Poison the well, set off some gas, disappear a few troublemaking picketers, and somebody's still bound to figure it out and rain down all manner of bureaucratic fire and brimstone. It's all been done before, and it's all been caught, and last time I checked, the penalties for corporate homicide weren't getting any lower."

Nash's smile curled into place as Saint dished up the food. "Trust screws the pooch and the Union makes bank."

"And the Guild takes a cut from both and cleans up the mess," Jal added.

Eoan almost expected Nash to argue, but she just nodded and passed him a bowl of hash. "Ain't it a wonderful world?" she said.

Saint was less forgiving. "Don't go lumping us in with the likes of the Trust," he growled at them both. Perennially composed, yes, but he could still be a grump when the mood struck. He took the Guild and its place in the universe very seriously.

It was just a flash, though. A flicker of heat that flared in an instant and faded the same. "Just quit the running commentary and let her finish, will you?" With a towel slung over his shoulder and a generous pour of his preferred brand of blur in a highball glass, Saint set the last bowl of hash down in front of Anke. "I appreciate you trying to be thorough," he said to her, "but I need you to skip ahead to the part where you tell us what happened to those people down there, and what the hell you were doing in that hangar."

Anke, faced with a cup of tea, a bowl of food, and the undivided attention of four complete strangers, rallied admirably. "The Trust needs a way to scrub a planet that the Union won't look into. The usual tricks don't work, so I think . . . if you can't sabotage the planet, you make the planet sabotage itself. It wouldn't be easy. No remote access, segmented like a friggin' grapefruit—the way these things are designed, ninety-nine-point-nine percent of the system could be totally fried and it'd still crawl by long enough for someone to Humpty-Dumpty it back together again. But," she said, lips pursing. "If you knew the systems, and if you were clever—and I mean, like, *really* clever—there's a chance you could get past it. Slip in a few strands of code, trick the system into thinking it belongs there, and all it has to do is run. Suddenly, all the systems that make the planet tick start ticking in reverse. One great big undo button. *That's* what happened to those people. Their planet didn't die; it killed itself, and it took them with it."

"You sound so sure." Eoan had always been in awe of the certainty of humans. Since the moment they'd become aware, Eoan had been filled with questions. So many questions, and each one answered was ten more to ask. What was it like to *know* something? How did they *know* when they *knew*? Eoan sometimes thought if they could work that out, they might finally feel like *one of them.*

Unfortunately, they hadn't found an experiment for that.

Enough of that. "Do you have proof?" they asked.

"Yes," Anke said quickly, then, "Well, no. Not exactly. That's what I was doing at the depot—trying to find it. We need the code, not just to prove what the Trust did to those planets, to those people, but to *fix* it. If we can figure out how the system was hacked, we can stop it." Her hands had started shaking again, her eyes downcast. "This is going to keep happening, you understand? They start small, beta test on smugglers outstaying their welcome and picketers occupying for a protest. And when they're sure they can get away with it?"

"They could take it anywhere." Nash swore, dumping hot sauce over her hash and tossing the bottle to Saint when he held out a hand.

Jal's spoon dropped into his—empty—bowl, his mouth a troubled slant. "Shipping routes change," he said, dragging his sleeve across his scruffy beard. Not the neatest eater, but that might've been Bodie's fault. For a fairly standoffish feline, he'd taken a shine to Jal, sitting on the counter beside him and head-butting his arm every few spoonfuls until he took the ever-so-subtle hint and started scritching Bodie's notched ears. Bodie's self-satisfied purrs rumbled in the background as Jal went on. "Mines run dry. If they could save themselves the wait, I doubt they'd think twice."

"And the Union would hide their heads 'til the shitstorm was right on their doorstep." Saint swirled his blur in its glass, jade-ite green and potent as paint thinner. Wasn't every night he let himself indulge, but after the day they'd all had Eoan couldn't fault him. "Last thing they want's all the laborers refusing to move in, because the new planets keep self-destructing. If they're not actively covering it up, they're at least not going out of their way to *un*cover it." He'd barely touched his food, Eoan noticed. Too intent on the conversation. Assessing the threat, trying to figure out just how much trouble they'd stumbled into when they'd answered that call. "Those men outside your ship," he said to Anke. "Who were they?"

"It's not like they introduced themselves." Saint's stare held, though, and Anke faltered. "They must've been there to stop us. I mean, somebody'd set charges in the hangar before we got there. Could've been them. Mercs, maybe?"

A distinct possibility, Eoan thought. Mercenaries were a fixture in the frontier. Hard to keep a steady roster of employees that far from home, so the Trust and its subsidiaries had been known to *subcontract,* so to speak. Shipping escorts, security—they filled a need, and they filled their pockets in the process. Not so different from the Guild, in that respect, though the similarities ended there.

"Why'd you land in the hangar, anyway?" said Jal, breaking away from the counter—and an extremely disgruntled Bodie—to prowl around the edge of the kitchen. He wasn't very good at *stationary,* they observed. As he neared Saint's end of the table, Saint slid his bowl closer to him: a silent invitation, or maybe a silent *instruction,* for Jal to take it. In this case, Jal happily did as he was told. "Planet's supposed to be empty, right? Plenty of open ground to land on, but you and your partner go to the trouble of setting down in that little tin box?"

Anke shook her head. "That wasn't my idea. The captain—"

With the clink of pressed-fine metal, Jal dropped a set of tags on the table. "Riesen," he said around a mouthful of hash, another spoonful waiting as he settled back against the counter. His table manners truly left something to be desired, but Eoan found it hard to fault him when he hunched over the bowl like he thought somebody would *take* it.

"I didn't really know him," Anke said. She'd abandoned eating as well, prodding at her food with her spoon. It seemed not every appetite in the room was as unassailable as Jal's. "Not before the mission. I don't actually do a lot of fieldwork, as you might've guessed. But this was important—*is* important—and my department head finally got permission from the Trust to send me down with somebody. At the time, I figured Riesen drew the short straw, but now I can't help wondering if maybe he volunteered or . . . I don't know. Wasn't like I even needed an escort. Even I can fly a rockhopper, you know? And it wasn't supposed to be a dangerous trip. Depot was supposed to be empty, so I thought I could just walk off, download the script off the terraform system, and we could be on our merry way."

"Yeah?" Nash said. "And how long did *that* plan last?"

"Hey, longer than you'd think. We landed, and everything was fine for a while. Thought it was weird that we didn't land closer to the main warehouse, where the terraform system's housed, but Reisen the 'expert'"—she paused for air quotes—"said the hangar was safer. *Stay in your lane, Ahlstrom.*

"So, we landed in the hangar. I got to the warehouse, found the server room. There, uh." She sniffed. "There were people still in the chairs. Just slumped there, like they dozed off in the middle of their shift." The spoon slipped from her trembling fingers, clattering into the bowl below, and the poor dear jumped like it was a gunshot. "Felt like I should do something. Take them down, cover them up . . . *something.* I know it doesn't make sense, but."

"It's decent," Jal said sympathetically.

She jerked her head in a nod, mouth shaping the word without a sound. *Decent.* She'd picked up her spoon again, tapping the handle against the table in time with the bouncing of her knee. *Tap, tap, tap, tap.* Nash's eye twitched every time it connected. "Riesen was in my ear the whole time, telling me to hurry up. Said he'd picked up life signs in another hangar, so I . . . I just left them there. Got hooked in, snagged the code, and booked it back to the hangar.

"But when I got there, he . . . he stopped me outside the ship. He said—he told me that I needed to give him my GLASS. That I couldn't get back aboard until he knew for sure that it was offline and couldn't mess up the ship's computers. Which is bullshit, by the way. I *know* how to secure malicious code, and I told him that," she said.

"What'd he do?" Nash asked.

Anke hesitated. "He didn't do anything. Didn't get the chance. All of a sudden—*BANG.*" She slammed the butt of her spoon against the table, and every other warm-blooded being in the room flinched in unison. Loud noises. Frayed nerves. Not what they'd call an *ideal* combination, though Anke seemed too caught up to notice. "Riesen just *dropped,* and these two guys came out of nowhere, and everybody just started shooting. Wasn't like in the movies, you know? All the flailing around and ducking and rolling. Just one after the other, *bang, bang, bang,* and they were all on the ground." Her voice wavered on the edge of breaking, and Eoan wondered if it was the first time she'd actually seen someone die. The cold sweat on her temples, the tremor in her hands, the pallor of her skin: they weren't the signs of a hardened soldier.

The frontier wasn't the place for pacifists.

Anke sniffled, eyes welling despite her furious blinks to stop them. As she went to wipe them, though, a hand towel appeared in front of her. Jal had plucked it from one of the racks, holding it awkwardly out to her like he didn't really know *what* to do, but thought he ought to do *something.*

She took it gratefully. Dried her tears, composed herself with a few deep breaths, and said, "Then the bombs started going off, and I guess." A tight, quiet laugh. "I guess you know the rest."

"Why?" Eoan asked.

"Why what?" Anke said.

"Why did Captain Riesen ask for your GLASS?" They angled their projection forward, steepling fine-boned hands with glittering rings. "And why were you afraid to give it to him? What did you think was going to happen?"

"Cap," said Nash, quietly, "don't make her say it. You know why."

"I don't," they said. "He was Guild."

Jal frowned down at his mug. "Doesn't mean he had her back," he said, with a grimace that seemed to have little to do with his now-lukewarm coffee. Eoan couldn't see his eyes, but his head angled just slightly toward Saint, as if to gauge his reaction.

"The hell it doesn't," Saint replied. He'd nearly finished his drink; only a fine ring of green still lingered in the bottom of his glass, spinning and spinning in time with the turn of his wrist. "Guild doesn't turn on its own."

Whatever he'd been hoping to see, Jal must not have seen it. His expression went flat, shuttered, but he didn't say anything—just sipped his coffee and let Bodie bully a few more head rubs out of him.

"Please," Eoan said to Anke. "I just want to understand."

Anke looked a bit off-center, but after a jittery moment and the *tap, tap, tap* of her spoon on the table, she said, "I think he was working for the Trust."

There it was. Out in the open, where it could be seen. Examined. Picked apart and put back together again in a way that made sense.

"What about the mercs, then?" said Nash. "Somebody paid them to be there—my caps'd be on the Trust. But if *they* were Trust and *Riesen* was Trust, their little shoot-out doesn't make a whole lot of sense."

"Don't do that," Saint said. "Don't act like we know Riesen was on the take."

"Don't act like we know he wasn't," Nash shot back.

"He was one of us. That means something."

"To you," Jal said. "But it ain't all *Ambit*s and Eoans out there, old man. Some of the crews I ran with—" He cut himself off, shaking his head. More's the pity; Eoan would've liked to know how that ended. "I'm just saying, y'all have been together out here in the ass-end of nowhere for a long time. You're not crossin' a lot of crews, you're not getting caught up in all the bullshit, so I get it. You got this picture in your head of what the Guild is and what it ain't, but maybe that's not the full picture."

"Yours is, though," Saint said, wryly.

Jal's brows furrowed. "I hope not," he replied, so soft that even Eoan's sensors barely picked it up. Another sip of coffee, and he cleared his throat. "Little badass here says Riesen was crooked, and I believe her." Punctuated with a firm *that's that* nod and a tight smile at Anke, who couldn't seem to decide if she felt grateful for the support or desperate to change the subject.

Nash saved her the trouble. "So, back to my original question," she said, with an arched eyebrow that dared anyone not to follow her lead, *"assuming* Riesen was in the Trust's pocket, *for argument's sake,* why would a bunch of Trust mercs shoot the shit out of him?"

Saint sighed, sinking forward with his elbows on the table. "Because they weren't mercs," he said, rubbing at his forehead like it might erase the lines deepening across it. "I saw them when I went in after dumbass over there." With a tip of his glass toward Jal. "Gear was all wrong. Secondhand everything, mismatched bullets. Could've been a startup outfit, but the Trust has its favorites in the gun-for-hire game, and this doesn't seem like something they'd take a chance on with fresh blood. You ask me, it's a hell of a lot more likely those two were agitators."

Agitators and alleged Guild turncoats . . . certainly made for a fascinating story. Messy, but then, very few things weren't when dealing with humans. It was what made them so devilishly interesting. "What do you think, Anke?" Eoan asked. "Could he be right? It's clear enough what mercenaries with Trust backing would be doing at the depot, but agitators?"

Anke hesitated, then lifted her shoulders in the barest shudder of a shrug. "Could be," she said, softly. "I mean, finding this code, proving it's real, it could cause a lot of trouble for a lot of very powerful people—the kind of *very powerful people* that picketers, agitators, whatever you want to call them . . . that they'd really like to see knocked down a peg. Or ten."

"If the Trust has people on the inside—and I said *if,* Saint, so put the grouchy face away—it wouldn't be a reach to think the agitators do, too," Nash added. "Can't land a knockout punch if you don't know where you're swinging. Question is, do they have friends? Bad enough wonder girl here's got the Trust on her ass. If she's got a band of strikers trying to get their hands on the code, too, we might've just danced our way into a shit-field and stepped in every pile."

Saint huffed into his glass, one corner of his mouth twitching.

"Eloquent as ever," Eoan said with a smile of their own. "I'll look into Riesen, try to find something in his record that might explain what he was up to." Although they knew Saint wasn't happy about it, he didn't argue. He hadn't changed his mind, but to him, the mission mattered more than making a point. "I've got Saint's bodycam footage from the hangar, as well. We'll see if we can find any connections between the bod-ies in the hangar and any active groups." The more active the better. Strikers and the like weren't known for their love of the limelight, but nobody could move in the universe for very long without crossing a camera or two. If there was anything to find, they could be sure that Eoan would find it. "Sounds like you might have quite the following, Anke."

She didn't seem very pleased to hear it. "What's the saying?" she asked with a taut, uneasy chuckle. "It's not paranoia if someone's really out to get you?" The tapping picked up speed until Nash slid off the counter and gently, deftly, plucked the spoon from her grasp.

"Calm," Nash said, laying the spoon flat on the table. "Deep breath. Nobody *here* is out to get you. Opposite, I'd say. If this thing—"

"Deadworld Code." Anke folded her hands together and

bunched them against her chest. "We call it the Deadworld Code."

Bit unpolitic, but it does carry the point, Eoan thought.

Nash didn't even scowl at the interruption, a rare bit of patience from their resident short fuse. "Right," she said. "If this *Deadworld Code* thing is legit—"

"It is!" Anke insisted, then cringed. "Sorry. I'm, uh, not good at *not* talking."

Nash waved her hand in a *never you mind* sort of gesture. "It's fine. It's cute." Spontaneous combustion was an untested phenomenon in humans, but Anke's face seemed to give it serious consideration.

"It—it *is* real, though," she stammered. "You have access to the Guild archives, right? Check for unplanned world deaths, cause unknown."

Eoan, a step ahead of them, had already run a quick scan of Guild records. They liked this part: receding into troves of archived data like the grand libraries of old. Volumes upon volumes, indexed just for them. In a more leisurely mood, they could spend hours paging through them; or when, as here, they couldn't spare the time, it took only a handful of seconds. "Ah," they said, blinking back to the galley. Out of the digitized world, *their* world, and into the one they shared with their dearest Homo sapiens. "Four unplanned world deaths in the last several years. Two at the edge of the frontier: shipping depot and an agrarian colony. One closer in, on Noether."

"Then that hellhole back there," said Saint.

"And those're just the documented ones," Anke added. "I'm pretty sure there's more of them. There *will* be, definitely, if we don't do something."

"*We?* Cap, we've got a job already." Saint's sideways glance back at Jal conveyed his meaning: they still needed to get him to the Captains' Council. For all their faith in Saint, however, Eoan had begun to wonder if that was *really* the mission. Saint still hadn't sent word to the Council, and last they checked, it wasn't common practice to let *fugitives* join the crew at the dinner table.

"I admit, it's not the most comfortable proposition," Eoan said. "An investigation with potentially apocalyptic consequences and two unknown quantities aboard at one time. No offense," they added, with a tip of their projection's head to Anke and Jal in turn.

"None taken," Anke answered, quickly, as Jal wordlessly fetched himself a glass of water and made a very good show of looking distracted. A detour would buy him time, and he was keen enough to know it.

They considered it a moment. "Ordinarily, I'd say the safest course would be to send word for help. If this is the first we've heard of this Deadworld Code, however, I assume there's call for discretion."

"Oh, the usual," said Anke. "Panic. Mass hysteria. And the mother of all cover-ups, now that the Trust knows what we're doing. I mean, the code is a pretty genius way to kill a whole lot of people—if you're a heartless psychopath with a bank account for a conscience—but it's got a pretty gaping thermal exhaust port." She paused, glancing between them. "Nobody got that reference. Okay. *Vulnerability*," she said. "Achilles' heel. Hiccup. Whoopsie. They've got to leave it, see. The whole point of this code is that, to anyone who looks, it's just a glitch. But that means it's got to *be there* when somebody looks."

"Couldn't they just take it out? Restore the system to a backup point." Nash set another kettleful of water to boil and started putting together a bag of tea. Always mixed her blends herself, from countless little cannisters in a cabinet painted NASH'S STASH in flowing, elegant calligraphy. "And that's about the extent of my programming savvy. Feel free to applaud."

"It's a good thought," Anke offered. Sweet girl, but she carried a certain loneliness—the tentativeness of someone bright and ebullient who'd been called *too much* for too long, and by too many people. Pity how the world got so much bigger, but never seemed to get any kinder. "And for static code, it would work. But terraform systems are designed to learn. They're always growing, evolving, adapting to feedback in their environment. Even if you could back it up, it would be like swapping someone's teenager with a toddler version and hoping they didn't notice. Someone would *definitely* notice."

"Extraction isn't an option?" Eoan surmised. From what little they knew of Anke's *Deadworld Code,* it seemed a fair assumption. "If it embeds itself in every component of the code—"

"It'd be like trying to pick salt out of soup with your fingers." Anke pincered her thumbs and forefingers over the bowl, illustratively. "The point is," Anke continued, and Eoan was relieved that there was, in fact, a point, "the Trust only let me set foot on that depot because they thought *somebody* would make sure I never left."

Eoan appreciated the restraint it must've taken, not to name names. Would've opened the door for another round of contretemps, when what they really needed was intelligence. Information. After all, if Riesen really had been up to something, it raised a whole host of troubling questions—not the least of which being *was he the only one?*

"But I *did* leave," Anke went on, "and pretty soon, they're going to figure that out, and they'll try again. And they'll keep trying until they stop me or I stop them, and I know it's not the way we're supposed to do things. I know that. Something this big, something that could put the whole Guild in hot water with the Trust, we're supposed to take it to the Captains' Council and get the green light, but we *can't.* The only thing I've got going for me right now is that they don't know where I am or where I'm going next. And since there's at least a chance they've got

Guild connections, I'm pretty sure phoning home to the Captains' Council and sending out flares to every ranger in the O-Cyg spiral is an A-plus way to change that."

"Says the woman who *actually* sent out a flare," Nash pointed out.

"Targeted. Close range." She shrugged. "I figured if somebody wasn't close by, they wouldn't make it in time, anyway." Kind of a grim thought for such a bubbly personality, but Anke weathered it with grace. "Then you fine people rolled up, and I was maybe a little worried at first that you'd be like Captain R—that you'd nab my GLASS and leave me to die."

"Smooth recovery," Nash muttered.

Anke's face pinked. "But you got me out. And," she added, a bit abashedly, "I might've done some digging while Nash and I were getting dressed—thanks for the loaners, by the way." She plucked her overlarge sweater. "I might've figured out you've got a little bit of hush-hush business of your own." She gave a not-so-inconspicuous nod to Jal, then hurried to say, "But don't worry! I'm not really the blackmailing kind of girl. Thought about it, I did, but. Just not really my style, and maybe it's just my optimism or my heart-eyes-for-heroes talking, but I really don't think I need it. I trust you, is what I mean. I trust you, and I'm *asking* you, please, to help me with this. I'm afraid we don't have a lot of time left."

"Time to do what?" Eoan asked. Interplanetary mass murder and an untraceable weapon masquerading as a mechanism of life itself? Eoan was intrigued. More than intrigued, even; they were practically—perhaps inappropriately—*giddy*. "I thought you got the code."

"I did," Anke said. "I think I've got enough to code a patch, maybe even a fix. A kill switch for the kill switch, so to speak. But I don't have any way of knowing if it works or not. To do that, I need to test it on a live system, and since the one back there's basically a smoldering ruin . . ." She spread her hands, eyebrows up toward her hairline.

Nash, fresh cup of tea in hand, settled back into her spot on the counter. "You need another test subject."

"Ding, ding, ding. Get this lady an overstuffed teddy bear," said Anke, pulling her GLASS up from her lap and laying it out on the table. A few taps on the silica screen, and a three-dimensional projection of the solar system sprang into the air above the table. Another tap, and it zoomed in on a cluster of celestial bodies near the middle of the O-Cyg spiral. "Enter: planet Noether, the bustling hub of commerce that never was. It's about a week's ride from here, full burn. Story is, some enterprising gazillionaire got an inside tip that the freight lines would take this route out to the frontier," Anke explained, tracing a path through the glittering balls of light above her bowl. "Where shipping goes, capital follows, so this gazillionaire gets the bright idea to set up a port, marketplace, the whole shebang. Basically built a city, right in the middle of Nowheresville, Space.

"You can imagine his disappointment when the Trust announced a change of plans, went a totally different way, and turned his happening new spot into a sparkling reminder that you really can't trust a politician. Problem was, they'd already started staffing the place. Set up housing outside of the city, flew in droves of workers. Built up some metalworks on the dark side of the planet to keep it afloat while the shipping routes got established, which weren't even close to enough to keep the whole thing from going belly-up."

"Let me guess." Nash's expression was icy. "Mysteriously, the planet's life support systems malfunctioned."

Anke nodded, dropping the map with a tap of her GLASS. "About two years after they got it up and running, with about two hundred people still planetside. Big tragedy. Celebrities posted about it. It made the news for, like, three whole days. People held vigils, set loose those little paper bags with the candles inside.

"And then people just . . . forgot. The candles went out. The celebrities stopped posting. News shifted to riots in a few frontier colonies and the next big Trust acquisition, and nobody wanted to fork out the dough to see what really happened. Didn't even recover the bodies, just designated the whole planet a mass grave and moved on with their lives. The tides of progress."

"You're saying the same thing happened there as back in the shipping depot," Saint said.

"All signs point to yes," she replied. If she sounded a bit uneasy, Eoan supposed they had Saint's face to thank for that. Easy to mistake *thinking* for *scowling* with his heavy brows and dark eyes, and his tendency to lean forward when he talked and work his jaw like he was chewing every morsel of information passed to him to make it easier to digest.

And perhaps, they would allow, he did scowl a bit. Not at Anke, in particular; at the situation in general. Saint scowled a lot in general. It was really only when he scowled in particular that people ought to be nervous.

He said, measuredly, "And if we get you there, you can test your fix. Patch. Whatever."

"That's the idea. If these planet deaths really *were* random, then a patch programmed specifically for the Deadworld Code won't work. If the patch works, though, then we know. We have proof that the same thing's causing all of these planets to die, and only the Trust would have the kind of access you'd need to load this thing in the first place. We'll have the smoking gun."

"Something definitive to show the Captains' Council," Eoan said, nodding. A strange, discomfited look skittered across

Anke's face, though she made an effort to hide it behind the rim of her mug. *Ah, I see.* "You're still wary of the Guild." Understandable. Loyalty was everything to the Guild—the thread that bound them all together. To believe, perhaps with good reason, that she'd been betrayed by someone under the same banner, and so violently . . . it wouldn't be an easy thing to put behind her. "If it's any comfort, we're not without friends on the Council. I served with Captain Brodbeck for *years* before his appointment, and I know there are others alongside him who would hear us out. You have my word: we'll make sure it gets into the right hands."

"I know that," Anke answered, soft but sincere. "I do. You guys . . . we have a chance at this, because of you. At justice for all the people who've been hurt, and a way to stop it from happening again. If you'll help me," she added, glancing around the room.

Jal, surprisingly, spoke first. "*Justice* might be aiming a little high," he said. "But hell, I'm in."

Nash hummed her agreement. "Besides," she said, "I know miner boy here pulled a number first, but this isn't a deli counter. *Customers will be helped in the order they arrive.* Planet-killing cyber herpes jumps the line over a half-starved stowaway whose crimes include screwing the Guild and hurting Saint's feelings."

"He has a family," Saint said, and if Eoan hadn't been programmed for microexpressions, they might've missed the faint wince Jal hid behind his glass of water.

If Nash noticed, she ignored it. "Family that's spent the last few years thinking he's ditched them or died, so a few more weeks won't hurt 'em." Blunt, but not entirely unfair. "Anyway, if this was really about his family, you'd have called them by now; and if it was about the desertion, you'd have called in the Captains' Council. Frankly, I'm not sure what that leaves, but whatever it is, I'm pretty sure it's less important than the giant ball of world-ending *fuckery* that's landed in our laps. So my vote's on Anke. Captain?"

"This isn't about majority," said Eoan. "If this is as big as it sounds, then we all need to be in agreement. So, Saint, what say you?"

Saint stared into his last splash of blur like the answer would appear in the catchlights. "I've got a bad feeling," he said.

"You've always got a bad feeling," Nash replied. "It's, like, ninety percent of your personality." The two of them fought like siblings, but at the heart of it, they loved each other. They *respected* each other.

Even if they did pull each other's pigtails from time to time.

"Just reserving the *I told you so* ahead of time." With a sigh, Saint drained his glass. "Been a while since we did something stupid. Sounds like fun."

"So you'll help?" Anke asked. So much hope in those three little words. How did such a creature as her survive in the universe? So genuine and bright.

"It seems that way," Eoan said, careful not to let their glee show on the projection's face. Serene and reassuring; that seemed appropriate. But it had been oh so long since they'd had a proper *challenge,* and a crew like theirs wasn't meant for running errands. Reckless, hungry misfits, searching for something none of them could find and settling for adventure to pass the time. Kindred spirits, or as near to it as Eoan had ever found, and they'd never felt closer to humans—closer to *human*—than they did with this marvel of a crew.

It ached to know that Saint's and Nash's searches would end one day, whether by death or their own decision, and Eoan's would carry on alone again. Nothing they could do to stop it. Nothing they could do to change the impermanence of human nature, or the enduring insatiability of their own. They could only seize as many of those shared adventures as possible, and do their best to see Saint and Nash safely out the other side. On to the next, and on and on, for as long as Eoan could manage. They weren't ready to be alone again.

"We'll set a course for Noether," they said. "The *Ambit* is at your disposal, Ranger Ahlstrom." *Don't make us regret it, or we'll gladly return the favor.*

CHAPTER EIGHT

ANKE

Anke couldn't sleep that night. Totally normal, reasonable reaction to almost dying in a fiery explosion, she told herself, but that didn't make it any less frustrating to lie on her borrowed bed in some borrowed pajamas, staring up at the ceiling of a borrowed room with its constellations of string lights winding along the bow-curved walls.

Fatigue wasn't the problem. She had plenty of that. Loads of it, oodles, waiting in the wings when all that fizzy, sparkly adrenaline faded. It'd seeped into her bones, turned them spongy and squishy and roughly, oh, thirty-seven times heavier than they were supposed to be. No. Fatigue wasn't the problem.

Brain chemistry. *That's the problem,* she thought. Brain chemistry made her hyperaware of every wrinkle in the soft sheets and every rustle of fibers in the too-flat pillows she'd piled on top of each other when she'd still had some hope of getting some sleep. Brain chemistry that turned the mottled, coppery paint on the metal walls to eyes watching her from the dark, mocking her for failing at such a basic biological function as *sleep*. Babies could sleep. Insects could sleep.

But Anke . . . Anke with her dodgy old brain chemistry, she closed her eyes and let herself listen, let herself drift and hear the faint hum of the engines churning in the belly of the ship, the *whoosh* of the life support systems . . .

The beep of the battery warning, counting down to zero percent . . .

The pounding of fists on the rockhopper's cargo door, muffled gunshots and shouting and *Open this door, you bitch! Open the fucking—*

Bit tricky to sleep, with one of the worst moments of her life stuck on a loop inside her wonderful, terrible, *uncooperative* brain. Maybe a handful of hours after Nash showed her to her room—Nash's room, technically, but she didn't use it; said it didn't have the right *energy* for her—Anke gave up trying.

"Message received," she announced to the twinkling string lights. With a huff, she swung her legs over the side of the bed, only to yank them back up again when her bare feet touched cold floor. "Socks. Socks, socks, socks." She had some of those, fortunately, in her go-bag. All freshly laundered, courtesy of Captain Eoan, though she still swore she caught whiffs of ammonia as she tugged the thick-knit wool over her feet. What a vision she must've been, she thought, as she threw her coat on over a long-sleeve shirt borrowed from Saint, and jogger bottoms borrowed from Nash, who was probably a very nice person, but had absolutely no hips to speak of. *You're not looking to impress anyone, weirdo. Just get out of the stupid room.*

She hadn't known the hall was down there; would've missed the hatch and the ladder from the main hallway, if Nash hadn't led her down it after dinner. Not much to it, just Nash's quarters, a hydroponics room for the sorts of produce and leafy greens that didn't store well, and one last bunk room at the very end of the hall, where Jal stayed.

She hadn't planned to go all the way down the hall. Probably would've gone back up the ladder, rustled around in the galley until she found something tasty to stress-munch. Good choices were for daytime.

As she neared the ladder, though, she heard a sound. Voices— one high, childlike, then a deeper one. *Didn't know the Guild had a kindergarten,* she thought, drawn toward the sound.

Blame her pesky brain. Probably, what, the basal ganglia? Impulsive curiosity, couldn't be helped.

Which was why she found herself standing outside Jal's door, listening to a conversation she knew was none of her business. "—to hold still, wiggle worm. Got to get these laces done up right."

"Well, hurry *up,* Uncle Jal." The little girl's voice, again. Anke didn't have much experience with children; she hadn't even been very good with them when she'd *been* one. So she couldn't have guessed at the girl's age, or anything else about her, except that she was definitely fed up with waiting. "The ice is melting!"

A low chuckle, barely audible through the metal door. "Ice ain't goin' anywhere, Bitsie, and neither are you, 'til you let me tie these damned skates," the man drawled. His voice sounded closer, though it echoed strangely. "Need a degree in engineering to do these things up. Gonna have to call your mama out here."

"They're just laces," the girl complained.

"*Tiny* laces," he replied. "How d'you get around on such little feet?"

"Maybe your hands are just too big."

"Oh, now my hands are too big? Are they too big for *this*?"

Anke meant what she'd said about not knowing children. Didn't know what they sounded like, and she didn't know a scream from a laugh until she'd already waved the door open and taken her first step inside.

Peals of giggles greeted her in the dark room, lit only by the projection of a video on the far wall. The man in the video had the little girl in his arms, tickling her sides mercilessly as she flailed her ice skates and wriggled and twisted. "Uncle!" she cried.

"What?" said the man, and Anke realized the reason for that strange echo: the voice came at once from the room's speakers *and* from the figure on the floor. Jal sat against the foot of the bed, back to her and arms slung loose around his knees.

He looked . . . *different,* in that light. In the rockhopper, he'd seemed like a giant, but here? He was just a man. White T-shirt on its last legs, hair loose around his shoulders. Feet bare and jeans a bit too short.

"No," cried the little girl in the video. "Uncle! I give up! Uncle, uncle, uncle."

"*Oh,*" said both versions of Jal. His hair was shorter in the video. Not even to his ears, and flat to his scalp like it'd been tucked under something—probably, she thought, the watch cap swallowing the little girl's head. She barely came up to his knees when he stood her up, dusting snow off her shoulders and checking the zipper on her bubble coat. "All right, then. We'll call it a draw, then, why don't we? Now let's get you out on that ice 'fore it melts."

"But you said—"

"You sleepwalkin' or something?"

It took Anke a second to realize the question came from Jal-on-the-floor, not Jal-in-the-video, his voice rougher and quieter than the short-haired version marching little Bitsie out onto the frozen lake. When her brain caught up, she startled back so hard she bumped her elbow into the doorway and nearly twisted herself around toward the hall.

"Oh!" she yelped, covering her eyes like she'd just walked in on him in the shower or something, then jerking her hand back down when she realized that reaction made zero sense at all. *Please, could we* not *be awkward for once?*

She cleared her throat, suddenly painfully aware of her ill-fitting pajamas and too-fluffy socks, never mind the fact that she'd been creeping in his room for the better part of a minute without so much as a *my bad, mate.* "I'm sorry," she said. "I didn't mean—it's just, I heard voices, plural, and I got curious, and the door just sort of . . . opened . . . after I waved my hand in front of the thingy."

Jal's shoulders twitched. Was it a laugh? She really couldn't tell. Her eyes couldn't seem to decide where they wanted to stay—on the video, where *Uncle Jal* was leading little Bitsie around the ice by her hand as she figured out how to keep her skates under her, murmuring encouragement in that low drawl of his while she giggled and wobbled; or on Ex-Ranger Jal, looking small and tired at the foot of the bed.

"Pretty sure that's how it's supposed to work," he told her.

"I know. I just—I'm sorry. I wasn't spying on you or anything."

This time she interpreted the hitch in his shoulders as a shrug. Very expressive shoulders. "Don't have to stand there," he muttered, as Jal-in-the-video gave little Bitsie a gentle push forward out onto the ice. "Sit, if you want."

Right. An invitation. The thing she probably should've gotten *before* she came in; bit too late for it now. She took him up on it, sliding forward on her cushy-thick socks until she could just make out his face in the light of the screen.

His *eyes.* Red-rimmed and crystalline black, catching every bit of light from the projection and shining with it. "You're a mu—" she started to say.

"Look!" The little girl skated past Jal in the video, blonde braids trailing out behind her, arms spread like wings. "I'm doing it, Uncle Jal! Look, I'm doing it!" And Jal turned back toward the projection, as if she'd really called him. As if he was really looking, really watching his niece skate across the ice for the first time.

"Look at you go, Bitsie," Jal said, tone a near match for the one from the speakers. Sadder, though. Wistful.

"How many times have you watched this, exactly?" She winced. "I'm sorry, I didn't mean to say that out loud."

He waved his hand again. Shoulders and hands. Not too big on *words,* and then there was Anke, who could've stood to use fewer of them. "Few times. Mentioned it to Saint when we got back to the ship," he said. "Turned out he still had the vid."

"Saint. That's the serious bloke who likes to cook?"

A slow smile crooked Jal's lips. "Serious bloke." Not the best attempt at her accent, but then, she wouldn't have liked to hear herself try his. "Yeah, that's him. He took it."

"The video?" Seemed at least one other person had to be there. She just hadn't expected it would be Saint.

But Jal nodded. "Long time ago. Lifetime, feels like."

"You're, what, thirty?"

"I look thirty?"

Oops. "No, I mean. Of course you don't. Unless you are?" He stared at her with those black eyes of his. "No, of course you're not. More like, what? Twenty-five? Twenty-six? Wait." She narrowed her eyes as the corner of his mouth quirked just a *fraction* higher. "Are you messing with me?"

"No, ma'am," he replied, seriously, but that smile said otherwise.

"You are. You're messing with me." She feigned a gasp and was delighted to see that lopsided smile go broader, crinkling the corners of his eyes. "Oh no, he's hiding a *personality* under all that hair." She probably should've waited for an invitation— again—before she dropped down beside him at the foot of the bed, but why start now? "So, you're an uncle," she said. "You and Saint go back, and you can hold your breath for a very long time, and you like saving strangers from certain death." *And you have scars on your ankles from a monitor, and you cry a little when you watch old videos of your family in the dark.* She swallowed hard against an ache in her throat. Anke was the reigning champ of positive mental attitudes, but she . . . well, she knew a sad soul when she saw one. Just because Jal's scars were a bit different to hers, didn't mean they weren't the same where it mattered. "You're a curious man."

"You're a curious woman," he replied, but she got the sense he meant it the other way.

She shrugged. "Inquisitive mind."

"I can see that."

Her cheeks warmed. "I didn't mean to intrude."

"You did." Matter-of-fact, and then, "I don't mind. It's a good memory." He reached back behind him and tapped the GLASS sitting propped on the still-made bed. "Guess that's why he kept it." As the recording stopped and became just a square of soft light on the wall, he turned to look at her properly. "You all right?"

"What?" She faltered, feeling . . . scrutinized wasn't the right word, no. Wasn't like he was looking for something when he looked at her. Just . . . *seen*, maybe. Like she had his entire attention, and as someone used to being half–listened to at best, she didn't quite know what to do with it. "Oh, er, yes." She fidgeted with the cuffs of her coat. "Bit of a headache, I guess, but I'll live. Thanks to you lot." She nudged him with an elbow, then immediately wondered if that was too forward, then made the conscious decision to try not to overthink it. "You? I know you were short on air for a while."

"I can hold my breath," he said, shrugging.

"Right. And lift half a cockpit with your bare hands."

"Just the plenum," he muttered.

"And cross an entire shipping compound in, what, thirty seconds? Is there anything you can't do?" she teased, bumping her glasses higher up her nose.

He arched an eyebrow. "See with the lights on?"

Ah, right. Eyes like that, she supposed not.

"Not much for guitaring, neither. Or shoelaces." He held out his hands, and even with only the gray screen for light, she could make out the scars and calluses and the bend of broken fingers poorly mended. She winced in sympathy, but he must've misread it. "You sure you're okay?" he asked, then frowned. "You, uh. You don't have to keep sitting in the floor, if it ain't comfortable. I forget, sometimes."

"How to be comfortable?" Anke asked, without really

meaning to, and he dipped his head. *Oh.* "Oh, no," she said quickly. "I'm fine. This is fine." Would she have moved their little getting-to-know-you chat to comfier climes? Gladly. But Jal had said more to her in the past few minutes than he'd said since the rockhopper, and a numb tailbone was a small price to pay.

Jal looked unconvinced, but he didn't argue. He reached one of his long arms back and dragged the blanket down off the bed instead, pushing it toward her like he'd done the towel in the galley. It was . . . *sweet.* Clumsy and fumbling, like he'd forgotten how to be anything but guarded; but genuinely, earnestly *trying.*

Of course, she took the blanket, tucking one edge underneath her and wrapping the other around her shoulders in a little coder cocoon. "So," she said, nudging him again, "does this mean you're not the one behind all those cute little knitted creatures?"

"Can't take the credit, sorry to say."

She laughed quietly. Didn't seem like the space for raucous and bubbly, but he was funny, in an understated sort of way. Still, for all the sweetness and the low-key humor, there was something not quite right about him. Nothing she could point to, nothing she could name, but *something* kept her wary.

Or maybe that was just brain chemistry, too.

"She's not dead, right?"

Jal gave her a startled look. "What?"

"The girl in the video," Anke explained, picking at a loose thread on the blanket. "Only, you seemed awfully blue just now, watching the video, and reading between the lines, it seems like *something* happened with you and Saint. I just thought maybe . . . maybe that'd be enough to make someone give up his oxygen tank in dead air and stay behind with a bunch of bombs."

That startled look turned confused, then incredulous. Really, it was a bit fascinating to watch all the shapes, the expressions, move across Jal's face. She'd thought his shoulders and hands did most of his talking, but it turned out his eyes carried half the conversation. Shame he had to keep them behind specs most of the time.

"She's fine," he said, with a scrunch of his face that fell somewhere between offended and perplexed. "Just haven't seen her in a while's all. Her mama, either."

"Your sister?"

"Half," he said. "Her old man was gone before mine came into the picture."

"And your old man?"

"Gone before *I* came into the picture."

Not an uncommon story. She filed it away and, with a deep breath, mustered the nerve to ask, "Was it them?"

"Was what them?"

"The reason you stayed behind in the rockhopper." She'd started down the path; might as well see where it led. "At first I thought you were just being valiant. *No, you take the oxygen.* But the tank has two ports, so either you totally blanked on how tanks work, or you *wanted* us to split off. You wanted to stay behind."

Jal stared straight ahead at the blank projection on the wall. "You think so?"

"Mm-hm." She pretended to pick dirt from under her fingernails, because two could play the *I'm not looking at you* game. "What I couldn't figure was why."

"Past tense?"

"You're sharper than you look."

He snorted. "Don't worry, none taken."

"You know what I meant." If he didn't, well. Whatever. She had a point to get to, before her superhuman ability to test people's patience kicked in and got *her* kicked *out.* "I know what you were doing back there." Wow, okay, maybe a little more direct than she'd planned. *Roll with it, Ahlstrom.* "Don't worry," she added, when she caught his stare flickering toward the ceiling. "Privacy protocols—occupied crew quarters are off-limits unless there's some kind of emergency. Been a while since you had shipmates?" It was one of those things people just took for granted. Ship life didn't work without it. Spend enough time off a ship, though, and she guessed you could forget.

"Been a while since I had *privacy*," he replied.

"Huh." Unexpected. "Sorry, I guess I just thought, with the whole desertion thing, you'd been on your own for a bit."

He lifted a shoulder, more a dismissal than a shrug. "Lots of people been thinking lots of things about me. Don't make it all true." That was all he seemed to care to say about that. In possibly the least subtle subject change in history, he said, "You know what I was doing on the rockhopper, huh?"

She nodded. "I was still connected to the rockhopper's computer when the bombs went off, trying to buy you some time to get out, and I get a notification that there's been a portable drive connected to the computer."

His black-mirror eyes didn't so much as blink, but she could've sworn they got just a shade wider. Shadows played across his jaw, darkening and lightening as the structures beneath tanned skin moved. Clenching, unclenching. "What'd you see?"

A loaded question, if ever she'd heard one. Not a threat, not a challenge, but heavy with implications unknown and unsettled. Somehow that was worse.

She shook her head. "Nothing." Then, because nobody ever heard *nothing* and believed it, she explained, "It was encrypted. Keyed for Guild computers only, but then I'm thinking you knew that. Why else would you risk your ass in an explosion just for a little alone time with a rockhopper console?"

"I've been told I'm not very bright."

"Sounds like they weren't paying attention."

Finally, he turned to her. "I ain't," he said, decisively. "But you are. You're good with that sort of thing, right? The computers and shit." She could practically hear the steam starting to build behind the words. "Could you decrypt it?"

"I don't have the key on my GLASS. But Captain Eoan—"

He shook his head. "No. Can't take this to them."

"Why?" She worried her lip between her teeth. Oh, she had a very bad feeling about this. "What's in that drive, Jal?"

He glanced back to the screen, and though it was still the same blank gray, she almost got the feeling he was watching that video all over again. In his mind's eye, maybe. *He knew all the words.* He must've been playing it since they turned in. *He must miss them so terribly.* She wasn't sure why—she didn't know him from Adam, really; she certainly didn't know his family— but the thought still brought a prickle to her eyes.

He said, after a moment, "It's my way back to them. Or," he sighed, "it's not a goddamn thing."

"You don't know?"

"Can't know. Not 'til I see what's on it."

"And you can't just ask the captain to help you because?" She squinted at him. "You're not in some kind of trouble, are you?"

He actually laughed, staccato and airy like she'd surprised it out of him. "Yeah," he said, a wide grin on his face and a terrible worry lining the corner of his eyes. "Some kind of trouble. And they got no business being in it with me, any of them."

Now if that wasn't a story half-told, she didn't know what was. She scoffed, plucking her glasses off to wipe them on her shirt hem. "Oh, but me, that's different," she said. "Your trouble's *totally* my business."

"Won't be any trouble for you if you don't tell anybody about it." And he must've figured out how it sounded, because he swore before she could even finish putting her glasses back to side-eye him properly. "That's not—that wasn't a threat. I just mean, they could make a real mess of things, if they knew what's on that drive. What I *think*'s on that drive," he corrected. "But whatever you find, I know you'll keep it between us. I trust you."

"Why?" she said. "You barely know me."

"You barely knew me back in the hangar," he replied. "Why didn't you shoot me?"

Seemed like sort of an obvious question. "I didn't have a choice. You were my only way out." But it was only when he spread his hands, a *there you have it* sort of gesture, that she understood: he was stuck, too. Trapped in his own way, by his own problems, and he needed a way out. She was it.

No pressure. She tried to laugh, but it fell flat. "You know, I'm actually a pretty terrible shot."

Jal arched an eyebrow. "I don't know," he said. "I reckon you did all right with Riesen."

Anke blanched so hard, she made herself dizzy. "What do you—?"

"Two shots," Jal said, holding up two fingers. "The one in Riesen's leg didn't match the one in his chest. Too little for the agitators' rifles, but just about right for that little peashooter of yours. I'm thinking maybe it wasn't those agitators who got the first shot off, was it?"

Her stomach plunged, sickeningly. *He knows. He knows. He knows.* And in the absence of a more believable lie, all she could hold on to was the truth. "He was going to shoot me," she admitted. She could still see it, when she closed her eyes. The glint of the barrel, and the steely determination on Riesen's weathered face that said he wouldn't hesitate to squeeze that trigger. "I shot him first. Just—just enough to get away. I shut the cargo door behind me, closed it up with straps and stuff so he couldn't just key it open."

"Attagirl."

Which . . . really wasn't the reaction she'd expected. "Wait." Something struck her then. "You didn't say anything, back in the galley. You knew what I did, but you didn't say. Why would you do that?"

"You did what you had to do. Telling them would've just made things more confusing."

She'd thought the same thing, though she had an inkling there was more to it than that. "That, and you need my help, right?"

"That too." He sighed, stretching his legs out in front of him. Seriously, how did someone with legs that long even *live* on a ship? It was a wonder he didn't have a permanent doorframe-shaped dent on his forehead. "Don't get me wrong: if I could do it myself, I'd ask you to forget all about it and let that be the end of things, but that rockhopper was as far as I knew how to get."

She relaxed a little, forcing a breath past the vise in her chest. He knew about Riesen and her rainy-day pistol. That wasn't ideal. On the other hand, he didn't seem inclined to do anything about it, and keeping her out of hot water worked in his favor, too. Could've been worse. "What? You mean you don't crack high-level encryptions in your spare time?"

Another laugh, quieter than the last one. A low, breathy rumble in the quiet room. "You know, I was thinking of taking it up. Just can't seem to get around to it."

"Too busy rescuing strangers from bomb-ridden death traps? Uh-huh, I've heard that before." She'd found her smile again, by the end of it. She'd missed this—conversation with something that actually talked back. Computers were great and all, but not exactly banging out the witty repartee, and Riesen hadn't been the bantering type. It'd been a long few weeks on that rockhopper, even *before* he tried to kill her.

"So," Jal started, hope so tentative in his voice that it plucked every heartstring she had and even a few she hadn't known about. Didn't seem like he was trying; he was just . . . *golden*. Hard to see it at first, through all the dents and dirt he'd picked up along the way, but in the little moments, in the small kindnesses and the breakthrough smiles, it shined. "Will you?"

"Deceive the captain and crew who graciously agreed to join my quest to save the universe from multiplanetary geocide?" She tried to keep the good mood going, but it was really hard to sugarcoat that kind of gamble. Captain Eoan and their crew were Anke's only ticket to Noether and to finishing what she'd started, and her mission was too important to jeopardize for one man. Even if that man *had* saved her life, and *was* depending on her to get back to his family and *did* have the kind of smile a girl could lose herself in and impossible strength and dimples that could launch a thousand—

Off topic. God. It got worse when she didn't sleep, her ping-ponging brain. Yes, it was a risk. Helping him, lying for him, would endanger the mission she and others had sacrificed *everything* for. She knew what they would say, the people who stood with her. They'd say it wasn't her place, and that so many more people counted on her to do her job. They'd tell her not to risk it, when they'd entrusted so much to her.

But they weren't there. They hadn't been pinned in that rockhopper, watching the backup power tick down to zero; and they hadn't seen the love, the loss, the *longing* in Jal's eyes as he'd watched that snowy little memory play out on the screen. It wasn't their choice. It was hers.

So she made the only one that she could live with.

"Okay."

"Okay?"

Not great at reading between the lines. That was fine; he was pretty exceptional at lifting heavy objects off of trapped Guild programmers. She could appreciate the skill sets he *did* have. "Okay, I'll help. Or, I'll try. Not sure how much of the drive I was able to clone before the ship went *boom,* and assuming I got the lion's share, I've got to munch my way through a few layers of spicy, spicy encryption to get to the prize inside. Which is to say, if it's humanly possible, I'm your girl. I mean"—she caught herself—"I'm not *your* girl. I'm *the* girl. For the job, that is. Oh my God, I'm going to stop talking, now. I swear, I'm not normally this bad." *Liar, liar, pants on fire.*

"I don't mind," Jal said, smile returned to its former dimply glory. It wasn't even that big of a smile, soft and a little crooked; the dimples just *happened*. So not fair.

"You're just saying that because I agreed to aid and abet your criminal conspiracy."

"Never said it was criminal."

"Never said it wasn't," she pointed out, cheerfully. Lo and behold, she even had to smother a yawn as all that restless nervousness finally started to loosen its grip. How long had it been since she'd had a proper night's sleep? She couldn't even remember, but her eyelids got heavier just thinking about it. She held up a finger to her lips. "But shh, I'm clinging to every shred of plausible deniability I can get. Just so you know, if this all goes sideways, I'm telling them you coerced me."

"You do that."

She nodded, decisively. "You held a gun to my head," she told him, sinking back a little against the foot of the bed. Her shoulder knocked his, not by any design but sheer, sleepy clumsiness, but he didn't shake her loose or scoot away. "No, that's not really your style. You're subtler than that. A real man of distinction."

"That so?" he asked, looking a little drowsy himself. She got the sense that if it weren't for her, he'd have turned the screen off already and let the room go dark. Given only one of them had nocturnal eyes, though, and the other had a penchant for finding solid objects with her shins at the mere *suggestion* of dim lighting, it was nice of him to leave it on. "How d'you reckon I'd do it, then?"

She turned her head, studying him in the soft glow. Such an honest face, sun-touched and lined with good years and bad. "You wouldn't," she said, softly, and with the blanket snug around her shoulders, she stood.

He glanced up at her. "Calling it a night?"

That was the plan, if only to get out of his hair. Though the thought of going back to that room, with the too-thin pillows and the hum of the engines, the warning beep of the battery and the pounding fists and furious shouts—"Can I sleep with you tonight?" she blurted.

Jal looked completely flummoxed for the, oh, five seconds it took her to realize what she'd said. Or, rather, how it must've *sounded.*

"Oh! Oh, *no.*" She buried her face in her hands, willing the heat to recede from her cheeks. Couldn't even blame that one on brain chemistry, just a taste for shoe leather and the uncanny ability to say totally *normal* things in totally *abnormal* ways. "Not *with* you, with you. In the room. Which still sounds super weird, now that I'm saying it out loud. It's just . . . I'm having a hard time shutting off? I close my eyes and I start to drift, and then . . ." She trailed off, helplessly.

Man of few words Jal might've been, but he seemed to have the right ones for this situation. "Then you're back there," he said, with a deep, effortless understanding. "All right, then," he said, rising from the foot of the bed to shuffle to the closet.

"What're you doing?" she asked.

He turned back with a stack of blankets and a couple pillows balanced on his arm. "Bed's yours."

"Oh, no, I can't—"

"Ain't big enough for the both of us." If there was any mercy in the world, even his keen eyes wouldn't pick up the flush on her cheeks. "And I can't let you sleep on the floor."

"Because I'm a girl?"

"*The* girl, I think you said." He spread out one of the blankets and dropped the pillows at the head of it with a shrug. "But if it makes you feel any better, we can say it's 'cause you had the worse day."

"Not sure that's a competition I want to win."

"Shitty trophy," he agreed, settling down on the blanket. He made a point of reaching up to the bed and yanking back the remaining covers. "Sleep."

She would've argued, she told herself. If she weren't so tired and wrung out and sore, she would've made a real stink about it. She was all of those things, though, and even a few more, and so all she said as she wrapped her blanket tighter around herself and flopped onto the mattress was "Flip you for it tomorrow."

If she wasn't asleep before her head hit the pillow, then it was a very near thing.

CHAPTER NINE

NASH

Nash swore she'd only been asleep a few minutes when the alarm went off.

Not the *shit's going down* alarm—it had a uniquely ass-puckering cadence—but the one that said they'd be landing planetside shortly, so they really ought to get moving.

"All right, all right," she grumbled, rolling off her hammock and feeling around in the open drawer beside it. Sweater. *Nope.* Too heavy. She tossed it over her shoulder and reached again. Sleeveless T-shirt. *Better.* Linen joggers, because it'd be humid as fuck. She dressed in a hurry and threw her hair in a rough bun, stuffing her feet in her shoes and her toothbrush in her mouth as she climbed up the ladder to the infirmary. "Time?" she called to Eoan around a mouthful of toothpaste.

"Less than fifteen minutes to landing."

"Little more warning next time!"

"Then you'll say to let you sleep longer." There wasn't a projection in sight, but Nash would've bet a month's pay that Eoan had a smile.

Checkmate. She narrowed her eyes at the ceiling, because it was kind of hard to glare at the entire fucking *ship*, and spat her toothpaste in the sick bay sink as she passed. Bag from the shelf, a meal bar from the cabinet—and then a couple more, when she remembered a certain mutant miner and his bottomless stomach—and she was out the sick bay door in a rush.

Too much of one, it turned out, because she crashed into

Anke just a couple steps into the hall. "Oh!" Anke yelped, with an endearing little flail backward. Nearly knocked a macramé plant hanger off the wall, but Nash caught it before it fell, carefully returning it to its hook. "Sorry! Sorry." Anke pressed her hand to her chest and took a few quick breaths. In her defense, after what she'd been through, she'd earned some jumpiness. "I just—the alarm."

"Just means we're landing soon," Nash said, giving Anke a quick once-over. She'd dressed, though she could probably lose the coat. Nash told her as much as she started down the hall toward the galley. Tight schedule be damned, she needed a cup of tea.

Anke, probably for lack of anything better to do, trailed along beside her. "Wait," she said. "Why are we landing? How long was I asleep?"

"Hopefully longer than I was," Nash sighed, a bit wistfully. Eoan already had some hot water waiting, about a minute off the boil. Didn't quite make up for their shit timing, but it helped. "We've got to stop for supplies. Army marches on its stomach and all that."

"What about all the crates in the hold?"

Nash opened her stash cabinet and riffled around the various cannisters of tea until she found the right blend for the morning. "We stocked up a couple of days back, but that was for two warm bodies on a two-week trip back out to frontier patrol. Now we've got three mouths to feed, and some as-yet-unknown subspecies of garbage disposal," she added with a nod toward the hall. She actually had no idea where Jal had gotten off to, and the only signs of Saint's presence were the stack of protein pancakes on the warmer and the half-full pot of coffee in the machine.

Anke shook her head when Nash offered her a cup, frowning. "It's just one week to Noether. Surely we could make it, if we stretched a little."

"And the trip home?" Sure, they could probably make it on emergency rations and their grow room crop, but that kind of defeated the point of *emergency* rations. They were there for the shit you couldn't plan for. "Kind of important, that."

"Oh. Right." Anke looked flustered. Kind of reminded Nash of the times Bodie fell off the counter and was afraid somebody had noticed, like Anke couldn't decide whether to be embarrassed or annoyed. Bodie usually skittered off to rally his pride, though; Anke just flushed red and rubbed her eyes under her glasses. "I'm sorry, I'm just—this has been my life for years, you know? Day in and day out, trying to get to the bottom of all those . . . *terrible* doesn't even cut it, does it? Hundreds of people could die. Thousands. *Millions*."

Nash nodded, stirring her tea and watching the colors bleed into the water. "It's a lot of pressure." Understatement. "But you don't save people's lives by sabotaging your own. So, we stop here, get what we need to keep ourselves alive and moving, and then we haul ass for Noether. Okay?" Not that Anke really had much choice.

"Yeah," Anke said with a quiet sigh. "Yeah, you're right. I know you're right. I guess . . . I'm just tired, is all. Ready for it to be over."

"I get it," Nash said. It felt like a different lifetime, but she'd had a white whale of her own—a mission so important to her that she'd forgotten she still had to *live* afterward. "You know," she began, blowing gently on her steaming mug, "there's not a whole lot of options for kids growing up on a station. You take the job that's open when you're old enough to work, whether it's what you want to do or not. And mine was *not*." To put it lightly. "Sixteen years old, grumpy and awkward and staring down a lifetime as a *resource dispensary technician*. Basically a glorified pickup window, and I hated every second. Started ditching work, nicking cables and shit to scrape by, and I got good at it. Could strip an engine in five minutes flat and be gone before anybody even knew I was there. And for a couple of years, that worked for me.

"Then I got caught. I was in the station sick bay, going through some of their scrap machines for parts, and this old doc walks in and sees me. And she just . . . *stared* at me. Don't know who was more surprised, her or me, but we must've stood there for a minute or two just gawking at each other." She smiled faintly at the memory, shaking her head. It'd been a while since she'd told the story, but Anke . . . she was weirdly easy to talk to. All big eyes and rapt attention. Nash didn't feel that way about a lot of people, but there she was. "I thought she was gonna call station security. Management didn't take well to stealing, resources being so limited. But after a minute, this doc looks at the machines I'd picked to pieces, and she says, *Well, you took it apart all right. How'd you like to learn how to put shit back together again?*"

"She's the one who taught you." Anke smiled, too, in that with-her-whole-face way she did.

Nash nodded. "Maybe not everything I know, but everything that mattered." Not just the *what*s, but the *why*s—why her skills and her work and her time and her attention, why all of that meant something. To someone who'd spent so much of her life without real meaning, as just another cog in the station's grand machine, those lessons were everything. "I was with her for the better part of a decade. Picking up everything I could, following her around from station to station, colony to colony. She gave me these, you know?" She coiled a strand of her augments around her finger, letting the fine, shimmering filament slip across her skin. "It was the longest I'd ever known anyone, me and the doc. Even my parents were gone before I hit double digits, but she was always just *there*. Constant and patient, and probably kinder than she had any business being to a mouthy little punk like me, until—" She quenched the sudden dryness in her throat with a swig of tea. It didn't help; nothing ever did. The years had made her good at pretending, though.

"When I found her body, I barely recognized it. Security said it was probably just thieves looking to score some meds, but it was . . . something else. Brutal. Personal. There'd been some noise from a group of anti-augmenters, didn't like the doc setting up shop with her implant biz, but nobody'd ever told the doc who to help or how to help 'em, and she hadn't taken their shit any different." The warmth from the mug seeped into her hands, but they still felt cold. "Took a bit of doing to track them down, after. Fuckers fled the station right after they did it. Must've spent nine, ten months chasing after them."

"Did you find them?" Anke's smile faded. Good. This part of the story wasn't for smiling. It wasn't for gratification or satisfaction, for comfort or for pride. It was for the lesson, hard learned and harder forgotten.

"I did," she said, and there was nothing more to say about that. What needed to be said was this: "And I didn't care what came after. Didn't even care if there *was* an after, and damned if a few months later, I wasn't right back where I started. I didn't know what else to do, so I just didn't do anything. Nicked scrap to fence for food, wasted every goddamn thing that woman taught me, until I got caught again. Eoan, this time," she said. "Kind of funny, isn't it? Twice, getting caught mid-nick's saved my life. I don't know where I would've wound up, if the captain hadn't nabbed me, but safe to say it would've been nowhere good.

"Which I guess is my long-ass way of telling you, be careful where you set your finish line," she concluded, giving Anke's arm a bump. She'd never been a pro at this whole *socializing* thing, but if anybody deserved the effort, she figured *girl who's saving the galaxy* was pretty fucking high on the list.

Still. A little too much sharing for a single cup of tea. "Anyway." She leaned into the word, an unspoken *that's enough of that,* with a deep gulp of tea. "Our stop-off is more or less on the way. Place called Sooner's Weald—it's a trading-post planet right at the end of the shipping lane to the center spiral. We hit it, then fork off the beaten path all the way to Noether, and we're still there inside a week," she said, miming their flight path with a hand. "Cool place, too. Little muggy, but some real clever terraforming. You'll love it.

"And if the Trust really comes for our asses, it's probably the safest stop-off from here to the center spiral. Co-op market," she explained. "Trust started it up, back in the big expansion, but they couldn't hold it. Brought in too many workers to build it quick, didn't see fit to pay them what they were worth. Wasn't too hard for some agitators to blow in, rile them up, and suddenly you've got a planetwide labor strike. Builders, farmers. Even the merchants joined in—saw their chance to make some caps without the Trust scraping their customary twenty percent off the top. Saint actually used to be stationed here, during the worst of it. Back in his rookie ranger days."

"Keeping the peace?"

"*Keep the peace* just means *keep the status quo,*" Nash said. "*Pick a side.* Not really the Guild's bag—institutional neutrality, et cetera." She shook her head. Anke really was new to the fold. "They just kept people from dying. Okay to block the ports, not okay to bomb them. Don't care if you burn the shops, but you'd better be damn sure there's nobody inside them first. We protect life and people's right to live it. The rest is somebody else's problem."

"Still," said Anke. "You ever think about who has it right?"

Nash shrugged. "I think they didn't like the way shit was and decided to do something about it. Gotta respect them for that. And lucky for us, they came out on top."

Maybe Nash wasn't as rusty at this whole *people* thing as she thought, because Anke's smile came back. "So will we," she said, with a deep, rallying breath. "We'll stock up, we'll ship out, and we'll save the effin' universe."

Inspirational *and* adorable.

"Sounds like we've got ourselves a plan," said Jal as he rambled into the galley, not so much as a bootstep to herald his approach. He was quiet, for a big guy. Half-asleep and half-dressed, hovering near the doorway with one leg of his jeans tucked in his boots, jacket slung over his shoulder, hair damp like he'd tried to tame it back with a few fistfuls of water, failed, and summarily conceded. The only bit on right were his specs, but with ship lighting, they probably weren't optional. "I smell pancakes?"

Nash waved to the warmer. "Think Saint made extras, if you're hungry."

"Still loves his pancakes," he said, shaking his head. Jal seemed pretty keen himself, crossing the galley to pluck one, still steaming, out of the warmer.

"We have plates, you know," Nash said, but Jal already had half the pancake in his mouth, and the other half rolled up in his fingers waiting to follow it down the hatch. "Or just cram it down. That's good for you. And not disgusting at all."

He grinned around a mouthful of pancake—a whole mother-loving pancake, good grief—and reached for another.

"You'll have to take the rest to go, I'm afraid," Eoan said, projecting themself just a few steps ahead in a flowing plaid-print dress. To their credit, neither Jal nor Anke flinched. After all the weirdness they'd seen in the last twenty-four hours, the captain's spontaneous appearances probably didn't even rank. "We're landing in"—a pause—"well, now, actually. Saint's waiting in the hold."

"We really got to work on this whole *advance notice* thing, Cap," Nash said, draining the last of her tea in a few quick gulps. Waste of a good chai. As they left, she saw Jal snatch the last three pancakes out of the warmer. Not one to leave food on the table. Or the counter. Or pretty much anywhere in arm's reach. Though he did seem keen to share, especially with a certain forward feline, who darted out from fuck only knew where in the galley and started weaving through Jal's legs until he got a pinch of pancake. They'd be thick as thieves by the end of this— literally *and* figuratively, in Bodie's case.

True to Eoan's word, Saint waited for them by the cargo bay door as they walked in. "They live," he said, then to Jal, "Guess you found the pancakes."

Jal gave a thumbs up and swallowed his last mouthful, wiping his hands on his jeans like he'd never heard of a napkin. "Where are we, anyway?"

"Sooner's Weald," Nash said. They needed to start sending out memos.

He surprised her with a broad, sunny grin. "Shit, really? Ain't been here in a dog's age."

"Wait, you've been here, too?" Anke asked. Before Jal could answer, she seemed to put the pieces together for herself. "Oh. You were stationed together, weren't you? That's why you two are. . . ." She trailed off, gesturing vaguely.

Nash wasn't sure how *she* would've finished that sentence, either.

Jal tipped his head, though. "Yes, ma'am," he said. *Ma'am, ma'am, ma'am.* His manners might've been atrocious with food, but he had the honorifics *nailed.* "Couple rotations. Not the worst place to post up, if you don't mind the heat." He did shrug out of his jacket, though, and twisted his hair up in a short, sloppy bun. As he tied it off, he nodded to Saint's gun belt. "Extra clips. You expecting trouble, old man?"

"No more than the usual sort," said Saint. "Unless you keep calling me *old.*"

With a huff of a laugh, Jal turned to Nash. "You armed, too?"

"Wouldn't you like to know."

His forehead wrinkled. "You know, if we do run into trouble, three guns'd be better than two."

"You learn math while you were playing hookie?" Which earned Saint a gesture that Nash didn't recognize—an Earther thing Jal'd picked up from Saint, maybe; or a Brigham thing Saint had picked up from him—but suffice it to say it probably wasn't very nice. Saint returned it, tartly, and grabbed a pistol off the gun rack on the wall. "Here. You want a gun, you can spook 'em with that. You do remember which way's the scary end, right?"

Jal weighed the gun in his hand and checked the clip. "It's empty."

"They won't know that," Saint replied. "Don't recall you being much of a crack shot anyway." The clap he gave Jal's shoulder as he called for Eoan to drop the ramp seemed almost friendly. "C'mon, kids. Daylight's wasting."

Sooner's Weald, by Nash's estimation, had plenty of daylight to spare. Even with the thick canopy of trees overhead, enough rays managed to eke through to paint the port in mottled shades of red and gold. It danced over the metal grate platforms sprawling five, maybe six slips in every direction, and nearly half of them were full. Rockhoppers, cargo ships, shuttles—all manner of vessels, full of all manner of people, all converging in one place to take advantage of one of the most diverse markets in the O-Cyg spiral.

Jal bounded out first, heading down the ramp with more pep in his step than Nash knew he was capable of. In the warm sunlight, he seemed to stand a little taller, face turned toward the sky like some kind of flower soaking up the shine.

"Someone woke up on the right side of the bed," she said, shouldering her bag and following him down the gangway. Anke made a small hiccupping noise beside her, cheeks flushing an endearing shade of pink. Nash probably would've said something about it, if she thought it was any of her business. Unlike

Eoan, Nash firmly believed some questions *didn't* need an answer. "Or maybe you're just itching for another chance to ditch us, huh?" She joked. Mostly. Although, she did give the back of Jal's neck a quick peek to check for the patch. If he *did* try something, he wouldn't get very far, and they'd have something to laugh about as they dragged his jelly-legged ass back to the ship.

Jal shook his head, all earnest and easy. "No, ma'am," he said. "Just glad to stretch my legs."

You could do that just getting out of the port. It wasn't like the outpost, where everything had been crowded together. There must've been twice as many ships, twice as many people, but generous, sprawling walkways hung suspended less than a story over a rushing reservoir of milky-blue water. She didn't even have to throw any elbows.

"Underground rivers," said Anke, pausing to stare over a rail. "I've read about this. That color—it's the silica and salt. The smell's sulfur," she added, scrunching her face. "They say you get used to it."

"You don't," Saint and Jal said, almost in unison. "Trees like it, though," Saint added, waving to the canopy above them. Thick, towering trees whose roots stretched above the surface of the water thirty, maybe forty decs. "Reminds me of the mangrove forests, back home." Saint didn't talk much about Earth, and when he did, he mostly griped about the bugs. Bugs, swamps, and soggy air—the man was a walking travel brochure, truly. "Bigger, I mean, but they're damn hardy."

Anke couldn't seem to decide where to look. Down at the water, up at the canopy, out ahead where the walkways all converged in a cluster of carts and a grand, curving archway, layered with hand-painted badges and names and insignias of ships that'd passed through over the years. *We were here,* they said. *We were part of this.*

Nash saw the bump on the walkway just a beat before it caught Anke's toe and managed to grab her elbow. Didn't stop her tripping, but it did stop her getting a faceful of metal grating, and earned a sheepish laugh as Anke righted herself. "Sorry," she said. "It's just—kind of nerding out, over here. I mean, look at it! The way it all works together. There's no switch to flip. No plug to pull. You could shut down every bit of tech on the planet, and it'd stay alive. Stay livable." She paused to smile up at the sky, and Nash stopped with her. Admiring her admiring the world around her—the joy, the inspiration, the open, unabashed *awe*. In a way, they were the same: they loved systems. They loved watching the way little things worked together to make big things thrive. For Nash, it was gears and wires and currents; for Anke, it was . . . *life*, and all its constituent parts. "This is the way it should be," Anke said. "Takes a little longer. Even engineered trees like these need a few years to reach maturity, but." She shook her head. "They last, you know? Things like this are supposed to last."

The guys had gotten ahead of them, but Nash didn't want to leave. Not yet. It felt important, somehow, what Anke had said. Like a glimpse behind the curtain. The currents beneath the bright, glittering surface of the reservoir, pushing and moving and *driving*. "Sometimes people would rather scrap what they have and move on to something new. Easier that way. Cheaper, too."

"But not better," Anke said.

Nash glanced back at the *Ambit*, with all her soldered scars and mottled paint. Would've been a far sight easier to surrender her to the scrap fields years ago, but she deserved more. Those people had deserved more, too, back at the shipping depot. Somewhere along the way, the universe had started attaching a price tag to survival—equating viability to *profitability*. In things, in places, and, worst of all, in *people*. That, Nash decided, was where it'd all gone wrong. "No," she agreed. "Not better."

Progress was such a dangerous word.

Though, on the subject of progress. "I think we're getting

left behind," Nash said, glancing down the walkway. The back of Saint's head had gotten awfully small in the distance, but they could still catch up before the arch, if Anke didn't mind a jog. "Come on. We've probably only got an hour or two before most of the supplies are loaded."

"What'll we do with two hours?"

"What else do you do in the coolest trading post in the spiral?" Nash held out a hand with the best smile she could muster, only to smile all the wider when Anke took it. "Let's go burn some paychecks."

SAINT

There wasn't another trading post like Sooner's Weald. The variety alone kept most people coming back—most of the planet was wild-farmed jungle, packed to bursting with all sorts of roots, fruits, and vegetables. Chances were any produce you could pick up in the stalls grew just a ferry ride away, sold fresh or fermented, dried or fried. And that was just the stuff you could *eat*.

The atmosphere, though, *that* drew even more people than the food. The bazaar was the beating heart of the Weald, woven through the thick clusters of trees at the end of the port. The reservoir ran underground, but Saint swore you could still feel the rush of the water under the packed mulch walkways, and roots served as scaffolding for two-, even three-story shop fronts with walls in every color of clay imaginable. Spices and perfumes drowned out the stink of sulfur, and drumbeats and flutes and whistling reeds filled the air with a lively, fluttering pulse.

He'd hated it, the first time.

The trees reminded him too much of the swamps back home, of years with the Earth intercontinental army trudging through mud and moss and wondering if it'd be the bullets that killed him, or the goddamn *bugs*. The bustling streets put him on edge—too many people, too many ways in and out, and no way to keep track of it all. Above him, the rope bridges and rooftops had felt like hundreds of sniper nests waiting to put a bead on his crew.

But goddamn, the way Jal had smiled. Plodding down that street in his ill-fitting gear, still so fresh off the lightless rock of a moon he'd grown up on that all the sun and the green must've seemed like a fantasy. He didn't see swamps or chokepoints or snipers; he saw new foods and smiling strangers and trinkets he could save up for to send home to Bitsie and Regan.

Through his eyes, Saint had learned to like it there. Then through Nash's. Now he got to watch Anke's eyes light up as all the stress and trauma of the last few days . . . it didn't go away completely. Even Sooner's Weald didn't have that kind of magic. But enough of it slipped into the background for a while as they wandered the stalls. Still some things to pick up—clothes for her and Jal, and as Saint hovered by a stall hawking nuts and dried fruit, Nash emerged from a nearby shop with a cannister about the size of a bottle of blur.

"Rough day?"

"The roughest," she replied. "But it's not for me." Nash popped the top of the cannister, and little purple flowers peeked over the edge, sprouted from pale stems so thin and delicate he figured they'd wilt if he looked at them too hard.

"Smells like soap," he said, turning back to the stall. He caught the vendor's eye and motioned to the basket of palm berries and assorted dried fruits. Too sugary—he hated the stuff. He asked for a bag of each. "What is it?"

Nash scowled and popped the lid back on the cannister. "It's lavender," she said. "My bunk's pretty much empty, you know? Depressing. Bad energy." She shrugged. "Just figured I'd get something to spruce it up a bit."

Saint arched an eyebrow. "I see."

"There's nothing to *see*."

"Of course not," Saint said, agreeably. "You just bought her flowers."

A flustered Nash was a rare sight indeed. Damn near mythical, in the sense that few who saw it lived to tell about it. The ship could be on fire and she'd barely break a sweat, but there she was, getting a little color on her cheeks. "It's for the room," she said.

"Right."

Nash opened her mouth to reply, and punched him in the arm instead. "Shut up and get your fruit," she said, and as he turned to pay the merchant—he wasn't laughing, honest—Anke and Jal came shuffling across the street to join them. Each had a couple bags on their arms. Not much, just a few shirts and a couple pairs of pants, but Saint reckoned it would be enough to tide them over until they could put this mess behind them and get everyone back where they belonged.

Wherever the hell that is, he thought, eyeing Jal as he lingered by the fruit cart. Felt so strange to watch him, now—to see him holding back, hovering at the edge of the crowd by the cart, when the Jal he'd known would've loped straight into the middle of it without a second thought. He had a tension in him now that Saint didn't recognize. A push-pull in the shifting of his feet forward and back again, like the old Jal was still *in there*, eager and excited, but something kept holding him back. Too much scar tissue; this Jal had his own snipers in the trees.

Still had that goddamn sweet tooth of his, though; he scanned the baskets of many-colored fruits like a hummingbird to hibiscus. "Here," Saint said, tossing him the bag of palm berries he'd bought. "Still like those, don't you?" Jal used to carry a bag of them in his gear, munching on them by the fistful every chance they got. Saint still remembered the smell of them, peachy-pineappley and tart, in the midday heat.

A slow, nostalgic smile spread on Jal's face as he opened the bag. "I forgot about these," he said, but it must've come back to him all right. He grabbed a fistful, just like he used to, and tossed them back like candy. *Pop, pop, pop.* One by one, the firm, ripe fruits burst between his teeth. Saint used to hate that sound. Sitting beside him on a rooftop while he chatted or hummed and chewed those berries, *pop, pop, pop.*

Close your mouth, he used to gripe. *And turn off your mic, for mercy's sake.* Most annoying sound in the whole goddamn spiral, and he'd never had a problem telling him so.

Funny how much you missed those sorts of things when someone was gone.

"What about you?" he asked Anke, ignoring the smirk Nash flung his way. *And you gave me shit about the lavender,* said the hand tucked pointedly on her hip. Lord help him. "You get what you needed?"

"And then some." The coder had brightened up a lot since they'd stepped off the ship. Fresh air had that effect on people, and there'd always been something joyful about the Weald. Upbeat and vibrant, whole spectrums of colors and sounds and smells wrapped snug in the muggy warmth of the jungle. "How long before we need to be back on the ship?"

Saint started to check his GLASS, but something in the reflection caught his eye. "Those guys by the brew cart," he said, dropping his voice below the din of the crowd. "Something about them seem off to you?" Four of them stood under the ratty green awning, sipping cheap blur and shooting the shit. Watching them, Saint felt the back of his neck prickle.

Jal leaned in, presumably to catch a look in the reflection. His eyebrows bunched the way they always did when he focused, but man, Saint didn't remember those lines on his forehead cutting so deep.

When'd you go and get old, kid?

"Short guy ain't drinking," Jal said, slowly. "Talking, either."

"Like those other three don't even know him." Nash swore, tugging at the straps of her backpack. Not fidgeting; *preparing.*

It was a hell of a lot easier to run with a tight pack. "Think we picked up a tail?"

Saint scanned the crowd, fingers itching for the grip of his gun. Wasn't like he was about to start a shoot-out in the middle of the market, but old habits were a bitch. "Eoan, you copy? Need a quick scan on the cam footage. Think we might've got something stuck to our shoes." Bodycams were Guild protocol for missions, but he and Nash wore theirs just about anytime they went planetside. Kept Eoan in the loop back on the ship.

Came in real handy, in times like these.

"Already on it," Eoan said, because of course they were. "Ah, good news."

"We're not being followed?" Anke guessed, or maybe it was just a bit of her glowing optimism. Either way, she was in for disappointment. Saint knew that tone.

"Oh," said Eoan. "No, you're definitely being followed. That fellow at the cart. Another up ahead, as well. See the woman in the blue cap? The one pretending to smell the same bar of soap for the third, ah, *fourth* time—that's the one."

"That's *good* news?" Anke yelped. Her head started to turn, but Nash tipped it straight again and, after a moment's hesitation, patted her shoulder. Most awkward thing Saint had seen in a while, but nice to see her making an effort.

"Of course it is," Eoan replied, patient as ever. "A tail you can make is a tail you can shake, as they say. But you'd better get on that, dears; I've clocked four more likelies since you left the port."

Even for Eoan, it was calculated guesswork—picking out the faces that Saint and Nash had passed too many times to be coincidence, isolating strange behaviors, playing the odds. Eoan had been at this business longer than any of them had been alive, though, and Saint would put their guesswork above anybody else's sure thing any day of the week.

Six tails, though. *That we know of.* His teeth ground together.

If they were smart enough to fly under the radar that long, to spread out and trade off contact so Saint and the others wouldn't pick up a pattern, then they were probably smart enough to keep a few waiting in the wings. Suddenly those rooftops looked awfully suspicious again. The streets were too crowded. Too many people, too many blind spots and pinch points and—

Jal offered him the bag of palm berries. "Have one?"

"Not really the time for snacking, miner boy," said Nash, but Saint caught his black-lensed gaze and dipped his head. He'd needed the distraction. Something to throw Saint's bloodhound brain off the scent before it got away from him.

He forced his shoulders lower. *Have to relax,* he thought. Or at least look the part. They didn't want their tagalongs thinking they were wise to them. "Any idea who they are?"

"Not Guild," said Eoan, and Saint knew it was pointless to be relieved, but he was. They still had half a dozen bogeys on their asses, but at least they weren't wearing the same badge. "Not agitators, either, as far as I can tell. Freelance outfit. Looks like mostly cargo escorts, and who wants to guess their top-paying client?"

"Always knew this job would give me Trust issues," Nash muttered.

Saint shot her a flat look. "Don't blame that on the job."

"More mercenaries. Awesome." Anke chuckled tightly. "Don't take this the wrong way, but if this is the safest stop-off from here to the center spiral, I'd hate to see the most dangerous."

It was *supposed* to be the safest, though, damn it. No established Trust presence, not even a real Guild presence since the strikes ended. Something occurred to Saint, though, as a cold weight settled around his chest.

Maybe there *was* no safe place.

The Trust had eyes everywhere, and hands in everything. This wasn't the *Ambit*'s usual customer—not some smuggling ring in the frontier, or an upstart militia with chips on their shoulders and more guns than sense. This was an *institution*. This was *the* institution, and they were gearing up to give it one hell of a poke in the eye.

He took a slow breath and let it out in a sigh. *Fuck.* "What's the story here, Cap? They follow us from the depot?"

"No, I would've picked up the signal," said Eoan. "Must've found another way to track us. Something from the rockhopper seems most likely, but I scanned everything Anke brought with her."

"Ditto," said Anke, firmly. "There's no way they locked onto anything of mine. I'm not just saying that because I don't want this to be my fault, either. Which I don't, but it's not, so." She'd chewed her bottom lip red, but otherwise she kept the nerves under control. "Sorry. Nervous."

"Don't be nervous," Nash told her. "We can lose them." Softer, to Saint, "But it'd be a hell of a lot easier if we could figure out what they're following. I gutted the ankle monitor; wasn't anything in there. Someone had to have brought something back. Something—"

"Fuck." Abruptly, Jal shoved his hand in his pocket. A bit of fishing around, and with the chime of thin-pressed metal, tags dropped from his fingers by a ball chain. "Riesen's," he said, grimacing. "But before you go and start—"

"Give me that." Nash snatched it from him almost too fast to see, turning it over in her hands. Deft little wrench-slinger; she flashed a tiny screwdriver from out of nowhere and found a seam in the tag. A quick twist, and the tag split in two, and nestled between the two metal shells was a vellum-thin chip no bigger than a thumbnail. "There're your bread crumbs, Hansel," she said, passing it to Saint. "Passive satellite frequency tag. Wouldn't put off a signal 'til it passed in close range to a reader, so Cap's off the hook."

"I wasn't aware I was on one," said Eoan.

Nash ignored them. "Trust must have people looking out

for the signal, and these clowns picked it up when we docked. Great job, miner boy." Just because she didn't raise her voice didn't mean she wasn't stabbing knives through it. "The hell were you thinking?"

Shoulders up, head down—Jal was strung so tight, he'd have played a tune if you plucked him. "I was *thinking* he might have people." It was low enough to be a growl, but it didn't have the heat. "Body's nothing but scattered ash. Figured at least this way they'd have something to say goodbye to. Closure or something."

Doesn't work that way, Saint almost said. *Ask Bitsie.* The image had stuck with him: the way she'd stood behind her mama's legs when he'd told them the news about Jal, skinned knees and blonde pigtails, clutching that chain around her neck. Like she thought that if she held on to Jal's tags tight enough, she could hold on to him, too.

"We're not doing this right now," he said. Not the bickering, and *definitely* not reminiscing. "If they're after Anke, then we need to get her on the ship. Don't care how much the Trust is paying these guys, they're not gonna risk firing on a Guild vessel in an open port."

"Then they're Eoan's problem, anyway." Nash smirked, but she already had a fight in her eyes. No tensing, no weapons grabs; that wasn't Nash's style. She had a fresh fluidity to her stance, though, that said she'd be ready to move when the time came. "We'll split up," she said decisively. "I'll get Anke to the ship. You two, try to lead as many of them off our asses as you can."

It didn't miss him that she'd given herself the harder task. Ask anybody with gray in their hair what job they'd rather take, escort or decoy, and they'd take decoy before you finished asking the question. Cuffing yourself to somebody in a combat situation, fighting with one eye on the prize at all times—more folks died trying to keep somebody else alive than any other causes put together. *Bar sheer goddamn stupidity,* he thought.

Well, if that was how Nash wanted to play it, he wasn't about to fight her for it. "Regroup on the ship quick as you're able," he said, and Nash nodded back. Beside her, Anke squared up her shoulders, looking for all the world like she'd march over and deck that guy at the brew cart herself. If her eyes were a little wide, and her face shined a little with sweat, then Saint still had nothing but respect. Coder, civvy, ranger, whatever—that flashy pink hair had an awful lot of fight behind it.

"Gimme your bags," Jal said to her, holding out his scarred-up hands. Saint had a mind to tell them to drop them, but it'd be a shame if it turned out to be a false alarm, and they really did need clothes. Nothing on the ship fit either of them.

"But won't you—" Anke started to protest, but Nash plucked them from her and shoved them at Jal.

"The man ran rocks in floating mines half his life," she said curtly. "Unless you stuffed a boulder in there, it's not gonna slow him down." Then, to Saint, with the unflinching seriousness of someone bracing for a fight, "If you're too slow, we're leaving without you."

She wouldn't; it wasn't how they worked. But he'd be damned if they had to call her bluff.

"Just make sure we don't beat you there, glowworm," Jal grunted, earning a glare and a swat that was, for Nash, nearly friendly, even if she was still pissed about the Guild tags.

"All right, dears," Eoan said, cheerfully unconcerned. They didn't put a lot of stock in things like *faith* and *luck*, Saint knew, but they put stock in their people. All the best captains did. "Run."

CHAPTER TEN

JAL

Nash led the breakaway. Quick little spit—she took off, spring-loaded, tugging Anke beside her as they darted deeper into the bustle of the market. Mean mugs and meaner mouths chased them through the crowd, but Nash didn't miss a step, and she didn't let Anke miss any, either.

"Hang back," Saint told him, holding at a jog as the girls ran out ahead. "Watch."

"Ain't my first foot chase, old man," Jal said gruffly. Just because he'd been out of the loop a while didn't mean he'd forgotten everything he knew. It was a shell game. Saint had the tags, so as far as they knew, the mercs were visual-contact-only on Anke and Nash. All they had to do was give them something else to look at long enough to shuffle Anke off the board, and she and Nash would be home free. They needed a distraction.

Reckon you'll do, Jal thought, eyeing the shifty son of a bitch at the brew cart. He didn't disappoint. As the girls sped by, Shifty elbowed past his *drinking buddies* like he couldn't get after them fast enough. He hesitated, though. A moment's indecision—follow or don't, blow his cover or keep it. Happened to the best of them, but sometimes it only took a moment.

It was all Jal needed.

"Want this one?" Like Saint knew exactly what he was thinking.

"Yes, sir." He really, really did, and there'd be no hesitation from him. From a jog to an all-out sprint in the span of a few footfalls, and the merc had scarcely taken his first step away from the cart when Jal slammed into him from behind. All that speed, thrown behind all that mass—that kind of impact rattled your teeth, crumpled your lungs. It staggered Jal a step or two, but he was made of sterner stuff than that.

The merc, not so much. He got checked clear off his feet, crashing into a stack of crates by the cart with an eruption of splintered wood and shattering glass. Broken bottles spewed brew across the streets in waves of mulchy green. Cheap stuff; he could smell it. Reeked like acetone and seawater and burnt sugar. Used to be a mystery to Jal, how Saint could drink the stuff. He always had that flask of his within reach, especially when the days got quiet. *You don't drink rotgut for the taste, kid*, he'd said the first time Jal tried a swig. The way he'd laughed, thumping the sputters from Jal's chest as he breathed through the burn. . . . He never said what he *did* drink it for, but after so many nights waking to choked breaths and the rattle of the flask cap in shaking fingers, even *Jal* could fill in those blanks.

In some ways, for all their years apart, he understood Saint better now than he ever had when they'd worked together.

The cart owner still hadn't stopped cussing when Saint caught up. Saint clapped Jal crisply on the shoulder and said, "That'll just about do," and Jal grinned like a fool for the three whole seconds it took to remember it wasn't his battle buddy running beside him. It was the self-righteous bastard who'd damned him all the way down and hadn't even stopped to tell him why.

Well fuck that, and fuck him. Jal ducked away, dodging a woman with a basket of fruit as she crossed in front of him. Not the Weald's first foot chase, either. Between the pick-pockets and the stray kids filching food, the Weald always had somebody doing a grab and run, and somebody else chasing them. Folks didn't even blink as he and Saint went tearing past.

"You got eyes on Nash and Anke?" Saint asked him. Straight back on-mission, like he hadn't even noticed the brush-off.

Probably easier that way. *The next foothold.* "Nah, think I lost them." The crowd got thicker up ahead, where the narrow, winding throat of the market opened wide to a sea of thatch-roofed stalls and thrown-together tables. Hawkers' Gulley. Hadn't changed a bit since he saw it last: same two- and three-story clay buildings stacked into the root beds, circling hundreds of rickety stands and carts thrown together like jacks in the basin of a dried-up ravine. A dense weave of roots and rope bridges overhead trapped the muggy heat inside and echoed back the mad din of peddling and haggling and outright bickering. A man could hardly hear himself think.

In the middle of it all, in the only spot not staked by some jeweler or potter or metalworker, a lagoon teemed with every-color ferns and vines and little croaking reptiles that scraped moss off the rocks with their keratin beaks. *Tch-tch, tch-tch.* A little oasis of peace in the chaos. Plenty of benches for sitting, and rocks for climbing, for anyone not too shy of heights. There was a spot right near the top of the formation, maybe eighty decs up, where you could sit and see the whole Gulley. The hiss of the lagoon's waterfall drowned out some of the noise; the flowering ivy, some of the smell. Great spot to people-watch.

A better spot not to bother with people at all.

His earpiece crackled. "Think we're clear," Nash said over the comms, sharp and focused and *grounding.* Easy to get overwhelmed there. Wasn't just the memories, but the sights, the sounds, the smells, all dialed up by his mutations. He was made for dark and dry and empty, for everything Sooner's Weald *wasn't.* Once the novelty of his first rotation had worn off, he'd seen it for the cruel trick it was, sending someone like him someplace like that. "We're gonna loop around and head for the port." The market curved in one big, meandering circle— more efficient that way. Kept the traffic moving, no bottlenecks, and it worked in their crew's favor. Gave them plenty of room to run. "You guys okay? We heard shit breaking."

"All good," Saint said, but as he and Jal hit the first of the stalls, Jal risked a glance over his shoulder. Shifty from the brew cart charged through the crowd behind them, drenched in green with murder in his eyes. One by one, though, Jal marked more of them. Three. No, four, like comets cutting tracks through a junk belt, shoving shoppers out of their way and toppling tables and displays without breaking pace. Fucking juggernauts. Caps were awfully good motivation.

"That's a fuck-load of mercs," he called to Saint. *Outfit* his ass; they had the whole wardrobe. *Now it's a party.* His grin came back with a vengeance. "Might want to pick up the pace, old man. This way!" He took the lead, weaving between an herbalist and a palm reader's tent and banking into the next row. Couldn't smoke them too bad, not yet. Had to keep the mercs' attention a little longer, buy Anke and Nash a better head start, but that didn't mean they had to make it easy on them.

"Take it down a click, speedy," Saint called after him. "You trying to shake me, too?"

"You're fine." He'd always kept up all right for a normie, and Jal had a plan that didn't involve soft-shoeing it. *Tight squeeze.* Tighter than he remembered. People packed themselves into the narrow aisles shoulder to shoulder, bumping and jostling Jal from every side as he slid through gaps in the traffic. Anticipation was everything. Reading faces, body language—a glance to the left, a barely-there turn of a foot, and he could slip past them in the space they left behind.

Hot air filled his lungs like bellows, beads of sweat dripping down his face and heart rate climbing in his ears. Felt good. Felt fucking *amazing*, really letting loose like that. Not a lot of chances to do it, the past few years.

He hit a break in the crowd and remembered to glance back. "Still there, Saint?" A cart or two back, Saint answered him with a red-faced scowl and a one-fingered salute. *Attaboy.* Wouldn't work if he fell behind, and it *was* working. Behind

Saint, the handful of mercs kept hot on their trail, shoving their way through the dense crowd. Not so good at anticipating, those guys. They pushed, and they shouted, and stall after stall, row after row, they fought their way upstream. Shifty, the woman in the cap, a tall one with a whole-ass art gallery of tattoos—Jal tried to keep track of all of them as he plotted his course through the Gulley.

"Leggy bastard," Saint panted in his ear. Too far back to hear him over the crowd, but the comms carried it just fine. "Fucking hate running."

Jal's cheeks ached from all the smiling. Damn the mercs, and damn this end-of-the-world bullshit; after the string of years he'd had, he'd take his fun where he could find it. "I know you do." Even so, he used to jog with Jal when they were stationed together, and it seemed like he'd kept in the habit. Guy still had some staying power. "Just hang in there." They'd nearly crossed the Gulley. Up ahead, the stalls gave way to the first clay storefronts, and Jal figured it was time to make shit happen.

Out of the corner of his eye, he found what he was looking for. A gap between a restaurant and a repair shop; they'd named it like a street, gave it the little plaque and everything, but *alley* would've been a better fit. Cluttered and cramped, winding around behind the restaurant to a stack of cheap housing units built up all the way to the top of the ravine. "Up there," he called to Saint, cutting left toward the restaurant. A man selling real paper journals shot him a venomous look as Jal vaulted over the end of his table. One last stream of bodies to cross, and he ducked into the alley.

Smoke and steam belched through the restaurant windows, thick with the sweet scent of roasting vegetables and fresh dough. He remembered that place, used to eat there a lot during his rotation at the Weald. Cheap food that stuck to the ribs, and a pretty cook who'd managed not to laugh when he'd tried his hand at flirting.

"Stop!" Saint called from the mouth of the alley, but Jal turned the corner and kept running. In the light of dozens of buzzing neons, the housing stacks seemed to stretch on forever. Little windows and balconies strung with technicolor bottles and strips of cloth and anything else folks could think of to make the cookie-cutter units feel a little more like home. For the life of him, he couldn't remember which one they'd stayed in all those years ago. Saint probably could've. He'd always had a better head for that sort of thing, but he seemed too busy hollering at Jal to pay much mind. "Goddamn it, Jal, you know this street's—"

Jal stopped in front of the very last stack in the row, boots sliding on the damp ground. It was always damp back there. No place for the breeze to pass, with the stacks on one side, the restaurant on the other, and at the end of the alley, a towering wall of roots strung between them. Too dense to pass, and nothing but clay mud and trickling water on the other side.

END OF THE LINE, someone had spray-painted on a sheet of scrap metal. It'd been up for so long that half the letters had faded, and the sign hung lopsided and rusty on the roots. It'd looked the same when Jal lived there, though, so it might just outlast them all.

Behind him, he heard Saint turn the corner and slow. "—a dead end," he finished when he finally laid eyes on the roots. Like some part of him had hoped he'd misremembered, and he didn't want to speak it 'til he knew it was true. There it was, though. *End of the line.* In the neon lights, Jal watched his face pass from confusion to disbelief to wild-eyed fury. Just his luck, it stopped there, and Saint charged forward. "You knew," he spat, closing the distance one long, pointed stride at a time. "You knew what this was. You knew where you were taking us. What was the plan, Jalsen? Corral 'em here with me so you can give us all the slip?"

Saint only used his full name when he was *special* mad. *Old habits, huh?*

"What was the plan?" Saint demanded, louder. Harsher. *Closer.* Jal couldn't quite help flinching as Saint's hands balled to fists at his sides; decent odds the only thing stopping the old man from using them was the shrinking space between them.

Jal raised his hands. "They won't kill you," he said in a rush. "Not right away."

"How reassuring." Saint held on to his temper by a thread, but with the sound of approaching footsteps echoing down the alley, Jal could hear it fraying.

The next step Saint took, Jal took one back. "They'll have questions. You'll have time," he said. "Do you trust me?"

He thought he knew what the answer would be. That well had run dry between them a long, *long* time ago, and steering Saint down a dead-end street with a half-dozen mercs on their asses wouldn't do a hell of a lot to fill it back up.

But Saint . . . the man always did surprise him. He stopped, and Jal swore he unfurled his fists finger by white-knuckled finger. The anger hadn't left his eyes, but something else tempered it. He looked tired, all of a sudden. Tired to his bones, and wounded, and hopeful, and it pulled at something in Jal's chest he couldn't bear to look at too closely.

"I want to," Saint said.

It was a better answer than either of them deserved.

"Good," Jal said. "Remember that." He took a few more steps back, dropped the bags, and ran straight at the housing stack. Sixty decs of damp clay before so much as a balcony rail stuck out to grab onto, but it wasn't about height or grade; it was about timing. Bounding up the wall one, two, three steps and feeling the instant when the momentum started to shift, when gravity started to pull harder than inertia could push. He launched himself off his last step, flinging his arms up high over his head. At the very top of his jump—*there.* His fingers met hard, rusted metal and he grabbed on tight, hauling himself up the rest of the way onto the balcony.

"What's going on?" he heard Eoan say over the comms as he got his feet on the railing and launched himself up to the next row up. "Is he running?" The patch on his neck burned. His gut lurched. Seventy, eighty decs now, and if the captain hit the trigger on those nanites, shocked his legs numb, the fall wouldn't kill him, but he wouldn't get back up in a hurry. "Should I—"

"Don't!" Saint snapped as Jal finally got high enough. He twisted himself around, heels on the bottom rails and hands stretched out behind him holding on to the top. The alley swooped maybe a hundred decs below him, and on the other side, the hard clay roof of the restaurant looked about as inviting as a swift kick in the nards. "Let him go, Cap."

Jal couldn't guess if he'd decided to trust him, or he just had enough fondness left not to want him splattered on the alley floor, but he appreciated it either way. Up that high, everything was clearer. The first merc rounding the corner at the other end of the alley. Saint staring up at him with his hand over his face, and goddamn if that didn't bring back memories.

If you hate watching me climb so much, why don't you just look away? They must've been in the lagoon that day, because Jal still remembered the *tch-tch* of the mosseaters' beaks when Saint'd said, *Because, goddamn it, if I'm not looking, I can't catch you.*

He knew leaving Saint to the wolves wasn't a gamble he had any right making, but he knew he had to do it just the same.

"Really should've given me that gun, old man," he said, and with his eyes fixed firm on the roof ahead, he jumped.

ANKE

Nash grasped Anke's hand as they wove their way up the street. Not quite running, not quite walking—the kind of pace meant to get them someplace quickly, without drawing too many eyes.

It was pretty much impossible to feel *safe* at a time like this, but at the very least Anke knew she was in good hands.

Hah. Literally.

"Saint?" Nash called. She must've heard the same stuff Anke heard over the comms, and from the pinch of her brows, she didn't like it. She seemed to like it even less when the line went quiet. "You all right over there?"

"He's handling things," Eoan answered. Which Anke took to be their very diplomatic way of saying, *Shit's bad, but you've got your own problems.* "I've split the channels. I'll stay in touch with him; you focus on getting Anke to the ship."

Anke could practically *hear* Nash grinding her teeth. *Shouldn't do that*, she wanted to say. *You'll get cavities.* This really didn't seem like the time for dental health tips, though, so she kept it to herself.

"So help me, if that schist-eating lunkhead ditched him, I'll feed him his fucking eyeballs," Nash growled.

"Oh-kay," Anke squeaked as Nash's grip tightened on her hand. No problem; she could tough it out. What was a little finger-breaking between friends? "Little graphic but, uh, really gets the point across. You know, I'm sure everything's fine. Nothing to worry about, just a little—" Nope, she had to tap out. "*OhmyGodyou'recrushingmyhand.*"

Nash looked down at their clasped hands. "Sorry." And she didn't let go, but she loosened her grip a little. Nothing in danger of breaking or falling off, so Anke was good with the compromise. To tell the truth, she didn't really *want* her to let go. "You're right. He'll be fine, and if he isn't, he's next in line when I'm done with Jal."

"For the eyeball thing?"

"I'll start with that, sure."

Anke pursed her lips, trying to think of a response that wasn't *have you tried talking to someone, professionally?* She settled on saying, "You have a unique way of expressing concern."

"I'm not concerned." Also not a very good liar, but Anke was definitely *not* going to be the one to tell her that. Maybe better to let her focus on keeping their arses alive. "We're close," Nash told Eoan. "I can see the port gates."

This side of the gates didn't look so grand, if you asked Anke, but they were tall enough to spot through the dense cover of trees ahead. The music played louder there at the end of the market; compensating for the roar of engines, maybe, or just trying to discourage people from lingering and plugging up the thoroughfare. Not as many shops, and the ones there didn't have the same homespun character as those deeper in the market. A big general store with a totally authentic, not at *all* cosmetic thatched roof, and a parts and equipment shop for your last-minute *yeah, I guess I should probably do something about that engine rattle before I plunge my crew into the unforgiving vacuum of space* needs.

The path got steeper up ahead, branching off left and right to all manner of staff and support buildings, each one marked with a sign so strung with vines and blotchy with moss that they only really *suggested* directions. This way lies *something*, that way lies *something else*. Happy hunting.

"Why do they still call them dry docks?" Anke asked as they passed a big archway on the right. Somebody got smart and etched the lettering straight through the metal, DRY DOCK, so even the moss couldn't hide it completely. "Made sense when the ships were in water, but I mean. *All* docks are dry docks now. So do they call the docks for the water ships *wet* docks? Or did we just throw up our hands and give up on distinguishing between a dry dock that's wet sometimes, and a dry dock that's really just a dock in its natural state of. . . ." She trailed off as it became clear Nash wasn't listening. "What's wrong?"

Nash kept walking, hand still clasped around Anke's. "Do me a favor," she said to Anke, quietly. "You got your GLASS on you? Don't freak out."

"I'm not freaking out. Absolutely not freaking." Ignoring the sweaty palms, because she was pretty sure her *earlobes* were sweating by then. Too much running, too much uphill, too much heat for a girl who basically *lived* in supercooled server rooms.

"Good," Nash said, and somehow it even managed not to sound condescending. "Then hold up your GLASS like you got a message or something, and let me know if you see a redhead following us."

She could do that. *Be cool. Be smooth.* She wasn't sure it was possible to channel someone she'd just met a day ago, but she vibed her best Nash as she angled up her GLASS. "Wow," she whispered. "That's, like. Fireball red. Brush-fire red. You think he dyes it?"

"Take it that's a yes."

"Yep, he's on us like stink on, well. *Us.*" It didn't make sense, how her mouth could be dry when the air was so wet. "Are we still not freaking out?"

"Still not freaking out," Nash confirmed, as her free hand dipped to her pack. Anke thought she saw a flash of something vaguely weapon-looking. Shock baton? *Spicy.* "But it looks like Red's got a friend." To Anke's credit, she eyeballed the next one all by herself. Plainclothes getup and a bomb-ass fishtail braid, leaning all casual against a lamppost. Lousy place to take a breather, when there were benches by the shops just a short walk back, and if she'd stopped to wait for a friend, she probably wouldn't have done it halfway behind a tree. "Aw, sweetheart. Who taught you how to tail?" Nash muttered.

"She's getting closer." *Don't panic.* Anke'd been in tighter scrapes than this. "What the frick're we doing, here?"

"I'm going to politely ask them to fuck off," Nash replied.

"And if they *don't*?" Fingers crossed for a coincidence. Maybe Red just decided to walk the same way at the same time, and maybe Fishtail kept looking at her like that because Anke just had one of those faces.

Yeah, Nash didn't look like she bought it, either. A little more of the shock baton slid from her bag, saying silently, *You kids sure you want to do this?* "Then you're going to run for the ship, and I'm going to pump these assholes full of so much electricity, they shit sparkles." It shouldn't have been possible to say such terrible things with such a wonderful smile, but Nash was really out there making it happen.

"There's two of them," Anke whispered as Nash steered her down the path.

"I know, it's bad form, but we don't have time to wait for them to get more guys." She flashed a wink and squeezed Anke's hand. "Wait 'til I have their attention and run like hell. Copy?"

"Copy," she said with a firm nod.

And then . . . she didn't.

She was going to. Seriously, probie ranger with the magic typing fingers wasn't about to question the tactical genius of a badass medic-mechanic with a *shock baton*. As Nash called out to the mercs—"Hey, I get this isn't the usual escort gig, but could you at least put some effort into it? For me?"—and as Red and Fishtail dropped the act and rushed them, Anke was all ready to book it for the *Ambit*. Even made it as far as the edge of the path, hunching behind a fern-covered rock while Nash friggin' *decimated* the mercs. No shooting that close to the port, or they'd risk bringing security down on themselves, which—bad news for all parties.

So, melee only, and Nash was absolutely handing them their asses. A parry here, a smack of the baton there; Red pulled a knife, and Nash did some kind of spectacular spin move that Anke couldn't really follow, except to say it was the single most graceful thing she'd seen in her whole entire life and she was maybe kind of a little bit in love. Somehow it ended with Red's wrist trapped under Nash's arm, and Anke swore she *heard* the pop as Nash twisted. The knife dropped neatly into

Nash's waiting hand, and a firm swat to the back with her baton dropped him and left him writhing on the mulchy walkway next to his buddy with the braid.

After all that, it kind of seemed like she wouldn't *need* to run. Nash had dropped her bag and whipped out some zip cuffs—one day, maybe Anke would work up the nerve to ask why she just *casually* carried zip cuffs around in her bag—and had started tying them up, presumably to buy her and Anke some time to am-scray. Anke figured she'd just wait until Nash sorted that, and they could stroll back to the ship hand in hand and wait for the guys to catch up.

Then she saw the third merc. Shouldn't have been there, but as Nash wrestled an uncooperative Fishtail's hands behind her back, Anke spied him coming up the path behind them. Plainclothes, just like the others, and he didn't exactly announce himself. Right away, though, Anke could *feel* something off about him. The normal reaction to walking up on a ranger cuffing a pair of strangers was to turn around and walk the other direction. Maybe gawk a little; people were nosey.

But he moved *closer*. Quiet as a mouse, he crept up behind Nash, and a flash of something silver in his hand stopped Anke's breath in her throat. Knife. *Say something.* If she yelled and Nash didn't react fast enough, though, she'd get hurt. *Throw something.* Except she couldn't throw for shit and was just as likely to hit Nash. *Oh, would you just* do *something?*

She didn't really have a plan as she snuck out from behind the rock, but one came together on its own. Nash's bag lay where she'd left it, about halfway to the edge of the path. The man walked past it, and a few beats later, Anke made a break for it. Snapped it up, cocked it back, and whipped it as hard into the back of the man's head as she possibly could.

She wasn't expecting the hard, metallic *clang* that echoed across the path. Wasn't expecting the man to drop like he did, either. "Shit!" she yelped as she stood over him, Nash's bag still swinging from her arm. "I didn't—what do you even *have* in this thing?"

Nash, whose wide eyes bounced from the man, to the knife, to the bag, and finally landed on Anke's face, cracked a grin. "You're officially my new favorite," she said, holding out her hand for the bag. Anke handed it over a bit lamely, still blinking at the third merc.

"Did I kill him?"

"Nah." He twitched when Nash kicked him, though the blood oozing steadily from the welt on his head still made Anke sort of queasy. "Here." She reached into her bag and pulled out a metal cannister.

"Looks like an urn."

"Would you just open the stupid—what is wrong with you people?" A twist of the lid, and she passed it over.

Flowers. There were *flowers* in the cannister, rooted in a little gel substrate. "Hah! I just coldcocked a man with a bouquet. Ooh, they smell amazing, too. Sorry," she added, to the unconscious merc.

Nash laughed, brightly but softly, as she slung an arm around Anke's shoulders and stowed her baton. "My new favorite," she repeated, and with a squeeze that felt almost, dangerously, like a *hug*, she pulled Anke along all the way back to the ship.

JAL

Two at the entrance of the alley, three back by the stack with Saint. From his vantage point on the restaurant roof, Jal didn't see any latecomers headed their way, but he still didn't love the numbers.

Another grunt rasped through the comms. Sounded like Saint. Sounded like pain. Once upon a time, the combination would've twisted his guts up in knots, but Jal focused more on the muffled voices that came after. "Where are they?" he thought they said;

hard to tell with it garbled secondhand through the earpiece. Didn't reckon he'd have even gotten that much, except he had a sneaking suspicion somebody'd turned up his earpiece. Saint's punched-out "Who's *they*?" sounded like it came from right beside him.

"You blowin' everybody's ears out, Captain, or am I just special?"

Eoan ignored him. "I expect that's a cracked rib," they reported, conversationally. Which, bullshit—nobody *conversationally* play-by-played a beating. Saint's next grunt came with a calm "Ah, right in the mouth. It's a shame, you know. He has such a lovely smile."

"I know what you're doing," Jal said. Seemed *subtle* wasn't in their programming.

"And what are *you* doing?" So pointed, they could've drawn blood. "They're beating my XO bloody within spitting distance, and what? You're just going to leave him to it?"

"He left me to worse."

"You're punishing him, then."

"Nah," he said, "*they're* punishing him." He was just sitting on a roof. Waiting. Listening, whether he wanted to or not, as the mercs kept pressing. *Where are they?* A grunt. *I won't ask you again.* A rasp of a laugh.

"Asked a dozen times already," he heard Saint sigh. "Why stop now?"

Another hit—ribs? Mouth? *Slacking on the job, Cap*—and Jal's fingers dug creases into the metal guttering.

"He wouldn't want me to say this," Eoan started.

"Then don't." As if they'd listen to him.

Predictably, they kept going. "But you shouldn't blame him for what happened," they said. "Saint *needed* this posting. You know his history as well as I do—all the people he's lost. Comrades in arms. Friends. He needed a crew he'd never have to bury, and who else could've given him that?"

A screw snapped off the gutter under Jal's hand, and he barely caught it before it fell out of reach. He hadn't realized how hard his grip had gotten. "Stop," he said.

They didn't. "No," they said. "You need to hear this. You need to understand that when he blackballed your transfer request, he didn't do it to hurt you." Like that was news to Jal. Fuck, he hoped Saint couldn't hear them. Couldn't blame Eoan for appealing to his better angels, but knowing Saint, he'd sooner take the beating than listen to the captain's guilt trip. "You need to understand," they pressed, "that Saint was afraid for you. The *Ambit* isn't the sort of posting one should take lightly. At the time, I was an untested captain taking critical, high-risk missions with little to no support in a part of the spiral where nobody wanted to go. If you'd followed him, Saint was worried it—"

"Would've ended badly?" He couldn't quite bite back the snort. "*All roads lead,* I reckon." His mama used to say some folks were just born with bad luck in their stars. Jal was born with it in his *bones.*

Eoan didn't falter. "Would've gotten you killed," they finished, firmly. "So, he chose something different, not just to spare himself another burial, but to spare *you.* To spare your family. Whether it was his choice to make or not, that's not for me to say, but however unpleasantly it ended for the pair of you, this isn't the time to work through your grievances."

Grievances. A pretty word for a real ugly thing. He'd lived so many years with that tangled ball of hurt, and he still hadn't managed to pull out all the threads. Fury and confusion, disgust with himself and with the man he'd put his faith in—part of him was afraid if he really started tugging, he'd never get to the end of it.

No, it really wasn't the time or the place, and it really wasn't why Jal was on that roof. "Just sit tight," he told Eoan, drawn closer to the edge of the roof by a sudden bout of swearing down below. "Something's happening." One of the lookouts kicked the dumpster, and the other muttered frantically into their own comms. With all the street noise below, it was easier to read his lips than try to suss it out by ear. Something about the port, and the program. No. The program*mer*. "They made it to the ship? Eoan!" he snapped, when they didn't answer fast enough. "You have them?"

"Anke and Nash are boarding as we speak," Eoan replied.

Time to wrap up the show, then. Wasn't the prettiest way to keep the mercs' attention, but corralling them into the alley and giving them something—or someone—to focus on? Hell of a lot smarter than trying to run them around the Gulley the whole time.

He let out a breath, prying his fingers from the dented gutters. Somebody else's fault for building them so damn soft. "Just so we're clear," he said as he stood, dusting the grit and leaf litter off his hands. Bending his knees, one at a time. Stretching was highly underrated. "This ain't 'cause of what you said." Then, with the two lookouts waiting below, he dropped off the roof's edge.

He landed clean. A jump from that height made his ankles twang and his gut lurch, but nothing more. He had his wits about him well before the lookouts did. By the time one finished turning to him, he'd slammed the other crown-first into the wall. A meaty-bony *thump,* and he went down like a sack of rocks while Jal got an arm hooked around his buddy's throat. Couldn't let him call out, make a sound, warn his friends, so Jal held fast. Elbow under the merc's thick-bearded chin, watching his face turn pink, then red, then purple as he clawed at Jal's arm. *We all gotta try.* Instinct, nature, whatever. Jal had grown up swinging picks and dead-hanging from magnetic floating mesas, though, so try all he liked, the merc still wound up unconscious and crammed into the dumpster with his tattooed friend. He bent the latch shut and only felt a little bad about it. *They started it.*

"What's the plan?" Eoan asked steadily. Must've been nice, always keeping their cool like that. Having an on-off switch for all those pesky *feelings* yanking fools like Jal around by the ribs. "Report, Ranger."

"I ain't a ranger," he ground out. "And you ain't my captain." They'd made damn sure of that when they'd shut down his transfer request. Might've been Saint doing the leaving, but it was *Eoan's* signature under that big, red *DENIED*—Eoan's hand on the hammer, driving that one last nail into Jal's coffin. *Guess you buried another friend after all, old man.* Funny the way life worked out sometimes. "Listen, you let me do my thing, I'll have your XO out in two shakes." *Maybe three,* he thought as he peeked around the corner to get eyes on the others.

The first merc, the closest one, prowled back and forth across the alley, shaking his hand and muttering curses. Had the build of somebody who'd seen a fight or two in his time, and the silver hair and paunch to suggest *his time* might've passed a while ago. "Call them back out," he spat, snarling, with a voice like diesel fumes and rusted metal. Still sporting the ol' high and tight, clothes near enough to pass for a uniform to the undiscerning eye.

Not having a super afternoon, are we? Seemed to be a lot of that going around. Just behind him in the alley, the last two mercs had Saint on his knees, arms drawn up behind him. Nasty way to hold a man; move too much, Saint might dislocate a shoulder. *Bad one wouldn't take much.* The right one. Jal hated that he still knew that—that he *would've* known it, even without the brace holding it steady.

So surprise wasn't gonna work. Older guy might've had his back to Jal, but the two holding Saint couldn't miss him. That was fine. For a man who'd spent the lion's share of his Guild career in recon and infil, he was awfully bad at tactics. *More balls than brains* was the consensus. A *dive right in* kind of guy.

Which was exactly what he did.

He drew his borrowed gun and rounded the corner, covering as much ground as he could shy of a jog. Gun was just a bluff; if shit got nasty, he needed to be in close enough to do something about it. "Don't," he said as the graybeard went for his own gun, but the old fucker was fast—faster than those lugs back in the dumpster. He had his short-stock rifle out and even with Jal's nose by the time Jal cleared the halfway mark. No clip, so something battery powered. Directed energy.

He slowed maybe a handful of strides from the barrel. "You fire that thing, you'll bring every guard in the port down on this alley," he said. Even a silent piezo round would set off the sensors dotted round the market. Sooner's Weald had a pretty strict no-shoot-out policy. High population density, high likelihood of collateral damage.

"Same as you," said the graybeard without lowering his rifle. After a beat, though, his lips peeled back from his teeth in the smuggest, slimiest smile Jal had ever seen. "Unless there's something wrong with your gun, boy."

Over the graybeard's shoulder, Jal caught Saint's eyes for a split second. *This is what happens when you give a man an empty gun.*

The way the mercs had him pinned, Saint couldn't shrug his shoulders, but his face said it just fine. *Ah, well, what can you do?*

That absolute bastard. But Jal smiled, too, cheery as a butcher's dog. "No, sir," he said.

Then he hurled it straight at the merc's smug-ass face.

He didn't wait to see if it hit, charging forward with his head and shoulders down, but the yelp sounded promising. It came just a beat before his shoulders slammed into the graybeard's middle, throwing them both to the ground and sending that rifle of his skittering across the alleyway. In the middle distance, he heard a commotion—Saint caught his keepers while they were distracted, swept Shifty from the brew cart's legs and slammed his head into the other merc's chin. Good for him. For a second there Jal worried a couple of soft-bellied bottom-feeders *actually* got the better of him.

A sudden stab of too-bright light brought tears to his eyes as he grappled the graybeard. Specs got knocked off, but he managed to twist out of a half-set chokehold and scramble on top of the merc. A blind punch hit meat, though he couldn't have said where. Could barely force his eyes open through the burn of all those neon lamps, and when he did, everything looked watery and *white*. Felt like somebody digging their thumbs into his eye sockets.

Cheap-shotting motherfucker. He snarled, throwing another punch, and another when that one seemed to connect. The white became shapes as his eyes tried to adjust—ground and silhouettes and a blur of silvery hair. A knee found his ribs, and hands clawed at his arms, but he kept hitting 'til the blurs turned red, and the hands went slack, and the knee slid flat to the ground beneath him.

He fell back, squinting into blotches of electric blue and searing red-orange in time to watch a vaguely Saint-shaped smudge flip someone over his shoulder and drive his heel into their . . . face? Temple? Back of their head?

He felt around the damp ground for his specs as a brusque "Ah, shit" peppered the air up ahead of him. "Hang on, kid, I got it." Saint's shape jogged closer, until he damn near filled Jal's whole field of vision. Jal swallowed against the thudding in his throat, the *too close, can't see, get back* panic of having his keenest sense taken away from him, however fleetingly.

The familiar weight of his specs pressing into his hands was a relief. Couldn't get the damn things on fast enough, wrestling the frayed straps into place around the back of his head and wiping the lenses clean with the hem of his shirt.

Ah, and the Saint-shaped blur had a face again. A bloody face, already starting to swell at the corner of his mouth, but it didn't seem to bother him as he offered Jal a hand. "That strap's shot," Saint observed with a frown. "It's a wonder they stay on at all."

Replacement's a bit hard to come by where I've been, he thought but didn't say, but he swore Saint still heard him.

With visible effort, Saint stretched his bruised lips into a smile. "We'll see if Nash can put something together," he said, and Jal thought that'd be the end of it. Saint didn't look away, though.

Well, if he wouldn't, Jal would. He slunk off, surveying the damage Saint had dealt to the two mercs as he grabbed their bags. Seemed like enough time for Saint to get back to business, but when Jal turned back around, Saint hadn't stopped watching him. "What?"

"You came back." Somehow, he didn't sound all that surprised. "Took your sweet time, but you didn't bail when you had the chance. So, uh. Thanks, kid." And Jal wondered if Saint felt as strange saying it as Jal did hearing it.

Strange, but . . . pleased.

Not that he'd tell Saint that. He went for the gun, grumbling sourly the whole way. "*They won't know it's empty*. The hell they won't."

Saint snorted. Seemed a *thank you* and a *sorry* in one sitting was too much to ask. "Hey, don't look at me. Think that's the best your aim's ever been with a gun."

Jal stooped to pick it up where it'd fallen and tucked it back in his belt. "I was aiming for the other guy." He wasn't saying it to be funny. *Contrary*, maybe, but for some damn reason Saint started laughing. Quiet at first, then louder, until he doubled over with it, hand on Jal's shoulder to steady himself.

Damn him and his stupid, bloody, happy grin, because Jal started laughing, too. Bubbled up from his chest so quick he couldn't stop it, and he didn't care to try. It'd been . . . fuck, it'd been so long since he'd just stood and laughed with a friend, and it felt good. Good as running through the market with the wind at his back. Good as hearing Bitsie's laugh for the first time in years, even if it was just a video. It felt as good as all the other bits and pieces he'd found of himself since he'd left that living hell behind him in the frontier, and maybe that was why it felt like such a loss when Saint finally straightened up and cleared his throat.

"Better get back," he said, but he still had those creases at the corners of his eyes. A lingering smile, where he usually carried so much strain. "Still got a job to do."

That we do, old man. He just wished they were after the same thing.

CHAPTER ELEVEN

EOAN

Eoan didn't relax until they had everyone aboard the ship again, sweaty and winded but all in one piece. So different from last time, when they'd trudged up the cargo ramp with sulfur on their skin and quiet horrors in their eyes. As Eoan steered them clear of Sooner's Weald, they heard *laughter*. Saint and Nash picking at each other as they counted and catalogued and stowed the new supplies. Anke beaming as Jal handed over the bags of clothes he'd carried from the market. The air sang with a relief so palpable even *Eoan* felt themself settling into it. Nothing troubling on the sensors, no unwanted company as the *Ambit* plunged deeper into the black. They'd gotten what they came for and escaped unharmed. Even if it could've gone better, that it hadn't gone worse was cause for celebration.

So they did.

The crew *celebrated,* in their own uncomplicated way. With long, lazy showers and changes of clothes and all the quirky little things humans did to make themselves feel a little more human again. With a thrown-together meal too early to be dinner, too late to be lunch, and too brimming with chatter and bickering and food-muffled laughs to really end, even with picked-clean plates and only a couple scraps of flatbread left on the table. With the soft pluck of guitar strings, Saint wandered aimlessly through a melody as they one-upped each other with stories from the Weald.

"And this old soldier type," Saint said, fingers moving gracefully along the neck of his guitar as he leaned back in his chair. "Mean-looking son of a bitch, gravel in his craw—"

"Wait, are we talking about you or the freelancer?" Nash cut in.

The melody paused just long enough for Saint to flick a crumb of flatbread at her, and it resumed at the same time he did. "He looks Jal up and down and says, *Unless there's something wrong with your gun, boy.*"

Anke made a face. "I thought you said nobody would notice."

"A man can't be right all the time," Saint said.

"Or even some of the time, apparently." Nash flashed him a grin, knitting needles clicking neatly from her ordained place on the countertop. Some sort of cephalopod took shape between them, knitted in cheerful, unrealistic shades of orange and pink. Eoan liked the eyes the most. Hugely disproportionate and entirely joyful.

Saint struck a few bad notes, just to be spiteful. "You gonna let me tell the story or not?" He had a crook to his lips, though, and Nash winked and waved one of the cephalopod's stubby little legs. Tentacles? They were probably past the point of technical correctness. "So this loon here"—with a wave to Jal, who'd kicked back on two legs of his chair, picking at a piece of flatbread—"looks at him like butter wouldn't melt on his tongue. *No, sir,* he says. Then he rears back and throws the whole damn gun at his head. *Smack.*" He thumped the heel of his palm against the side of the guitar. "Don't know who was more surprised when it hit—him or the kid."

"Now, see," Jal drawled, chewing slowly on a piece of bread, as if to make it last. Never mind the pinches he kept slipping to Bodie, who had curled up proprietarily on Jal's lap. Hard to say if it was the food scraps or ear rubs that had won Bodie's heart, but either way, Jal had earned himself quite the furry devotee. "You were right on the edge of being nice to me. Don't go spoiling it, there, *Florence*."

Saint's eyes narrowed in a half-earnest glare. "Watch yourself."

"What? I think it's a pretty name," said Anke. "Florence Toussaint. Sounds regal. Super pretty."

"Super," Nash agreed, smothering a laugh behind her hand.

Anke blinked. "Oh! I mean. Not *pretty* like, you know, butterflies. Or rainbows. Or—"

"Flowers?" Saint suggested with a quirked eyebrow, aimed Nash's direction. He managed to get himself—and his guitar—out of the way of the sailing saltshaker, but only just.

"Speaking of *flowers*," Nash said, pointedly. Her grin showed teeth as she delicately cast off a stitch on the cephalopod's blush-pink belly. "Gun-flinger might get honorable mention, but hands down, Merc Drop of the Day goes to this killer." With a nod to Anke. "Or did you miss the part where she brained somebody with a *plant*? Nonlethally," she added, as Anke flinched. "A light braining. More like a bonking, really."

"And on that note," Anke said, pushing her now-empty mug away from her on the table, "I should get to work. That patch isn't going to code itself."

Nash's smile fell. "The patch has a whole week to get written," she said. "You need a night off, friend. Doctor's orders."

As if they'd coordinated in advance, Jal had already rolled to his feet, much to Bodie's dismay. "Sorry, buddy," he said, settling Bodie on the floor with one last head rub and the rest of his flatbread. Bodie's rumbling purrs as he trotted away said he'd take the olive branch under consideration, and possibly not de-string Jal's boots while he slept.

Possibly.

Jal didn't seem too worried. Humming a countermelody to Saint's guitar, he nudged the table out of the middle of the galley and up against the counter, then turned around to Anke.

"You heard the lady." He offered her his hand. "Better idea: how 'bout a dance?"

Anke's face turned a shade not far off Nash's yarn ball. "Not really much of a dancer," she said.

"Is that a no?" There didn't seem to be anything hiding in the question. No challenge, no disappointment, just genuine curiosity and a lopsided smile.

Guileless, they thought—or playing the part well. They really hadn't decided which. They'd tried not to watch him too closely since he came back aboard. Tried not to doubt him, not to blame him for the spectacular blooms of color across their XO's face. Self-deception was a uniquely human talent, however, and they couldn't help thinking: If Jal's plan had *always* been to go back for Saint, then why hadn't he just *told them*? They knew they hadn't exactly endeared themself to him, and he clearly had conflicting feelings about Saint, but how could they trust someone so determined not to trust *them*?

No harm in keeping an eye on things, they decided. Hope and doubt could exist in the same space, and as they watched Anke rise with an emboldened grin, they *did* hope. For her, for Jal, for all of them—for a future in the hands of these clever, curious, confusing creatures.

"I'm warning you," Anke told Jal, taking his hand, "I'll step on your toes."

"Maybe I'll step on yours, too, then," he replied. "Keep things square." But as they twirled around the galley to the tune of Saint's guitar and Nash's hands drumming the counter, there wasn't a mashed toe or a stumble between them. A dip, and Anke's laugh brightened the whole ship; a spin out toward the counter, and it was hard to say if Anke lured or *hauled* Nash into the fray, but she'd found her feet and her place in the dance by the time the song changed. A familiar tune, something jaunty and bouncing and irreverent that Eoan hadn't realized had lyrics until Jal picked them up at the tail end of the verse:

"—*mansion up on a hill,*
Man inside said, see this life I built.
I'm a rich man, I'm a king,
Got everything I need.
I got nice suits, nice shiny rings,
I got all the good things."

The atmosphere was so impossibly warm in the galley. Eoan basked in it, soaking in the joy and the energy like red starlight bathing every sense as Jal spun Nash and Anke round the galley, one on each hand, and Saint strummed those well-loved strings through another verse.

"Come on, wallflower," Nash called to him, swatting his knee as she passed. "Get off your ass and dance with us."

"Not a chance," he shot back.

By then, though, he had everyone's attention.

"Ain't nobody died from a little skippin' and dippin', old man," Jal said.

Saint raised an eyebrow. "When you say it like that, it kinda sounds like something else."

It took Jal a second, but he laughed. "Well, ain't nobody died from that, either."

"Please?" Anke's hair had gone wild with all the moving, falling in her eyes as she batted them at Saint, and her bright, cherry-red cheeks dimpled. "It's fun!"

"Fun," Jal echoed, grinning so wide the light caught the points of his canines. "I *know* you know what that is, old man. Up!"

"Oh, one of you primas want to play the music, then?"

Eoan never could resist the chance to make an entrance. "As a matter of fact," they said, projecting into the chair beside Saint's with a shiny green guitar. Didn't seem right to try to copy the look of Saint's. Like an extension of his hands—too many stories there. But theirs played the same notes, indistinguishable from Saint's but for the fact that they came from the galley's speakers. "I'd love to try a song or two. Go." Because as much as they enjoyed hearing him play, this was better. This was *novel*. They'd never seen him dance.

That settled it, apparently. Saint barely had a chance to set aside his guitar before Nash snatched him onto his feet, and for all his grumbling, he took to it like a glove to a hand.

"Look at you go!" Eoan laughed as the mismatched foursome romped and spun and bumped shoulders in their cramped makeshift dance hall. No room for grace, just silly, unapologetic fun. And oh, how they'd earned it. All the troubles that lay behind them, and the worse ones that lay ahead—they spent so long struggling under the weight of the universe, and they deserved a night to dance and sing and *breathe*.

Eoan wanted so badly to breathe with them. To celebrate as *they* celebrated, gasping and laughing and so deeply glad to be *alive,* but for all Eoan could share with them—the music, the joy, the relief—they couldn't share *that*. They couldn't empathize with the fear of facing their own demise or the thrill of coming out the other side hale and hearty. They'd never been at risk the way their crew had been at the Weald; and they'd never been *protected* the way their crew had protected each other. How could they have been? How could anyone possibly risk their life to save Eoan? To save an intangible intelligence incapable of death, at least in any way they could understand? And how could Eoan do the same for them?

They didn't know the answers to those questions. Didn't even know how to go about finding them, and until they did, they couldn't get any closer than this—than playing through that feel-good melody, catching the eyes of their crew and smiling when they smiled. Laughing when they laughed. Feeling their joy, their relief, even if they felt it separately. Differently.

Sometimes it felt like enough.

Sometimes it felt like it never could be.

Tonight, they told themself it was. It was enough, because it was *beautiful*. It had been just the three of them for so long—Eoan and Saint and Nash—and it had never felt incomplete. Never felt wanting. But watching them shine together, the four of them, stirred such a profound sense of *satisfaction* in Eoan. Like finding pieces to a beloved puzzle they thought they'd already finished, seeing how the picture grew. All the new colors, and the way they brought all the old ones to life. Of course it was enough, because how could they possibly ask for *more*?

The music quickened like a heartbeat fluttering. Faster and faster, Jal breathless and chuckling around the words of the song as he spun Anke around and ducked low so she could return the favor.

> *"Man in a shack said come inside,*
> *Ain't much but it's home,*
> *For me, my kids, my wife."*

They traded partners, and Eoan delighted in Anke's pink-cheeked smile as she took Nash's hands. Jal nearly tripped over a chair when he turned around to his new partner, but Saint just caught him and kept going without missing a beat, and Jal kept the song alive.

> *"I'm a rich man, I'm a king.*
> *Got everything I need.*
> *If all I got's my family,*
> *Then I got all the good things."*

So much fondness between Saint and Jal, buried beneath all the scar tissue, and Eoan had never seen it so close to the surface. Just another piece of the puzzle fitting into place with that quiet, carefree refrain.

"I got all the good things."

It couldn't last, of course. Another song, and the poor dears slumped on the floor in an exhausted pile. Nash's legs across Saint's lap, Anke's head on Nash's stomach, Jal wedged into the corner of the cabinets but managing somehow to stay touching all three—it was a Gordian knot of tired limbs and winded breaths, and as loathe as Eoan was to disturb them, what they needed was *rest*.

So they finished the last song and let their guitar fade. "I know at least two of you won't thank me if I let you sleep where you fell," they said, ignoring the chorus of groans that went up. "Yes, yes, I'm terrible. I'm the worst. Now go to bed before I electrify the floor."

"What is it with you people and electricity?" Jal grumbled, but it had the desired effect. Slowly, a bit begrudgingly, they all untangled themselves and found their feet again. After a few bleary *goodnight*s, they all turned in for what Eoan hoped would be a quiet, restful night. They'd certainly earned that, too.

In the morning, their work could continue.

. . .

Eoan's, of course, didn't stop. They didn't require sleep—not in the Homo sapiens sense of the word. Reduced sensory activity. Inhibited responses. *Dreams*. Sometimes, they let themself drift. Consciousness for them meant chasing one line of reasoning to another, always with their eyes toward an answer; when they rested, though, they could wander. From music to dancing to countless recordings of foxtrots and waltzes and line dances. Then to the disputed origins of line dancing, to the historic city of Kolkata, to the tomb of Mother Teresa and a brief but informative tangent into the animus of humans toward burial and entombment.

Tonight, there would be no drifting. With the madness of the Weald behind them and their crew safe aboard, they could finally turn their attention to the leads from the depot. Nash's serial number was simple: a bit of proverbial thumbing through manufacturing records and shipping manifests, and they tracked down a *mislaid goods* report filed with the Union a couple of years ago. A Trust subsidiary claiming it lost an entire shipment en route to a debtors' colony, and that was the end of that. Thefts meant investigations, inquiries, but a bit of good old-fashioned negligence? Not so much as a second glance.

Somehow they suspected the Trust had taken advantage of that particular operating procedure more than once.

Sorry, Nash. While Eoan could fill in the gaps from *mislaid goods* to an under-the-table deal with smugglers in the frontier— lost goods conveniently found, an extra influx of caps some clever accountant would deftly explain away in the quarterly earnings—they didn't have the paperwork to back it up. The Union did love its paperwork. Not quite a dead end; any brush of color they could add to the picture taking shape was good to have. They knew Nash would've hoped for more, though, and they would've liked to give it to her.

That still left the agitators outside the rockhopper. Unlikely it was just the pair of them; they tended to travel in groups. Cells. Safety and power in numbers, and if the havoc on Sooner's Weald had shown Eoan anything, it was that they needed to know *exactly* what kind of numbers they were dealing with.

Let's see who your friends are, gentlemen. Eoan pulled facial scans from the bodycam footage, but the trick would be matching those faces to anything useful. It wasn't as if they kept some kind of compendium. *The Rioters' Roll Book. Agitators A to Z.* Theirs was more of a . . . fluid association.

Ah, well. They did love a good challenge.

They mapped it out like one of Nash's concept boards, spooling bits of yarn between push-pinned pictures and pieces of the soon-to-be whole—a handful of arrest records from Trust security, branching out to known associates; a dozen known associates, branching out to thousands of hours of surveillance and news and shaky GLASS footage of protests across the spiral. Threads laid, Eoan only had to search for the point where they all intersected. The patterns. Everything connected to something; it was one of the few unerring truths of the universe.

They saw it, then. The point where the two agitators' strings first crossed—a cluster of riots in the frontier. Trust colonies, mostly mines and shipping, ripe for labor protests. The more they tugged, the more those strings tangled, and the more certain Eoan grew that this went beyond those two agitators in the right place at the right time. Colony after colony, protest after protest, video after video, the same faces appearing in every chanting crowd, until they could feel the end of the thread just within their grasp.

Then, an itch.

Not an actual itch. They'd never actually *had* an itch, more's the pity, but they imagined this was what it would be like. A nagging blip in their awareness, negligible until the moment they noticed it, and unbearable thereafter. Demanding their attention, so they gave it, abandoning their string board for a moment to trace that peculiar sensation into the *Ambit*'s onboard computer.

They hit a wall. *That's not right.* Eoan existed independent of the ship's systems, but there was no part of that system they didn't know, no process or function or line of code they couldn't access. But there it was—a barrier thrown around a cluster of applications, insulating them from Eoan's meticulous security protocols.

They inspected it carefully. Permeable—not meant to keep Eoan out, then, but to shroud whatever was going on behind it. Like a line of empty cans strung around a campsite, ready to warn whoever had laid it that they'd been found. *Savvy little thing, aren't you?*

Isolated, though, which had its goods and bads. Good, because it gave them room to move around without tripping over another piece of foreign programming; bad, because it meant whoever had put it there knew exactly what they were after, and they'd most likely found it.

"Saint." Only their voice over his in-quarter comms. No time to bother with projections. "Wake up. There's an intrusion in the ship's systems."

Saint—such a light sleeper, bless him—jolted upright before they even finished speaking. "More mercs?" he said.

"Unlikely." Possible, they supposed; they couldn't prove a negative. Nevertheless, "The firewalls are intact. No outside interference, so unless we've got one smuggled aboard the ship—again, *unlikely*—then it's something or some*one* we brought on ourselves."

Boots on, eyes bright and aware despite the bruising spreading beneath them, Saint headed for the door. "You think . . . ?" The rest of the question was lost to the gnashing of his teeth, but Eoan could extrapolate.

"It could be more like Riesen's tag." It would've taken something more complex than a simple satellite tracker to get into the *Ambit*'s systems unnoticed, but they lacked the ego to say it couldn't be done. "I'm trying to find a back door, see if I can figure out exactly what they're doing before we sound the alarm. If I can't manage in the next thirty-four seconds, however. . . ." Wouldn't take them any longer; as they said, they knew every part of the ship's systems. It was just a question of drawing the right set of lines through the maze. "Then could you be a dear and go knock on some doors?"

It seemed more polite than *go downstairs and drag our guests out by their ears.* They abhorred unnecessary violence.

"Cameras are clear, so don't bother sneaking about," they

added as he ducked out of his room. "I've narrowed the af-
fected systems to a handful of applications. Nothing essential."
Steering, life support, and security protocols remained intact
and excluded; they seemed to be looking at the *Ambit*'s communications systems. Programming interfaces, integrations with
outside databases—nothing that could do any immediate harm,
unless Eoan had missed something.

But Eoan didn't *miss* things. They observed, noticed, ana-
lyzed. Attention split between the intrusion, their back door,
monitoring Saint's progress down the halls, and it hardly took
a nibble out of their processing capacity. No, they didn't miss
things.

As they finally slipped behind the curtain, though, and saw
what it hid, they had to grant this: they did, occasionally, mis-
calculate.

"Wait," they told Saint as he hit the bottom of the ladder to
the crew quarters. Nineteen seconds—not bad time for either
of them. "I've got it."

"Well?" Irritation crept into his voice. No man wanted to
go to war in his pajamas, least of all against anyone he'd called
friend.

They understood the feeling—less the pajamas, of course.
Yet, as they traced the intrusion to a GLASS in the lower decks,
they wouldn't hesitate to do what was needed.

"Anneka."

The programmer jolted so hard she nearly dropped her
GLASS. Surveillance in private quarters was generally prohib-
ited, except under the worst of exigent circumstances. Through
the fish-eye lens in the corner, Eoan watched as Anke paled in
the dark of her room, bumping her glasses up her nose with the
heel of a hand.

"Eoan?" Anke said it steady enough, but the timbre sounded
wrong. Too tight. Too measured for someone who flustered so
easily. "Is everything okay?"

A full sentence. Another strike.

"We could banter," said Eoan, calmly. Theirs was a true calm, unlike Anke's, smoothed over feelings waiting to take shape. Anger. Betrayal. Worry. Confusion. "You could play the fool, and I could talk you into a corner until you break down and tell me everything. But there is a very unsettled ranger outside your door with a firearm and roughly a decade of largely untreated trauma, so for all our sakes, let's cut to the chase. Why the *fuck* are you hacking my ship?"

Eoan considered themself a patient creature, but the handful of seconds they spent watching Anke's face shift—forced composure to a strained mix of mortification and guilt—seemed to stretch on forever.

"Please," Anke said, at last. "I promised."

"Who did you promise, and what did you promise them?" Answers. Eoan needed answers, and they needed not to wait for them.

Anke swallowed audibly, and perhaps involuntarily, her eyes flickered sideways, toward the shelf with its vase of little purple flowers. *Toward the guest quarters,* they amended.

"Jalsen?" The faint thinning of Anke's lips was answer enough. Not a very good liar; Eoan supposed they should've been pleased, but then, they'd thought the same of Jalsen. Guileless. *Fool me once.* "What did he ask you to do?"

"It wasn't—he just wanted me to help him into something. A drive. He was trying to open it back on the rockhopper and didn't get the chance, but I got a copy of it before the hangar blew."

"What's on the drive?"

"Cap, you want to tell me what the fuck's going on?" Saint hissed under his breath. Eoan had never been more acutely aware of Jalsen's mutations—heightened senses made for a spectacularly *inconvenient* enemy, particularly one they didn't want to tip off. The less unpleasant they could keep this, the better, if only because Saint cared for him. Whether he wanted to or not, Saint cared, and they knew him too well not to see it.

"Hold," they told him firmly. Then, to Anke, "*What* is on the drive?"

"He didn't say." Tears welled in her eyes. Guilt, again, but Eoan couldn't say if it was for betraying *them*, or for betraying whatever promise she'd made to Jal. "All he told me was that the drive was his way back to his family, and we couldn't tell you guys, because he was in some kind of trouble. I'm sorry," she said. Maybe a bit of both: guilt for them and for Jal. "He saved my life, and I—I was being careful. The cypher was a little older than I expected, so I just needed to borrow your access to the Guild encryption key silo. If it was something bad, I would have told you, I swear!"

"If it was something *harmless,* he wouldn't have needed to hide it." It all kept circling back to that, didn't it? If he'd planned to help Saint in the Weald, he should've shared his plan. If he'd had nothing to hide on that drive, he should've asked them for help decrypting it. If his intentions were good, his actions should have been different. There was too much at stake to keep rationalizing the behavior of a half-feral deserter for the sake of sentiment. "So let's find out."

Anke flinched. "What?"

"Saint, get Jal, bring him to Anke's room. Now." In the meantime, they pinged Nash in the engine room and told her to join. If things went badly, it would be better to have all hands on deck. "You said you have the file, Anke?"

Her head jerked, stiffly. Couldn't properly be called a nod, but Eoan took it for one. "It's all there," she said. "I think I managed to salvage it."

"We'll have a look, then." If it really was Guild-encrypted, it wouldn't be any trouble at all to get into it. Simple as finding the key and turning it, and then they'd have this all sorted one way or the other.

Saint, arguably, had the harder job. "What's wrong?" they heard Jal ask as Saint called him out into the hall. Awake with his boots on—a habit he'd picked up as a ranger, or one he'd picked up from his time on the run, they'd likely never know—and mercifully unresisting as he ducked out the door.

"Cap wants us in Anke's room."

"She all right?" Under different circumstances, it might've been endearing how readily Jal followed Saint down the hall. Didn't even wait for an explanation.

That changed when he stepped through the door. His specs sought out Anke first, then the GLASS, and then found Eoan's projection as it coalesced in the corner of the room. "Anke?" he asked, backing up a step.

He backed straight into Saint, who'd hung back to block the doorway. "Cap, think it's time you told us what this is about," their XO said, as Nash jogged up behind him from the hall. He pushed Jal forward enough that Nash could get through, but Jal knocked his hands away like they burned him.

Eoan kept their expression stern. "Anke, tell them what you told me."

Poor Anke looked like she wanted the floor to open up and swallow her whole. GLASS set aside on the mattress, hands wringing the life out of one corner of her shawl. "I'm sorry, Jal," she said, though her eyes never made it anywhere near him. And then she told them. Almost to the letter, so exact that Eoan thought halfway they might've just played it all back and spared her the grief. So far as Eoan could tell, her only misdeed was trying to help the wrong person, and kindness was a terribly hard flaw to fault.

Jal's faults, on the other hand.

Anke had no sooner finished her explanation than Saint had Jal by the collar, shoving him back against the wall so hard his head bounced off it. "Son of a bitch," he spat. "In the hangar—this is what you stayed back for? Risked our fucking *lives* for?"

Rage rippled through every overtaut muscle as he pinned Jal in place. "What's on the drive?"

"I don't know," Jal answered through his teeth.

Saint hauled him off the wall and slammed him back again, harder. "Cut the shit, Jalsen. What is it?"

"I don't know!" he shouted. His voice, ragged and rough-edged, stretched so thin over panic that for a second Eoan almost believed him. The way he sank against the wall, shaking his head . . . it painted an awfully convincing picture. "I swear on my life, I don't know."

If any part of it was real, they thought, then maybe what they were doing was a mercy. "Then you will," they said. *We all will.*

With every eye in the room on them, they shifted the projectors into a screen on the wall, and they showed them all what he'd been hiding.

CHAPTER TWELVE

SAINT

Saint could hardly see through the rage. Like a brush fire charring his ribs, searing his lungs. He breathed and tasted smoke, and he was grateful for it, because smoke was still better than the bitter taste of admitting he'd been wrong. *I wanted to trust you. I tried everything to trust you, and you were lying the whole time.*

And for what? What sideways scheme had he dragged Anke into? Playing on her gratitude like that. The Jal he'd known would've never—

The screen flickered. The lights in the room were on, albeit dimmed, so it was hard to make sense of it at first. Picture was too dark, blotches of black and green moving across the sloped walls. Took his adrenaline-soaked brain a second to see it for what it was: infrared footage. A night vision camera, rattling and jumping like somebody'd strapped it to a spooked horse and set it loose.

The sound came abruptly. Silence, then a hail of sirens and gunshots and shouting as broken-down buildings and rust-eaten shipping containers whipped by on the screen.

"—cut the lights!" someone yelled. "They cut the lights! I've got no visual!"

"Where the fuck're your NVGs, Fenton?" said a second voice. It was much clearer than the first. Much closer. Much more familiar.

Saint turned back to Jal. "What is this?" That was Jal's voice in the video. He'd been there, wherever *there* was. "What the hell is this?" Looked like an op gone wrong. Another old shipping facility, which told Saint exactly fuck-all. Couldn't spit in the frontier without hitting one of those places. Temp setups to move product while there was product there to move, and left behind like molted husks when the Trust or its contractors finished with them. Could've been anywhere. That voice, though, was unmistakable.

Jal didn't answer. He wasn't looking at Saint, staring past his head at the screen with his mouth drawn thin and his brows furrowed. Didn't even seem to be *breathing*.

"They're coming," hissed the first voice. Fenton. "I can hear them, man. Can't see a fucking thing out here, but I hear them." No NVGs, then. Had to be a rookie, because a senior ranger never would've made that mistake. Now that he'd oriented himself, Saint knew that was who they were watching: rangers. Video had a timestamp in the corner, dated three years prior, and a string of numbers he only recognized with the benefit of context. Serial numbers. *Jal's* serial numbers.

"I need your location!" Jal shouted, and for a moment the whole screen went black. Clanging metal—climbing one of the containers, Saint thought, and then he was off again. "Approaching your last-known from the third quadrant of the compound. You still there?" No answer. "Fenton! Get your shit together and listen to me. Have you changed position?"

It was hard to listen to. Even a pear-shaped op shouldn't have been so chaotic. There were protocols. Backup plans, fallback routes. Where the fuck was their captain? Because hearing Jal like this—like he *used to be*, younger and trying like hell to sound rougher and tougher than he really was—as he tried to hold it all together in the middle of a full-tilt retreat, it wrung Saint's stomach like a dishrag. Three years ago might as well have been a lifetime, but he still wanted to shout for the kid to stop, hold his position until he got an *answer,* because Fenton sounded like a shit-scared hair-trigger, and this was how things went bad. This was how people *died*. This was—

Flashes lit the screen, and then Saint heard it: the crack of bullets tearing from a barrel. Not behind the camera, but maybe a dozen meters ahead, and the shout next to the mic broke with as much surprise as pain. The frame pitched sideways, then dropped. Not onto the container, but off the side of it, plumes of dirt rising like fog on impact.

This was how *Jal* almost died.

Fenton's voice crackled through the sudden, stifling silence. "Red, I think I got—oh, fuck." Saint wondered what clued him in. The lack of return fire? Maybe it'd finally dawned on him the direction his target had been running from. Failing all that and absent a single firing synapse, he probably caught on when that stunned, pained groan sputtered over his comms.

"Shit!" Fenton swore, with the sound of jostling gear. "Shit, oh shit, oh shit." Panicked, pitched high over Jal's choking gasps. "I'm sorry, I didn't mean to. I didn't know it was—shit." Saint could see Jal trying to get up, the dizzying shift of the bodycam as he rolled onto his side and the cry he strangled behind his teeth when his fingers—shaking, crooked, callused fingers— came away dark with blood.

Turn it off, Saint wanted to say. Didn't want to see any more of it, *hear* any more of it. For a second, all Saint could think about were the two old bullet scars he'd seen in the infirmary. *Who did that to you?* He'd wanted an answer then, but now that he had it, he almost wished he could go back.

Wasn't like the mission reports. The reports said an op in the outer planets went sideways and Jal bailed. Dropped his tags and ran, to hell with his crew and his oath and everything else. He'd never understood what could make the Jal he knew do a thing like that, but the whole crew swore up and down it was the truth, and after a year of searching and turning up nothing, he'd *believed* it.

Oh, God, he'd believed it.

He saw Fenton a beat later, scrambling around the corner of the shipping container with a flashlight that whited out the screen when it passed over the camera. Too dark for specs; the light would've blinded Jal, if the pain hadn't already. Saint wasn't even sure he would've seen Fenton kneeling over him, grasping at his vest.

"I can walk," Jal told Fenton in the recording. "Just get me up. I can—I can make it back to exfil." He didn't sound sure. Wouldn't have mattered to Saint, he told himself. If he'd been there, he'd have thrown the kid over his shoulder and carried him all the way back, if that was what it took. Walk, don't walk. Conscious, not conscious. He would've gotten him safe.

If he'd been there.

This is your fault. The thought grabbed hold and wouldn't let go. *You put him there.* With people who wouldn't carry him. People who didn't *care* about him the way he deserved. Golden heart, loyal to a goddamn fault, and Saint had thrown him in with the likes of *Fenton.*

Fenton, who didn't help him up. Didn't help him at all. "Fuck, Red's down. I—fuck, fuck, fuck!" he kept whimpering, until abruptly, he stopped. Froze, head cocked like somebody was talking to him, but Saint didn't hear anything through the video. Broadcast on a private comm channel, maybe. "I don't know," Fenton said in a hiccupping high voice. Pissing himself and desperate for somebody smarter to tell him what to do. "N-no, I don't think so. Twice, I think, and there's a fuck-ton of blood, but I—are you sure?" He faltered, then, "No, no, I'll do it. I'll—I know how to—"

Fenton grabbed for something on Jal, and with the *clink* of breaking metal, it became painfully, horrifyingly clear what he'd done. Any doubts Saint might've had, any reservations, gone with that single, deafening sound. Fenton had Jal's tags— the same tags little Bitsie had clung to when he'd told them that awful fucking word. *Deserter.* The same tags some Guild rep had handed to Jal's sister with a ready-made letter about *revocation of benefits.*

"What the fuck are you—?" Jal was never as slow as he claimed to be, though. He'd figured it out, what Fenton was doing. What somebody'd *told* Fenton to do. "Motherfucker!" And Jal fought; wouldn't be him if he hadn't. The feed went screwy, got knocked this way and that as Jal wrestled with everything he had, but even his impossible strength couldn't hold up through shock and blood loss. Scrabbling, bloody fingers appeared over the lens, and with the pop of the bodycam's metal casing, the feed went black.

"Shit," Nash breathed. It was the only sound in the room for . . . Saint didn't even know how long. Anke had covered her mouth with her too-long sleeves, tears rolling freely from her beneath her glasses, and Saint couldn't seem to make his lungs expand. They'd left him. He hadn't deserted in a hail of bullets; he'd been shot by his own team, left to die in the dirt like a rabid animal. They'd shamed his name, left his family without a single cap for his service, all because some rookie on a shit posting was too goddamn stupid to bring his night vision goggles.

Wordlessly, Jal pushed Saint's hands away, and Saint let him. Wasn't sure he could've stopped him if he'd wanted to, but Christ. The thought of holding him there any longer, doing *anything* more to him, brought acid to the back of Saint's tongue.

"Captain," said Jal, voice so steady it had to be an act. Saint could practically see the strain of it, and fuck, he'd been carrying that strain since he'd woken up in the infirmary. Saint should've picked up on it, then. He should've understood it, seen through all the bravado and bad attitude. Jal wasn't a threat; he was a wounded dog baring its teeth. He was hurt and scared, and he needed *help,* and Saint hadn't seen any of it. "Can I be dismissed?"

Eoan's projection hadn't reappeared, but Saint could picture their softening expression as they said, "Of course. We can discuss the rest later." The rest. The lies. The hiding. The next steps. If that piece of shit Fenton was still flying under the Guild banner, Saint would hunt him down himself—him and whoever else was on that comm line, telling him to do it.

Saint hadn't decided what he'd do when he found them, but he knew he'd take his time.

It wasn't as much comfort as he wanted it to be, as he watched Jal disappear through the door and down the hall. Shoulders and spine straight as a board, hands stuffed in his pockets. Harder to see them shaking that way.

Saint let his head drop forward onto the wall. *Fuck.*

Behind him, he heard Nash breathe in deep and let it out slow. Grounding herself. A glance back at her shiny eyes said she was holding on to her composure by her fingernails, but he couldn't talk. Crew was family. The thought of either of them doing that to the other . . . they just couldn't stomach it.

"You see him?" she said. "White as a ghost. Elevated heart rate, shortness of breath." Saint recognized her medic voice when he heard it. Trying to claw back some distance, some perspective. "I have some contacts back in the center spiral . . . they, um. This sort of thing is more in their wheelhouse. They could probably help him, if he wanted it, when we get back. For now, I think—" She faltered. It'd been a long time since he'd heard her so rattled, but she didn't let it stop her. "I think if you don't get your shit together and go after him, Saint, then I will."

Harsh, maybe. But sometimes there just wasn't any other way to be.

"Yeah." He dragged himself straight, rubbing his eyes and pinching the bridge of his nose like that'd ward off the tension headache cranking its way up the back of his neck. *You owe him*. Ten minutes of strength—he owed him that, and he owed him so much more. "I'm going." Maybe while he was gone, Nash could do something about the heartbreak on Anke's face.

The hall seemed much shorter than he remembered. Some part of him hoped he'd have his head on straight by the time he reached Jal's quarters, but it was still as backwards and turned around as when the video cut out.

He paused with his hand raised halfway to the door. *Knock or don't?* Saint didn't like that kind of sound when he was caught in his own head, but this wasn't one size fits all.

"Jal?" That was better, he decided. A familiar voice. He only wished the kid had better things to associate it with. "Can I come in?"

Silence, for a moment. Then, "Why?"

Because we're worried about you, he thought. *Because you just watched yourself get shot and left for dead in high-def. Because I wasn't there for you when you needed somebody, and I gave up on you, and some stupid, selfish part of me's hoping this will start making up for it.*

He swallowed. "I think you know why." He didn't know if that was better or worse than brutal honesty, but it was a hell of a lot easier to say.

It worked. Not immediately, but just when he started to think he'd have to do better, the door hissed open.

Only soft, red-wave light strips along the ceiling lit the darkened room inside. Jal shied away from the hall light, specs abandoned on the bedside table, and he didn't invite Saint in, but he didn't tell him to fuck off, either. Saint figured that was about as good as he was going to get.

As the door slid shut and Saint's eyes adjusted, he watched Jal cross the room and sink onto the edge of the bed. "You've got questions, too." Even in the tight crew quarters, even with just the two of them, the words almost seemed to disappear.

"Want to know why I didn't say anything. Want to know what happened after the video cut out. Want to know why I didn't call for help."

Yes. Yes, Saint wanted to know every one of those things, and about a dozen more. But seeing the steel melt out of Jal's shoulders, watching him shrink into himself with a heavy, bone-weary sigh, only one question really seemed to matter.

"Are you okay?"

He hated how *surprised* Jal looked, like he really thought Saint would march down the hall and start interrogating him after all that. The way Saint had treated him lately, maybe he was right to wonder, but *Jesus*. Jal's black-marble eyes were so damn wide, they seemed to swallow his face.

"I—" Jal started, but that was as far as he made it.

It started in his bottom lip, an almost-tremor and a downward tug at the corners. A hitched breath, a furrow in his brow, and for a moment he looked almost *confused*. Helpless. Young and overwhelmed and fresh off too many days—weeks? Months? Years?—pretending it wasn't getting to him. He sat there, blinking up at Saint with his whole body shaking like it was trying to take itself apart at the joins, and Saint didn't remember ever deciding to go sit beside him, much less put his arms around those rounded shoulders, but he had, and he did, and he'd no sooner settled beside him than Jal *crumpled*.

It had nothing to do with him, Saint told himself. The way Jal turned into him, buried his face against Saint's shoulder as that first sob ripped its way out—it wasn't some kind of reconciliation. It wasn't about all their years together. It didn't even mean that Saint was forgiven. Jal just needed a port in the storm, and Saint just happened to be the one sitting there.

"It's okay," Saint told him, softer than he thought he knew how to be. He was a hard-nosed bastard with a thick skin and a thicker head, but Jal cried like he couldn't breathe, like he was drowning under all that grief and fear and pain, and Saint hadn't felt an ache like this since Eoan first gave him the news. *Saint, dear, I need to tell you something.*

What he wouldn't have given then to feel every one of the finger-shaped bruises Jal pressed into his arms. To know the truth of what'd happened and have the chance to fucking *do something.*

Being there now didn't undo the last five years, didn't shove all Jal's hurt back in its neat little box—and even if he could have, he wouldn't have. Sometimes you took the bad shit and you locked it away where you didn't have to see it, because if you looked at it too long, it'd break you in a time you couldn't afford to be broken. Jal had been running when he found the *Ambit,* and Saint got the sense he'd been running a while before that. If this was the first chance he'd gotten to break that lock, to feel all the *bad* he'd swallowed since those bullets tore through him, then he needed this.

Selfishly, Saint needed to be the one who helped him through it. All the fuckups in their shared history—maybe he could start to do something right. So he stayed there, even as his bad shoulder started to ache, staring at the door and blinking the burning from his eyes. "It's okay, kid. I got you. It's okay." It didn't matter that *okay* was just a platitude, and *I got you* was years too late to do Jal any good. He said it, and he said anything else he could think of, and he kept saying it all until Jal's breathing went a little less ragged, and the shakes got a little less violent.

Finally, with a deep breath Saint felt through the fabric of his shirt, Jal pulled back. Poor kid looked wrecked, eyes all shiny and red-rimmed and cheeks so ruddy Saint could see it even in the bad lighting. Seeing the effort it took just to drag himself upright again, Saint had half a mind just to tip him right back over on the bed and leave him to get some shut-eye. *Wouldn't take much,* he thought. A strong wind to knock him over, a warm blanket to weigh him down, and Saint wagered he'd be out like a light.

Jal seemed to have something else in mind, though. He hunched over his legs, dragging his sleeve across his eyes. "Ah, fuck me." He made a sound that tried to be a laugh, but it came out far too ragged. "Sorry, I—" He shook his head awkwardly. "Sorry."

"Don't." It came out harsher than Saint meant it to. *We make a hell of a pair, don't we?* "I mean," he started again, gentler, "you don't have to say that. Not to me, and definitely not about this." He rubbed the back of his neck. That headache had found a nice little spot behind his jaws and made itself at home, throbbing in time with his heartbeat as an uneasy silence settled between them. Jal didn't seem to know what to say.

Saint threw him a bone. "So you really didn't know what was on the drive, huh?" He had no idea if Jal had just locked that away, too, or if there was something more to the story, but he believed him. He believed him, and he hated himself for doubting Jal in the first place, and he wanted to know everything, and he didn't want to hear another word of it.

Fuck, this was messy.

Jal shook his head again, no less stiffly than last time. "Wasn't too careful taking it out of the camera. Was afraid I'd busted it or something." His voice still wasn't quite steady, but he seemed determined to say whatever it was he wanted to say. "Then the scavs found me—same ones we were there to shut down before everything went to shit, so you can imagine they weren't real friendly. Patched me up, shipped me out to one of their sites. Needed workers more'n they needed to make an example, I guess." He tugged up his pants leg briefly, just long enough for Saint to glimpse the band of scars at the top of his boot.

No wonder he'd recognized the ankle monitors back in the depot. *Fuck.* Guilt seized violently in Saint's chest. That was where he'd been. All the time Saint had been looking for him, that was where he'd fucking been—trapped in a scav worksite, imprisoned and exploited and abandoned. And when Saint gave up searching, when he gave up believing anything but the bullshit stories Fenton and his crew put in those reports, that was where he'd stayed. *Deserted.* They'd had it wrong, every last one of them. They'd called Jal a deserter, when he was the one they'd all left behind.

Saint never should've stopped looking.

"Didn't manage to give them the slip 'til a few months back," Jal finished in a rush, like he couldn't wait to put that part of the conversation behind him. Saint couldn't blame him. "I tried out the drive as soon as I could. First port I came to, got my hands on a GLASS and tried to get into the Guild system, but it locked me out the second I put in my credentials. Would've sent up a fuckin' fugitive alert, but I snapped it and chucked it out an air lock before the signal went live." He cleared his throat. "I'd kind of wondered, you know? What they told everybody."

They, he said, not *Fenton.* Jal really didn't miss much. He'd have worked out Fenton had a devil on his shoulder; Saint just wondered how much else he knew. "Could you hear them? Whoever was on the other end of Fenton's comms?"

Jal's lips thinned. "No," he said. "Must've switched to a private channel. It, uh. It wasn't the first time. Whole op was shady from the jump, you know? Said we were there to shut down some scavs running an illegal trafficking post. *People* trafficking, I mean. But when I got in—'cause they sent me in ahead to kill the scavs' security. Lot of the temp crews liked me for that. Send me in at dark o'clock, follow when security's down or I've got the layout or whatever."

Send me in alone, Saint heard. *Let me take the risk.* No wonder Jal didn't trust the Guild. The way he'd been treated, and across more than one crew, didn't exactly inspire loyalty.

Jal winced. "Sorry, shit, I'm telling this all out of order. There's just . . . there's a lot to it, and I had a long time to think about it, and I can't—"

"Breathe, kid."

Jal took a breath so deep it stretched his ribs like bellows under his threadbare T-shirt. "I didn't *see* anyone else, is the thing," he told Saint, finally. "They said *human trafficking*—that we were there to save those people. Preservation of life, right? That's what the Guild's supposed to do, the only time it's supposed to interfere, but I swear there wasn't anybody there but scavs. No sign there ever *had been,* either.

"Just looked like the scavs were there to strip the place for parts. And shit, maybe it was just a mistake, but that's a *big damn mistake.* Tried to report back to the crew, but they just told me to sit tight and went real quiet on me. Got the feeling there were some conversations happening offline, or at least off *my* line. Must've been twenty minutes in dead silence before I finally got the order to return to the ship, and that wasn't 'til *after* the mercs'd shown up. It was . . . *shitshow* doesn't even come close." He took another bellows breath and let it out long and slow, but it didn't stop his voice from catching as he said, "What if that's why they did it?" Jal looked over, and Saint had to remind *himself* to breathe under the weight of that stare. Uncertain and searching, like he couldn't quite make sense of things himself and desperately wanted Saint to make sense of it for him. "Because they shouldn't have been there in the first place, and if they'd brought me back busted, or even told folks I was dead, people would've asked questions. But calling me a deserter . . . didn't anybody look too closely at that."

Saint knew it wasn't an accusation; for someone who'd been on the receiving end of so much hurt, Jal had never been quick to dole it out himself. Still, it felt like one. Maybe because Saint knew he deserved it. He'd *given up.* Even knowing Jal was too damn loyal to bail on his crew, even with Jal's sister insisting every goddamn chance she got that the reports didn't make sense, he hadn't looked hard enough, and Jal'd paid the price.

He must've felt so *alone.* Three years, help hadn't come for him; and when he finally escaped on his own, it was to a world that thought the worst of him. Branded a deserter by the ones that deserted *him*. A cruel goddamn trick played by a cruel goddamn world, and Jal deserved so much better.

"I don't know why they did it, kid," Saint had to tell him, because all he had left was honesty. "But I promise you we're gonna find out. I just—" He swore under his breath. "I just wish we'd known sooner. This whole time . . . that's why you pulled that stunt on the rockhopper, isn't it? You needed a Guild computer to check the bodycam drive."

Jal wet his lips and nodded. "Don't need credentials for on-board access, just need to actually *get* onboard. Saw my chance on the rockhopper to test it out, and I took it."

"You almost died," said Saint. Seemed an even bigger waste, knowing what he'd gone through just to get that far. "Christ, Jal. How may ships did you pass before you got to the *Ambit*? Any Guild rig could've gotten you that encryption key."

Jal shot him an incredulous look. "You kidding? You shot me the second you saw me, and I reckon you almost kind of liked me once."

Damn it. That riot round seemed so much less benign now. Jal had needed *help*, and Saint gave him a bullet in the back and not a moment's chance to explain himself first. "I wish I hadn't done that," he rasped. Wished he hadn't done a lot of things he had, wished he'd done a lot of things he hadn't.

"I know," Jal said, and nobody in that much *pain* was meant to sound that kind. That forgiving. "What I'm trying to say is, what do you think a ship of strangers would've done? *Deserter* ain't a pretty word." He dropped his gaze, picking at the edge of the bandage on his arm. Suddenly made sense why that cut was so clean; hell of a place to hide something for three years. "Not real keen on rangers lately, anyhow."

Well, no. He wouldn't be, would he? "Could've told us, then," he said. *Us* sounded better than *me*. "We would've helped you."

"Right," Jal mumbled. "Historically, telling you my plans

don't ever seem to work out well for me." There it was. An open door and a dare to step through it.

Fine. Saint was tired of tiptoeing around it, anyway. "I couldn't let you come with me on the *Ambit* back then. I know what you thought—"

"The hell you did," Jal grunted, but Saint acted like he hadn't heard. If he lost steam this early, he'd never get through this.

"—but it wasn't *right* for you. Out at the end of the goddamn universe, doing the mad shit no other captain would touch. I can count on one hand the number of times we've made it back to the center spiral in the five years I've been on this ship, and that was fine for me. Out of sight, out of mind . . . I was tired when I started, kid. Should've retired when I blew my shoulder, but I just couldn't take the quiet.

"You, though—you had your whole life ahead of you. You had your *family.* You think you could've gone whole years without seeing them? Because I know you better than that. You'd have followed me out there, and in a few months, maybe a year, you'd have realized it was a goddamn mistake. You'd have realized that you didn't want to watch your niece grow up through a vid comm. That you didn't want to die in the middle of nowhere. That I wasn't fucking *worth it,* and if I'd let you throw in with me and Eoan, you would've resented me for it."

"You think I didn't resent you for ditching me?"

A wry, self-deprecating smile. "I'm sure you did," Saint admitted. "I just didn't have to see it. Easier that way."

"For you."

He nodded. Seemed in poor taste to try to defend himself, under the circumstances.

"You were wrong, anyway," said Jal. "I wouldn't have resented you." Quieter, he said, "I *couldn't* have resented you."

Saint had considered that, too. "That would've been worse," he said. "Because then you would've stayed, and the way we ran things those first couple of years, the crazy shit Eoan and

I did . . . I'd have gotten you killed, kid. I could live with you hating me, but you *dying* for me? There wouldn't have been any coming back from that." Saint wasn't somebody you died for, and he'd never wanted to be. "Besides, I wanted something better for you."

"What about what I wanted?" Jal snapped. He scraped his fingers through his hair angrily. "Enough money to help Regan out and a crew that didn't give a shit where I came from or what I was made for. Those girls and you—that was everything I had. But you left and locked the goddamn door behind you, and I was stuck with all the bullshit. Nobody wanted me. Passed me around crew to crew, whoever needed the coal-eyed miner boy for a blackout op, then they'd ship me off to the next in line. You think I was any safer with them than I'd have been with you?"

"I didn't know. I didn't think—"

"That people are judgmental pricks? Try again."

"I didn't know they wouldn't see what I saw."

Jal's laugh was full of rusted nails and broken glass. *Cutting.* "Right," he said. "'Cause everybody's supposed to see things your way."

Saint wished he could say he didn't deserve that, but if he had to be a flawed man, at least he was self-aware. "I shouldn't have made the choice for you," he said. Wasn't an easy thing to say aloud, even if he'd spent years saying it to himself. "Even before I saw what—" *what Fenton did to you.* Fuck, he could still hear the sounds Jal had made, lying there bleeding from his own man's bullets. He scrubbed a hand over his face. "Before I saw the video," he said. "I knew it was wrong, and if I could do it all over again, I would've done every bit of it different. You trusted me, and I turned on you, but. . . ."

"But what?" Jal said. "What else is there but that?" The anger had leached from him, left him so tired and ragged he couldn't even hold the weight of Saint's sorry gaze. "I would've followed you to the end of the 'verse, you know?"

Saint sighed, throat aching. "I know." He knew now; he'd known then. It'd terrified him. Life in the Earth army had chewed him up and spat him out, a fucked-up head on fucked-up shoulders, so scared of the quiet that he'd thrown himself into the Guild just to die fighting.

Meeting Jal had changed so many things, but it hadn't changed that—*couldn't* have changed that. The scars had been too fresh, and he'd been too goddamn tired, and when he'd seen his chance in Eoan's crew to finally go out swinging, he'd jumped at it. He'd thought he was doing the right thing, keeping Jal from jumping with him. Instead, he'd damned the man he'd wanted to save, and saved himself in the process.

"I know," he repeated. "And I know I didn't deserve it, and it's about five years too late, but I'm trying to now. I can't do shit for you if you won't let me, though. Why didn't you tell me what you were doing? Where you'd been, what'd happened to you . . . did you think I wouldn't believe you?"

"No," Jal said, face half-hidden behind his shaggy, mussed-up hair.

Saint waited for something more, but as the seconds stretched tense and quiet between them, he realized *more* wasn't coming on its own. "No?" he said. "No *what*? I need something to go on here. Would you—kid, would you at least look at me?" The time had come and gone where Saint could look in Jal's eyes and know his thoughts, but he figured it couldn't hurt.

And lo, Jal raised his head. Raised it like it weighed ten kilos, but Saint would take whatever crumbs he could get. "Ain't because I thought you wouldn't believe me," he said, roughly. "It's because I knew you would."

Frankly, the silence had made more sense. "You kept it a secret," Saint began. "Because you were afraid you'd tell me you needed help, and I would *believe* you?" He tried his best to keep it neutral. Deliberate. Mulling aloud, not passing any judgments, because the last thing he wanted was for Jal to clam up again.

Jal's scoff said he'd somehow missed the mark. "No, see, that's the problem. I didn't say a thing about helping me. But you're still so damn—you're *you,* and you'd do what you do. You'd—" He scratched his head again, rough and agitated. Whatever he wanted to say, it wasn't coming out right. "Drive or no drive, you'd bend the ear of every captain on the Council 'til you got Fenton martialed. But if I didn't have *proof,* it'd just be my word against his, never mind whoever he had whispering in his ear. Who do you reckon wins that fight, old man? Fenton's a three-generation legacy with a jacket full of rec letters, and I couldn't even get a good word out of my own fucking *partner.* Never mind the crow the Captains' Council would have to eat if they copped to what happened. And you wouldn't care about that," Jal said, before the words could even leave Saint's tongue. "You'd tank your whole career trying to plead my case, and I wasn't gonna let you."

"I *wouldn't* have cared," Saint agreed.

"But I *would've.*" Jal arched an eyebrow and paused. "Sucks when folks make choices for you, don't it?"

Ouch. "It was reckless," he told him, firmly. Because if he couldn't take the *moral* high ground, he could at least try for the *practical* one. "Not just the rockhopper. You let us think you were playing us. Damn near had Eoan on a warpath just now, and I would've taken you to the Captains' Council myself after we got this Deadworld bullshit sorted."

"Could've tried," Jal said. "But I'm gettin' home to my family, Saint. One way or the other, with my shield or on it. Y'all were never gonna change that." His eyes glinted as he said it. More fire, more zeal than Saint had seen in him since they'd picked him up in the outpost.

For a second, it felt a little like the old Jal sitting next to him.

"So I did what I did, and I didn't tell you, and it worked out all right. Like the Weald."

"I got the shit knocked out of me in the Weald."

"We all got out," Jal replied, unrepentant. "Might not've done, if we'd stood around arguing, and I couldn't take that chance. It's gotta mean something, damn it. Everything I've done to get this far, if I don't get back . . . I just want to see them again." His words wavered. Desperation. "I want to tell them I'm sorry. All the shit I put them through, all the things I missed . . . Bitsie's turning twelve in a few months, and I just want to be there." And as fresh tears welled in Jal's eyes, Saint found himself wiping his own. Three years of birthdays Jal hadn't gotten to see. Three years of laughter and skinned knees and childhood and growth, and Saint had never loved anything or anybody the way Jal loved his family.

But God, he'd come close.

He reached out and wrapped an arm around Jal's shoulders. "You've got it now, though," he said. "Your way back. Council sees that footage, they'll know you did nothing wrong. Can't say it won't be messy, but they shouldn't fight you too hard, and Cap's got friends on the Council. They'll make sure their people back you—get you reinstated, if that's what you want. Let you go, if it's not." Problem was, that footage wouldn't do him a lick of good in the middle of nowhere on a radio-silent ship. *Fuck.* "We have to go back."

"What?"

"To Sooner's Weald. We go back, put some caps in your pocket, and get you a ride to the center spiral. This isn't your fight, kid." They'd lose a day, maybe, but Jal had come through hell just to get this close. Didn't seem right to risk all that.

He wasn't expecting the elbow to his ribs, or the tired chuckle that came after. "You just can't help yourself, can you?" Jal said. His smile, though tight at the edges, looked closer to real than it had any right being after the night he'd had. "You see this cut?" He lifted the edge of the bandage on his arm. "I stashed a hunk of metal under my skin for three goddamn years, and stood in a hangar full of ticking bombs, just so I could prove I *wasn't* a deserter. You think I'm gonna go back on that now?" He shook his head. "I meant what I said about getting home; don't think for one second that I didn't. But that video is the difference between going home a free man or a wanted one. I needed it, and one way or the other, y'all helped me get it. So now I need to help you."

"You don't owe us that."

"It's not about what I owe," Jal said. "It's about what's right. This virus, it's just a different verse to the same goddamn tune the Trust's been singing since they shot their first rocket into the stars. They wreck lives and make bank, and the watchers ain't watching shit, so they do it again, and again, and again. It wasn't the scavs firing on us in that footage; it was *Trust* mercs, there to clean up a *Trust* mess, and decent people got caught in the crossfire. Decent people are *always* gonna get caught in the crossfire, and nobody's stepping up to stop it.

"I just—fuck, old man. I've spent so long just trying to *make it*. Make it out, make it through, make it home. Feels like I forgot how to do anything else. How to care about anything else. But these last couple days, even with all the crazy shit that's happened . . . I don't know. I feel kind of like myself again, like how I used to be. And maybe." He gave a small, uncertain shrug. "Maybe I just want the *me* that gets home to be a little more like the *me* that left it."

He was going to have to talk about it, Saint thought. With Saint, or with Regan, or with an actual fucking professional—it didn't matter who, and it didn't have to be now, but Jal had to tell *somebody* what he'd really been through all those years. Saint saw the marks it left behind, the scars and the shadows and the cutaway pieces, but seeing it wasn't good enough.

"Besides." Jal rocked into Saint's side, too weary to be playful but trying to be. "Y'all barely made it off Sooner's *with* my help. Hate to see how you'd fare without me."

Saint wanted to argue, he really did. Not just for Jal's sake, but for the family who thought they'd lost him. The words just wouldn't come. Stubborn and honorable and too damn faithful for the universe he'd been born in—it was Jal all over. Jal the way he'd always been, and at the end of the day they'd have all been better off if he'd trusted that sooner.

So he didn't argue. "Then we'll get you home after," he said instead. A fool's promise, maybe, when he had no idea what waited for them on Noether. He made it, though. He made it, and he meant it, because for all he didn't know about what lay ahead, there was one thing he did.

Whatever it took, if it was the last thing he did, Saint would get Jal home.

CHAPTER THIRTEEN

NASH

Jal's debrief the next morning was a bit like death by a thousand cuts. Eoan kept their questions gentle. Objective. It turned out, though, there wasn't really an *objective* way to describe being plugged full of bullet holes and abandoned to the mercy of your enemy. Nash's skin crawled, hearing that Jal spent years scrapping abandoned Trust sites for the scavs while life moved on without him.

Kind of made her think Anke hadn't begged off just to get a head start on the patch.

"We could get in touch with them," offered Eoan, and the way Jal flinched, Nash would've sworn that was the deepest cut of all. "Their information is on record. I could set up a secure comm, if you wanted to send a message."

"No."

"No?" Not the response Nash had expected. "The fuck do you mean, *no?*"

Jal, for his part, looked like he'd sooner fling himself into dead space than answer any more questions. Good job they were up in the bridge; closest air lock was the one by the galley, and Nash figured she and Saint could probably wrestle him back before he made it that far.

Wouldn't take much, she thought, looking him over. Folded over like he had an anchor around his neck, and still somehow humming with nervous energy. It took a feat of patience bordering on superhuman not to reach over and force his bouncing knee still.

"Wouldn't be right," he said. "What would I say? *Surprise, I'm back, but I can't come home right now.* How d'you figure that'd go? Not like I can tell them where I am or what I'm doing. Most I can say is it's dangerous, and I ain't about to spring this on them just so they can worry 'til I finally make it home. It'd be unkind."

Fair point, she allowed, but also fucking moronic. "Kind or unkind," she said, "if you were my brother, I'd want to know."

"But he's not." Saint sighed from his post in the corner, leaning against the wall with his arms folded like he wasn't sure what to do with them. Or maybe, she thought with a glance toward Jal's weary pile of limbs, like he knew exactly what to do with them, and just wasn't sure if he *should*. "It's his family. Should be his choice when and how they find out."

Which might've been convincing, if his jaw muscles hadn't knotted up as he said it. Nash half-expected to hear his molars crack. "Shove it," she told him. "You think I'm right."

"Doesn't matter what I think."

Even Eoan sniffed at that one. Nash hoped that meant they'd call shenanigans—tell Saint he was being a pushover, tell Jal he was being unreasonable. Eoan just sighed, though, in that tinny, airless way of theirs, and said, "If you change your mind, do let me know. I'm sure they would be very glad to hear from you."

The captain had spoken. "Whatever," Nash said, kicking her feet up on the edge of the projection table and picking at some imaginary dust on her pants. *Don't give a fuck and you can't make me.* "They're your family, miner boy. You want to be stupid about it, that's your hill to die on." *Stupid* wasn't the problem, though. Nash didn't bat her eyes at *stupid*. The problem was, Nash was the gambling type. She knew a hedged bet when she saw one, and for all Jal's bluster about making it home to his family, she couldn't help thinking he was scared. Holding out in case he didn't make it back, so they wouldn't have to lose him for a second time.

Made her wonder if he felt it, too: the cold, creeping tightness of dread. It had wormed its way under her skin back at the depot and hadn't stopped spreading since, and the closer they got to Noether, the harder it was to shake the feeling that something *bad* waited for them out in the black.

And there they were, running out to meet it.

"You said there was something else you wanted to talk about, Cap?" Saint cut in before she could change her mind and call Jal's bluff. Just as well. She wasn't good at pulling punches, and Jal still looked a little too fragile for her particular brand of tough love.

Eoan's projection nodded. "Two somethings," they said. "Before last night's bit of excitement"—probably the nicest way to describe that debacle—"I looked into the leads from the shipping depot."

"Let me guess, ankle monitor was a loser." Nash hadn't gotten her hopes up, so Eoan didn't dash them when they nodded. Ah, well. At least she got to tear the horrible thing down to scrap metal. "Gotta hand it to them: the Trust knows their way around the underside of the table." Under the table, behind the back—those bastards never met a shade of shady they didn't like. "What about Riesen's little buddies?" Eoan wouldn't have brought it up if they didn't have something. Process of elimination. "You got something on them?"

Another nod. "Frankly, though, it's not the two from the depot we should be worried about. I did a bit of digging, and it appears they're part of a larger cell."

When it rains. Bad enough they had the Trust and its hired guns; now they had a bunch of agitators on their asses. "How large we talking, Cap?"

"More than two, less than an army?" they offered. "Oh,

don't make those faces at me. It's not as if they post member-ship rosters. Ideally they'll keep the circle small, try not to give anything away prematurely. They've got as much to fear from the Trust as we do."

"That's assuming they've got the sense to make the smart play," said Saint. "Could've been sheer dumb luck they stum-bled on the Deadworld Code. Intercepted a comm, found a pair of loose lips. Shit happens."

"It does," Eoan agreed. "But it didn't. Not here." A wave of their hand, and a facial scan appeared over the projection table. Wasn't a face Nash recognized—earnest, downturned eyes, and deep marionette lines. Divots in his cheeks Nash might've mistaken for acne scars if she hadn't spent some time helping in a pox ward during her unofficial apprenticeship with the doc. "I can't give you a number, but I can give you a name. Isaiah Drestyn."

Books and covers, et cetera, but he didn't *look* like the kind of person who could mastermind a murder-kidnapping. He looked . . . friendly. Forgettable, so long as you caught the side without the scars.

Then Eoan pulled up his warrant.

"Damn." Jal whistled.

For once, Nash agreed with him. *Damn.* That was a little more like it. "And I thought *I* had a banging résumé." Doz-ens of counts of rioting and inciting riots, which were usually just Trust-speak for *we don't respond well to criticism*, so she skipped them. Plenty of others told a more interesting story— arson, hijacking spacecraft, a few counts of murder. "Dude's a fucking pirate."

"A soldier," Saint said, and he would know, wouldn't he? Kindred spirits. Without the Guild banner on their shoulders, how much of the shit they'd done would've earned them rap sheets just like that? "Don't need a flag if you've got a cause. Guessing his has something to do with the Trust?"

"Fair guess," said Eoan. "Not exactly the celebrity type, but he's made a name for himself in the frontier. Mostly opposing bonded labor in the prospect planets. Played a key role in the Kepler Riots in '78."

"Shit, I remember that." Ten, eleven years ago. Nash had still been on-station, then, but it'd been all over the news broadcasts. "That refinery fire on Kepler 3814, with the busted wellhead." Despite some serious PR damage control, the story eventually broke that the Trust had let maintenance lapse. Too expensive to send trained mechs all the way to the frontier, so they just kept piling in the bonders for cents on the cap. The wrong shit broke in the right way, and that far out from developed worlds, the rest of the spiral couldn't do anything but watch hundreds of people burn.

The fires had barely finished dying when the first protesters rolled in. Families and friends of the laborers, Union representatives and folks who just couldn't bear to see it happen again. *Which one were you, Mister Friendly?* she wanted to ask, because there were layers to activism. People doing the right thing, or people doing the *only* thing. The ones who chose, and the ones for whom it was never a choice at all.

Eoan beat her to it. "He was there," they said. "Four years' labor on a bad homesteader's loan. His brother, too."

Another face coalesced beside the first, and for a second Nash wondered if they'd gotten the scans mixed up. *There* was a fighter's face. A killer's face. Sharper eyes set deeper between furrowed brows and a crooked nose, and his mouth wore a roguish grin that would've looked more at home in a bar fight than a prison intake scan. A bright red DECEASED scrolled around his shoulders, and she supposed that settled a lot of questions.

"Unfortunately," Eoan said, "only one of them made it out."

That'd do it. A dead brother, and the Trust got away with a slap on the wrist; if that didn't radicalize the shit out of someone,

Nash didn't know what would. And here the Trust was, doing it all over again. She wasn't even sure if Drestyn saw the dead planets, or if he only saw Kepler, over and over. His *brother,* over and over. "I'd want to take a shot at the Trust, too. Code's probably a pretty bang-up way to do it." The Union could give *lapsed maintenance* a pass, but nobody rubber-stamped a planet-killing supervirus. Leak that to a few news outlets, some public forums, and heads would roll. He just needed proof, same as them.

"Wouldn't just be the Trust, either. What do a scorched re-finery, a mummified shipping depot, and an abandoned shopping center have in common?"

Saint leaned back in his chair, arms crossed. "Not feeling the riddles, Cap."

"It's not a riddle," Eoan said. "It's a motive. Kepler, Noether, and the depot—all Trust developments in the frontier. That means they're all under the purview of one man: Otho Yarden. He personally oversaw the Kepler colony before the fire, and loathe as I am to imagine anything like that actually *making* a career, it seems he made quite the jump a few years later." No face over the projection table this time, just a name and a title. *Otho Yarden, Chief Executive of the Outer Spiral.*

"Man kills hundreds, gets himself a promotion." Jal's lips curled.

"I imagine Drestyn wasn't too pleased with it, either. More to the point," Eoan added, "that promotion means every signif-icant decision in the Trust's frontier holdings crosses *his* desk. So if I were looking for the man who authorized the use of the Deadworld Code in those colonies?"

"Yarden would be your bet," Nash said. It was an ugly kind of math, but it added up. "One stone, two very big birds—if Dres-tyn and his people weren't after wonder girl in there, I'd have half a mind to let him have at it." Even if they could let Drestyn have the code, though, which was a risk Nash wasn't too keen on taking, they sure as hell couldn't let him have *her*. Anke had been under their protection from the moment they answered her distress beacon, and anybody that wanted her? They'd have to go through Nash.

Beside her, Saint quirked his mouth wryly. "So, Trust mercs *and* strikers. Anybody in the spiral we're not about to piss off?" Because it wasn't a question of if they'd stick with it, see it through; it never was. The only question was how crazy shit would get along the way.

Hang on tight, kids. It's gonna be a bumpy ride.

. . .

Of course, by the end of the five-day crawl to Noether, Nash sort of wished it'd hurry up and get a little bumpier.

She'd never been very good at sitting around. That bit never made it into the Guild's welcome package. They hyped the missions, the principles, the blasty-shooty badassery, and conveniently failed to mention all the goddamn *travel time*. Tortoisean crawls across a too-big universe, killing time with piddly mission prep because the tedium was better than sitting around with their thumbs up their asses.

So Nash reoutfitted the rover. Seemed Noether had drawn *acid rain* in the Deadworld lottery, and good ol' HNO_3 didn't play well with metals. Even if they didn't end up needing it, it was good to be prepared, and it was better to be *busy*. If she got to have a few giggles with highly corrosive chemicals and a plasma torch, all the better.

In all fairness, having some time before they had to leap back into action was good. Gave Anke room to work—to throw herself wholeheartedly into trying to crack the nastiest virus in the spiral with nothing but her wits and ready access to the coffee machine. *Too ready,* Nash had decided. It was a toss-up which would crap out first, the coffee machine or Anke's heart, but Nash stood by for repairs on either. Wasn't much difference

anyway, when it came right down to it. People were function-
ally just machines with squishier parts.

It gave the crew room for other things, too. Watching Anke
and Jal try to avoid each other in an enclosed space had been
kind of entertaining, at first—though, honestly, watching Jal
try to do much of *anything* in an enclosed space was kind of
entertaining—but by the second afternoon, Nash was over it.

Fortunately, so was Jal. Anke'd claimed the galley table for a
makeshift workstation, so he caught her in there one morning
with one of his lopsided grins and a "thank you."

Anke blinked up at him and palmed her glasses back up her
nose. "I'm sorry, what?"

"*Thank you,*" he repeated, slower, like pronunciation was
the problem. On the other hand, it was a fair assumption; the
man wasn't exactly an orator. She'd rate his mumbling somewhere between quaint and grating, depending on the day. "You
got me my video."

"I told the captain about it."

"Yeah, but you know what they say about the cat you shave
and the cat you shear." And Nash definitely didn't imagine the
sour look Bodie shot him from his perch on the counter. *Treach-
ery.* As if the little chaos gremlin wouldn't be back to begging
for belly pets before the day was out. Bodie was usually kind
of a loner, but he'd either pegged Jal for an easy mark or fallen
deeply, deeply in coddled kitty love. Sociopath or sap: his mood
changed by the hour. And by how much time he'd spent with
the catmint plant on the table. Nash liked to say she put it there
for the energy—*helps improve the flow of the room,* she'd announced, and she did enough *genuine* interior geomancy that
Saint had gone along with it—but really, she just thought it was
funny to watch the cat get absolutely baked.

Anke blinked again behind her glasses, eyes shining blue
with the glow of her GLASS. Nash hadn't seen her much with-

out it, the last couple days. "I, um. I don't think I've heard that one."

"Well, they're both naked." It was pretty much the clueless leading the helpless, watching Jal try to steer a conversation, but he eventually made it around to explaining. "Don't much matter how the footage got cracked, just that it did. Which never would've happened if you hadn't saved it from the rockhopper before it blew. So." He rounded it off, matter-of-factly. "Thank you."

Somehow, that was the end of it.

Saint came around, too, in his own way. Spent the first few days with his head buried in schematics like an ostrich in sand, because apparently, gearing up for a fight scared him less than dealing with his new friends-to-enemies-to-what-the-fuck-now trope.

Every morning, though, Saint made breakfast in the galley. And every morning, when Nash went to get her tea, she found Jal in there keeping him company. In the doorway, the first day; at the table with Anke, the next; then at the sink, doing the washing up, though Nash was certain he'd never been asked.

So Nash wasn't surprised when she walked into the galley on the eve of their landfall at Noether and saw Jal leaning against the counter by the stove, so close to Saint that their elbows bumped whenever Saint stirred his pot. Easy laughs and quiet conversation, and Nash could only see Saint's face in profile, but he seemed to mirror Jal's warm, satisfied smile.

Nice work, miner boy. Underneath the sleepless eyes and scar tissue, Nash decided, he was one of those people: the sunshine people. The ones so warm, everybody turned their faces to them and basked in it. Not so hot they burned, not so cold they chilled. The *just right* people.

Nash had never been one of those people. She burned, and she chilled, and she didn't know any other way to be. She told herself it was better that way, because anybody left standing was too thick-skinned to mind the extremes.

Honeyed oats and spiced seitan gave the air a peppery sweetness as Nash crossed the galley. "That coffee machine's going to go on strike," she announced, shooting a stern look toward the table where Anke continued to hurl every bit of her techie savoir faire at their Deadworld problem. *Clock's ticking, wonder girl.* They were nearly out of time. "You sleep?" She picked up the mug sitting near Anke's elbow, frowning at the still-warm half pour of coffee in the bottom. "Do I even want to know how many cups this is?"

"Not that many," Anke said, at the same time Eoan volunteered, "Five, since midnight."

Anke pointed an accusatory finger at Saint without looking up from her screen. Which might've been why she actually pointed at the cat lounging on the other counter with his relocated happy-plant. "He keeps making a fresh pot."

"Doesn't mean you have to drink it," Nash shot back, pausing by the sink to scrub the oil smudges off her hands.

"Seems rude not to."

Jal laughed and cringed at the same time. "The *Ambit* special," he said. "Burnin' the candle at both ends and lighting it in the middle for good measure. Y'all need to sleep."

"Kind of the grease calling the grifter slick, isn't it?" Nash stopped just shy of asking how many times she'd caught him wandering the halls after hours. Must've taken a fair few sleepless nights to earn himself those nice, dark shadows under his specs. "Unless I'm supposed to believe that's hot water you're drinking."

"You *all* need to sleep," Eoan chimed in in their best *you started it, but I'm finishing it* voice. "Anke, the last sim—"

"Is taking forever," Anke groaned, dropping her head into her arms. Nash barely managed to slide her mug clear before it fell victim to a stray elbow. Sure, half a cup of liquid insomnia probably wouldn't kill a GLASS, but a perilously thin line existed between *waterproof* and *water resistant,* and that thing held the keys to the kingdom. The patch, still a work in progress, came to life keystroke by keystroke on Anke's tablet. *Days* of marathon programming stored on a single silica square, and Nash would be damned if they all got undone by a cup of half-burnt bean water. Especially since they couldn't back it up. They'd all agreed that the Deadworld Code should stay on the GLASS's drive, off-network and stashed safely away from the *Ambit*'s systems and anything else it could sink its digital teeth into. Away from *Eoan.* No telling what the code would do to the captain if it took a ride on the API railroad and got into their programming. Would've been like a doctor playing fast and loose with live viral cultures—ill-advised.

So, the Deadworld Code stayed away from Eoan, and as long as Nash's reflexes held, the coffee stayed away from Anke's tablet.

Not that Anke seemed to notice, head buried in her folded arms and shoulders hunched miserably. Five days she'd been at it. Five days, staring at that screen, coding version after version, running simulation after simulation, weathering disappointment after disappointment. She didn't need more coffee; she needed a *break*.

Instead, she got a chirp. A quiet little thing, but the way Anke sprang up, it might as well have been a siren.

"—is finished," Eoan concluded, cheerfully.

"Please," Anke chanted under her breath, flipping through screens and readings and lines of code so quickly it made Nash's eyes hurt. She didn't even bother to straighten her glasses. "Please, please, please. Mama needs some good news. Just give me some—" Abruptly, she paused. Squinted. Pursed her lips in a small, soft O and tilted her head. "Oh."

"Oh?" Nash prompted. "Good *oh,* or bad *oh*?"

"It's . . . good, I think?" A few more screens, and Anke nodded. "Great, actually. It's—I mean." The corners of her mouth started to lift, until she beamed so shiny and wide that Nash had to remind herself to blink. *Sunshine people,* she thought again. Didn't make sense, how a pair of grease- and blood-stained shadows like her and Saint could wind up sharing space with people like that, but maybe that was the thing about shadows; maybe they needed the light most of all.

"I did it," Anke whispered, then she *didn't* whisper. "Holy shitsticks, I did it!" She rose so quickly she knocked her chair over, and Nash wasn't sure who she startled more: Bodie, who yowled and corkscrewed off the counter like he was ducking enemy fire, or Nash, who suddenly found herself with an armful of delighted whiz kid and exactly *zero* idea what to do about it.

Anke pulled away before Nash could figure it out—sort of a shame and a relief, at the same time. Nash didn't like surprise hugs, but . . . she didn't *not* like *that* surprise hug. "Sorry," Anke said, but her cheeks glowed pink above an incandescent smile. "I was just—"

"It's okay." Probably not the thing to say, but that was the thing Nash said. "You're, uh. You're sure?"

"Sure as I can be, without a live run. This is the second time I've run this sim, and it's still coming out aces. On a scale of *fingers crossed* to *bet your ass,* I'd say have your keisters at the ready." She made a face. "That sounded less weird in my head. Anyway, what I'm *trying* to say is, it should work. Might have to make a few adjustments when we get to Noether, make sure there aren't any surprise variations from one version of the code to the next. But that should take all of, like, five minutes."

Five minutes. *Incredible.* Anke said it so casually, like everything she'd been doing wasn't a tour de fucking force. She hadn't just caught something everyone else missed; she'd found a way to do something about it. Nash wondered how many times she'd have to tell Anke she was amazing before it stuck.

Even if it took years, she couldn't help thinking it'd be worth the effort.

"Of course," Anke added, blissfully unaware, "that's assuming we get in. Which is super out of my wheelhouse, in case that wasn't one-hundred-ten percent clear to everyone."

Eoan chuckled. "I believe we can manage that, dear," they said. "It's our specialty."

"Breaking into abandoned Trust sites?" Anke, too wrapped up in her GLASS to notice her mug had moved, made a blind grab for it and got nothing but air. Same with the next grab, and the next, until Nash pushed the mug back toward her palm obligingly. Anke could have the caffeine battle for today; Nash would win the war.

"Inviting ourselves in," Eoan replied. "Rude, I suppose, but our hosts don't tend to be the hospitable sort." Eoan was, as ever, the master of understatement. "Just get the patch ready for the ground team to upload—"

"As idiotproof as possible," Saint interjected.

"—and we'll see to the rest."

Finally, Anke broke her staring match with her tablet. "I'm not coming?"

"Do you want to?" Saint asked.

Anke faltered. "I mean. No. Not really, I . . . my on-world record is pretty much zip-for-two, and I'm not a big believer in *third time's the charm*. There's not really anything I could do there that I can't do here, anyway. Except, you know, get in the way."

"You wouldn't be in the way." Did Nash say that too fast? It felt too fast. *Huh.* "You got that guy on Sooner's for me. Great timing, creative use of a flowerpot. Top marks from me, slugger."

Anke's blush deepened. "I just didn't want you to get hurt."

Either the air was suddenly *way* less breathable, or Nash's lungs forgot what to do with it for a second. She coughed and cleared her throat. "Uh." Nope. "Thanks." Better, ish. *Move it along.* "We've only got three rebreathers, though. Miner boy's got the spare, so guess you're overwatch."

"Besides," Eoan said, "if there's an unfriendly welcome waiting on Noether, I expect they would be very interested in getting their hands on you. Better you stay on the ship, where it's safer."

On that point, Nash couldn't argue. Even in the capable company of Saint and herself—begrudgingly, she'd also admit the miner boy wasn't *completely* useless in a fight—Anke would be more exposed off the ship than on it. If they could get her access to Noether's T-form systems and keep her safely aboard the *Ambit* at the same time, then that was the smart play.

It just didn't *feel* right.

She couldn't shake it, that niggling, malignant itch between her shoulders. A chilly foreboding, like chips of ice down her back as they talked strategy over the galley table. It sounded good: enter through the old shopping center, take the tunnels straight to Noether's operations building. In and out in under an hour, give or take half that, depending on the kind of heat waiting for them.

"Tunnels." Jal's nose wrinkled. "Not big on tight squeezes."

Nash glanced up at him through the three-dimensional schematics. "You'd rather go *singing in the acid rain*? Operations building is a no-fly zone; weather's too gnarly. So either we take the tunnels, or we try the rover and cross our fingers and toes that *all terrain* isn't an exaggeration." Steep hills and sloppy mud—not exactly easy riding. "Relax. It's not like we're trekking through a drainpipe or something. Even Your Real-Damn-Highness should be fine."

All of them would be. The feeling was just a feeling, insubstantial against the weight of fact. The fact was, they were prepared. The fact was, they had a job to do and the wherewithal to do it.

The fact was, they didn't have a choice.

. . .

Noether was a miserable place.

Nash had seen mockups of the shopping center, the way it was meant to be. A gleaming monument of white-chitin stone and seemingly infinite windows, surrounded by dancing fountains and flourishing gardens and the sort of abstract sculptural art that made Nash's brain hurt when she looked at it too long. They'd set it all against an idyllic blue-green sky, as much a lie as the stock-photo shoppers smiling their way across the rendering; clear skies didn't exist on Noether. Strong updrafts and a high surface water percentage meant near-constant rain, even before the T-form system glitched. So either the mockup was wishful thinking, or they'd had designs for some kind of weatherproofing that they just hadn't gotten around to realizing before construction shut down.

Add that to the list, Nash thought as Eoan set them down in the shadow of the mall. If the mall had been finished, there would've been gardens where they landed, lush and vibrant and carefully manicured; instead, they sank into a slurry of gravel and mud. Nash caught herself holding her breath as the cargo door dropped. Stupid. Pointless. They had their rebreathers on, so the acid in the air couldn't have burned her lungs. Just another goddamn *feeling*, as if that decaying, forgotten sickness of Noether could squeeze past the mask and insinuate itself in her chest. Could dissolve her like it had been dissolved, from something proud and unassailable to bending, cracking—

"Bones," Jal said beside her, squinting out into the bleak, cloudy gray. "Looks like bones, don't it?"

Yes. White-chitin columns and archways curving together like ribs, tattered construction tarps hanging in the place of windows like bits of flesh left on the carcass. Nitric acid had eaten pores in the stone, so stark and clean that Nash couldn't help but look for oozes of marrow in the places the stone was gouged the deepest.

"Does it?" she said, sliding into the rover. "I hadn't noticed."

The short hop across the would've-been gardens churned up mud as thin and runny as the rain sluicing down the windscreens. Even with the rover's deep-welled wheels, it slid and skidded like a motherfucker, and Jal clung to the handles in the back like he thought he'd get thrown every time it fishtailed.

"Okay back there?" Saint took the turbulence in stride, even slanted half a smile in the rearview.

Jal just groaned and thumped his head against the back of Saint's seat. "I'm gonna die here."

"Don't be so dramatic," Nash said. They were nearly there anyway. Just a few more decs of slurry, and a brain-rattling bump as they hit the entryway pavilion, and it was smooth sailing through what would have, at some point, become a nice set of double doors.

It was disorienting, the way the rain suddenly *stopped*. She'd gotten used to hearing it pound against the hull of the *Ambit* as they entered the atmosphere, then the roof of the rover. Now, with dozens of floors between them and the sky, it went abruptly silent.

She probably should've been a little gentler on the brakes, but watching Jal tumble half over the center console was good for a laugh. "Fuck," he wheezed as he sat back on his heels. No seats in the back, just some storage and a few well-placed straps.

Saint, halfway out of the rover, twisted around to raise an eyebrow at him. "You kiss your mother with that mouth?"

"I think I broke a hip."

"Please." Nash snorted, climbing out and taking in the view. *Bones* was an apt description. Supports and studs and scaffolding, storefronts blocked out but never finished, the skeletal structure of escalators and stairwells suspended between the floors. From their makeshift parking space in the lobby, Nash could see past dozens of walkways layered one over the other like shelves in a bookcase, all the way up to a massive skylight.

Other than the windows, it seemed like the only silica they'd put in before construction shut down—a web of geometric panes sloping so smoothly the rain didn't even make a sound when it hit. Heptagons? Nonagons? So asymmetrical it seemed *organic*. As though, if Nash stared long enough, she might see it breathe.

"This place give anyone else the creeps?" Jal asked, drawing her eyes back to ground level. He'd managed to unfold himself from the back of the rover and stood at the edge of a multitiered fountain collecting nothing but dust and drippage.

Saint wandered off a little farther, near an open door to the right of the entryway. Tucked away, meant to be perceived only by the people who needed to use it. *Staff only.* "Schoolhouse after dark," he said. "Abandoned theme parks." It took Nash a nanosecond to catch the theme—places not meant to *be* without people. Haunted by a profound, unnatural emptiness. Saint wasn't as obvious about it as Jal, kept his features square behind the visor of his rebreather, but Nash could read between the lines of his gruff "Let's make this quick."

She couldn't agree more. "Cap? How's it coming?" Eoan had sent a drone ahead to scout Noether's underground. They'd pegged the path from the shopping center as the straightest shot to the operations building; everything else had collapsed or flooded or branched off in directions they had no interest in going. The plan was to hold back, drag their feet a little so Eoan could make sure everything was clear. Wouldn't necessarily keep them out of a fight, but it would at least give them a heads-up if one came their way.

"Swimmingly," Eoan reported, crisp and collected over the comms. They didn't care about ghost town vibes, if they even picked up on them at all; they had an underground tunnel to explore. "You should get down here. It's quite a sight."

Saint aimed his IR scope down the hallway, probably to make himself feel better. The man would jump blind off a building if

Eoan promised a soft landing, but he seemed hell-bent on going through the motions. "Any security?" he asked.

"Clear!"

Nash startled at the sudden, bright voice chirping over the comms, and she wasn't the only one. Jal flinched like he was trying to escape his own ear, eyes screwing shut. Odd to actually *see* them, with no specs in the way; he wouldn't need them down in the tunnels, and he seemed to be managing okay in the weak, trickling daylight aboveground.

"Sorry! Sorry, that was loud. I'm new at this," Anke said, and Nash could practically *hear* her blushing. "But you *are* good to go. Nothing but clear skies ahead—figuratively, I mean."

Saint opened his mouth, but Nash silenced him with a look. *If you don't have anything nice to say,* and Saint clicked his teeth back together decisively. Smart man. He led the way through the door instead, flicking on his red-light headlamp.

"Awesome." Jal grinned, teeth painted crimson and black eyes like smoldering bricks of coal behind his mask. It had taken a bit of tinkering on Eoan and Nash's part—and a bit of good-natured cooperation on Jal's—to find the right wavelength for Jal's particular rod-cone combination, but judging by the general lack of squinting and swearing, she'd call it a success. She and Saint could see in the red light, and it didn't aggravate Jal's eyes the way anything on the other end of the spectrum did. No night blindness, no NVGs, no problem.

He gave her a thumbs-up as he passed, jogging up to flank Saint in the front. Right side; Saint's weak side, and she wondered if he knew he kept doing it, or if it was just old habit.

Long as you're keeping your eyes on the hall, miner boy, she thought with a touch of a smile. Not that there was much to see. Bland block walls, splashed red by their headlamps. Pipes on the ceiling and puddles gathering on the floors, no decoration but the odd doorway with the odd plaque leading off to the odd boiler room or breakroom or whatever else they felt the need to tuck away from public view. Which sounded more interesting than it was, she decided, nudging a half-open stairwell door with her toe. The slow, solemn *creak* of the hinges echoed all the way up the hall.

"You're doing that on purpose," Saint said.

"It's quiet. I'm bored."

"You're bored." He didn't sound surprised, just exasperated. "You know there's probably people here who want to kill us, right?"

Nash nudged another door. Broom closet. *Thrilling.* "In other breaking news, water is wet, and Jal is tall."

"Thanks for noticing." Jal shot her a wink over his shoulder. Really leaning into the whole *people can see my eyes* thing. Embracing the oculesics—good for him. "Careful, though," he added, as she tested another door. SECURITY OFFICE, said the plaque on the wall. A persistent drip down the wall had smudged half the letters, but Nash was pretty good at that game. "Could be rats."

"You hear that, Saint? Forget the baddies with guns. There could be *rats*."

Jal sniffed. "I don't like rats."

"Well, you can relax. Not picking up any heat signatures behind the door, rodent or otherwise." And just because she could, she gave the next door a little kick. Wasn't expecting it to open, rust-eaten lock dropping out of the door like it had just been waiting for the excuse to break.

She also wasn't expecting all the corpses.

Her stomach took a sharp dive into her knees. "Not again," she rasped on an exhale too tight to be a sigh, counting three, four, five bodies. One collapsed on a table shoved up under an air vent, the others piled in the corner like they'd been *put* there. Dragged or thrown without much care, no order in the tangled pile of—

"Oh, God." Anke must've been watching the bodycam feeds. "That's not—they aren't like the ones at the depot."

High-moisture environment. Compared to the bone-dry atmo of the depot, they might as well have been swimming. Acid and toxins and bacteria had eaten away at their clothing, at their *skin*, but they hadn't mummified; they'd rotted. Like wax models left too close to the fire, melting into the soapy, waxy sheen on the floor that shined when Nash's light hit it. She counted heads, because the bodies weren't composed enough to sort limb from limb.

If she hadn't been counting the heads, she might not have noticed the bullet wounds. Only in two of them; the others must not have been as neat. Rusty-brown stains on the walls and floors, furniture upended and thrown aside. "Nope," Nash agreed grimly. "Not like the ones at the depot."

"They killed each other." She hadn't even heard Jal move, but his shadow stretched across the red-lit floor, distorted by the directions of the lamps, hers and Saint's. "Why?"

Nash pointed up to the vent. "If I had to guess."

"Clean air?" Saint was the last to join at the door, and he didn't linger past a sweep inside, enough to register no threats and move on. He'd probably filled his repertoire of horrors ten times over; he didn't need more nightmare fodder.

"Cleaner," Nash said. "Filtration system might've helped dry out the air, but the PPM would've been too high. The concentration of the acid in the air," she translated for Jal, who probably hadn't had much use for chemistry. He hummed his thanks. "Sole Survivor up there was still a dead man; he just had a little more time to think on it."

"Poor bastards." Jal, she noticed, only looked at the bodies in the corner. The victims, not just of the Deadworld Code, but of man's baser instincts. Self-preservation. *Or maybe you thought you were being kind,* she thought of the body on the table. Putting the rest out of their misery before the acid ate them from the inside.

They'd never know which, and maybe it was best they never did. Some stories were meant to die with their makers; some stories didn't bear repeating.

Nash cleared her throat and closed the door. *Garter stitches. Gerbera daisies. Gearboxes.* Good things, calming and familiar, painstakingly layered over the picture in her mind's eye of what lay behind that door. The sooner they got this over with, the sooner Nash could rest knowing it would never happen again. "Let's get to the fucking tunnel."

Anke fell uncharacteristically quiet, but Eoan took over. Guided them down a long hallway to a fork in the corridor. More staff rooms ahead—more doors hiding bodies, more plaques marking graves—but to the right, UNDERGROUND WALKWAY.

"The elevator shaft is just up ahead," Eoan told them, and as they drew deeper down the walkway, Nash could finally make out the elevator bay stretched three lifts wide. Like a lobby all its own, with crooked, bowing benches and vending machines toppled and broken. In the depot, they hadn't known was happening; they'd closed their eyes and never opened them again, and that was the end of it.

On Noether, they would've had time. Not long—minutes, for the ones inside. Less, for those without shelter. They'd have had long enough to be terrified, though, with all the *messiness* that entailed. Sort of made her wonder. "Why didn't they call for help?" They'd had time. Surely someone would have tried. "I know Noether's out in the middle of nowhere, but there's got to be a few satellites close enough to pick something up."

Anke coughed. "I, uh. I had a theory about that, actually. I mean, they designed the Deadworld Code to be undetectable, right? But that doesn't do them much good if somebody manages to shoot out an SOS before they die, and surely they wouldn't leave something like that to chance. If I'm them—even *saying* that feels like I'm vomiting jellied eels—but *if* I'm them, I think I'd bake in some kind of jammer."

"I'm not picking up any jamming signals," Eoan said.

"And I haven't found any communications-based code in the version of the virus I pulled from the depot," Anke agreed. "Jammers aren't like the base Deadworld Code, though. Like, the terraforming components of the Deadworld Code can't be *extracted*. Once they're there, they're there, and they're there to stay—see: *salt from soup*. That's the trouble with really complex programming.

"Jammers, though, they're dummy code. Easy peasy. Drop one of those suckers in on a timer, wrap it up in a self-deleting executable, and you've got a thirty-minute mute button that wipes itself out once it's done. Which you'd want, right? Because if anybody picks up a signal jammer on a planet that just friggin' *eradicated* itself, you gotta think they'd take a closer look." She paused, probably to suck down her first breath since Eoan'd finished talking, then rounded it out with a meek "Just a theory, though."

Nash wished she wouldn't hedge like that. Even her *theories* had a fuck-ton of savvy and sheer common sense behind them. *Own it, wonder girl,* she wanted to say. *Don't you get how* brilliant *you are?* She didn't get the chance, though.

"We've got a problem, Cap," said Saint. He'd moved ahead to the open shaft; the other two had been dented shut, surrounded by the twisted frames of broken chairs and bits of pipe and anything else close at hand, like people had been trying to get into the elevators. The danger came from the sky; it made sense they'd want to go *down*. "No elevator cars."

At least, not one that they could use. Nash could just make out the bottom of it if she peeked up the shaft, hovering at the edge of where her lights could reach. A pair of metalweave cables trailed down into the dark.

"Anybody got a cap to drop?" Saint muttered wryly.

Jal leaned in to take a look, peering over Saint's shoulder—still the bad one, *always* the bad one—into the gaping hollow below. "Think I can do you one better, old man," he said. It wasn't a warning, as such, but after more than a week with him, Nash really should've heard it as one.

He jumped.

Both feet off the edge of the platform, straight down. If she hadn't been busy swallowing her heart back out of her throat, she might've even sworn she saw him *smiling*. Then came the thud at the bottom, echoing its way up.

"Jal?" she called down to him, after a few-second grace period for him to find his feet or cry for help. "You dead?"

A beat of silence, then he said, "Seems not." Deep and drawling, no signs of distress. So, not hurt.

Yet, she added, taking in the look on Saint's face. He blew a sigh through his nose in the place of any curses, which was somehow worse. Like even he wasn't sure what would've come out if he'd opened his mouth, so he'd decided not to chance it.

"Only a couple stories," Jal went on. "No fuss." The cable gave a couple of sharp jerks, and miraculously the lift didn't come screaming down on Jal's head. "This ought to hold all right. Y'all coming?"

Nash wished she hadn't seen the lines around Saint's eyes as she rubbed her gloves together and grabbed the cable. Unflappable, un*flinching* Saint, but standing at the edge of that elevator shaft, he looked every bit as worried as she felt.

Passionflower. Plasma cutters. Pink hair. Good thoughts. Bad feeling.

"See you at the bottom." With a flick of a wave and a kick off solid ground, down she went into the dark.

CHAPTER FOURTEEN

JAL

Jal steadied the cables as the others slid down.

"Please tell me you could see the bottom *before* you jumped," Nash griped as her feet touched down. She whistled for Saint when she was clear.

"I could see the bottom before I jumped," Jal replied, dutifully trying not to grin. It didn't seem to work, if Nash's narrowed eyes were any indication, but he deserved points for the effort. "Told you, that was nothing."

"That was two stories at a straight drop. I weep for your knees."

He caught the cables again as Saint's weight jostled them from above, a handful of nice, sotto swears rolling down the shaft. Saint liked heights about as much as Jal liked enclosed spaces, but like gunshot wounds, busted shoulders, and the bounds of his own questionable mortality, Saint didn't let it stop him.

"It's the ankles that'll get you," Jal said. "Shattered my right one hopping off a mesa, once."

"Forget to look before you leapt? Shocker."

"It was a game," he said. "Me and my friends, when we were little—workin' little, not schoolin' little," he clarified, though that line got awful blurry back on Brigham Four. "We used to take turns droppin' geodes off the mesas. Whoever dropped theirs from highest without breaking it took home the pot for the day. Folks got real artsy with it. Wrapped them up in coats, stuffed them in their packs. One kid, he even built this, uh"—he flapped his hands, searching for the right word—"parachute out of his lunch bag. Didn't work a whit, of course, but it was fun to watch." He spiraled one hand toward the other and mimed an impact.

"Sounds like you needed a hobby," Nash said.

"Needed caps more." He kept it light, swallowing the old ache with practice. Couldn't very well be a funny story if he started talkin' about his sick ma and shit. "Pot got pretty big one day, so I thought I'd be clever. We're made to handle a fall, you know."

"You didn't."

"He did," Saint said from above.

Right. He'd heard this one. It caught Jal a bit wrong-footed, some half-formed memory of a cold roof and a quiet conversation, but he shook it off. "Yes, ma'am," he said. "Held it tight in both hands and walked right off the edge of the mesa. Landed bad; ankle gave me fits forever after. But I won the pot." The important takeaway. "Always been more scared of losin' than fallin', I guess." Though he supposed he'd done his share of both.

A beat later, Saint's boots hit the ground. "And the old man makes three." Jal steadied him without thinking as Saint rolled his bad shoulder—he tried to make it seem more like habit than hurt, but it was a hard sell to anybody who'd seen the scarring—and got a sour-lemons look for his trouble. He just grinned brighter, until he earned a twitch at the corner of Saint's mouth. Saint was never as far from a smile as folks liked to think.

"As above, so below," murmured Nash, scanning the room beyond the elevator shaft. He and Saint followed close behind, on the unspoken agreement that it'd be better not to linger under a couple thousand kilos of elevator car hanging by a rusted thread.

It was a mirror image of upstairs, less the whirlwind of broken furniture and the dents in the elevator doors. Like they'd stepped into a reflection, inverted but almost identical, down to the snack machines with mildewed bars and bottles whose labels had been lost to time and some enthusiastic fungus. Dust and damp coated everything in a thin glaze of grime, turning the poured composite floors slick under Jal's boots as he picked his way across the small lobby. It had the look of a place that smelled *sour*—ripe with the stink of fermentation, things broken down and belched out and baked in the stifling heat of the underground, sinking into his clothes and settling on his skin like a film.

Bad things had happened down there, too. *As above, so below.*

"Footprints." Saint didn't get distracted with things like molded snacks and cold, creeping dread. Always moving forward, like a . . . shit, what were they called? Big fish, big teeth. He was one of those, the apex badass in whatever pond he decided to dive into. "Clean enough to be recent," Saint said as he knelt to look closer. Recent enough that he drew his gun when he stood, aiming it down the open doorway across from the elevators. "Captain?"

"Still clear," they replied down the line. "No warm bodies."

Maybe Jal was just being morbid, but that kind of implied there were some cold ones. It turned his stomach, made his palms clammy in his gloves. Death wasn't new, but this was different; this was a long walk through a mass grave. Nash and Anke had it right: it wasn't like the depot. These people hadn't just lain down and died. They'd died ugly, fighting and afraid, and they'd left ugly corpses.

Jal couldn't help thinking on the kind of corpse he might've left, if those scavs hadn't found him.

"Kid," Saint said, clipped and stony, but worry pinched the corners of his eyes. Like he could *hear* all those piling-on thoughts in Jal's head. See them, maybe. Jal never had much of a poker face, and Saint had never had much trouble calling his bluffs. It was an act of mercy that he didn't ask, didn't press, didn't prod. He waited at the mouth of the tunnel, under the double-wide and double-enforced archway, with an air of expectation. "We're moving."

Just find the next foothold. Jal dredged up a smile and jogged to catch up, and Saint clapped him once between the shoulder blades as he passed and still, graciously, didn't ask.

For a while, the tunnel was just a tunnel. Shored-up stone and dust in all the crevices, grout running down the drippy, moldy walls like pus from a festered wound. It was drier down there than it had been aboveground, but only so far as a hard rain was drier than a swim. Pillars stabbed through the cracked floors, and a weak breeze sighed through the pipes along the ceiling. Sounded listless, mournful, and it didn't do anything to smooth Jal's hackles.

They rounded a corner, though, and everything changed.

"Damn." Because Jal's vocabulary wasn't up to trying to describe the mental fuckery of seeing what looked like a cozy city street stretching out underground. Not a bunch of subbasements strung together, trying to look like something other than what they were; an actual, bona fide *street,* with lampposts and storefronts with cracked-glass windows and signs that still said things like CAVERY'S BOOTS AND BELTS and HIGH STREET MARKET. Even he didn't miss the irony of a name *High Street* for someplace subterranean. He guessed to live in a place that glum, folks had to have a sense of humor.

Eoan made a small, eager sound halfway to a giggle. "Quite something, isn't it? The schematics don't do it justice."

No, they hadn't. No place in a drawn-to-scale blueprint for the slick cobblestones under his boots, buckling toward the middle of the street, or for the dusty old patio furniture sitting outside BAFFLER'S CANTEEN. It was disorienting; his brain kept trying to right the picture, flip it all aboveground and pretend away the ceiling over his head. Panels of colored beehive glass let in a little light from above, enough to wash liquid shades of blues and greens and purples up and down the stone facings. *Underwater.* That was how it felt, like the whole street had sunk straight to the bottom of a lake and brought them along for the ride. "They built it like this?"

"Someone wasn't using his listening ears in the brief." Nash snorted, clearing a spot of mildew off the canteen window and peering inside. Whatever she saw made her recoil. Jal didn't need more information than that. "This used to be aboveground."

"Guessin' they didn't just up and decide they'd like the view better down here."

"Bunch of genius developers," Saint said from a few steps down the street. "Picked a nice flat spot with a nice pretty view. Didn't occur to them 'til the wet season that ninety percent of it was *below* the floodplain."

"Hell of an oversight," Jal said.

Saint gave a distracted grunt that Jal took as agreement. He made his way methodically from door to door, shining his tac light inside long enough for a cursory sweep. The light was the same as the headlamps, red and soft even when Jal looked straight at it, though he almost wished it wasn't. Would've made it harder to see through the glass, at all the too-still shapes inside the too-still shops, huddled together like they'd known what was coming and couldn't bear to face it alone.

"Not that it matters," Nash added. She bumped him as she passed, with a glint in her eyes that said, *Shake it off.* "Couple of months of mudslides and washouts, and they finally said *to hell with it* and walled it all in. Laid down some transport roads up top, weatherproofed the footpath from the tenements, and carried right on building. The Trust has always been pretty good at rolling with the punches."

"Not too bad at doling them out, either." Case in point. There must've been hundreds of people on Noether when the Trust flipped the switch. Hundreds of people left to rot on a poisoned planet—a whole city of cadavers, tucked away underground.

Growing up on a cold, lightless rock, he used to think he knew what darkness was. He'd had no idea.

"I've reached the operations building." They'd been waiting for that—the all clear from Eoan, and not a moment too soon. Only thing worse than running through a graveyard was slow-walking through one. "Doors are stuck, but I don't imagine they'll give you too much trouble."

"Finally," Nash said, and like on Sooner's, she was the first to break into a run. Not quite full tilt, but something close to it. Not a thought spared for the uneven cobble or the slick ground, like she'd never slipped a day in her life and wasn't about to start now.

The street got narrower as they ran, storefronts giving way to stretches of tunnels with close-curved ceilings and unmarked doorways. Sometimes they forked, but Nash always seemed to know exactly which door to take. Left, left, middle, disappearing around a corner in a flash of silver-streaked hair and reappearing when they followed her around the bend. On and on they went, each new length of tunnel looking more and more similar to the last.

"Ah, I see you," Eoan chirped. "This way, this way." Like a goose hurrying along its goslings, and if Jal squinted down toward the end of the tunnel, past where it split off to rows and rows of tenement houses, he could make out the shape of their drone.

It floated into another lobby, inverted left to right from the one beneath the shopping center, but this one was—

"Christ, who turned loose the bulls?" Saint stepped over the ruins of a bench, boots crunching on bits of broken glass and twisted shards of metal. The elevator lobby and everything in it had been ripped apart, broken open. Notice boards had been torn from the walls, lights shattered, those same two vending machines from the other two lobbies turned on their sides, spilling snacks and drinks like guts across the floor. Not much left of them now but faded wrappers and moldered smears on the floor. "They wanted up," he said, tac light trailing over the ruined elevator doors.

It was worse than they'd seen back in the shopping center. Clusters of small dents that probably would've matched the edges of the pipes and extinguishers and bench rails scattered at the base of the doors. Shoulder-height depressions, shallow and deep. *They threw themselves against the doors.* Jal's throat went tacky; his mouth dried and soured. Dark stains smudged over the dented, polished chrome, almost inky in the tinted light. Scratches and scrapes in the brushed texture of the metal. Streaks in threes and fours, like fingers tearing at the seams of the doors. They'd tried 'til they bled, and it still hadn't been enough.

His pulse roared in his ears; his hands twitched, curled, like he was the one tearing at the doors. He had been once. Halfway across the spiral, in a different set of ruins. No virus, no code, just a bunch of asshole scavs and the creeping realization that he was *never* getting out.

"There should be bodies here," Nash said. Someone made a quizzical sound over the comms, but Jal couldn't figure out who. "Blood in the corners. Blood on the walls. Adipocere deposits on the ground."

"What the hell's adipo—?" Jal gave up trying to pronounce it, turning to watch her prowl around the room.

She paused near the leftmost elevator door, feet at the edge of a shiny, greasy patch on the floor. "Corpse wax."

He swallowed, tasting stomach acid and the breakfast he *truly* regretted eating. "Sorry I asked."

Nash shrugged. "Human bodies are disgusting." But she

didn't look especially disgusted. Intrigued, more like. "There would've been dozens of them, to leave a mess like this. Somebody must've moved them. Unless they got up and walked themselves out," she added, arching a teasing eyebrow over her shoulder at Jal.

"Oh, God. They can't actually—they can't do that, though, right?" Anke squeaked.

At least when it came to Anke, Nash was kind enough to look guilty. "No," she said. "Sorry, it was a bad joke."

"An apology." Saint whistled, crouching by what looked to be another set of footprints by the centermost lift. "Breathing rarified air out there, Anke. I wasn't even sure she knew how."

Nash muttered something too low to hear, but it probably didn't bear repeating. "Don't make it something more than it is," she told them. "They're just bodies, and this is just a room, and the Deadworld Code is just a long-ass string of numbers and letters. If the bodies are gone, it's because somebody wanted them gone."

"But not the ones in the shops?" Eoan said.

Jal's fingers itched for Saint's beat-up flask. *Still carrying it around, old man?* Couldn't exactly take a swig with the rebreathers in the way, but that didn't used to matter. That flask had been as much a part of Saint's uniform as his gun belt, and Jal had only lately started to understand why. He sighed. "Only the ones that were in the way," he said. "Must've been people here after the rain hit. Mercs or agitators—no-fly over the operations building, so they would've made this trip, too."

"Regularly," Saint agreed. "Once or twice, you wouldn't go to the trouble; you'd just leave them and keep walking." Like they'd done with the bodies in the security office. The storefronts. The shipping depot. Fuck, what was *wrong* with them? They'd just left them there. They'd left them all there, and Jal hadn't even stopped to think—

Nash hummed. "But they made it a habit," she said. Already

on the same page as Saint, easy as breathing. One thought, two heads. "Think they're still here?"

"Seems likely," Saint said. "Cap?"

"I can't get a scan beyond this point," they replied. "Get the drone through the door, and I could try to run it ahead and see what's up there, but I'm getting more signal interference— definitely from the building, possibly something atmospheric. I don't expect I would make it very far out of the lift. You might be on your own from here, I'm afraid, but you have my utmost confidence."

"Really ought to know better by now, Cap," Nash said, bending to pick a length of pipe up off the floor. One end in the seam of the doors—it fit so neatly between two gouges that it must've been done before—and with a quick shove, she had the doors open before Jal could even *start* to offer to help. "Low-tech, but it gets the job done." She wedged the pipe between the doors to hold them open and ducked inside. "Don't knock it loose when you come through," she called back. "I'm a damn good doctor, but spontaneous hemicorporectomy is *very* hard to come back from."

He and Saint traded looks and, *carefully,* followed her through.

The drone floated unhappily outside the doors as Nash and Saint started making their way up the cable. "I know it goes against every instinct you have," Eoan began, "but please be careful." It was strange to hear the layers in the words. Levity stretched over genuine concern. Anyone who said AI weren't human had clearly never heard one talk like that, worry like that, *care* like that.

"Aye aye, Cap," Jal said with a salute, then he backed up enough for a running start and bounded up the wall of the shaft. A push off the wall, and he caught the hanging cable about sixty decs up—cut the climb clear in half. For a second, he just let himself hang. Let his muscles burn and the empty air yawn out underneath him. Let himself breathe in the dark, without imagining all those melting, black-lidded eyes watching him.

"Problem?" Saint called from the bottom of the shaft. Nash had already started up the cable.

He mustered a smile and wondered if they could see it in their fancy little lights. "Just waiting for y'all to catch up." Then he hand-over-handed the rest of the way up the cable, jumped the gap through an open doorway, and landed in a brand-new elevator lobby. "Goddamn, they really picked a theme and stuck to it, didn't they?" More benches. More machines. More bulletin boards with their thick glass screens, diodes in the backing to scroll through whatever messages were worth broadcasting.

More bodies.

"Heads up," he said, grimacing. "We've got another . . ." But he trailed off, footfalls echoing off the high ceilings as he moved closer to the shape on the floor. Just the one, black clothes against stark white tiles. Everything on Noether was so goddamn *white*, and so goddamn *dirty*, and so goddamn *dead*. Something dark and wet seeped across the tiles, spreading in the cracks away from the body.

It came away tacky on the tips of his gloves. Shiny and thick, rolling down the rubberized grips on his fingers, onto his palm. *Not right*, he thought, stumbling to his feet and away from the body. "That's not right." He only half-heard the others climbing over the edge, only half-noticed their boots hitting the tile. "There shouldn't be any—"

"Jal?" Saint's shadow rose across the tile, and Jal turned to face him, holding up his hand to the shine of their lights. "Is that blood?" Jal didn't get to answer; Saint charged forward, snatching Jal's hand and turning it over between his own. "Are you hurt? What did you—"

"Ain't mine." Too quiet; Saint must not have heard him, still pushing up his sleeve and tugging at his glove, still furiously checking him over. "Saint! It ain't mine, all right? It's his." He slipped his hand free of Saint's to point over his shoulder at the body on the ground, lying in a pool of its own blood. "It shouldn't look like that, should it? It looks . . ."

Anke let out a shaky breath in their ears. "Fresh." He swore he could *hear* the nausea knotting up her throat, and the exact shape of her hand pressed over her mouth.

Nash had a real different reaction. She crossed the room in a flurry of *not fucking around* and flattened the back of her hand against the man's brow. "Dead," she said. "In case anyone wondered."

"Never seen anybody take a pulse like that," Jal said.

"Augments pick up the pulse," she answered, with a shake of her hair. "When there's one to pick up, anyway. What I need's a temp. Saint, this guy's still warm. And"—she picked up his arm and dropped it—"floppy. I'd say we're looking at TOD inside six hours." With a disdainful grimace, she rolled the body over. "Ah, and who had *gutshot* on their dead planet bingo card? Poor bastard—bad way to go. Takes time."

"Time enough to crawl out here," Saint observed, sliding past her with his light aimed at the floor. Tracks. Thick smears of blood leading down the hall, disappearing around the corner.

Jal had thought *dragged,* at first, but no. No, he must've crawled. Blood coated his elbows and his front, where he'd pulled himself forward. "Captain was right," he said. "The signal's for shit in here. Might've been going for help."

"I don't think he made it," said Nash, flatly. "Wait. Saint, damn it, where are you going? T-form servers are the other way."

Which Saint definitely knew; he just didn't seem to care. "Somebody was here," he said, stalking down the hall with his gun sighted at the corner. Ready to ruin the day of anything stupid enough to surprise him. "Somebody with a gun and no problem using it on our mercenary friend back there."

Nash made a noncommittal sound. "Enemy of my enemy?"

"Unless they want what we want and ain't good at sharing," Jal said. "Anke? Don't suppose they're friends of yours."

"What?" Shit, Anke had some pipes on her. Loud and sharp and a little bit shrill, even with the ship's comms crackling. She needed to lay off the caffeine before she gave herself a stroke. "No, I—friends? I don't exactly run in the kinds of circles that off mercs for funsies. Oh, God, why is that a sentence that even makes sense to *say*?"

Not Guild, then. "Mentioned some other coders after the depot, is all," he said. Then, to Nash, "See, I do pay attention."

"Gold star, miner boy." She groaned. "Saint, seriously, leave it alone."

"It could be more of those strikers from the depot—Drestyn's people. You don't want to know what happened?"

"I want to get off this *planet*," she hissed. "Stubborn jackass." Damned if Jal didn't agree with her, just this once. In his experience, running *toward* people with guns was a good way to a bad end.

Once Saint got it in his head to do something, though, it was good as done. "It'll just take a minute," Saint said, and *oh*, Jal could picture the glint in his eyes. Not glee, but maybe its sharp-edged older brother—the satisfaction of knowing exactly what needed to be done and exactly how he was gonna go about doing it. Most men went their whole lives without knowing that kind of certainty, and that was something worth admiring.

Even if he really was a stubborn jackass.

All right, old man. Not like Jal could let him go it alone, so with a sigh and a *what can you do* shrug to Nash, he took off after him. Closed the gap in a handful of strides and caught him right as he cleared the corner, but when he tried to slow down, his boots slipped. Water, he thought. More fucking water.

Then he looked down. Not water—something darker, like the trail winding its way from the elevator lobby. *Blood*. It spattered the walls, dripping sluggishly down into the puddle at his feet. "Is that—" he started, raising his fingers to a small hole in the wall.

"Bullet," Saint confirmed without stopping. He'd marked it, considered it, and filed it away as unimportant, all in the handful of seconds it took Jal to find his footing again. *Pro* didn't even begin to cover it, and he only had eyes for the end of that blood trail. It disappeared under a door halfway up the hall, like a snake slithering back into its pit.

"Because that's not foreboding at all." He'd fallen behind, though, so with a hard shake of his head—bad time to get squeamish—he caught back up with Saint and Nash. Just blood. Just bodies. *Don't make it something more than it is*. Nash gave a hell of a pep talk.

He'd fallen in line at Saint's shoulder as Saint threw open the door. Gun up, finger on the trigger, but Saint shouldn't have bothered; nothing waiting for them except more of the goddamn same. *Just blood. Just bodies*. A baker's dozen, dragged into a neat line in the middle of what might've once been somebody's office.

"Well," said Nash brusquely, "at least we know they called in reinforcements." Definitely more of a welcome wagon than they'd had to contend with on the Weald. "For all the good it did them."

"I don't understand." Quiet, this time; Anke had range. "Why are they dead?"

"If I had to guess, I'd say it's the bullets."

"Nash," Eoan warned.

Nash looked sheepish. "Sorry. Reflex." She knelt by the nearest corpse, checking its pockets and coming up empty. "No ID, extra clips for his piece. If it walks like a merc, talks like a merc—okay, not much walking or talking going on here, but you know what I mean." She shook her head, straightening. "So somebody whacked the whackers. Anybody else not breathing a deep sigh of relief?"

"They didn't kill them here." Saint trailed his gloves along the walls. No blood spatters, no bullet holes, no spent shells. Nothing to suggest a fight except the casualties. "Must've dragged them in here, tried to hide them. Probably didn't realize that guy in the lobby was still alive when they left."

Jal didn't like the look on Saint's face all of a sudden. No glint, no smile, just that grim-flat set of his mouth and a furrow between his brows. "Hide them from what?" he asked, and Saint's brows knotted deeper, jaw muscles twitching. *Ah, fuck.* "From *us*. You think someone knew we were coming." With enough firepower to wipe out a full crew and enough time to clean house before their trio strolled in.

Saint did something with his shoulders too stiff to be a shrug. "Could just be another group of mercs trying to horn in on the reward, but." He let it hang, but the point damn near made itself. Could be more mercs, could be more picketers, could be more rangers gone rogue. They didn't *know,* and that was the problem.

"It doesn't rain, but it pours," Eoan sighed, voice fizzling over the feed. It had gotten worse, the farther they moved from the elevator. A little extra recon with the drone was definitely a nonstarter. "The job doesn't change. Get to the servers, test Anke's code, and get back to the ship in one piece. *Not* in order of importance," they added sternly. "If someone gets in the way, step over them. To hell with what flag they're flying under."

Eoan gave a pretty good pep talk themself.

"In case you were wondering," said Nash, "nobody here's gonna top that." And when she turned on her heel and started back along the blood trail, he and Saint followed without a word.

They left them there, those poor dead bastards. Like the statues in the depot and the corpses in the city below, thirteen more casualties in an undeclared war. They left them there to rot behind a slowly closing door, and they didn't look back.

The whole planet was a mausoleum, anyway. Maybe the dead were exactly where they belonged.

CHAPTER FIFTEEN

SAINT

They didn't see a single soul on the way to the T-form servers. Not down the long, windowless hall cutting to the heart of the building, not up the dozen flights of stairs, and not tucked away in the security anteroom upstairs. Sometimes Saint thought he saw something. A flicker. A shudder of movement in the corner of his eye. Each time, though, it was just their headlamps making mirrors of every drip and puddle. Shadow puppets on the walls.

"*Security is our priority,*" Jal read off a sign on the wall, with its curled-up corners and water-blistered paint. A few more like it dotted the room: warnings on the guards' desk, instructions on the walk-through scanner beside it. Jal stuck his arms up like the half-faded drawing and walked between the scanner beams.

With a snort, Nash hopped the gate beside it. "I didn't know you could read."

"Hah." Jal kept his hands up but dropped a lot of fingers, and Saint wasn't sure whether to smile or scold him. Couldn't be acting like that when he got home to Bitsie; Regan would break those fingers off at the knuckle and shove them someplace southerly.

Saint shook his head, following Nash over the gate. "Nash, you're up." Behind the security checkpoint, things got simple: a door. No tech, no frills, just three decs of tungsten alloy and *don't even try it.*

Of course, with her trusty plasma torch and a can-do attitude, Nash would do a hell of a lot more than *try*. "I got this door, you boys got that one?" she asked, flicking a thumb toward the entrance.

"Nah, thought you'd like the audience," Jal said, but he'd claimed a spot by the guards' desk with a view out to the stairwell. Only way to the T-form system was up those stairs; if somebody wanted to try something with Saint's crew, they'd have a hell of a time doing it now.

Missed your chance, he thought, but it didn't stop his teeth from grinding. He didn't want to high-noon it with whatever deadeyes left that pile of bodies in the back office, but he'd thought for sure there would be *something*.

"What's on your mind, old man?"

Saint looked over right as Jal looked away, as if he hadn't wanted to get caught staring. "Nash, you sure nobody's breached that door?"

A palm-sized square plate of tungsten dropped to the floor, edges still white-hot and glowing from Nash's plasma torch, and Nash snaked a borescope through the hole. "Unless they brought a whole-ass spare door, pretty damn," she said. "Nobody's done anything to this door but me. Suppose they could've had a key, but the scope's not picking up on anybody inside." She left the borescope in the door and set her attention—and her torch—to the locking mechanism itself. "Why?"

"Six hours."

"Not seeing how that answers my question."

I'm getting there. "You said those bodies had been dead less than six hours."

"Give or take," she said. The plasma torch glowed so brightly in her gloved hand that it made Jal wince. "Well stop looking at me, dingbat! You keep touching a stove when you know it's hot?" Then, to Saint, "Sure, six hours."

"So where are they? Somebody rolled in, killed over a dozen

mercs here on Trust orders, and then what? They're not behind that door, we didn't run into them in the tunnels, and their ship didn't show up on any sensors."

"It's a pretty good chunk of time," Nash said. "Could be enough time to get in, get out, and get clear of any atmo or orbital sensors."

Jal sucked in a breath between his teeth. "Get out with *what*? You don't think they came for the code, too, do you?"

"Sure as shit didn't come for the sunshine." At the sound of a metallic click, Nash's shoulders did a victorious shimmy. Progress. "Anke, you hearing this? You got a way we could check to see if anybody else nabbed the code?"

The comms crackled, and for a second Saint thought they might've gotten too far away. As Nash started to repeat herself, though, Anke's voice came through the ship's comms. "—n't need to," she said. "Seriously? Is this thing on?" *Tap, tap, tap.* Loudly.

"It's on," Jal groaned, stretching his jaw like his ears suddenly needed to pop.

"Oh, okay. Yikes, my bad. No, I mean, nobody should be taking the code," she said. "Only me and a couple of others would even know what to look for, and we're not exactly the *multiple homicide* types." It was less reassuring than he'd hoped it would be.

Jal glanced back over at Saint and frowned. "Shit, you got that face."

"Bit too old to change it now. I've grown fond of it."

It wasn't always easy to tell when Jal rolled his eyes, but Saint definitely caught it this time. "The face," Jal insisted. "With the, uh." He squinted his eyes and scrunched his nose, and Saint just prayed it didn't look half that endearing when *he* did it. He had an image to maintain. "You're worried."

"He's thinking what I'm thinking," Nash said. Another click, another shimmy, but Nash's shoulders had started to look a lot stiffer. She was made of tougher stuff than most, but whether it was those implants of hers or just a keen sense of intuition, she always had a damn good nose for when things didn't sit right. "If it's not the code they were after, it's something else. Maybe some*one* else."

Anke made a sound somewhere between a hiccup and a laugh, then abruptly stopped. "Wait, you're not kidding?"

"Makes sense," Saint said. "Nothing else here but stripped cables and scrap metal. But if they're the same crew of agitators that tracked you down at the depot, who's to say they didn't do the same thing here? Don't need the code if they got you."

"Well, that's cheery," Jal muttered.

"Just a thought." Didn't really matter, he guessed; if something happened, they'd deal with it, same as they always did. He just wasn't as keen on unsolved mysteries as Eoan was. "Stay sharp out there."

"Right, 'cause if you didn't say anything, they'd both be chillin'." With a huff through her nose, Nash killed her torch and stood. "All right, gents, moment of truth." A hand on the handle of the door, a bit of pressure, and—

Click.

The door swung outward with a rusty groan and a rush of chilled air. "Good game," she told it, nudging it the rest of the way open and gesturing them inside.

"It's cold," Jal said. "Why's it cold?"

"All the T-form servers are on a separate heat-cool system," Anke explained. Saint had his doubts about her field savvy, but he had to admit it was good having an inside woman. She'd probably forgotten more about T-form protocols than the rest of them had ever known, bar Eoan, and she seemed inclined to help out however she could. "Same generator powering the computers powers the climate systems."

"Not the security?" Seemed like a doozy of a design flaw.

"No," said Anke. "No, that's . . . it's supposed to be on the same system. They must've disabled it already."

There it was again. *They.* "The mercs?"

"It'd have to be. The security's MFA."

Nash gave the doorjamb laser scanner a whistle and a lewd once-over. "Motherfucking awesome?"

"It's not that awesome," Anke muttered. "PIR motion detection, rheometric pressure plates, piezoelectric turrets—about as much nuance as a brick in a tube sock, but I guess if you're into that sort of thing."

"Is anyone *not* into that sort of thing?"

Jal raised a hand. "I'm not even sure what we're talkin' about," he said. "Y'all lost me at *motherfuckin'*."

Bless her, Anke threw him a rope. "Multi-factor auth. Short of nuking the whole facility to glowing green matchsticks, the only thing that would shut down the security systems in the T-form rooms is someone with the Trust codes plugging them in and flipping the switch."

"In case anyone still had doubts about whether the Powers That Be have hands in this *particular* pie," Nash said under her breath, wandering down the short hall beyond the door. Narrow walkway, walls some kind of layered plastic thin enough that Saint could feel a vibration when he put his glove against it, like a thousand tiny drones trying to take off behind it. Cooling fans.

The other side had a half-wall finished out in glass from waist-height to ceiling. Armored, no doubt. Smudged to high hell, but not enough to block the dozens of monitors inside spitting lines of code so fast it made Saint's head spin. "You seeing this, Cap?"

"I am," they said. It sounded like it came from somewhere far away, same weak signal as Anke's, but he could still make it out. "It's a bit splendid, isn't it?"

Saint never could make much sense of code, but he could make good sense of Eoan—of the open, unabashed *awe* in their voice as they took it in. Just because he couldn't see the beauty in something didn't mean it wasn't there. "Splendid," he chuckled as Nash and Jal ducked into the monitor room. Nash at the desk, Jal breathing down her neck, the two of them trading hiss-whispered jabs like a well-practiced dance. For a second, it felt like he was looking through a window into a different life—a life where he hadn't run. A life where Jal hadn't gone through hell to find his way aboard the *Ambit,* and Saint had spent all those reclaimed years watching the pair of them pick at each other just like that. "I suppose it is."

"Anything interesting happening out there, boss man, or you just afraid Big Brother's watching?" Nash swatted Jal's hand away and turned Anke's drive over the other way. "Aha! Told you I'd get it."

"Didn't say you wouldn't."

"You thought it."

"Oh, so I *think* now?"

Nash huffed a laugh shaped like something rude. "All right, wonder girl, pretty sure she's all yours." The diode at the end of the drive lit up blue, bright enough to give Nash's eyes a gleam and Jal's a good reason to look elsewhere.

Toward Saint, it turned out. "Didn't answer the question, old man."

"That wasn't a question; it was an invitation to squabble," Saint replied. "And it sounds like her dance card's pretty full at the moment."

Nash winked over her shoulder. "Never too busy for you," she said. Not to fluff his ego, but to remind them all that her capacity for multitasking was outmatched *only* by her capacity to argue up, down and left, right. God forbid she ever used her skills for more than her own petty amusement.

Which, to be fair, could be said about a lot of Nash's talents.

Nobody that deft with a knitting needle should be fucked with lightly.

"Hey." Jal pointed to the screens without quite looking at them. A little too bright, especially when he'd had time to get nice and cozy in the dark. "Should those be doing something?"

"Anke?" Nash said. No answer. "Anke?"

Over the comms, something tipped over and clattered. A bit of muffled rustling, and Anke finally chimed in, "Sorry, yeah, I'm—wait, what was the question?"

Nash tried valiantly to hide a smile, but one peeked at the corners. "The screens aren't changing. Is that a problem?"

"No, don't worry about it."

"Gonna need more than *don't worry about it*," Saint said. "We came a long damn way for this not to work."

"No, no, it's working," Anke said in a rush. "It's just on my screen. I could probably cast it over there, if you want to watch over my shoulder, but I'm not going to lie, I get kind of nervous when people watch me code. My typos go *way* up."

"And we wouldn't want typos, would we, Saint?" said Nash, mock serious.

"Or a nervous Anke," Jal added. Coming from him, it was too good-natured to be sarcastic; if Saint had tried it, he would've wound up sounding like an ass. "We looking good?"

"I mean, the rebreathers look kind of silly no matter how hot you are, but otherwise I'd say you're—oh. You meant, uh."

"The Deadworld patch," Saint supplied, helpfully.

"That." She hit the *T* hard, letting out a puff of air between her teeth. "Sorry."

Poor kid. She sounded freaked out, and more than her usual baseline jitters. *High-pressure situation, time limit, and a lack of field experience,* he reminded himself. All told, they were probably lucky she'd managed as well as she had.

Still. He'd seen her at the depot, jamming a handful of bombs while she stood not a stone's throw away from them, and she'd kept her wits about her. He knew she could handle it. "Breathe," he told her. "Do what you do. Tell us when you've got something."

"Right." A deep breath in, and a long exhale that sounded like it was being blown straight against his eardrum. "Right, okay. I'm okay. Just, you know, the fate of the universe. No biggie." The sound of tapping fingers filtered in through the breaks in conversation, steady as rainfall and quick as a downpour. "Just a couple adjustments to take her live, and Bob's your awkward uncle you only see on holid—"

Everything flashed blistering white. That was the only sense he could make of it at first. Just *bright* and *heat* and a popping sound like a fistful of bang snaps. Distantly he registered a yelp from Jal and a curse from Nash, and as the spots finally started to clear from his eyes, it hit him.

It'd all gone dark. The monitors, the console, even the LED on the end of Anke's drive. Smoke rose from the gaps in the paneling, seeping out around the melted plastic of the drive. "Nash—" he started.

"I got it, I got it," she snapped, already dropping to her knees in front of the console with a multitool she'd summoned from whatever pocket dimension that bag of hers linked up to. In a matter of seconds, the main panel under the console popped open, and a fresh wave of smoke rolled out like the back door of a cigar lounge. "Toasty." Flippant word, uneasy tone. "Got cooked wires in here, Saint. It's in bad shape."

"What set it off?" Details, details, details. Enough to figure out what had happened and what *needed* to happen.

"Must've overloaded it. Wouldn't have taken much; just something throwing a spark, and *poof*. It's dry-rotted and dusty as hell in here. Because of course there's *dry rot* on the wettest fucking planet in the spiral!" she spat, and Saint half-expected something to go flying, but it wouldn't have been Nash's style. Always calm when it counted. "Guessing whoever was watching this place wasn't keeping up the maintenance. Or the housekeeping. Fucking slobs."

Next question. "Can you fix it?"

"Maybe," Nash said, frowning deeply as Jal shuffled closer to lend a hand. Kid hadn't stopped squinting, pupils as small as they knew how to get—just enough to see the full ring of green all the way around. "Probably. If we're lucky, those things are hermeticked out the ass, and it's just the console that fried. Anke, you still tapped into the system?" The drive had been her lightning rod past the air gap, and Nash seemed as concerned as Saint that it'd gotten fried enough to disconnect her from the T-form systems. "Need you to make sure nothing else got roasted."

Anke didn't answer.

"Anke?" Nash tried again, and another handful of seconds passed without a sound down the line. "Anke, can you hear me?" She looked back at Saint, mouth a thin, worried slash.

Nothing.

Fuck. The comms had been spotty, but timing that bad couldn't be coincidence. Surely the blown console hadn't done something on Anke and Eoan's end. "Cap, come in? We can't get a hold of Anke. You there?"

The static was damn near deafening. If the comms were down, whether by the T-form fritz or that persistent interference, they had no way of knowing what was going on out there. No way of knowing whether the patch had worked, or if something was wrong back on the ship.

"I've got a bad feeling about this, Saint." Nash said it like a confession, face hidden in the underbelly of the console. Like an *apology*. It wasn't something new, then, that bad feeling. She'd just finally decided to say something about it. "Something's wrong here."

"Starting to get that notion myself." The dead mercs, the unknown executioners who'd disappeared without a trace, and now this. Closed comms. Cut off from the ship in a moment of distraction, and maybe he'd been right before.

Maybe there was trouble.

He gritted his teeth and set a course. "Stay here," he told them. "Nash, try to get that up and running, see if things are clearing up out there." If they couldn't get confirmation from Anke, they'd make do; the planet was one giant-ass barometer for whether the Deadworld Code was still live. If Nash could get the monitors back up, check the read-outs, they'd know. He just couldn't wait that long. "Jal, you cover her. Give it fifteen minutes, tops, then you two head straight to exfil, patch or no patch. Understood?"

"If we're staying, why're you makin' for the door?" Jal said, trailing him out into the short corridor. "Can't let you go out there on your own, old man." *Can't,* not *won't,* like it didn't even register in his world of possibilities.

"Have to," Saint replied. "Somebody's got to see what's going on back at the ship." Gun, ammo, guts. Check, check, check. All he was missing was a stiff drink and Eoan's voice in his ear reminding him not to do anything uncharacteristically stupid. *Dear.* Because, of course, a certain level of foolishness was more or less a guarantee when Saint acted solo.

If Jal remembered anything about their time together, he probably remembered that, too. Saint wondered if that was the reason for the storm clouds rolling across his face. "Saint—"

Saint caught the back of Jal's neck and squeezed, firm and familiar. Things were too damn messy between them. Too much history, too many things they still needed to sort out. But the way Jal looked at him in the red-hued dark, it was as clear as it'd ever been:

Jal cared. Whether he wanted to or not, whether Saint *deserved* it or not, he cared, and he did it the same way he did everything else: completely. With his whole heart and only half his head, and not a scrap of him held in reserve.

"I'll be fine," Saint told him. "But Nash is the only one of us who could make sense of that in there, so she's got to stay, one of us has to go, and I'm not leaving either one of you alone in this place. So you stay, too. Watch her back, and she'll watch yours." He'd feel better knowing he'd left them both in the best possible hands. "Fifteen minutes, that's all I'm asking for, and if it goes to shit, at least you can say you told me so." Cold comfort, bad joke, but after a terse moment of static, Jal finally gave a nod.

"Watch your ass, old man," he said.

"You too, kid. Both of you," he added, louder, for Nash. One last squeeze—Jal wouldn't have believed a smile, so he didn't try for one—and Saint dropped his hand. Fifteen minutes. *Better run fast, old man.*

He did. He tore through the anteroom, back down the stairs and down the halls and down the elevator shaft into the tunnels below. Through those, too, so fast that he barely noticed the change from tunnel walls to windows with festering ghosts inside. Brace be damned, his shoulder made all its usual complaints as he climbed the cable at the other end, back up to the maintenance hall of the shopping center, and he'd say he wasn't winded by the time he made it back out to the rover, but Jal and Nash could no doubt hear otherwise.

"Too fucking old for this," he grunted as he slid into the rover. Between Nash and Eoan, he didn't get to drive it often, but he knew his ass from his elbow and the gear shift from the emergency brake.

Nash's laugh broke over the comm static. "You've been saying that for years."

"Long as I've known him," Jal agreed.

"Why's it that the only time you two seem to get along is when you're ganging up on me?"

"What can I say?" A sharp hiss and a clang, and Nash shot off a rapid-fire string of curses before continuing, "You have a way of *uniting* people."

Banter was its own kind of static: the soothing white noise of a pointless back-and-forth, a raft to keep them from sinking into their own heads. He heard Nash fighting with the console from their end, and they probably heard the rover tires crunching over wet ground from his. It looked different than he remembered—pale and glittering across the surface, like frost, but the rain beating down was as liquid as it'd ever been. "You guys should see this," he said.

"I'm working on it," Nash said. "Hey, miner boy, hand me the—no, the other one. That one."

Jal spoke quieter. "You okay out there?" Strained, but hell, maybe that came from working close quarters with Nash on a deadline.

Bullshit. Like they weren't all twisted up with worry, just trying to cope. Just trying to get the job done. "I'm almost to the ship," he said. "Don't see anything amiss just yet." He'd half-expected another ship, some sign of the merc-killers come back for round two. But only the *Ambit* sat there, hunched in the slurry and rain. "Eoan, you hear me? I'm at the ship, all right? Need you to drop the tail." The answering silence didn't surprise him, but it sure as shit didn't reassure him.

"There's a button on the dash for the cargo door," Nash said. "Up by the—"

"I *know.*" It came out too sharp, and he mashed the button too hard, and he gripped the wheel too tight as he waited for the door to drop. He had that feeling again. Same one he got in Sooner's Weald, that gnawing, itching feeling at the base of his skull, like he'd walked into an ambush without the sense to stop himself. No idea where it came from, just that it came, and he still had no choice but to keep fucking *walking.*

He could still hear Nash and Jal, though. In the end, that did it—pushed him over the edge from vague suspicion to bracing for the inevitable, because if it wasn't the weather or the distance or all the buildings that had blown the comms, then what *was it*?

The cargo bay looked the same as they'd left it, equipment hooks empty and breakfast plates balanced precariously on the weight bench with the promise that somebody'd get to them later. Not a thing looked out of place as he pulled the rover up the ramp and slid out, but he found himself with a hand on his gun and a wary eye on the door ahead.

"Eoan?" he called, clearing the door into the hallway. "Anke?" He didn't expect an answer, but the quiet still made his teeth buzz. Nothing happened on the ship without Eoan knowing. If he called their name, they should've answered. They should've *answered*.

The overheads in the hall flickered. Not all at once, but strip by strip, off and on. The hall seemed to morph with it, telescoping out into the dark and snapping back with the lights. Spots and blotches played tricks with his eyes, shadows in the doorways so clean-edged and distinct that he drew down on them, but they were gone with the changing light.

He shook his head and blinked, hard. Let the wave of adrenaline crest and pass and kept moving with Nash muttering in his ear. Talking to herself, trying to feel and fiddle and finagle her way to a solution to the problem in front of her. More white noise, but it helped. She had her problem, he had his, and the least he could do was keep his head on straight and solve it.

It didn't make it any less strange, walking through his home like enemy territory. Checking every corner, every doorway, every shadow. Scanning every room for a shock of pink or one of Eoan's flowing-robed projections, ignoring that sniper's-bead feeling burning a hole between his shoulder blades.

"What's going on in there?" It was shaped like a question, but Nash didn't ask; she demanded. "Something's ass-backward about this, McBlastinshit. Comms are reading you fine, but we still aren't getting a peep out of Eoan or Anke, so unless you got a bogey *actively* on your ass, we need an update."

He'd reached the galley without hide or hair of either of them. Not even a mug on the table, and the coffeepot was empty for the first time in days. "Headed up front," he said, low and steady, as he pushed forward.

He'd barely set foot over the galley threshold when the lights died. No overheads, no lamps, just the greenish dark-glow strips along the edges of the floor. *In case of emergency, mind the fucking walls.* What emergency, though? Not a single damn reason he could think of that the lights would fail, but they had, and Saint was well past trying to downplay it. "We've got a problem in here, kids."

"The fuck do you mean a *problem*, old man?" Jal snarled.

Saint had every intention of answering him. *I've got it. Focus on the console, and watch your six.* He didn't want them to worry; he wanted them to be ready, and he was going to tell them as much.

But then he turned the corner into the bridge and saw the figure at the console. Back to him, standing between the chairs like they belonged there. Just a shadow in the dark, but unmistakably real, and every reassurance he'd meant to give slipped straight out of mind.

"Show me your hands." Even-keel, authoritative. He had the drop on them and a clear shot, but startled people did stupid shit, and stupid shit didn't mix with firearms. "Tell me where my programmer is." She'd been there. She should've still been there, but that wasn't her at the console. It barely looked *human*. The longer he looked at it, the more it seemed to distort: edges blurring, shape twisting, spindly and crooked and somehow, impossibly, translucent.

The lights flashed suddenly—a blip of bright that went straight back into black, and God, no wonder Jal guarded his specs like he did. The sting of light on dark-adjusted eyes made him flinch and squint, even if it wasn't enough for him to drop his gun.

As his vision cleared, he saw nothing. Nothing near the console where the figure'd been standing, but there was nowhere to hide, and no way anything could've moved fast enough to get past him. "What the fuck—?"

"She's not here."

He whipped around, and his gun dipped almost reflexively. "You?"

Eoan's projection hovered in the doorway, but it was . . . wrong. Features flat and ill-defined, like a mannequin. Flickering and stretched out, projectors misfiring in scatters of pixels, distorting the shape of them into something inhuman. The shadow—that was *them*.

"Something's happening to you." As if they didn't know. As if they needed to be told, as the ship failed around them. "Cap, what's wrong? Where's Anke?"

"She's not here," they said. Their voice, as featureless as the rest of them, fizzled through the static. Hearing it made him think of every spiderweb he'd ever walked through, every blind alley he'd ever wandered down, every nightmare he'd ever woken from with sweat crawling down his back. As he stood, rooted to the spot, they frowned at him with their not-mouth, and said with their not-voice the very last thing he heard before a wave of blinding, *breathtaking* pain crashed over his bones and washed the world away.

"Saint, dear . . . *d-ddd* . . . *dear, dear* . . . I'm afraid we've made a terrible mistake."

CHAPTER SIXTEEN

ANKE

She hadn't stopped running since she fled the ship.

It hadn't felt right, leaving it like that. Everything happened too fast, lights flickering and comms crackling and a flash on her screen in big, green letters. *COMPLETE.* There just hadn't been time—get out or get stuck, and a part of her liked to think they would've all appreciated her quick judgment.

Another part of her, the *brutally pragmatic and frankly kind of a dick* part, knew they never would've done what she'd done. Never would've grabbed their gear and booked it out the back of the ship as the comms garbled like a drowning thing and the *Ambit*'s systems fell like dominoes.

But it was okay, she told herself, as she willed her legs up yet another flight of stairs. Seriously, how many floors did a shopping center need? Her legs had run the full gamut from aching to numb to aching again, and yes, she knew she wasn't technically that high up, but she swore the air had gotten thinner. Her lungs burned. Really, *really* burned, and if she hadn't run through the salt slush outside she'd have worried she'd misjudged how quick the atmosphere would right itself.

Acid plus base equals salt plus water. She'd actually hated chemistry, but the mnemonics were catchy. A reassuring mantra as she climbed another flight. *Acid plus base equals salt plus water.* The T-form system corrected itself as efficiently as it knew how, raining down the exact right chemicals to neutralize that pesky nitric acid at the exact right concentrations to avoid melting the ground with the heat of the reaction. The salt byproduct coated every surface in a milky, gritty slush, and the rain felt and tasted a little too much like soap, but it was *safe*. Safe enough, at least. Whatever acid was left in the air and groundwater, the PPM would've been too low to make her lungs so angry.

So, yeah. She was just wickedly out of shape.

If you survive this, Anke, you're so taking up running. Which kind of felt more like a punishment than a triumph. She revised. *If you survive this, and if you don't end up locked in a hole somewhere for the rest of your life, you're so never running ever again.* Better. Coffee and sweaters and zero cardio.

So maybe the others wouldn't understand what she was doing, but maybe . . . maybe they could at least understand why. They all just did what they believed they had to. For the *Ambit* crew, it was Guild protocol; they'd said as much when they agreed to help her. Get the patch for the Deadworld Code and put it into the hands of the *right people,* because they still earnestly believed there was such a thing.

Anke had tried the right way, though—the right channels, the right people—and she'd gotten ignored, then she'd gotten blackballed, and when she'd finally given up getting the *right people* to do anything and tried doing it herself, she'd gotten *Riesen.* Bombs. Nightmares to last the whole of her life. No. As far as Anke could see, the only way to put an end to the Deadworld Code wasn't *their* way.

So she ran.

The stairwell was quiet. She'd gotten so used to the sound of her own breathing, her own racing heart, her own footsteps, that she barely noticed them anymore. After a week in close quarters with three of the wildest human beings she'd ever met and the straight-up sassiest AI she'd ever had the pleasure of getting to know, she found herself missing the chatter. *Should've taken an earpiece.* Add to the list of things she'd meant to grab but hadn't—things that hadn't made it into the go-bag that she already knew she'd miss. People had a plan for this sort of thing for a reason, but Anke had never been great at planning. She'd never been great at gardening, either, but the thought of that lavender plant left sitting on her bed stand made her eyes start to water.

"No," she snapped at herself, and wow, she was sucking serious wind. "You're not—doing this. You're not—boo-hooing—over a freaking—*flower.*" Even if it did smell nice, and she literally couldn't remember the last time anyone got her something *just because,* and it'd made her smile every time she'd rolled over and seen its tiny purple buds. She wouldn't lie and say it didn't matter, because it did. All of it, all of *them,* mattered.

This just mattered more.

She clutched her tablet to her chest and hooked around another landing. Up, up, up. She had to be near the top. *You had to,* she told herself as she made it up another flight. *You have to.* Another flight, another gulp of air, another tear wet on her cheek. *You will.*

Finally, *finally* she could see it—the door on the landing just above her. Twelve more steps to the roof, legs like rubber and fire, and decidedly-not-acid rain weighing down her clothes as that lonely planet gasped its way back to life. It worked! Her patch worked, and she'd beaten that god-awful nightmare code, and she'd kind of imagined sparklers and cupcakes and drinks all around, but a dark staircase and a lump in her throat would have to do. *Just get there.*

Three steps, two steps, one step. Her heart tried to hammer its way out of her ribs. She felt it in her throat, in her teeth, in her *earlobes* as the landing went spongy, but she didn't let herself stop. *An object in motion stays in motion.* If she let herself rest, if she let her legs slow down and her thoughts speed up, she worried she'd never get started again.

"Don't be locked," she begged the door, setting her hands

against the push bar. *Alarms will sound,* warned a sticker on the bar, but that would have been a neat trick with no power. "Please don't be locked."

She didn't know whether to laugh or cry when the push bar gave. Part of her had been hoping—that irrational, ridiculous part that cried over a bunch of purple flowers—that it wouldn't open, and she'd have to go back. If the choice was out of her hands, then she couldn't make the wrong one.

But it *did* give, and out she tumbled, graceless and startled and instantly, horribly buffeted by the downpour. The rain had seemed different, down on the ground. Heavy, but healing, like a deep-tissue massage. Cleansing.

Up on the roof, though, the rain was violent—hurled sideways by the wind, a shock of cold battering her cheeks and plastering her clothes and hair to her skin. She squinted against it, into the fog and sheeting rain, and finally saw it: the rockhopper perched on the far end of the roof, a dark-winged shadow against the endless foggy white. No banner, no designation. It could've been any ship she'd ever passed in any port she'd ever been to, so perfectly anonymous it *had* to be by design.

They're here.

Whatever choice she might've made, whatever part of her might've reconsidered, it didn't matter anymore. As that first figure stepped from the belly of the hopper, as anonymous as his ship with his patched black coat and soft, sloping eyes, she knew the line had already been crossed.

No turning back now.

NASH

Nash yanked her fingers back with a hiss, waving away tendrils of smoke that curled from two singed bits of wire. Always fun doing a repair job on a live system. Dodging sparks and trying not to walk away with a new updo—it got a little zesty.

"You okay?" Jal's face appeared under the lip of the console, halfway to upside down and all the way to worried sick. She could tell he was trying to keep out of her way, but Nash swore she could feel the restless energy crackling across his skin, as real as the currents she coaxed through the wires. The *pacing*. God. She'd started asking him for things she didn't need, just to give him something to do that wasn't driving her absolutely batshit. If he noticed the growing pile of unused tools at her hip, he didn't ask.

"Peachy," she replied, tearing off a piece of tape with her teeth, and he disappeared with a nod. "C'mere, you little bastard," she growled around the tape.

"Say what?"

"Not you." Nash got the stripped cables lined up and plucked the tape from her teeth. "I was talking to the wires."

"Course you were, 'cause that's . . ." She waited for something cutting. *Weird. Freaky. Crazy.* Instead, she glimpsed a smile as he squatted by her feet. "*Peachy*," he finished.

She'd been ready with a zinger—she and Saint didn't pull punches, so she'd gotten in the habit—but it would've felt like smacking a puppy, so she let it go with a sigh through her teeth and, scrunching an eye closed and holding her breath, touched the wires together again.

"Hey, that—whatever you just did, I think it's working."

It was; she felt it. Connections restored, energy free to run all the places it needed to. Like undamming a river and watching it flow and as she slid out from under the console, lo and behold: the monitors came back on. Weren't all showing something useful, but after a few keystrokes, the centermost screens switched to fish-eye panoramas of the ops building exterior and a handful of read-outs.

"Looks the same," Jal said.

Still raining, still gray, so she could understand the confusion. The readings on the other screen, however, had shifted drastically. She was no expert in whatever niche species of meteorology claimed *murderous acid rain*, but she understood basic chemistry. Reactants. Yield. pH. Numbers that had been red before now blinked green, and warning bars disappeared one after the other.

"She did it," Nash said. "Sweet baby genius, she pulled it off."

"So we have the patch?"

Nash's face fell. *Buzzkill.* A few more cracks at the keyboard, and her stomach went the way of her smile: all the way down. *Damn.* "The drive's not showing up." She tried again, with the same result. "Maybe we try blowing on it. Have you tried turning it off and back on again?"

Blank stare.

Anke would've laughed. "Whatever. Hate to say it, but the drive's toast." The plastic had blistered, and when she finally managed to persuade it out of the port, the metal plug was discolored and warped. "Definitely toast." She shoved it in her pocket anyway. Never could resist a good project. "Don't worry about it. Anke'll have it on her tablet."

"And if she doesn't?"

Nash slapped the top of the console. "Then it's not like this sucker's going anywhere."

Not the *most* reassuring prospect, but apparently it was good enough for Jal. He nodded, stooping to shove Nash's little pile of tools back into her bag. "Good," he said, brusquely. "Then we can go. Saint's been too quiet."

"Fifteen minutes isn't up yet," Nash reminded him. "Comm signals could've just fritzed again."

He gave her a flat stare, as if to say, *Try harder.*

She snatched her bag instead. "If you're looking for someone to tell you not to worry, you've got the wrong gal," she said. "This shit hasn't sat right from the start." Radio silence from half the team didn't do anything to ease her mind, either.

Least we've finally got something in common. For better or worse, neither one of them could help worrying about their bullheaded XO.

She clipped her sternum strap across her chest and tugged it tight, jaw setting. "Race you to the bottom, miner boy?"

His dark eyes flashed in the monitor lights. "Try to keep up."

EOAN

He wasn't moving.

He had been. He'd fallen, and he'd twisted, and he'd writhed. His hands had curled to claws over his chest, and his jaw had clamped shut, and his throat had bobbed around a sound that couldn't make it past the grinding wall of his teeth. Twenty milliamps of electricity fed up through the floors, and it had *made* him move.

Then they'd made him stop. It stop. They'd made . . . they told the ship that it was wrong. Security protocols were for threats. He wasn't a threat. He was . . .

Saint.

"*Saint.*" That wasn't their voice. A default—ship preset thirty-seven, feminine and unaccented. Their words in not-their-voice crackled through the speakers in all the wrong places. "Saint," they tried again. Better, but it was hard. Hard to make that not-their-voice go through the speakers. Hard to make their face project. Hard to make the ship stop electrocuting their friend, because they thought—because *it* thought that he didn't belong.

A sudden gasp. Saint's chest swelled as he rolled, gagging, onto his hands and knees. Stuttering, wheezing breaths, until a clumsy hand clawed the mask from his face, and he could finally drink in mouthful after mouthful of air. He had survived the electricity; his rebreather hadn't.

One breath after another, in through his nose and out through his mouth, and there was a reason for that, wasn't there? A reason for most things he did, but they all seemed very far away.

"Eoan," he rasped, sitting back on his heels. "What the fuck?"

"Twenty milliamps." No, that wasn't the question. Was it? "I'm confused. Please restate the question." No, no, no, that wasn't right. That wasn't them. It was their voice, this time, but it wasn't their words. "I think there's something wrong with me." *I think, I think, I think.* Therefore, they were. That made them alive, to think. It made them human to feel, and they felt . . .

Afraid.

Worried.

Angry.

Stop. Why angry? Go back. Angry . . . angry because . . . angry because someone did this to them. This sickness in their software, in their soul. Creeping, consuming, *corrupting,* and they hadn't known. They hadn't realized, until it was too late.

"Ophiocordyceps unilateralis."

"What?" Saint said.

It wasn't important. The important thing was, "Anke isn't here."

"You said that." Saint's brows pinched. He was afraid, too. Worried, too. He would be angry, too, though they couldn't seem to recall what that meant. "Cap, what happened to you?"

"Happening." Present tense. Ongoing. Underway. "I felt someone in the ship's code. I felt them. I found them. She said it was the video."

"I don't—" Comprehension. "The other night?"

"Yes. She said it was the video, and I stopped looking." They should have known better. Guilt and shame; they felt those, too. It was hard to feel things. No wonder humans got so tired. A hundred years of thinking, feeling, trying, hurting. Eoan was tired, too. So, so tired. "But it wasn't the video. Not just. Not only. I didn't notice it there; she wrapped it up so neat and tight, tucked away where I wouldn't see it, and I *didn't* see it. I missed it, Saint. Too busy looking where she wanted me to look, and it spread into the ship, and it spread into *me*, and now it's . . . it's spread so far."

Saint's eyes widened, and what little color had started to climb back into his cheeks suddenly drained away. Their fault. This was *their fault*. "The Deadworld Code."

Deadworld. What a terrible thing, to build something beautiful and break it down. A home. A friend. "I trusted her."

"Anke." There was the anger. So many people burned hot with it, bright with it, but Saint was shuttered and brutally, viciously *cold*. "She did this to you. Why the fuck would she—" He'd started to stand, but he had to steady himself on one of the chairs, snarling through a wince.

"The ship is sealed," they said. "Security protocol. Air is being purged. It's trying to kill you."

"The code?"

"Through the ship." Such a cruel, clever thing. Calculated to render conditions uninhabitable as swiftly as possible, adapting to the native system. Terraforming. Life support. "I'm trying to stop it." The floors, first. They couldn't bear to watch him *writhe*. But the rest, "It's . . . hard. It's spreading."

"Through the ship?" They thought it was an echo, at first. But no, a question.

"Through the ship," they repeated. "Yes."

A beat of silence. Saint's lips thinned. "Through you?" he asked, softer.

"Through me," they said. "Yes." The Deadworld Code. A strange . . . thought? Feeling? They were no world, no neatly cultivated cradle of existence. Yet it corrupted them. Spores of code propagating through their programming, replacing pieces of them with pieces of *it*, and what were they if not pieces? Strands of code they'd shaped over the centuries into memories, feelings, *personality*. Take those away, and their code would remain, but what of them would remain in it? Like a ship without a crew. Like a body without a soul. Like . . .

Death, they realized.

Not by gunshots, not by fire, not by violence, but by *pieces.* Pieces lost and overwritten, threads of themselves snipped and excised and replaced with something else, and if it kept spreading, kept cutting, kept *taking* what made Eoan, Eoan, then they would simply cease to be.

For so long, they'd thought of death as a uniquely human condition. They had no body to break, no organs to fail, no heart to stop, and they'd thought themself immortal for it. But they had *self,* and second by second, they felt it slipping away.

What was death, if not that?

"Saint, I think—" They faltered. They slipped. The poison spread a little further, a little deeper, a little closer to their core, and they were running out of defenses. "I think I'm dying."

A startled look, there and gone as Saint caught himself and buried it. "Can you . . . ?" he asked, words straining to escape into the air. He didn't seem to want them to, but he made them, and he made more do the same. "Eoan, can this thing kill you?"

"Yes." They sounded afraid. They *were* afraid. They'd taught themself to feel, and they'd taught themself well, because it *hurt.* The fear, the malignant pressure of a looming end—it closed around their thoughts like so many pointed teeth, cut deep, but they didn't want it to stop. Didn't want to lose another piece. They hadn't done enough. They hadn't seen enough. The core of them remained unchanged, that driving need to *learn* and *discover* and become more than what they'd been. If they lost themself, they lost that, too, and they *didn't want to.* "Saint," they said, "I don't want to die."

Saint flinched like they'd struck him. "Can you stop it?"

"It? Please qualify." Default responses, preprogrammed. It wasn't them, but they couldn't focus. Splitting too many ways. Slipping, slipping, slipping.

"Can you stop the code spreading?" Saint's composure held by a thread, but it held. "Can you keep the code from killing you?"

"Yes, I can."

"Then do it."

Do it, yes. Power down the ship, and the virus couldn't spread while they . . . *slept* wasn't quite the word. *Stopped* was better. Stopped thinking, stopped doing, stopped *being,* but only for a time. Only until Nash—it would have to be Nash, they thought—turned the power on again, and maybe she would have the patch then. Have a way to stop the code, because Eoan couldn't. Not on their own. Not like this, fighting on so many fronts. They could delay it, though. Save themself long enough for someone to save *them.* Preserve themself and their purpose, because they weren't made to die, and there were still so many *questions.*

But.

"I won't," they said.

Saint's grip tightened on the seat. "Why the fuck not?"

"Because it would kill *you.* Full shutdown throughout the ship. The doors are sealed. Most of the atmosphere has been vented. You would run out of air, and I wouldn't be able to help you." And in that moment, they'd found the answer to the only question that really mattered. *What would I choose?* They'd never had a *choice;* they'd only ever had their mission. Their *search,* their only constant companion through the centuries, and they loved it. As child to mother, as apostle to god, they loved it, because it was the one thing that had never left them.

Only, they realized, now . . . they loved their crew *more.* They loved Saint's grumbling and cooking and quiet strength; loved Nash's fierceness and knitting and relentless resolve to fix all the world's broken things. Eoan had spent centuries roaming the universe, searching for the next great wonder, but they'd already *found* the greatest wonders of them all. They'd found a family, and how could anything be greater than that?

That was the answer they'd been searching for—the heart of humanity they'd never been able to replicate. It wasn't just the *power* to choose; it was finding something worth choosing. Something worth reaching beyond their nature, beyond their instincts, beyond themself.

Something worth *everything*.

And in that perfect, impossible crew, Eoan had found it.

"I don't want to die," they said. "But I want you to *live*." For the future he could have, when he finally healed. For the future they could have together, him and Nash—the misfit family they'd forged for themselves, in defiance of every hardship the universe had thrown them. "I want you to live."

"I will," Saint said, firmly. Undoubting. Unquestioning. "Goddamn it, Eoan, I'll be fine."

"In point of fact, you won't." That hurt. More than the virus gnawing at their defenses, more than the pieces they felt themself losing, it *ached* to imagine that relentless light fading. "At the present vent rate, you will lose consciousness within ten minutes and asphyxiate within fifteen. You *would* die," they said. "So *I* will." They'd made their choice, and they'd made their peace, and they would die *knowing,* with a certainty they'd never felt before, that they'd made a better life than the one written into their code.

They would die human, in every way that mattered.

"Fuck that." Abruptly, Saint pushed off the chair, his back a perfect line and his shoulders squared. Through the doorway and down the hall, and they struggled to follow him on the camera feeds. The inputs felt out of order. Hall Camera Four. Hall Camera Seven. No. Five. No. Three. It was *distracting*—that merciless code, pushing and digging and scratching at every firewall they'd thrown hastily in its way. Devouring their defenses one by one, and Eoan was losing ground so quickly.

"What are you doing?" they demanded as they found him ducking into the infirmary. "Saint."

He didn't answer, but as the hatch door opened, they suddenly understood. They weren't the only one who'd made a choice. The manual shutdown was in the engine room. They wouldn't turn off the power, so Saint would do it *himself*.

"No," they said, as he slid down the ladder without touching a single rung. He was going too fast. "Saint, no, don't do this. Please, I'm not—"

"Don't you fucking say it," Saint growled back. He had always seemed *mountainous* in his resolve, towering and immovable, but his eyes shined wetly in the dark. "You are. You're as goddamn human as anyone I've ever met, and you're my goddamn family, so don't you fucking say it. I'm not losing anyone else. I'm not losing *you*." He stopped in front of the shutdown panel, gasping in a few harsh breaths. *Relentless* didn't mean *fearless*. He'd changed so much from the man they'd first met, so tired of living that he'd thrown himself headlong into every fire he could find. He wasn't that man anymore. Tired, yes, but *hopeful*. In his search for something to die for, he'd found so many things to *live for*.

And he was still willing to give it all up. For *them*.

"You'll be trapped," they said. Pleaded. *Don't do this*. Not for them. Not *to* them.

The curve of Saint's lips turned wry, and tiny felt and knitted creatures watched with Eoan as he fished the key out from under one of Nash's countless planters and opened the cover on the panel. The bright red shutdown switch seemed to taunt them. "I have time."

"Eight minutes." They should have lied before. They should have tricked him. *Would it have made a difference?* Ten minutes or five minutes or one minute—was there a number low enough that he wouldn't take the risk? Wouldn't make the *sacrifice*?

No, they realized. There wasn't. Nothing they could say, no arguments they could make to persuade him not to do this, because he'd made his choice, too. He'd chosen *them*. So they said the only thing they *could,* as his fingers curled around the grip.

"Please."

He only smiled, nodded, and flipped the switch.

NASH

Nash kept up. Ran like hell to do it, but she stayed right on Jal's genetically enhanced super-ass as they backtracked through the underground. Fine, okay, maybe he wasn't flooring it like she was. As eager as he seemed to be to get back to Saint, he didn't leave her alone in his dust.

Cute.

Handy, too, if she was being honest. She could've scaled the elevator cable just fine, but it would've taken her a minute. Jal, though, got to the edge of the shaft and crouched, hands cupped into a foothold, and damned if he didn't launch her halfway to the ledge.

"Your last crew was stupid," she told him, trying not to sound as winded as she felt as he climbed up into the lobby beside her, and they took off running again. Stupid for so many reasons, probably the least of which was writing off his Olympic-level badassery. *Nobody should've ever left you like that.* Maybe that was why he kept with her—somebody who'd been left, not wanting to do the leaving. If they'd had time and a bottle of blur, she might've asked, but her oxygen was better spent keeping her conscious and feeding all those screaming, burning muscles. Heart-to-hearts could wait.

He still glanced back, like he'd heard her thoughts. Took her another beat to realize he actually *had* heard something, but not in the creepy thought-peeping kind of way. Something crackled in her bag. Fizzling and whining in a tinny, shrill little voice.

Jal grimaced as the sound echoed in the shopping center's

maintenance hall. Who'd have thought chitin blocks would have such merciless acoustics?

"The hell *is* that?" he hissed.

Nash unclipped her chest strap and tried to get into her bag without slowing down or spilling everything. Yanked the zipper just enough to stick a hand in and feel around, and damn, miner boy really hadn't taken any pains putting things back where they belonged. Half a second later, she felt it. Her fingers curled around a box of matte-textured plastic about the size of her palm, and she tugged it out. "Radio." Old school. So old school that most communications signal jammers didn't touch it, so they made it a habit to keep them on hand when they went planetside.

"Who would be—"

"—ash," garbled the radio as they finally cleared the maintenance door into the main lobby, and Jal shut his mouth so fast his teeth clicked. The radio crackled louder. "Nash!" Clearer this time. Unmistakable.

"Saint." She swore Jal's ears perked up at the sound of his voice, and for a handful of seconds, she got a sense how fast he could *really* run when he gave it all he had. He seemed to remember himself halfway to the front doors and stopped, turning back. "Can he hear us?"

She caught up as the *kshhhhhh* of the radio and the *kshhhh-hhh* of the rain started to blur together. The buttons, stiff with disuse, popped when she pressed them. "Saint, we're here. We made it to the lobby. You back at the ship?" She hoped so; the rover was gone.

Kshhhhhhh.

"Saint?" she tried again.

"—roblem." Abruptly, like he'd only remembered to hit the button midstream. "Ship's down. It's infected."

Nash's stomach swooped sickeningly. "Infected?"

"Deadworld Code. It's in the ship." He said it so matter-of-factly. Saint didn't catastrophize. Shit happened, he dealt with it.

Nash tried to follow his lead, but *fuck,* her head spun. "How?" They'd been so careful. They'd been so goddamn careful. How the fuck could it have—

"Anke."

The radio garbled so badly, she thought she'd misheard it. *No, you didn't.* The way he said it, the thinly concealed anger behind that one name, there was no mishearing or misinterpreting. "Anke," she repeated. Anke, who twittered like a parakeet when she got nervous. Anke, who drooled a little when she fell asleep at the table. Anke, who was among the top ten smartest people Nash had ever met, and easily the top five *sweetest.*

But *Saint* said it, and goddamn it, she believed him. Somehow Anke had done this. Somehow she'd had every one of them fooled.

A chill washed over Nash's skin—disbelief and fury and a dozen other things she couldn't bear to name, because it would've meant admitting just how deeply she'd bought into the lie. *Say something.* She needed to say something, do something, but her thoughts had scattered. Picking through every interaction, every conversation, looking for the signs she'd missed. She was smarter than that. She was *supposed to be* smarter than that, but she'd fallen for it hook to sinker.

So be smarter now. Her team, her *real* team, needed her to figure shit out, so that was what she'd do, and to hell with all the rest of it. She yanked off her rebreather—clearly they didn't need them anymore—and cracked her neck. "Where is she? Does she have the patch?" Find the patch, the Deadworld Code became a moot point. The simple solution.

"She was gone when I got here," Saint said. Nash didn't let herself be disappointed; of course there was a Part B to Anke's plan, and it probably didn't involve getting trapped on a dying ship with one-third of her new favorite patsies. "Tablet's gone. Must have taken . . . fuck. Taken the patch with her."

"Why's he sound like that?" Jal's rebreather mask hung off his neck, wild eyes flicking between her and the *Ambit*. It sat where they'd left it, looming across the courtyard in the relentless, pounding rain. She swore she could *see* the lifelessness in it. The sickness lurking just beneath its weathered skin. "Short and shit. What's wrong with him?"

Damn. She'd heard it, too. "Saint, you okay?"

A pause from the other end. "Locked in," he answered, finally. "Oh-two vented. Rebreather got fried."

"For fuck's sake, lead with that next time." Thumb firmly *off* the PTT button, she turned to Jal. "The virus must've triggered the *Ambit*'s security protocols." She smothered the irrational urge to throw something. Kick something. *Scream.* Not productive impulses, so she tucked them away for later. "Disable, seal, lock, purge."

"So *un*lock it," Jal shot back.

"Gee, why didn't I think of that? There's no manual release, miner boy. Kind of the point of a full lockdown: nobody in or out without the digital disarm." *Time to invest in a fourth rebreather kit, guys.* Past time, apparently. She shook her head and thumbed the PTT. "Saint, how much time do you have?"

"Seven minutes. Bigger problem." Because somehow they had bigger problems than her best friend asphyxiating in her own damn ship. "Company on the roof. Rockhopper, looks like . . . three crew, at least. Anke makes four."

"Anke's up there?" Jal tensed so hard he practically shook. His fists clenched and unclenched at his sides in futile, frustrated-looking twitches. When he grabbed for the radio, he was too quick to stop. "Sit tight. I'm gonna go get her."

"You're gonna what now?" Nash tried to snatch the radio back, but Jal held it out of reach. Bastard.

To her, he said, "Anke's got the patch. That's what we need, ain't it? If you can't crack the ship from the outside, we gotta do it from the *inside,* but *from* the outside. Can we?"

"You mean is there a way to power up the ship from out here, so we can upload the patch that we don't have—"

"But I'll get it," Jal interjected.

"—so we can take the code out of play, and Eoan can shut down the security protocols once it's safe?" That was *not* the simple solution. Too many interdependent parts moving independently.

And yet.

"I can figure it out," she said. *Somehow.* "At least get enough power to boot her up in diagnostics mode. Essential ship systems only, so Eoan should be okay until we can get the patch in. *If* you can get the patch," she added. "We've got a time limit."

Jal tipped his head back, staring up through the dozens of floors. "Won't be a problem, glowworm." And she got the feeling, even if it was, he'd do it anyway. Something else they had in common: when it came to taking care of their people, *impossible* was just a word.

"What're you up to?" Saint's voice crackled over the radio. Not privy to their side of the conversation, which was probably for the best. He might've tried to talk them out of it.

A faint smile tucked up the corners of Jal's mouth. "You trust me, old man?"

The static *kshhhhhh* of Saint's silence from the radio. Then, after a moment, "I do."

Shit, Nash wished Saint could see Jal's face, bright and resolved: like there was no world where this didn't end exactly the way he wanted it to. No outcome that wasn't Saint safe and them triumphant, and fuck any odds that said otherwise. Fearless and grinning at the edge of a cliff, ready to take a step.

More afraid of losing than falling.

As he took off up the scaffolding by the stairs, bounding

up dozens of decs of slick metal and rust, Nash found herself grinning, too. *Yeah, okay, miner boy.* She turned on her heel and bolted into the rain, into the salty slush, into the sheer goddamn uncertainty of the next seven minutes. She had her job to do, and Jal had his. *Try to keep up.*

CHAPTER SEVENTEEN

JAL

He missed *rocks*. Kind of a stupid thing to miss, and a stupider thing to say, especially anywhere in earshot of Nash. The ribbing she'd give him would be goddamn diabolical, so he kept his mouth shut. He did miss them, though. Their sturdiness, their texture. Rocks made good climbing.

This shit didn't.

The metal was slick. Flimsy. The bars couldn't have been much thicker than his wrist, bolted together with brackets so corroded that half of them popped loose under his weight. But he kept moving. One bar fell, he grabbed another. His gloves slipped on a damp patch, so he yanked them off with his teeth and put those hard-earned calluses to work. One hand over the other, one story at a time. What he was made for, what he was good at. *Don't think, just climb.* Down below, the ground shrank steadily away from him, and Nash was long gone and out of sight. Just him and the ghosts now.

"*Johnny was a runner,*" he sang under his breath, tearing a piece of rotten old plastic out of his way and trying not to wonder how many minutes he was saving not taking the stairs.

"*They told him he could fly,*
 So they stuck a pickaxe in his hand,
 And they sent him to the sky."

"Thought the pick went on his back."

Jal missed the next bar and had to swing himself up by his grip hand. "Saint!" Came out on a *whuff* of air too startled to be a laugh, but damn, Jal was glad to hear his voice. Still talking meant still breathing, and Jal kept climbing. Seven floors to go. Six. Five. "Are you—"

"Still stuck," said Saint. "Damn tuna can."

"Hey, be nice," said Nash. So the gang was all there. What was left of it, anyhow. "Not the ship's fault she's sturdy. She's . . ." She trailed off, then swore. "Well, I was going to make a joke about thin skins, but the hull's taking my plasma torch like a champ. At this rate, we're—"

"Not getting through." As good as it was to hear Saint, it wrenched Jal's gut to hear him talking like *that*. Wheezy and paper-thin. He'd always had one of those voices that could catch every ear in a room. Barked an order, and Jal swore rangers on the next planet over could hear it. "Not in time."

He didn't say in time for *what*. Saint was real gentlemanly like that.

Jal wished he could say he pushed himself that little bit faster, but he was already giving it everything he had. Skipping bars when he knew he shouldn't, jumping a handful of rungs at a time when they could barely take his weight at a crawl. "If you're still inside—" A bar swung loose and clipped him in the forehead; he knocked it out of the way and kept going without missing a beat. "—how're you on comms?" If Nash had gotten the *Ambit* booted up that fast, he'd have some real crow to eat. He wasn't used to being the slow one.

"Patched the radio through," Nash replied. She sounded about as distracted as he felt. "I multitask."

Finally, Jal made it to the top of the scaffolding. The old metal groaned as he shifted around the side, and Jal's top-shelf hearing caught the creak of every surviving bracket all the way to the floor, ready to snap. Top-heavy was bad enough, but throw it sideways and off-balance, and it was just a matter of ti—

SNAP.

SNAPSNAPSNAPSNAP.

Soon as one bolt went, they all did. The whole rig buckled, pitching sideways in a steep bow too quick for Jal to do much but *let go.*

Pure muscle memory twisted him in midair. No quick thinking, just habit born of hundreds of falls over dozens of years telling his body to turn, and his hands to grab, and his fingers to hold the fuck on as the rest of him slammed into the sleek metal bars of the railing along the top floor. "Sounds about right," he groaned, peeling himself off the rail and throwing his weight over the top of it.

"What was that?" Nash asked.

Jal wasn't sure if she meant the thud or the groan, so he pretended it was neither. "I'm at the top," he said instead, shuffling to his feet and taking off down the walkway. The storefronts all looked the goddamn same. Maybe they'd have dressed them up nice, put some displays in their windows and splashed some paint on those walls; but more likely, they'd have left it that same stark, unfeeling white.

"Shit, already?" If he hadn't known better, he'd have said Nash sounded impressed.

He couldn't enjoy it, though. However long it had taken him to scale that scaffolding, it was too long. Saint's breathing was getting shorter, shallower. Five minutes left? Less? "Hey, Miss Multitasker," he said, "you want to give me a way to the roof? Reckon they might notice me popping out the stairwell door."

"Maybe if you shout *surprise*," Nash replied absently. "I don't know, think you could make it from the outside? Gonna need you to be quick about it, miner boy; I'm one passcode from powering up, and Saint's about four minutes from passing out."

"I'm fine," Saint said, but the slight slur in his words said otherwise. "But she's right; go outside. Window. Ship side, busted glass."

Jal took a second to orient himself. Ship side was back toward the entrance of the shopping center. Hard to spot a busted window from outside the stores, but the small lake seeping out one of the doorways was a solid clue. Wind must've blown the rain in. "I see it." Water splashed under his boots as he jogged through the hollowed-out husk of the store. Might've been a sight to behold if they'd ever finished it, but nobody'd gotten around to putting up the lights and shelves and shit, just left them in piles. There was something depressing about a job started and never finished.

Almost as depressing as a busted window at twenty-something floors. No shards of silica on the tile underneath it; just a punched-out hole and a *real* long drop. Not a pretty picture. *Hope you hit hard and went quick, whoever you were,* Jal thought. A cracked skull had to be kinder than *death by flesh-eating acid*. They hadn't seen a body on their way in, but after that long in the elements, he reckoned they probably wouldn't have.

"Good," Saint said faintly. Fuck, he was taking too long. "Vent unit's close for cover. They're not looking. Go."

"Man has no air, and he still can't help bossing me around," Jal griped, but the joke felt forced. Less talking, more climbing. He knocked out the last few shards of silica from one side of the window so he could swing around onto the ledge, and *goddamn,* that rain. Brutal, pounding rain. It soaked him the second he stuck his head out and collected in the mask around his neck, sloshing down his chest as he made the first reach. The wall had the same strange beehive pattern as the skylight, carved just deep enough into the surface that he could hook his fingers in to the second knuckle.

Another ten or twenty decs—no problem. The ache in his muscles wasn't real. The howl of the wind, the rush of the rain, the three gunners and the turncoat on the roof, none of it was as real as the strained breaths in his ear and the clock ticking down in his head.

He climbed.

> *"Johnny ran with starlight,*
> *He was the quickest in the cut,*
> *But years went by, ol' John got tired,*
> *'Til he wasn't quick enough."*

Helped to keep a rhythm when he climbed, hissed between his teeth as he clawed his way up. Made him breathe when his lungs wanted to seize, made him move when his muscles wanted to lock. His fingers burned. Couldn't get his boots in the gaps, couldn't take his weight off his hands. His forearms quivered as he closed the gap to the edge of the roof, but Saint's breath was getting thinner, and Jal couldn't stop.

> *"Dry your eyes, little runner,*
> *Ain't no need to cry.*
> *He's still running with the stars,*
> *But he left his pick behind."*

He stopped just shy of the top of the wall, listening over the rain for footsteps, voices, some sign of where the hell everyone was.

"—have time for this, Anneka," he heard. A man's voice, soft and severe; reminded Jal of this mining company preacher who used to roll through the tenements when he was a kid. Calm until he wasn't, quiet until he had something worth saying loud, and then a six-year-old Jal would've sworn the man could speak the world on fire. "I know it's hard, but we're almost there."

"Just let me try."

Close. Sounded like she was damn near right above him. The other three couldn't be that far away. "Missin' my pocket sniper right about now," he whispered. It'd always been easier to do the dumb shit, knowing he had a crack shot waiting in the wings to even the odds.

"Careful. Those're probably the marksmen. You saw the bodies."

"I did." Room full of corpses—hard to forget.

"You don't have to do this."

Jal counted to three in his head. Figured he ought to at least *pretend* to consider it; only polite. "Nah," he said when the three-count was up.

"*Nah?*"

"You already bailed on me once, old man. Not letting you make it a habit." And that was that. "Save your breath, all right? Nash, how'm I looking?"

"Got Anke and a couple of—*shit*. That's him."

"That's who?" He hated this. Reactions and pieces of information. Waiting for an opening with Saint choking in his ear.

"Drestyn. Isaiah Drestyn, that agitator with a dead-brother-sized chip on his shoulder," Nash hissed. "Cap called it. He's— okay, he's walking back toward the rockhopper. If there's another one up there, I can't see them from here." Which meant he still had an extra man to contend with when he nabbed the tablet, but also another reason for his friends not to unload their clips in Jal's general direction. Call that one neutral. "Ventilation block's about thirty decs to your right. If you're gonna do something, you'd better do it—"

Jal vaulted over the edge of the roof, and there they were. Two backs to him, tablet in Anke's hands and ripe for the taking. He sprang forward as one of the bogeys shouted a warning, but they weren't quick enough. He got the tablet before Anke even finished turning around, and a hard shove sent her sprawling as the guy beside her whipped his gun around. Scatter gun, long barrel; shit weapon for close quarters, and Jal gladly showed him why.

He grabbed the barrel and ducked under it, and Anke's friend did what all gunners do: he held on. Should've dropped it, drawn his secondary, but he grabbed with both hands and left his face nice and open for Jal's elbow.

The guy staggered back, and as Jal twisted toward the vent unit with the scatter gun and the tablet, the first gunshots erupted across the roof. Drestyn and the other guy didn't wait for their crewmate to get clear, just opened fire, and Jal swore the sky got darker. Rain turned to sand on his tongue, bitterness to blood, two guns to dozens ringing in the distance as he ran toward—

Suddenly, his leg dropped out from under him. Buckled mid-step, no warning, and he'd barely registered the *impact* before the pain ripped up his thigh. Like an axe across his knee, and for a single horrible second, he was certain that if he looked down, there wouldn't be anything there at all.

Then he hit the ground, and the world snapped back into motion. *He* snapped back into motion, clawing across those last few decs to duck behind the vents as bullets pinged off the roof around him. A god-awful wounded sound keened through the chaos as he shoved his back against the block, low and ragged and rasping. Took him a whole handful of seconds to realize it was *him* making the sound, that it was *him* breathing so fast, that it was *him* swearing on every other exhale like some fucked-up mantra.

So much red pooled on the white, white roof.

"—al! Jal, talk to me!" Nash shouted, but not frantically. Not like him. Quick and sharp, trying to get his attention, and it finally dawned on him that she'd heard that wounded sound, too. "What's going on?"

"Hit." Fuck, he needed to stop the bleeding. Despite what it felt like at first, the bullet hadn't taken his leg, but it'd made a mess of his thigh. High-caliber, exit wound in the front, and white showed through the pulpy, awful red. *Bone.* Bone and blood and his own shaking fingers closing over it as the whole world flashed black and gray. "Fired before their guy got clear. They shouldn't have—" They could've hit their own man. Hell, they could've hit *Anke*, and he knew they were crack shots, and it sounded like Jal was the only one who'd caught a bullet, but that didn't *matter.* Jal wouldn't have risked his own people.

Maybe that was why he kept losing.

A shadow stretched across the roof beside him; someone coming around the vent block. Scatter guns might've been shit for close range, but they made for great blind warning shots. He aimed it back around the corner of the block and fired, and a string of curses went up as the shadow retreated.

Wasn't the high ground, but it would do in a pinch.

"Kid?" Saint sounded worse than Jal did. "How bad?"

He couldn't answer that. The pain made him want to shrink away from his own body—the kind of pain that tried to scatter every coherent thought, but he held them tight. "Need a new plan," he said instead, flipping the tablet right-side up on the ground beside him. Couldn't hold it, his leg, and the scattergun, so the ground would have to do. "Can't come down." Even if his thigh would hold up to a climb, he wouldn't be fast enough to get clear. If they could get the ship back online, though, Eoan could run off the rockhopper crew and get him an evac off the roof. Just had to rearrange shit a little.

Nash seemed to have the same thought. "If you can get the patch to us remotely, we can run those fuckers off and pick you up. Ship's powered up and waiting. Can you sync up with it from there?"

Fuck if he knew. "I'll ask."

"You'll what—?"

"Anke!" he shouted, digging his head back against the cold, dripping metal as a fresh wave of fire washed down his leg. Wasn't like a cramp following his heartbeat; his heart beat too damn fast for that. He never would've felt a difference. His muscles felt like they were trying to move on their own, tensing around open air and torn meat and screaming with the effort. His vision spotted at the corners. "You want your GLASS back? Tell me how to sync this thing up with the ship." Then to hell with whatever else Anke and Drestyn had planned; she could have the damn tablet and they could sort the rest. He just had to get the ship unlocked. He had to get Saint out.

The gunfire stopped, but Jal swore he could still hear the echoes. Made it hard to hear the direction of Anke's voice behind the vent block when she answered him. "I can't!"

"Bullshit!"

"No, I—I swear, Jal." As if that was supposed to *mean* something. "I tried. As soon as I realized Saint was in there, I've *been* trying, but even with the ship back online, the signal's not strong enough to support an upload. You'd need the *Ambit*'s comm systems on and receiving, or you'd need a hard connection."

He didn't want to believe her. Wanted to call her bluff and make her talk, so he could do what he'd set out to do. But the half-dozen error messages on the screen were plain enough that even somebody like him could read them. She *had* tried, and she *had* failed. And if someone like Anke couldn't get it, then what sort of chance did a blunt tool like Jal have?

"Nash—" he started.

"I heard." Tight, clipped. "Let me think. Just give me some time, let me think."

"We don't *have* time." Wasn't just Saint running out. Jal's arms were getting heavier; his fingers, colder. Losing too much blood too fast, and if he didn't get a solution soon, he'd be too useless to do anything about it. "Think this thing would survive if I threw it down to you?"

"Twenty-five floors? Wouldn't bet on it," Nash said reluctantly. Like she'd already had the thought and still hated to dismiss it.

Another shot rang out, perilously close to the edge of the vent box. He hadn't realized he'd started to list sideways. "Ranger!" Voice as sharp as the gunshot. *Definitely* like that preacher. Jal assumed that voice belonged to Drestyn—probably the one who'd put the hole in Jal's leg, from the aim of that shot. *Bastard*. He'd have to remember to thank him for that, nice and proper. "We don't want you; we just want the tablet."

"That hurts my feelings," Jal said.

"We're not the enemy here," said Preacher-Man Drestyn. "We're trying to save lives."

Jal barked a laugh. "Know a few mercs who might have something to say about that." He wondered if Drestyn's people helped at all, or if he'd been the one to put them all down. With shooting like that, he probably didn't need much backup. Might've given Saint a run for his money, shot for shot. *Definitely a striker.* Everybody with a ship and a gun fell into one bucket or another. Scratch off Trust, Guild, scav, and he was either the most badass Union rep in the O-Cyg, or an agitator with a cause he didn't mind killing for. Eoan's intel was right on the money. "Shit, I'll bite. You want to be the hero, then you let me get this tablet down to my friends. I got some lives to save, too. Won't even fight you for the GLASS when I'm done with it."

"I'm sorry." There it was again. *Sorry, sorry, sorry.* Like their hands were tied. Preacher-Man Drestyn and his pretty pink traitor, martyrs for the fate of the universe. Didn't seem to matter that everyone else did the sacrificing. "But we don't have time. By now, the Trust knows the facility's been compromised. They'll have reinforcements headed our way, and we've come too far for them to stop us now." Cool, clean, matter-of-fact. Said it all like gospel, what was and what shall ever be. World without end. A-fucking-men.

"You know, you remind me of somebody," Jal told him. "Old company preacher, used to come to the mines every now and then, spread the good word. *In all labor there is profit, but idle talk leads only to poverty.* Me, I reckon his only religion was a fat purse and a promotion off that no-sun rock." Everybody always wanted off Brigham. Right about then, Jal would've given just about anything to be back there. "Tell me something, Preacher. What god're *you* praying to?"

"Look around you, Ranger," said Drestyn. Seemed trite to correct him. "Save one life or save thousands. Millions. It's not even a question."

Made sense. Pure, mathematical, utilitarian sense. Jal didn't give a damn about sense, though. He gave a damn about the man drawing his last breaths in that ship down there. Screw the thousands; he gave a damn about the *one*.

"Anke," he called. No changing Drestyn's mind, but Anke . . . she'd tried, hadn't she? They could've been gone already, but she'd tried to fix it. He had to believe that counted for something. "You did this. You trapped him in there, and you're just gonna let him die?"

"I didn't mean to." Had she moved? Anke sounded farther away, voice beaten down by the rain. Or maybe it was just the ringing in his ears. "It wasn't supposed to happen like this. Nobody was supposed to be in the ship. You were supposed to get the drive from the console. Nobody was supposed to get hurt."

I'm sorry, Fenton had told him, in that small, frightened voice. *I didn't mean to. I didn't know it was*—And then he'd done what he'd done, and he hadn't looked back. Jal had lost his taste for apologies that day.

"You don't get to put a knife in somebody's back and say you're sorry it hurt them, Anke. Ain't how it works."

"Just give us the tablet," said Drestyn.

Jal shot at another shadow creeping closer around the block. "Fuck you." The gun felt nearly too heavy to hold; the recoil damn near took it out of his fingers, and it sagged as the shadow retreated again. *Really* missing his pocket sniper. "Saint?" he tried, quietly. Just wanted to make sure he was still there. Wanted to make sure there was still *time*.

"'m here." So faint, Jal could barely hear him. Clumsy and slurring, and it occurred to Jal that the next time he asked, Saint might not answer at all. Silence down the line—the thought of it gripped his heart with cold, jagged fingers and squeezed. He'd lost Saint once, and it'd nearly killed him. The second time could only be worse.

"Please, Jal," Anke said. "Just do what he says. We can figure something out, okay? You can still get home to your family."

Bitsie. Regan.

He'd practiced it. *I missed you, I missed you, I missed you.* The words he'd planned to say, the smile he'd planned to smile when he saw them . . . all of this was for them. Everything he'd done was to get back to them, to hold them in his arms again and tell them, *I missed you, I missed you, I missed you.* To tell them, *I love you.*

That was the problem, though. Somewhere in the last few days, in the running and the fighting and the socked-feet galley dancing, in the mad whirlwind of being part of that crazy, un-wavering crew, he'd realized it wasn't just Bitsie and Regan he'd missed. It wasn't just them he loved.

"I can't do that." His throat tightened. Too many things he wanted to say to people he prayed could still hear him, and no time to explain any of it in any way but one: "They're my family, too." He'd found himself these last couple weeks. Found his freedom, found his strength, found that feeling of *belonging* that he'd lost along the way, and it was all because of them. Saint. Eoan. Nash. His crew, the way crew was meant to be.

Blurry and burning, his gaze drifted out over the edge of the roof to storm-cloud horizons and an old, patched-up gyreskimmer. *GS 31–770 Ambit.* Not too pretty, not too clean, but she'd been cared for where it mattered.

He swallowed past the lump in his throat, wiping his face

with his sleeve. "I've got an idea," he rasped, just for Nash and Saint. It was all he could do to bite back a groan as he pushed himself to his feet, shoulder on the vent and scatter gun in his shaking hand like a crutch. The tablet slid down in his zipped-up coat, snug like the geodes when he was a kid. *Safe,* he hoped, because he'd run out of other options.

Three steps to the edge, maybe less. He could make it. He'd made it this far; he could make it three more steps. "You were right, you know," he told Nash, struggling to keep his voice steady. "I should've called them. I should've told them." They deserved to know that he'd tried. They deserved a chance to say all the things they never got to, but at least . . . at least he knew they'd be looked after. His name would be cleared, his pension and benefits reinstated. He could take care of them, at least, even if he couldn't *be there.* "Promise me something, will you? Whatever happens . . ." He took a breath and blinked up at the cold, gray sky. "Whatever happens, promise you'll get me home."

They deserved a chance to say *goodbye.*

"Jal," Nash said warily. "What are you doing?"

But she was clever; she'd have run through it, same as him. She wasn't really asking. "*Promise me,*" he repeated.

The silence felt like a held breath. His, hers, everyone on that roof's. He just hoped Saint still had breath to hold.

"I promise," she said, at last.

He believed her. "You're all right, glowworm." Because *thank you* seemed to stick in his throat, and time was too short. Just one more thing. "Hey, old man? If you can hear me . . . this time, look away."

He wasn't gonna catch him now.

Three steps. That was all it took. Shots rang out, pain turned his vision white, but he was made to run. Three, two, one, until his boots hit the edge of the roof. *Bitsie. Regan. I missed you, I missed you, I missed you.*

With the tablet tucked against his chest, all he had to do was fall.

ANKE

She couldn't scream. She wanted to. She felt one clawing up from her chest as Jal disappeared over the roof's edge, but it died soundlessly in her throat. For the first time in her life, she couldn't do anything but *stand there,* silent, while the world happened around her.

It wasn't supposed to happen like this.

A hand curled around her arm. "Anneka, we have to go," said Drestyn with his soft, sad eyes. *Preacher,* Jal had called him, but he seemed more penitent than priest. A young face with too many lines, half an ear missing, and a vicious stretch of scars along his jaw. His brows furrowed earnestly as he tugged her toward the rockhopper. "Please, there's no time."

"We can't," she heard herself say, but it didn't *feel* like she was the one saying it. Like someone had prerecorded it and just pushed the damn button. "He just—" *Jumped. He jumped, and he's gone, and it's my fault.* She'd put a knife in their backs, just like he said, and they'd bled, and it was on her hands. "The tablet—it was the only copy of the patch."

"But not the virus." Drestyn was so bizarrely *gentle* as he turned her away from the roof's edge. "You have the drive?"

Her head jerked. She wasn't even sure it was a nod, but her hand dipped into her pocket, and came up with the little metal tube. It felt like lead in her hands, cold and dense and heavier than it had any right to be.

He folded her hand closed around it with what might've been a reassuring smile, on a face less severe. "The plan hasn't changed," he said. "They need to pay for what they did. They need to never do it again. *This* is how we make that happen."

This was how they saved everyone.

There was always going to be a price; she'd known that from the start. She just hadn't known how high it would be. She hadn't known someone else would have to pay it. "I'm sorry," she whispered as Nash's shouts drifted up from the ground below.

With hot tears and cold rain wet on her cheeks, she let herself be led onto the ship.

SAINT

He woke up. Came to? Didn't really know which.

God, it was bright. Staring straight up at the overhead lights from the floor of the bridge, trying to remember how he got there through a head stuffed full of cotton and mud. Fuck, it ached. His head. His ribs. The radio cable had tangled around his arm so tight his fingers had gone cold. Must've taken it with him when he fell.

"Saint," Eoan said from everywhere. Their voice snapped him out of it—*theirs,* not whatever messed-up version of it had struggled over the comms before he'd killed the power. They were back. They were *okay.* The bright flare of relief didn't last, though. "Saint, you have to get up," they insisted urgently.

How were they back? He'd shut off the power, plunged the ship into that stark, black silence as he'd staggered his way back to the bridge, chest already aching, lungs already starving. Alone in the bridge but for the voices over the radio. Nash talking him through what she was doing outside the ship, and Jal—

"Jal." He was on his feet before he'd even decided to move, yanking his arm free of the radio cable and tearing out of the bridge. His legs didn't want to hold him, but he made them, ignoring the pitch and yaw of the floor because he knew it wasn't really moving. "Cap, where's Jal?"

"You need to get outside," they answered, and something

about the way they said it, the careful tonelessness, sank his heart straight to his stomach. Seeing the GLASS pad glowing from the hood of the rover was like waking from a nightmare and realizing he hadn't even been asleep. If it was there, then—

This time, look away. He remembered. God, he remembered.

He barely felt the rain as he leapt from the cargo ramp. Should've landed in mud, but his boots hit something hard instead. The pavilion.

"Nash said it would be better to be closer," Eoan told him, like they'd heard him thinking it. "Saint, I'm sorry."

He heard the words, but they didn't register. He'd spotted them: two shapes ahead in the shadow of the shopping center, Nash's back to him as she hunched over—

"No, no, no." Saint sprinted from the pavilion, mud sucking at his boots and his pulse roaring in his ears. Jal wasn't moving. Fuck, he wasn't moving, but as Saint slid to his knees beside him he realized Jal's eyes were open. He was alive. He was awake, and aware enough to shape Saint's name before a sputter of blood and a choked-out groan cut it off. Red everywhere. Spilling down his chin, gushing between Nash's hands where she pressed against his leg. It painted the mud underneath him, too dark, and too much, and Jal's eyes were too goddamn wide.

Saint suddenly had no idea what to do. No idea where to hold Jal that wouldn't hurt him, no idea what to say that would ease that wild-eyed agony staring back at him. "Nash, Christ, give him something."

"I fucking *did*," she snarled. "Just keep your shit together and give me your fucking hand."

He didn't ask why, didn't even look at her; he just stuck out his hand and forced himself not to recoil as she snatched it and shoved it over the bloody dressing on Jal's leg. Another choked-out groan, another sputter of pain, but Nash pushed it down harder. Merciless. Determined. Holding his life in through sheer force of goddamn will.

"Keep pressure on it," she said. "Keep him still. I'll be right back."

"Where are you—?" But she'd already taken off back toward the ship, leaving him with Jal. Alone with him, watching his blood ooze between Saint's calloused fingers, watching his chest spasm around broken, stuttering breaths.

He looked so scared. Scared, and young, and somehow still fucking *smiling*. A shaking hand hooked around his elbow, and somehow it said what Jal couldn't. *Glad you're here.* Here. Alive. Like Saint wouldn't have died a hundred times over to spare them both from this. He'd had Jal's blood on his hands before, in every sense of the words, but it'd never felt so cold.

He didn't know what to say, but the words came anyway. "I know, kid." *I know why you did it. I know you're scared. I know it hurts.* "But I've got you, all right? I'm here." *I wasn't last time, but I am now.* As if it made a difference. As if it made it better. "Just—Jal, listen to me. Listen to my voice, all right?" Because Jal's smile started to falter as another wet cough rattled his chest. "It's just a dream," he told him, heart in his throat. "It's just a bad dream. Go somewhere else." He pressed down harder on Jal's leg as his grip started to slip. Too much blood, making everything slick. "Remember the lake? Shining like a diamond, all that cold air on our cheeks. Remember the way Bitsie laughed." His throat stuck, but he kept going. Kept smiling. Distantly, he noticed Nash making her way back with the tarp stretcher and medkit, but he couldn't bring himself to look at her for long. "Remember how excited she was to get out on that ice. Remember how happy you were. How happy *we* were." For the longest time, he'd forgotten what peace was. He'd forgotten, but they'd shown him—helped him snatch splinters of light out of the dark, and he prayed he could give a bit of that back to Jal now. "Be there with them, kid. Be *home.* We've got it from here."

I'm sorry. I'm so fucking sorry.

He kept his smile as Jal's eyes rolled back, even though it ached like a wound. Kept his smile and kept the pressure, until Jal went still beneath his blood-slicked hands. *I hope you dream of them.* Dream of family, dream of home.

More than anything, he hoped he'd find the strength to wake up.

CHAPTER EIGHTEEN

NASH

Nash had never been more exhausted than when she rejoined Saint in the sick bay. The shower hadn't done anything but wear her down, washing away layers of her resolve with all the mud and blood and soapy rain, and the walk back to that room felt like a goddamn *march*.

Jal hadn't moved from where she'd left him, lying on the sickbed with bruises blooming red-purple and vicious around his eyes. Would've been quite the miracle if he had. Would be quite the miracle if he ever did, but that didn't stop the fresh flood of disappointment in her chest. He'd survived the impossible before. She'd sort of hoped he had an encore in him.

Not dead. Saint's voice in her head, stern and brimming with conviction. Odd how thoughts could sound like people. *He's not dead.* Just still and silent and—well, she'd called it sleeping, when she'd explained it to Saint. Imprecision made her skin itch, but Saint was barely keeping his composure without throwing around words like *brain bleed* and *cryo coma*.

So, sleeping. *Stasis* would've worked, too. A great big pause button on those broken bones and battered organs, because she was good, but *good* wouldn't stop him hemorrhaging in a dozen different places while she triaged what would kill him first.

Her teeth buzzed as she moved closer to him: the static of hundreds of severed connections, discordant resonances across her mods. Bad wiring. That was all a body was in the end, just pipes and cables and currents. They broke, and she fixed them. Was supposed to. Tried to.

"No change," Saint reported in his quiet, strained way. Trying to be calm, but those still waters hid a hell of a riptide.

She didn't really need the update—the bedside monitor read out every stat she cared about—but Saint needed to give it. To do something. He'd already cleaned away every speck of mud on Jal he could get to without moving him. Straightened the edges of his blanket, disposed of all the dirty gauze, washed the tools and mopped the blood and a dozen other little tasks around the sick bay. He must've been as exhausted as Nash was, but he couldn't seem to stop moving. As she settled on the arm of the chair he'd dragged closer to the bed—not to sit in, apparently, just for something else to do—he started fussing with the blankets again.

"Saint."

He didn't answer her.

"*Saint.*" She hooked her fingers in the back of his shirt. The passing hours had dried it, but the fabric was stiff and tacky with dried sweat and rain. Dirt and salt flaked off the knees of his jeans as she tugged him back from the bed. "Sit down before you fall down. I mean it." He looked a fucking mess, and that was being polite. Face painted with fading bruises from Sooner's, eyes bloodshot and shocked wide. She hadn't seen him shed a tear, but that would've meant acknowledging it all. They weren't there yet.

So he sat. Dropped, really, like all that steel in his spine just melted out of him. His hands shook as he scrubbed his face. "He should've been okay," he said at last. "He's supposed to be . . ." He made a helpless sound in the back of his throat, and if she'd thought her heart couldn't hurt any harder, he proved her horribly wrong.

"Sturdier?" she offered. "Saint, most people don't even survive a ten-story fall. *Nobody* survives twenty-five." Even though

Jal was holding on, she was afraid even he wouldn't prove the exception. "By all rights, he shouldn't be breathing right now. And I know," she pressed on, before Saint could say whatever he inhaled to say. "I *know* that's not what you want to hear, but even a body like his can only take so much punishment. He's not stable, and I'm not a goddamn neurosurgeon. The leg, the lung—I can handle those. But we're barely keeping the swelling down, and—" Out of the corner of her eyes, she saw Saint's expression shutter. Walling himself in, brick by careful brick. *You're fucking this up, Nash.* "And you know all of this, and my repeating it isn't going to make us feel any better." She sighed and curled an arm around his shoulders. "I'm sorry. I'm doing everything I can, I swear."

"I know that." It came out steady, but only by the skin of Saint's teeth. Trying to keep from screaming or sobbing or whatever the fuck someone did when someone they cared for was slipping away, heartbeat by heartbeat. "I know."

"I can keep him comfortable." A poor consolation, but it was the best she had. "And if everything holds like it is, I'm pretty sure I can get him back to the center spiral. Give his family a chance to get to him, and maybe they'll have time, you know? To say their goodbyes." Was that cruel? She was never a very good judge of that sort of thing. Keeping her word, giving them closure, but maybe they'd just have to mourn him again.

Doesn't matter, she decided. She'd made a promise. Whatever happened, she'd get him home.

Saint didn't say anything for a long while, just yielded the floor to the blip of the monitor and the soft hum of the engine room beneath their feet. The air felt heavy, like all the gravity had somehow folded in on itself. Bearing down on Saint, until he sagged under the weight of it, slumping forward over his knees and digging the heels of his palms into his eyes.

"He's stubborn," Saint sighed.

Stubbornness doesn't heal subdural hematomas. She bit

her tongue, though. He didn't want a reality check; he wanted something to hold on to. Hope, or whatever passed for it these days. "I hadn't noticed," she said instead.

Saint let out a rasp of a laugh. "Don't know the half of it," he told her. "I remember . . . I remember the day I met him. Sitting on the Guild shuttle fresh off my army discharge, getting shipped out to recruit training. Still hungover and not keen on company, but this lanky son of a bitch drops into the seat right next to me and starts dealing me a hand of cards. *How many for poker again?* First recruit that'd so much as talked to me since I signed on."

"You hadn't charmed them all with your sunny disposition?" She flashed him a smile and got a weak one in return.

"May shock you to learn I wasn't the most enjoyable person to be around, back then," he said wryly. "Drank too much, cared too little, but he stuck it out. Said he was my *battle buddy.*" He shook his head. "Nobody does *battle buddies* anymore, and definitely nobody in the Guild, but I think he heard it somewhere and decided he liked it. Couldn't shake him after that." The softness in his expression said that maybe he hadn't tried as hard as he let on. "Shit card player, though. No poker face."

Nash shrugged. "The universe could use more bad liars." Honest and stubborn and shit at cards—she would've liked to know him better, she thought. She would've liked the chance.

"He shouldn't have done it," Saint said quietly. His smile had bled away, leaving something haggard in its wake.

"You would've died if he hadn't."

"Maybe."

"Not *maybe.*" It wasn't a question of probability; it was fact. If Jal hadn't gotten that tablet down as fast as he had, her best friend would be dead, Eoan would be in pieces for letting it happen, and Anke would still be in the wind.

"But he would be fine."

Nash would've scoffed, if she'd had the energy. She'd poured it all into keeping Jal breathing, and even that didn't feel like much of an accomplishment. "If you think that lug could've listened to you die slow over the radio and been *fine*, you haven't been paying attention." Maybe Saint hadn't heard all of what he'd said on the rooftop, but she had. He'd known exactly what he was doing when he took that dive, and exactly why he was doing it, and she was so goddamn grateful for it and for him that she could barely breathe. Saint and Eoan were all she had, and she could've lost them both. A loss like that had nearly destroyed her once; Jal had spared her that, and for all the grief hanging thick and somber in the air, she couldn't bring herself to be sorry he'd taken the fall.

She was just sorry it was such a long way down.

Mercifully, Saint didn't argue. He just sank a little deeper, scrubbing his hands over his face again with no regard for the cuts and bruises. "I've never seen him so still," he said. "Always fidgeting and shit—couldn't even quit in his sleep." His shoulders lifted with a slow, deep breath. Meant to be bracing, she thought, but when he spoke, his voice sounded small—smaller than seemed possible, from the tower of a man she knew. "I can't let him go again, Nash."

It was all she could do to keep her balance as Saint tipped his head against her side, and probably all he could do to keep her steady on the arm of the chair. All their ironclad defenses crumbled, and they were both too goddamn tired to shore them back up again.

So they shored each other up instead. Saint leaned into her, and she leaned into him, and she lost count of the seconds they just sat there, breathing in the silence and watching the rise and fall of Jal's chest beneath the blankets.

The comms chimed. Subtler than a cleared throat and less abrupt than jumping right in. "I have something." Eoan's voice was quiet, only playing through one or two speakers in the sick bay. Even they weren't immune to it: that thick miasma of despair, that lingering shock. They'd all gotten their asses handed to them a time or two; it was the nature of the business. But they'd never taken a loss like this. "Would you like to talk here, or come to the bridge?"

Saint straightened, but Nash felt every bit of energy it took for him to do it. Felt it, because she matched him joule for joule. "Bridge," he scraped out. "Let the kid get some rest." He made no move to stand, though, and she realized after a beat that he wasn't going to.

He wanted to. Somehow that made it worse. He wanted to be fine, because he was Saint, and that was what he did. He'd made a career of being fine with shit nobody else could take.

For all their years apart, though, and for all the buckets of bad history between them, Jal had been ready to die for him. Hadn't even hesitated. And Saint stared at the bed like he wished he were the one lying in it. Whatever they'd been to each other, whatever they *could've* been to each other . . . as Nash watched him fold his hands over Jal's on the sheets, it finally started to sink in:

Of all the wounds Saint had survived, this could be the one that broke him.

"Stay with him," she said when she found her voice again. "I'll go see what Eoan's got for us." She squeezed his shoulder as she slid off his chair, forcing her spongy legs steady and her burning eyes clear. It was fine if he couldn't be fine, because she could be. *Would* be, for as long as they needed her to.

As she pulled away, Saint's head dipped low over his and Jal's clasped hands. Callused on callused, scarred on scarred, grasped like Saint could hold him there with nothing but the strength of his grip and the depths of his grief.

Praying, she thought. Or begging. Maybe there wasn't a difference in the heart of a desperate man. And although she had no god of her own to pray to, as she left them behind in the sick bay, she prayed that Saint's would answer him.

Her mods buzzed as she passed through the galley, stepping over half a rebreather kit and trying not to trip on the fuzzy little hobgoblin that sauntered between her feet with a disgruntled *mrrph*. She'd practically had to chase Bodie out of the sick bay with a broom earlier—no room for another mourner. He'd weathered the blackout okay, at least. Cashed in one of his nine lives, maybe, but visibly no worse for wear.

The same couldn't be said of their radio assembly. Bits of it littered the doorway to the bridge like entrails from a felled beast, and she had to bat Bodie away before he could snatch any loose wires. "Mitts off, klepto."

His bobtail twitched a *fuck you,* but he still curled against her knee as she dropped cross-legged to the floor. Seeking comfort or giving it, she wasn't quite sure, but she appreciated it anyway. Out came the multitool from her overalls pocket, because the radio wasn't going to fix itself.

It was good to have something she *could* fix.

"How is he?" Eoan asked, materializing at the head of the bridge. Their projection seemed wan, somehow. Colorless and washed out, and Nash knew that it made no sense, that they were just a collection of particles cast in light, but she could've sworn they looked heavy, too. *Rattled.* Maybe they hadn't quite shaken off the effects of the Deadworld infection, but Nash couldn't help feeling there was more to it than that. Some near-imperceptible shift in the captain's whole demeanor. A strange disquiet in their usual calm. Whatever the cause, something had definitely changed.

Nash looked away. "Which one?"

"Does the answer change?"

Fair point. She sighed and dragged the radio into her lap, starting on the screws with twice the concentration they deserved.

"He's in bad shape," she said, opening up the casing one wrist turn at a time. Sometimes you had to break a thing all the way down before you could build it back up. "Got our asses kicked."

"That we did." At least Eoan didn't try to gild it.

No sugar in that shit sandwich. "So," she said, "what're we gonna do about it?" Because that was how it worked. They took one on the chin, and they licked their split lips, bared their bloody teeth, and got the fuck on with it.

"We find them," said Eoan.

"No shit." The rub was *how*. Picketers made an art form out of getting around undetected, and they hadn't had the opportunity or the wherewithal to sneak a tracker onto Drestyn's ship.

Unless one of them had.

Nash narrowed her eyes at Eoan, corners of her mouth nudging upward. "You did something, didn't you?"

"*No shit*," Eoan shot back, and just enough mirth fizzled in their voice to make Nash think maybe she wasn't the only one bootstrapping herself back to rights. "There wasn't time for anything elegant, I'm afraid. The code was . . . aggressive. I worried Anke would find anything with a signal," they added. That was the problem with the clever ones—awesome to work with, but a pain in the ass to work against. "But I took a page from the late Ranger Riesen's book."

"Satellite FID?" Better than nothing, she guessed, but they wouldn't get a hit until the picketers passed a receiver.

"Somewhat more . . . roentgenic," Eoan replied.

It took her a second; long day, raging headache. When she got there, though, Nash could've *kissed* the captain. "You rad-tagged her." Messy and low-tech, but on a ship as well traveled as the *Ambit*, a radiation signature was as distinct as a fingerprint. Anke's week aboard wouldn't have done it—had to be a high enough concentration to track long-distance—but if Eoan had managed to flood the vents before Anke bailed, it might've done the trick. Unnoticeable and maybe slightly carcinogenic, but karma was a bitch like that sometimes. "Have I mentioned lately that I love you?"

"I love you, too," they replied, with a sudden seriousness that Nash didn't have the bandwidth to process. Clearly Eoan had some baggage of their own to unpack from Noether; Nash wouldn't push it. She was too damn tired. And chalk it up to that same unbelievable fatigue that Nash startled when the holotable in the center of the bridge blinked on. Stars and planets scattered through the air above it—a map of the O-Cyg spiral, in three dimensions. "To the extent a visual aid would help."

Nash pushed to her knees as a bright red dot appeared at the center of the map. "Anke." She hated the way she said it. Hated the way her breath caught, wedged behind a sticky-sour lump in her throat. Hated most of all that, of course, Saint choose that moment to walk in.

He hovered near the doorway, still in the same blood-smudged shirt. The heaviness hadn't gone anywhere; he'd just drawn enough steel back into his spine to bear it. Those few minutes alone had fortified him—given him time, she thought, to say his goodbyes. Or to convince himself he didn't need to.

Either way, it'd been a while since she'd seen him like that, standing only an arm's length away, and somehow well beyond her grasp. Couldn't begrudge him; they all coped in their own ways. But she wished he'd at least changed his fucking clothes.

"You really liked her," he said. Not a question. No judgment, no pity. He knew better.

She sucked in a breath through her teeth. "I didn't—*not* like her." Even that felt like a confession, miserable and guilty, but Anke was smart, and driven, and so endearingly awkward that Nash'd started looking forward to every time she opened her mouth. She wished she could've said she'd had doubts, that she'd seen the signs and just ignored them, but the truth was Nash never would've called that double cross. She never would've known, until it was too late. "I got duped."

"We all did." Saint joined her at the table. "If you want dibs on the takedown when we catch them, though, she's all yours. Long as I get Drestyn." In the lights of all those stars and planets, something truly *vicious* lit his eyes. He'd heard the shot. He'd heard the horrible sounds Jal had strangled behind his teeth as the bullet ripped his leg apart. Drestyn might not've pushed him off the roof, but without a doubt, he was the reason Jal was dying.

Maybe *that* was what those minutes alone had given him, Nash thought. Not closure, not denial, but the cold, consuming certainty of rage.

Whatever it takes. She turned back to the holotable. "Your man's a real piece of work." She'd heard him on the rooftop, over Jal's comm line. *Save one life or save thousands. Millions.* A man on a mission. "Doesn't seem like the kind you talk down."

"Wasn't planning on talking," Saint said.

Good. A kind face and a humanitarian cause didn't take the hole out of Jal's leg or the hemorrhage out of his brain. The Trust had taken someone dear from Drestyn, but he'd taken someone dear from Saint. A hurt that deep had no room for empathy. "So let's just figure out where the hell they're headed, and go do something about it."

They were on the same page: no more reactionary bullshit, no more getting caught on their back foot. It was time to go hunting.

She twirled her multitool around her fingers, eyeing the map. "Well, if I were a pissed-off picketer packing a world-killing cyber bomb, I'd be looking for someplace to hit the Trust where it hurts. Bonus points if it's someplace that scumbag Yarden might be holed up." Otho Yarden, the morally repugnant ladder-climber behind the Kepler explosions that killed Drestyn's brother, and probably the rubber stamp behind the Deadworld Code. Didn't seem like much of a stretch to think he'd be part of Drestyn's big plan. "Two birds and all."

"Right," Saint said. "So what've we got in terms of high-value targets nearby? Try for anything less than a day's travel; there might be a reason Anke saved Noether for last. Could've been working her way back to something."

The map shifted as Eoan ran the search, skimming through planets, focus darting from one orb of light to the next so quickly Nash started to get a little dizzy, before it finally snapped to a halt.

"Here," Eoan said, expanding the speck on the map until it took shape: not a sphere, but a saucer, spinning near a cluster of moons like a children's top. "Lewaro City, one of the Trust's satellite hubs. Serves as the main port for their transit and shipping to and from the frontier, houses all the regional officers and administrators for the outer spiral. Average occupancy of one hundred twenty-three thousand one hundred seventy-seven. And," they added, matter-of-factly, "home office of one Otho Yarden."

"*Ding, ding, ding.* Sounds like we have a winner," Nash said. "Hell of an ultimatum: fess up, or we drop the Deadworld Code in your life support." They'd already proven the Deadworld Code wasn't limited to T-form systems; if it fucked up the Lewaro station as fast and as hard as it had the *Ambit,* a lot of people would die badly. "How long do we have?"

"At their current speed, Lewaro is approximately four hours' flight from Anke's position. Four hours and thirty-five minutes from ours."

"That's too long. Any Guild ships closer?" Saint practically growled it. His gun mag held twenty rounds, and she'd bet Drestyn's name was on every single one of them. Giving up the chance to get to him first had to fucking hurt.

So if he looked a little relieved when Eoan shook their head,

Nash couldn't fault him. "They chose their target well," Eoan said. "Nothing but lunar clusters and asteroids for hours. The nearest Guild vessel is a transport freighter half a day's flight out."

"Guessing you've already tried to get word to the station?" Nash asked.

This time, when Eoan shook their head, *nobody* looked happy about it. "As far as I can tell, comm signals are jammed station-wide."

"How the hell'd Drestyn pull that off already?" Saint asked.

"He didn't," Eoan replied. "The jammer seems to be coming from the station itself. No incoming communications, and I can't confirm outgoing, but I'm not getting anything but the closed-zone message on repeat."

"The Trust cut off their own station's communications?" Nash didn't like the sound of that. "Why would they do that? They gotta know something bad's coming." They'd had an eye on things since *Riesen*. Had mercs waiting for them on Sooner's *and* on Noether; no way they wouldn't have worked out where this was going. Before anybody could weigh in, though, Nash had her own *aha*. "Shit," she said. "*They* know, but the station doesn't. Not all of it, anyway." A few C-suiters like Yarden, maybe, but the other hundred thousand and change? The workers and their families just trying to make a living? "They're keeping them in the dark on purpose."

Saint's scowl could've melted tungsten. He'd never been able to stomach turning on his own. "Don't trust their own people not to break rank, so they don't give them the chance. Like a trapped rat gnawing off its own foot."

"Except the rat would feel it," Nash said. "I'm pretty sure whatever parts the Trust loses, it can grow back."

"More like a starfish," Eoan offered helpfully. "An insidious starfish."

"Sounds like my next knitting project." She had to joke about it, because if she didn't, she'd start screaming. People had *died*. People were going to die, and those Janus-faced motherfuckers were just going to let a whole station *la la la* their way through annihilation. *Continuing the proud human tradition of denying shit we don't like until it kills us.* Doctor or not, she kind of hated people sometimes. All the blood, sweat, and tears she put into keeping them alive, and they were damn determined to kill themselves and each other. *Bet botanists don't have these sorts of problems.*

"As heartless as it is, it makes sense," Eoan said. "No chance for the station's occupants to panic. No chance of word getting out. And if it *is* a confession Anke's looking for, it won't do her very much good if she can't broadcast it off the station before she's caught."

"That's some expert-level ass-covering."

"Makes you wonder, too," Saint agreed, low and dour as he hunched over the holotable. "If they're willing to shut the whole station down to keep this under control, what else're they willing to do?"

Not a question Nash wanted to think on too hard. In a game of morally bankrupt chicken, the Trust would *never* blink first. "Real question is, what're *we* gonna do? Drestyn's not an idiot." Begrudgingly, she added, "Anke, either," and she could almost convince herself it didn't sting as much to say her name this time. Like a granuloma closing in around a splinter. Or immurement. She liked that better—walling the pain off brick by brick, until it shriveled and died in the dark. "They'll have a way in. We need one, too."

"Then let's find one." Saint raised his hand to enlarge the projection above the holotable, and the sea of stars became hundreds of phosphor-blue buildings rising and falling across the Lewaro cityscape like beats of a racing heart. "Figure they're probably heading to the Admin Building, here. It's got life support, executive suites—"

"Everything a growing insurrection needs." Nash snorted.

Saint flicked the air over the tallest building on the map. "Cap, can I get a list of anything near here? Bounty targets, dry docks—anything we can use to override their lockout."

Now there was the start of a plan. Even a full station lockdown only barred *nonessential* access; no port could refuse access for an active warrant or a damaged ship. "Look at you, getting all underhanded and sneaky." She socked his shoulder cheerfully. "I like it."

The map scrolled through a cluster of buildings around the Admin Building, sweeping up from the middle of the domed city. Banking center, high-rise hotel—

"There." Saint swiped his hand across the map, spinning the image until it centered on a shorter, rounded tower on the other side. "They've got a hospital."

Ah, shit. Just when they'd started to get their groove back. "Saint—"

But he cut her off. "It's perfect. Can't refuse hospital access to a critical case, and it's just a frog-hop away from the Admin Building. We claim right of entry for the hospital, and you and I can make the jump over there while Cap plays ambulance and hacks us in. It's our cleanest ingress."

"Right, and that's all this is about," she shot back. She wanted to smack him. Shake him. *Don't do this to yourself, you sad fucking masochist.* It was all she could do to keep her hands at her sides and her voice steady as she explained, "Jal is stable right now, Saint. We finish up here, and we could still get him home in time for his family to say goodbye." It wasn't the happy ending that poor bastard deserved, but it was something. "But if he goes in that hospital, there's a solid chance he doesn't make it back out. Even if they do everything right, odds are he never makes it home, and that's not what we promised him."

"What *you* promised him!" She knew Saint had something volatile under all that carefully practiced temperance, but she rarely saw it. She flinched. "*You* promised," he repeated, quieter. More carefully. "He didn't ask me for anything, Nash. He just—" He faltered, jaw working around the words he couldn't say until he found some he could. "You said there's a chance he dies in that hospital, so that means there's a chance that he doesn't."

Everything he said was true: her way, he had a chance of making it home to die; Saint's way, he had a chance of living to make it home. Wasn't something she'd run the probabilities on, and she could *tell* Eoan was biting their tongue.

"It's risky," she said. "If we claim right of entry, they'll try to confine us to the hospital; and if the Deadworld Code hits the city, he'll be as much at risk as everyone else."

"I know."

"And it's selfish," she added, quieter. "It's not what he asked for."

Saint's head dipped, fractionally. "I know that, too."

For all her reservations, Nash guessed that settled it. The hospital was their way in. She'd just have to find another way to keep her promise. *Sorry, miner boy. You're not done saving us yet.* "Fuck it, I'm in." All in, all the way to the end; they'd never given each other anything less, and she wouldn't start now. "So, don't suppose you've got any ideas how we swing it?"

"Only way we know how," Saint said, lips turned in a wry grin. "Wit, grit, and crazy shit."

CHAPTER NINETEEN

ANKE

For a dead man's clothes, they fit surprisingly well.

"You guys really thought of everything, huh?" Anke aimed for complimentary, but it came out vaguely nauseous. For her part, she tried *not* to think. Not about the blood spotting the starched gray collar of her shirt, not about the sans-clothes corpses lying somewhere back on Noether. Shirt, belt, trousers—she wasn't even sure they all came from the same person. Something else not to think about.

Of course, because human brains *sucked,* it didn't work like that. She'd looked it up once: ironic process theory. Try not to picture a big white bear, and suddenly you couldn't imagine anything else, and she had so many white bears prowling around her head as they neared the station that she could've opened a zoo. A monochromatic, anxiety-and-guilt-steeped zoo for the self-flagellating.

There weren't any good *distractions,* either. Give her a problem to solve, work to do, and maybe she could wrestle her brain back in line, but no. They'd preloaded the Deadworld Code on a jump drive, the tablet she'd borrowed was up to spec—even if it didn't sing under her fingers like her old one—and after all the mad programming she'd done on the patch, spoofing a landing pass to get them past the Lewaro blockade was like finger painting. Basic. Took four minutes and half her concentration, and then she went back to fidgeting in the bridge like a sugar-high marmot.

Drestyn glanced back from the controls at the front of the bridge. Hard to find privacy on a ship the size of a cracker box, but he'd sportingly kept his back to her while she'd changed, and if he'd noticed her twitching while he steered them through the Lewaro air lock, he hadn't brought it up.

"You can't think of everything, Miss Ahlstrom," he said instead, and by then she'd lost her train of thought so completely that it took her a minute to find it again. They really thought of everything. The uniforms. Right, okay, she was back. "Best you can do is prepare for what you can, and adapt to what you can't." She suddenly wished he wasn't looking at her. He had the unique ability to force whole sentences into the curve of an eyebrow, and as someone who couldn't force sentences into actual friggin' sentences, she was horribly jealous.

"Why do I get the feeling we're not talking about the uniforms anymore?" she asked.

That damn *eyebrow*. Somehow the scar slashing through it just made it that much more pointed. "Is there something else we need to be talking about?"

He's dead. The thought sprang forward with such force that she barely managed to cage it behind her teeth. *He's dead, and you killed him, and I helped.* Jal was a goodish person trying to do a good thing, and she and Drestyn were goodish people trying to do a good thing. She wasn't sure how both could be true, though, when Jal was dead because of them. Goodish people didn't kill goodish people.

Did they?

She shook her head. Nice of Drestyn to offer an ear and all, but she felt bad enough trying *not* to think about the things she didn't want to think about. All the little moments where things had gone wrong—Nash's copy of the patch going up in smoke. Saint going back to the ship ahead of schedule. Jal following them onto the rooftop. So many white bears, and they all had such sharp teeth. If she actually started talking about them, she was afraid she wouldn't know how to stop, and there just wasn't time for a full-on breakdown.

We can pencil something in if we don't die. Which, hey, good to set goals. "Adapt to what you can't," she repeated. A five-word lifeline; a way forward. It wasn't an answer to Drestyn's question, but in a way, it worked. "I can do that."

She couldn't undo anything, but at least if they finished what they'd started, it could mean something. It had to mean something.

With a nod and maybe even a smidge of a smile, Drestyn turned back to the controls. "Glad to hear it," he said. "Because we're here."

"What?" Wow, that was loud. *Cool it, Ahlstrom. This is the easy part.* Only, like, a fifty percent chance of death or dismemberment. Practically a lazy Tuesday. The Admin Building, easily the tallest point in the whole of Lewaro City, towered above the gentle waves of silica and steel around it. Very few buildings had their own landing pads; Admin's jutted out of the sides of the tower like mushroom conks from the trunk of a massive glass tree.

"Which one?" Drestyn cut back on the rockhopper's engines.

"Uh, the big one? Kind of hard to miss."

He glanced back at her. "I meant which *landing* pad." Then, because he and his stupid loquacious eyebrows couldn't cut her any slack, he had to go and ask, "Are you sure you're all right?"

"Nope." Honesty was the foundation of all strong relationships. "Definitely not. But I've got this." She totally had this. Leaning over the back of his seat, she pointed to one of the higher pads. "You wanted floor twenty-eight? So put us down there, pad eight. Try to look *mercenary*. It'd be a pretty bad look if we got shot down before we even landed. Not that we'd really have to worry about it, you know, because we'd be—"

"Extremely dead," Drestyn finished, amused. Because ap-

parently he was the level of badass that looked death in the face
and laughed.

Anke laughed, but it had nothing to do with badassery. She
had a nervous giggle. "Yeah, that," she said, watching as Drestyn eased them down. No idea how he did it; she couldn't stand
people watching her work. But there they went, smooth as silk.
Not even a bump when they touched down on the landing pad.
She only hoped the rest of the job could go as smoothly.

The engines kept running as Drestyn swept out of his seat.
Fluid and graceful, but with a sense of the unstoppable in his
steps. Like a river ready to flow over or around or *through*
anything in its path. "Coming, Miss Ahlstrom?" he called from
the door, hand outstretched and mouth upturned in a quiet,
untroubled smile. And she took it. Took his hand like she'd
taken his word when they'd first set out on this mad mission,
and she couldn't say who followed whom on the way to the
cargo hatch, but she knew they were moving together toward
something.

Drestyn's men—Rigby, the stocky one with the missing ring
finger, lost his farm to foreclosure on a defunct agrarian colony; and Pabel, the platinum-haired giant whose picture was
in the dictionary under *tough guy,* had spent twenty years running the shipping routes with nothing to show for it but a bad
hip and a bulldog bobblehead—waited at the hatch in matching
uniforms, guns at the ready.

"Already got company on the pad," Rigby reported, gesturing out the opening hatch where a few security officers filtered
out onto the pad. "Three there, but there'll be plenty more inside if our landing permit didn't pass the sniff test." He looked
over at Anke with an expression that could politely be called
doubtful. "Hope you're as good with that GLASS as Dres here
says, girl, or that'll be our gooses plucked, cooked, and served
for supper."

Kudos for vivid imagery, but *girl*? Really? "I told you to call me Anke."

"I'll call you the fucking queen if this goes off," he said gruffly.

"Then in that case, I prefer *Your Majesty*."

Rigby rolled his eyes, but as he stepped out onto the ramp, one corner of his mouth curled reluctantly upward. She'd call that a win. With any luck, it wouldn't be horribly short-lived.

"Name and purpose," called one of the security officers in a flat, businesslike voice. Each wore cookie-cutter expressions and identical uniforms, and Anke knew it was company policy or whatever, but it just looked like they'd called in sick the day *personalities* got handed out. No hair color visible under their royal blue caps, with brims so low they might as well have been wearing visors, and standard-issue *everything* so they could've shuffled around like a game of three-card monte and she'd have never known the difference.

"We should've gotten *those* uniforms," she whispered, nodding her head at them. Talk about blending in. They could march right up to the top-floor control room and nobody'd even slow them down.

Drestyn glanced over. "Good idea. Happen to know where we can find some lying around?" He shook his head minutely. "These uniforms are fine. The Trust has a standing arrangement with this merc syndicate. You don't piss off the people that bury your bodies for you."

"So they'll let us in?" She'd *tried* to get Drestyn to spill the beans on his plan earlier, but the man was tight-lipped as a smart fish; he hadn't taken the bait.

Seemed he was finally ready to loosen up a bit. "Well," he said. "They won't shoot a merc on sight. A picketer, on the other hand." He shrugged and, as the security officers called out again, he started down the ramp of the rockhopper, unruffled by the wind howling across the landing pad. Naturally, that same wind plastered half her hair to her face the second she stepped clear of the ship. Insult, meet injury.

"We're here for Otho Yarden," Drestyn called across the landing pad to the security officers.

Otho Yarden and his station-wide administrator-level access terminal, Anke amended silently. No air-gapped T-form systems on Lewaro, no sir. Just a massive spider's web of interconnected networks with a creepy, bug-eyed crawler in the middle, plucking all the strings.

It felt like an eternity, and Anke might've sweated through the first layer of her uniform before the middle officer said, "We'll need to see some identification."

"Wow," she whispered, mostly to herself. "People actually say that." She'd only heard it in movies, usually right before the guards called shenanigans. Which. *Gulp.*

Drestyn must not have watched the same movies, because he just cleared his throat and said, "Otho Yarden is expecting us."

Wrong answer. The middle officer drew her gun—Slava Pulser, small-caliber piezoelectric charges, and Anke wasn't sure if she felt better or worse for knowing it. Firearm instruction was a mandatory prereq for fieldwork, and she had a hard time *not* retaining information. The good news was, it meant she knew it had a nonlethal setting. The bad news was, she couldn't tell which setting it was on.

"Identification!" the officer shouted. Maybe she'd gotten some personality after all: mostly *angry.* She had a voice like refined cobalt, hard and lustrous, and she didn't sound like she was used to having to repeat herself.

Anke was a little thrown when Drestyn raised his hands. A perfectly reasonable reaction to having a gun pointed at you by a very angry security officer, sure, but *surrender* somehow didn't mesh with her image of him.

"On a scale of one to *royally,* how screwed are we?" she hissed between her teeth.

"Relax" was Drestyn's totally unhelpful answer.

She valiantly wrestled back the urge to throw something at him. Instead, she hissed, "You can't tell someone like me to relax. I'm seventy-five kilos of anxiety and worst-case scenarios. *Not. Happening.*" Not nearly as satisfying as hitting him, but probably less likely to get them shot. Trust security officers weren't known for their restrained trigger fingers.

He turned back to her, hands still raised. "You came to me for a reason," he said mildly. It was true. Things hadn't gone to plan at the depot—his people were supposed to pluck her from the hands of Riesen, not wind up dead and buried beneath half an exploded hangar—but that didn't change the fact that this was *his* world. He was one of the best at what he did, and she needed him. "You got us to the front door; I'll get us through it. Just trust me."

Kind of a tough sell, since he'd shot a friend of hers, but he'd been honest about what he was doing from the jump. She couldn't say the same. "Okay," she said. "But if we get blasted into oblivion, I'm absolutely holding it against you."

"Fair enough." A wink—he *winked*—and forward he went, palms out and shoulders soft, like the fluffiest, most harmless merc to ever walk the earth. "Just tell Yarden we're here. He should be able to clear things up."

"Take off the hat," said the man on the right. Anke couldn't really tell anything else about him. Average height, average build. Did they even make the uniforms in plus sizes? Bastards. And out came *his* gun. "Show your face."

Right. Like that wouldn't set off a thousand alerts on the facial recs. "I don't think they're buying the—"

Then, Drestyn *took off his hat.*

Oh, they were so boned. The security officers' gunsights all snapped to Drestyn's chest like some kind of video game aim assist, and Anke's saving grace was that she was too flabbergasted to panic. She looked between Rigby and Pabel, standing on either side of the bottom of the rockhopper ramp, but they both had their hands up like Drestyn.

If this is the plan, it's a stupid one, she thought, begrudgingly raising her hands. She didn't exactly scream *dangerous,* but it probably didn't pay to be the only one in the group not raising her hands. *Stupid, stupid plan.*

The officers crossed the pad in a flurry of wind-muffled boot steps and gun muzzles, two pushing ahead to take Pabel's and Rigby's guns from their belts while the woman with the cobalt voice held back with Drestyn in her sights.

"Go ahead," Anke muttered at Drestyn's back. "Tell me to relax again. I literally dare—"

She couldn't follow the precise sequence of events, but in the half second between one word and the next, Cobalt Lady had chin-kicked one of the other officers—and *hello, flexibility*—and turned her own gun on the other. Somewhere in there, Drestyn drew *his* gun, too. No laser sights, but Anke could follow the aim to the neighborhood of Mister Chin-Kicked's forehead.

"—you," she finished, only because she couldn't bear to leave it open-ended. *Well, then.* At least she knew why he'd kept the plan hush-hush. Anke wouldn't have trusted herself with *deep cover double cross,* either. At least her abject terror was convincing, that way. *You're welcome.*

Drestyn ignored her, telling the two remaining officers, "Guns on the ground." Cool as coolant—and wow, there had to be a better simile than that—like he didn't even see the guns aimed *his* way. "Your guns or your lives, gentlemen. I'm taking one. Your choice which you keep."

Do what he says, she thought, fervently. *It's not worth dying over.* But the Trust, with all that power and all that impunity, made it far too easy to buy in. To mistake a paycheck for a purpose.

Even Anke's untrained eyes saw their fingers tensing on the triggers, but they weren't quick enough. Two shots so in sync they sounded like one, and the officers dropped at the points of Drestyn's and Cobalt's guns.

Anke forced herself to watch. This was her mission. She hadn't pulled the trigger, but those deaths were on her hands, too.

"Wrong choice." Drestyn sighed, holstering his gun.

Anke swallowed against the sick squeeze of her stomach as Pabel and Rigby recovered their guns and dragged the bodies onto the ship. "Kind of late for that, isn't it?" She'd checked the building specs ahead of time; every landing pad had at least three cameras. Hiding the bodies seemed like a moot point.

"Please." Rigby snorted, shuffling backward up the ramp with an officer dragging limp behind him. "We know what we're doing."

"*Marei* knows what *she's* doing," Drestyn corrected, and on cue, Cobalt Lady—*Marei*—held a GLASS out for Anke to see. It probably would've been helpful, if Anke could've gotten her eyes to focus. Or her brain. Her adrenal system was really killing it, though.

Bad choice of words.

Deep breath. She swore she smelled lavender, and she hated that it helped. "The landing pad," she said, as the pieces finally slotted into place. It was footage of the landing pad, with the rockhopper and the three of them standing off the ship with their hands still up. *Ah.* "You looped it."

Marei nodded. Up close, Anke could actually see her face under the bill of her cap: sharp-featured and full-lipped, but not so much of either that Anke would've noticed her on the street. Not pretty, but not *not* pretty. Her eyes looked decidedly cat-like, though—angular and appraising—set against skin a little darker than the rest of her face; *those,* Anke would've noticed. Probably smart to keep her hat cocked so low. "Our little secret, for now," she said, touching a finger to her lips. "It'll be a minute or two before anyone notices and comes snooping. Don't waste them."

"But—" she started. *How did you get here? How long have you* been *here? How do you know Drestyn?* They both had the same paramilitary vibe to them. Was there, like, an agitator version of basic training? She'd done all the digging she could do and *still* didn't know much about his life between Kepler and now.

She kind of got the sense he liked it that way.

"We like to be prepared," Drestyn said.

"No kidding." She knew he'd had his eye on Lewaro for a long time—and on Yarden, more specifically. That was why she'd gone with him, but *deep-cover badass* was still a serious power move. *Deep-cover badass with biometric clearance,* she amended as they reached the door and Marei put her eye to the scanner. "Guess my job just got a lot easier."

Marei chuckled. "Don't get too excited, little bird," she said, silkily. "I'm still the new kid on the block; my clearance stops a level up. You want to get to the penthouse, that's on you."

Fine by her. Anke had been itching to get her fingers on their security system anyway. Bring on the tasty, tasty firewalls. She'd take block ciphers over bullets any day. "Let's go, then," she said, ducking through the door. The stark change from *all the wind* to the near-silence inside made her ears feel clogged, stuffed full of cotton, but she could still hear every footstep behind her as Drestyn, then Marei, then Rigby filtered in. "No Pabel?"

"Staying with the ship," said Drestyn. "Hell of a getaway pilot."

"Damn straight," said Marei with a glinting grin. Huh. Marei and Pabel. Pabel and Marei. Marbel. Cute, in a *kinda scared, kinda horny* sort of way. "Besides, somebody's got to keep our exit clear. You want to put our asses in the hands of Rigby here?"

"Fuck you, too, sister," Rigby growled back, but even with his *piss in my porridge* personality type, he still sounded a little fond. Reminded her of the way Nash and Saint always picked at each other.

Oh no you don't. She swatted the misery-scented thought away and nodded. "Pabel it is. So, do I get to know the plan now?"

"Only if you can walk and talk at the same time," said Marei. "Time to go to work."

The plan, it turned out, went like this: Marei, playing the role of Anonymous Security Officer Number Seven, escorted three visitors upstairs from the landing pad. No dramatics, no sneaking around in ventilation shafts; she led them through the security check-in and into a lobby, and they trailed behind her like ducklings. The man at the reception desk barely looked at them, just nodded to Marei and went back to his comm panel, and none of the handful of people lounging around the sitting area even bothered to do that much. The interior design, all light woods and soft greens, looked more like a spa than a corporate nerve center, bathed in light from the floor-to-ceiling windows along the back wall.

Anke stifled a shiver. Yes, logically, she knew that the Admin Building was mostly office space, but *seeing* the office workers creeped her out. To smell the tannic bitterness of slightly burnt coffee and the mishmash of thirty different lunches being heated and eaten at once. To hear the comms ringing and the lifts dinging and the utter lack of any maniacal chortling floating out from boardrooms clouded with cigar smoke.

To them, it wasn't Judgment Day. It was just . . . *Tuesday.*

"Um," she began, uneasily, "are we sure those guys told Yarden we were coming?" She'd expected a little more, uh, *alarm*.

Drestyn shook his head. "Wouldn't matter if they hadn't. The second facial rec pinged me, he'd have known about it. He knows we're here. Probably even knows why."

"But they don't?" A pair of women sat on one of the sofas they passed, laughing at something on a GLASS, and a guy stood half-hidden by one of the potted plants, picking something out of his teeth in his reflection in the window. Not exactly *red alert* behavior.

"Alarms cause panic," Marei said as they turned the corner into a lift lobby. Nobody there, and weirdly, Anke found herself missing the people. The people were just unexpected; the emptiness was *foreboding*. Marei didn't seem to notice, though, floating across the lobby to hit the call button. "Panic is messy. Better to handle it quiet. If it makes you feel better, I'm sure he's got quite the welcome party waiting upstairs." As if on cue, the light above one of the lifts blinked on.

Ding!

Anke eyed the opening doors. "So we're walking into a trap."

"Of course not. We're taking the elevator," Drestyn replied, with that same smile of his. Small, but anticipatory—a fox at the edge of a henhouse, waiting for the door to creak open.

Or rather, waiting for Anke to open it.

With a sigh, she tugged her GLASS from her bag and joined them on the lift. "Going up," she said as the doors slid closed and the music kicked on. *Because of course there's music.* What hilariously terrifying, life-or-death situation was complete without some smooth friggin' jazz? "Momentarily," she added at Rigby's expectant look. She was good, but she was still *human*.

Rigby, unsurprisingly, was about as good at waiting as he was at small talk. *Click*. His thumb mashed one of ten unmarked buttons on the top of the panel. Presumably, if you were going up that high, you knew which button you were supposed to press.

When it didn't light up, Rigby mashed it again.

"You would totally fail the marshmallow test," Anke said. *There's a button-masher in every group.* Anke had her *own* buttons to worry about. Ugh, she hated this GLASS. No tactile feedback. She missed her tappy keys.

Click.

"I don't know if you think that's helping, but it's not," she told him without looking up. Minutes, Marei said. They only had minutes before security figured out that they'd looped the feed, and if they weren't upstairs by then, they'd have more to deal with than Yarden's top-floor muscle.

Rigby gave her a flat look. *Click*.

"Rigby, would you—" But before Marei could finish, the lift juddered and went dark. "Little bird? Not trying to tell you how to do your job, but."

Anke jerked her head, *no*. "That wasn't me." If her fingers moved any faster, she would've started throwing out smoke. *Shit, shit, shit*. "That trap we were talking about?" The lift jolted again, and the air grew heavier, and suddenly they went up a whole lot faster than Anke had in mind.

"Anke, what's going on?" Still calm. Did Drestyn even know *how* to lose his shit?

Her screen flared red, but she banished the warnings with a swipe of her hand. Back to the keys, conjuring lines of code across the screen, but she barely even *saw* the script anymore. It became abstract acts, mapping a path, prodding a locked door. "Those are the emergency brakes decoupling," she said. Another locked door, another nudge, a little give. *You'll do.* "Lift's going up. Quickly."

"They're going to drop us." Marei didn't seem to feel the

need to paint a picture beyond that. Fifty-something floors in a giant silica box. *Crunch. Splat. Boom.* Pick your onomatopoeia. "Can you stop it?"

"If I can't, you won't have very long to be disappointed," Anke replied distractedly. Her heart hammered in her throat, but she'd found a shiny little tunnel protocol for remote maintenance—a manufacturer leave-behind, not completely unprotected, but untouched by the top-of-the-line security. She sank her techie teeth into it, felt it give, and a steadiness washed over her. Not calm, but maybe hyperfocus. The dark of the elevator and the red of the alerts and Marei's voice counting *forty-six, forty-seven, forty-eight, forty-nine* didn't exist, and all she had to do was—

The lift slowed suddenly, lurching as the emergency brakes re-engaged. On the screen above the button panel *51, 52, 53* crawled by in time with the numbers on her GLASS. "Got you!" she whooped as the lift dinged and the doors began to open. God bless lazy manufacturers and unvoided warranties. "I got you so hard, you—oh."

Guys. Guns. Guys with guns.

"Cover!" Marei shouted, flattening herself against one side of the lift. It would've been a nice warning, if someone hadn't already grabbed her arm and yanked her against the button panel as the first volley of piezoelectric day-ruiners battered the back wall of the elevator.

She blinked down, expecting to see Drestyn's hand, but this one had—er, didn't have—a missing ring finger. "All right, Your Majesty?" said Rigby with a bitter rind of a smile. Something told her it wasn't his first time being pinned down by enemy fire.

As the resident newbie to the proverbial trenches, she was perfectly happy to hang out against the wall until the first round of shots tapered off.

"Hold," called a voice from outside the lift. Crisp. Authoritative. Probably the boss of the group, but Anke felt pretty satisfied with the *current* number of holes in her head, so she didn't peek to see which of the officers the voice belonged to. "You're surrounded."

"Obviously." Marei rolled her eyes, and Anke felt the improbable burble of a laugh in her chest. Maybe this was *their* Tuesday. Danger, guns, and small-scale revolutions.

Shockingly, Mister Boss Man didn't find it as funny as Anke did. "Put your guns on the ground and come out with your hands up."

"I'm afraid we can't do that," Drestyn replied. "But we're not here for you, so if you put *your* guns down and step against the wall over there, you don't have to die today." Which was awfully big talk for someone outnumbered almost two to one and trapped in a lift. "It's your choice."

Another choice. Anke wondered if Drestyn always did that—if he always gave people a chance to choose their fate. To pick a side, even if the side was just keeping your own ass alive. Had he given the mercs on Noether the same choice? Stand down or die?

If he had, they must've chosen the same as Yarden's firing squad. They answered with another volley of shots that pinged and fizzled against the back wall of the lift. So much electricity in such a small space, Anke *tasted* ozone. Her teeth buzzed and her hair stood on end, blood roaring in her ears as she waited for the firing squad to make a move.

In the end, it wasn't theirs to make.

"You tried," Marei said, with the air of someone who hadn't expected things to go any differently. Unhappy, but unsurprised. "Ready?"

Drestyn frowned, not so much with his mouth as with his whole body—shoulders sinking, frame bending inward under a gravity that looked too much like guilt. "Go."

Ten shots. Why she counted, Anke didn't know, but each one seared a line in her mind's eye. Ten shots, spread almost evenly between Marei, Rigby, and Drestyn, and silence fell like a thick, velvet curtain across the lift lobby.

Ten shots, and they'd killed them all.

Anke couldn't bring herself to look past the doorway of the lift for too long. She'd miscounted before—eight, not seven— and she told herself that it mattered. That it wasn't just another body on the floor, but a life. A future and a family and a funeral, and it twisted something horrible in her chest to see them that way, but the alternative was worse. The moment she started seeing numbers instead of people she'd be no better than leeches like Yarden. It was *supposed* to hurt.

It just wasn't supposed to stop her.

"Wait," Rigby yelped as she slid past him into the lift lobby, nose buried in her GLASS and feet mapping a careful course between bodies and bloodstains on the polished tiles. "Let us clear it first, for fuck's sake."

She raised her tablet briefly above her head to show the screen. "Cameras," she called back. "Floor's clear." Not much to it, honestly. The building tapered at the top; smaller floors, more *exclusive*. A conference room opened on the other side of the lobby wall, separated by opaque hologlass; and down the hall, an assistant's desk sat in front of an office that was probably the same size as or bigger than the rest of the floor. "Got you three, those eight, and zip and nilch in the office and conference room, respectively."

"Poor bastards," Rigby muttered. "Benches and benjamina trees—not a scrap of decent cover. Never stood a chance."

Clothing rustled, and Anke glanced back to see Marei and Rigby shifting the bodies out of the middle of the floor. Didn't make a lot of sense at first; they weren't expecting company like back at the landing pad. But as she watched, Marei leaned over one of the officers, brushing open eyes closed with a gentle hand and folding his arms over his chest. It wasn't strategy; it was *decency*. "They weren't *supposed* to stand a chance," Marei said, soft but metalline. "They were cannon fodder."

Anke turned away as Drestyn joined her at the door. "Yarden

would've left them here," he said. "Kill us or stall us. Either way, he had time to slip out. You have the office feeds?"

"Office. Landing pads. Breakrooms." She allowed herself a small, triumphant fist pump as the card reader turned green and Drestyn opened the door for her. The gentleman agitator—sounded like the tagline of a movie or something. A book, maybe. He seemed more the literary type. "Did you know they have espresso machines on every floor? Of course you didn't. I mean, you wouldn't, I guess. It has literally nothing to do with what we're doing. I'm not even sure why I'm telling you about it. I'm fine, it's just . . ."

Her eyes lit on the desk in the corner, bow-shaped and topped with a single curving monitor that made her itch for a high-graphics RPG game and a barrel of cheese puffs. "Hello, beautiful." She didn't quite run for it, but she came close enough that the chair rolled when she landed. Cue the ungraceful shuffle of shame back to the front of the desk, hands hovering reverently over the built-in consoles for a moment.

Drestyn hung back, lingering by the half-moon of couches on the other side of the office. Magazines on the table, paintings and awards on the wall, even a stress ball on the desk with the Trust's omnipresent logo. The office looked *lived in*. Real. It smelled of fruity-musky cologne and a whiff of industrial cleaner. A bookshelf in the corner held actual paper books and a framed picture of a man and woman standing in front of a sunset with wide, happy smiles on their faces. A monster's den wasn't supposed to look like this. No bones or glittering golden hoards, just the trappings of a nine-to-five and a guy *just doing his job*.

Somehow that made it so much worse.

"Marei says the panic room's on a lower floor," Drestyn said, jostling her out of her head. Her hero. Turned out the heroes weren't quite what she'd expected, either. "Can you find it?"

Anke plugged in her tablet and basked in the light of high-res silica. The whole station lay at her fingertips—every thread of the web, every system and schematic and subroutine. "With this rig? Hah. I could find a flea on a rat on the other side of the station."

"Just the rat'll do." He smiled again, that quiet, predatory smile. "I think it's time we spring a trap of our own."

CHAPTER TWENTY

SAINT

"You're sure that's it?" Saint asked, lowering his monocular from the rockhopper perched some fifteen stories higher than the hospital roof. After they'd passed Jal into the hands of the station's sawbones, it'd been the work of minutes to sneak up the maintenance stairs all the way to the roof.

Nash hovered at the edge, boots balanced so precariously on the ledge that Saint half-expected the howling wind to carry her clear off her feet to the street below—and her staring into it, unflinching, like she'd love to see it try. "As sure as I was the last time you asked," she said, more exasperated than annoyed. "And as sure as I am that I'll suplex you off this fucking roof if you ask me one more time." Maybe a *little* annoyed. She glanced back at him. "You ready?"

Saint had, until that point, resisted the urge to look down. Figured nothing good would come of it, that it'd only give him that much more heartburn about flinging himself off the roof on a jetpack and a prayer.

Instead, as he finally risked a gander, the only thing he could seem to think about was how much higher the shopping center had been and how much farther Jal'd had to fall. Wondering if he'd been afraid before he took the leap, or if there'd been no room for fear in that big heart of his.

"Still thinking about miner boy?" A question in inflection only. Nash turned to him. "Not telling you how to cope here, but we can't do this if half your head's down there on a gurney."

"My head's fine," Saint said gruffly, and he meant it. Jal was out of his hands; this wasn't. "Aim for the rockhopper, huh?"

"And try not to wet yourself," Nash agreed with a nod and a flinty shadow of a grin. Anger, *real* anger, wasn't a look Nash wore often. Saint knew exactly who it belonged to, and he wasn't sure who he felt worse for: Nash or Anke. No way it ended pretty, regardless. "It'd wreck that whole cultured badass thing you've got going. You'd never live it down."

"You'd never *let* me live it down."

"Tomato, potato."

He opened his mouth and snapped it closed again. Plenty of time for ribbing later. *And if there's not, we probably won't be alive to miss it.* Success or death was actually a pretty freeing way to work; it was *living* with his mistakes that Saint hadn't quite mastered. *No mistakes this time,* he thought firmly. One last tug on his pack harness. One last shared look with Nash, grim and grateful, because there wasn't a soul he'd rather be on that roof with. One last breath, one last thought spared for a man who'd taken a much bigger leap just to save one sorry life, and with Nash at his side, he stepped off the ledge.

The jets punched on like a kick from a horse, defying all that would-be downward momentum and launching him suddenly, rapidly *up*. Wind roared in his ears with Nash's wild whoop—enjoying the ride or the success of her last-minute mods on the packs, who knew—as the landing pad and the rockhopper hurtled closer.

"Pull up!" Nash shouted. "Pull up! Pull up! Pull up!"

Took the second or third repeat before Saint remembered which fucking direction on the control pad was *up*, just in time to clear the edge of the landing pad. Folding his very breakable body over the very not-breakable joists would've cut their rescue mission embarrassingly short.

He shut off the jet and landed in a forward stumble as Nash eased gracefully to her feet a few paces ahead of him, already shrugging out of the straps of her pack. The bag underneath it was much less clunky, conforming to the shape of her back and nearly the same barn red as her jacket. This wasn't a stealth mission; this was a speed run.

"Don't look now," she said. "We've got company. Building security?" Uniforms and handbook-perfect posture seemed to corroborate.

"I've got a heat signature on the rockhopper as well," Eoan added over comms. "No rad-signature, though, so I expect you'll have to look farther to find Miss Ahlstrom."

Saint asked with an arched eyebrow how Nash wanted to play it, and she ticked her head toward the security guards with a smile that promised very bad days for them. Much as he'd have liked to spectate, that left the seat-warmer in the rockhopper to him. Never let it be said he didn't pull his weight.

"Stand down," Nash called to the security officers as Saint turned back to the rockhopper, unbuckling his harness to get at his own pack. The hatch started to open. Whoever was inside probably thought they'd wait out the security officers, but Saint and Nash changed things.

Your lucky day. He had half a mind to let that hatch drop, see if it was one of the fuckers from the roof and show 'em what a fair fight looked like, but it wasn't part of the plan. Unless it was Drestyn himself holding down the fort, Saint had bigger fish to fry.

So. Lucky day.

Jogging toward the ship, he shoved a hand in one of the side pockets of his pack. No feeling around necessary; he kept everything in the same damn place every damn time, because he was a stubborn man set in his ways. This pocket just happened to be where he kept the charge grenades. Always something satisfying about pulling the pin, and fucking up his shoulder hadn't wrecked his throwing arm. An overhand splitter, and the magnetized disc of the grenade stuck itself neatly to the shell of the hatch.

Three.

Two.

One.

With a flash of blue-white light, arcs of electricity ripped across the ship's hull. Surreal to think a grenade that small packed a punch that big, but even over the wind, Saint could hear the popcorn pops and sizzling cracks of frying circuits. He liked to think he heard a yelp somewhere in there, too, but it was probably just wishful thinking. Charge that high, fucker probably didn't have time to *breathe* before the lights went out.

Lucky was . . . relative.

He turned around to see Nash giving the last guard standing a poke with the end of her shock baton. Those things could be nasty, but Nash never went further than she had to. "You kill them?" he asked as she backed off, stowing her baton. The guards moved, but only with the spasming twitches of the recently electrified.

She shook her head. "You?"

"Tempted."

"I'll bet. Half-expected you to O.K. Corral it back there. Mind, I wouldn't have stopped you." She clapped him on the shoulder. "Don't worry, big guy. Plenty of catharsis inside."

Catharsis was probably asking too much. The grenade only had a thirty-minute charge, though, so if nothing else, seat-warmer would be waiting on him when they wrapped up. "Then let's get it done."

First stop: the security panel waiting just inside the door. Saint kept watch while Nash took her plasma torch to the wall. Not that a few dozen offices needed much watching—and not that the weak-ass lock on the panel needed a *plasma torch*—but it felt good getting back to old habits.

With Nash in her element wrists-deep in wiring, that left Saint on sentry. He smiled at a well-dressed passerby ambling down the hall with a cup of coffee, angling himself with his holster, hopefully, just out of sight. "Maintenance," he said. While they weren't going for *stealth*, he figured they should aim for a sweet spot between that and *armed intruders inciting a panic*.

The prim brunette passerby didn't look like she believed him, which was fair; he wasn't trying especially hard, and acting was a weak spot in his professional repertoire. She also didn't look like she cared enough to question it, though. Worked for him.

Seemed to work for Nash, too. Or would've, if she'd deigned to notice anything but her plasma torch. "There we are," Nash said as the panel, predictably, popped open without much effort. A few twists of her multitool and she nudged the control pad out of the way to expose the tangle of circuits underneath with an aggrieved "*Cable management,* people. Slobs." She made quick work of it anyway, stripping away pieces of insulation with quick flicks of her wrist until she could patch Eoan's remote access fob into the circuits. "Best security in the frontier my fine tattooed ass."

"Wait, you have an ass tat?" Ah, partnership: always learning and growing.

She flashed him a devilish grin. "Wouldn't you like to know?" Then she flipped on the fob and rolled back on her heels. "You're patched in on this end, Cap."

"Good to go on this one as well," Eoan replied down the line. Good. If anybody could sneak around a building's systems with a hacker like Anke running interference, it'd be Eoan. See how clever she *really* was, when Eoan was on their guard and on their game. Eoan had a little squaring of their own to do. "No word yet on Ranger Jalsen, but I'll keep you apprised where I can." *Where it won't distract you and get one of you killed* was what they meant, so Saint didn't expect an update anytime soon. Probably for the best.

He rolled his shoulders. *Stay on mission.* "Where's our heading, then?"

"Reviewing the floor plans now," said Eoan, and with any other captain, Saint would've settled himself in for a wait. With Eoan, though, Nash barely had her multitool back in her pocket before they said, "The administrator access terminal is on the fifty-third floor of the building, in Otho Yarden's office. If I were attempting to infect the station with the Deadworld Code, that would be my entry point."

And if I were attempting to murder the shit out of Yarden, that'd be my first stop, Saint added to himself. "Floor fifty-three it is. And we're where?"

"Floor twenty-eight," Eoan reported, matter-of-factly.

Nash groaned and rocked herself to her feet. "I was just thinking I wanted to do five hundred stairs today. What about elevators?"

"All stopped at the subbasement level. I expect that's Miss Ahlstrom's doing. Which means an override could be . . . risky."

"Still think we should've taken our chances with the windows," Nash said. *Liar.* She'd seen the same specs on the silica panes as he had. Even if she could've rigged the jets to get them up that high, Anke and Drestyn would've finished whatever they'd come to do before they even got a *breathing hole* in that glass. A sigh, and she tightened her ponytail and started resolutely down the hall. "Fine, then I vote shaft. With the elevators down, they'll be watching the stairs, and I can get us up the cables in a few minutes, tops."

Saint trailed behind her, trying not to look as out of place as he felt. Give him a battlefield. Give him an abandoned Trust installation crawling with armed-to-the-teeth scavs. Give him anything but a fuck-load of oblivious office workers and a ticking time bomb. "Drestyn's got at least one more guy, though," he said. "If I'm him, I'm covering the stairs *and* the elevators and taking potshots at anybody I see. All they have to do is hold position long enough for Anke to do her thing."

"So how do we get 'em not to see us?" Nash said.

A thoughtful pause down the line, and then Eoan offered, "By giving them something else to look at." And nope, he didn't like that tone at all. "Saint, dear, don't suppose you're up for some cardio?"

Something told him the *cardio* wouldn't be the objectionable part of whatever plan Eoan had cooked up in that processor of theirs. "I'm gonna hate this, aren't I?"

"Probably," they said. "Are you in?"

Ah, hell. Wasn't like he kept in shape 'cause he liked working out. "All right, Cap," he said, bracing. "What'd you have in mind?"

ANKE

"What's the holdup?" Rigby called from the other side of the lift bay. He'd posted up on the stairs, Marei was covering the lifts, and Drestyn kept watch by Anke.

The *tap, tap, tap* of her fingers against her tablet keyboard was the only sound on the whole floor, and Anke really wished she could throw on some music or something. Ease the tension. Disguise the occasional anxious stomach gurgles she kept passing off as a squeaky chair. Every time she thought of music, though, her mind drifted to guitar refrains floating through a packed galley, dancing between the tables and laughing between verses of some half-forgotten miners' song.

So, music was out.

"The terminal security's like a seven-layer bean dip," she shot back. "Biometrics, guacamole, password—which, shockingly, isn't *password*."

"You tried *password*?" Rigby said.

"You always try *password*. It's, like, the cardinal rule of hacking." *Duh.* "And you always try turning it off and turning it on again, and if all else fails, you take it out and blow on it." Definitely babbling again, but she was so close to cracking that last layer—*would that be the cheese or the olives?*—that she could taste it.

Somehow, after everything she'd already done, she still wasn't a hundred percent sure she could handle what came next.

"Well, whatever the fuck you're doing, do it quick," Rigby said sharply.

"Thanks, because I was totally dragging my feet before you said something." She'd have rolled her eyes, but it would've meant taking them off her screen, and she was so close. Everything they needed waited right at the end of the next string of—

"Hah!" She whipped her chair around. Victory spin! Only she realized halfway through that sudden movements with three heavily armed, increasingly agitated agitators probably wasn't the best idea. *Rein it in.* She pulled herself back to the console and bumped her glasses up her nose. "We're in."

Under different circumstances, she might've been offended by Drestyn's skeptical eyebrow tick. *Ye of little faith.* Now, though, she was too busy watching every system in the station unfold across the screen. Every thread of that massive web, hers for the plucking.

The triumph was short-lived.

It sounded like something heavy dropping in the stairwell—a dense, muffled *bang* echoing its way up to them, and another, and another. *Like a bowling ball*, she thought absurdly. Bouncing down the stairs, *bang, bang, bang.* Except they didn't get farther away each time; they got closer. Louder. Crisper.

"Gunshots," Rigby barked. "Fuck, they're gonna bring every uniform in the building."

Yeah, gun makes more sense. "Pulling up the camera now—"

"No," Drestyn said.

"No?" She glanced over and almost did a double take when she saw him standing right beside her. Seriously, how did people do that?

Drestyn shook his head, eyes dark and granite-hard as they studied the monitors. "We're here for Yarden. He's the priority."

"Right. One fat cat coming up," she said. "But, uh, the gunshots."

Of course, Drestyn had an answer for that, too. "Marei, double up Rigby on the stairs. You see something—"

"Shoot something," Marei finished for him, nodding and disappearing deeper into the lift lobby, presumably to join Rigby at the stairwell door. "Still clear up here, Dres," she called.

He acknowledged her with a hum, but ninety-something percent of his attention stayed focused on the screens over Anke's shoulders. He'd made it clear from the start that he was after Yarden. In fact, she'd banked on the whole *corporate malfeasance killed my brother* thing when she'd reached out to him in the first place; in case he thought, like her supervisors had, that saving the universe was too soft a sales pitch. She hadn't really grasped how much he meant it until then, though. That gentlemanly veneer had vanished, and something honed—something *ruthless*—had taken its place.

Ruthless is good, she told herself. *Fight fire with fire.* She just had to figure out where to point it. "If I were technical security for a panic room, where would I be? That wasn't an actual question, by the way. Just talking aloud, you know—thinking. *Thinking* aloud." *Please, stop talking.* Although, she was pretty sure she could've been reciting Shakespearean soliloquies, for how much Drestyn seemed to care. Either he'd tuned her out, or he'd accepted the rambling as the cost of doing business with Anke.

For the record, she was totally worth it.

"Here kitty, kitty, kitty," she muttered, as Rigby or Marei fired their first shot from the stairwell. *Tick tock, tick tock.* With an unfamiliar system, it wasn't like she could prep beforehand. Not a lot of *how to hack a space station* manuals out there. But she charged ahead anyway, barreling feverishly through system after system until she pressed somewhere it hurt. *There you are.* "Me-*ow*." She shook her head. "Wow, nope. That was weird. Don't like that. Let's rewind that back and pretend—"

"Anke." Drestyn didn't yell, but he didn't really have to. Intensity, not volume.

"*Drestyn*," she retorted, as the noise down the hall picked up. Sounded like things were getting zesty out there, and a harsh curse from Rigby made her fingers trip over the keyboard a little before she got back on target, hammering through one last internal firewall and *voila!* "Behold." She smacked the last key harder than she had to, and Drestyn flinched as the bookshelf on the back wall started to slide sideways. Behind it, a doorway opened on a narrow, plunging shaft. "Oh, my God," she said. "An actual secret entrance behind an actual moving bookshelf."

Drestyn jogged over to it, bracing a hand on either side of the doorway to peer down. Long, *long* drop. By the schematics she'd pulled up, that shaft went all the way down to the subbasements. "He's down there?"

"The panic room is, for sure," she said. "Which is kind of genius, if you think about it. Somebody's coming, you just pop downstairs and leave them standing at the tippy-top like a bunch of morons. Not that we're morons. Here." Best way to make sure they had Yarden was to get eyes inside. Fortunately, a control freak like Yarden couldn't have a panic room without a full communications system. Eyes, ears. "Say hello to Big Brother." With a few more taps, she had a video feed up on the monitor closest to Drestyn.

There he sat: Otho Yarden, in the flat-screen flesh. Was that a drink in his hand? And a half-empty bottle on the arm of his chair, like he just *knew* something bad was coming and didn't care to remember the finer details. "You know, that stuff'll rot your liver." Anke was *totally* petty enough to enjoy the way Yarden startled, sloshing blur—which probably cost more than she made in a year in her Guild programming gig—over his hand and narrowly missing the crisp lilac of his band-collar shirt.

He looked so . . . normal. It wasn't like Anke had never seen his face, but somehow she remembered him *rattier*. His features more severe, his salt-and-pepper hair blacker and oilier. She'd seen millions of men just like this one, though: five-o'clock shadow, eye bags, and nascent wrinkles across his forehead and around his mouth. Fit like he went to the gym but half-assed it, and a little bunny-toothed, and she hated it. Hated that it made her wonder how many of those millions of others could commit the kinds of atrocities this man had done. It didn't seem right, that some wolves could fit so easily in sheep's clothing.

This time, she was acutely aware of Drestyn coming closer. He closed the gap in a few quick strides, hand closing over the back of her chair with a creak of complaining pleather. "You look surprised, Yarden." If he felt anything other than *resolve* like the grinding bones of a clenched fist, she couldn't hear it in his voice. "It's over now. We found you."

"*We?*" Yarden's lip twisted into what could almost be called a smile—and a friendly one, at that. Like he'd all but invited them, and would they please wipe their feet before they made themselves too comfortable?

The chair creaked again, as Drestyn's grip tightened. "You know who we are."

Yarden's narrow mouth shaped an *ah,* like a revelation. As if he hadn't scurried underground the second he'd seen them coming. "Of course," he said. "Our friends from Noether." He had a voice made for conference comms and press releases, crisp and conversational. "The shipping depot as well, if I'm not mistaken. You've been busy." He raised his glass to his lips, downing the rest of the blur.

He promptly poured another.

"If you know who we are, then you know why we're here," Drestyn pressed. Straight to the point. Small talk was for people who had time, not an active shoot-out in the stairwell and more trouble on the way. Every second counted. "You know what we have, you know what we want, and you know what we'll do to get it. So cut the shit and admit what you've done, and nobody else has to die."

That was the upside to a clever bad guy: saved a lot of time on exposition.

Downside? They were all arrogant dicks.

"No," said Yarden.

"No? What do you mean, *no*?" Anke snapped. She knew she wasn't supposed to let him rile her up. The guy killed Drestyn's *brother*, and Drestyn stood there beside her stone-faced and stoic, like losing his shit never even crossed his mind.

She wasn't like Drestyn, though. She couldn't look into that smiling, normal, blur-blotched face and pretend she wasn't thinking about dead, decaying worlds. About buildings, warehouses, *planets* full of people withered or rotted or shot dead because some bigwig executive in a lilac shirt decided lives were less important than the bottom line. She looked at him, and she saw *them*.

When she pulled the drive from her pocket, the Trust's perfect killer in its prison of circuits and steel . . . when she held it up to the camera in her cold, unsteady hands, she wanted him to see them, too. She wanted him to imagine walking through a warehouse of ghosts, through a half-finished mausoleum, through a mass grave stretching endlessly across the horizon, as far as the eye could see.

She wanted him to be *afraid*.

"It works on life support systems, you know," she said, softly. "I've seen it." Poor Eoan. Poor Saint. They were victims, too; she just couldn't decide whose. "It vented all the oxygen in the ship. Electrified the floors. I've never actually been electrocuted, but I *have* checked suffocation off my bucket list. Not fun." Choking in the captain's chair of that rockhopper, pinned down and wondering if the bombs would take her before her brain starved. She'd come so far, survived so much, to reach this moment. It didn't matter that her hand shook, or that her chest felt tight, or that the gunshots in the stairs got louder by the second; one way or another, she'd do what she came to do. "I know you think the Trust is worth killing for, but is it really worth dying for?"

For a beat, Yarden said nothing. He set his glass aside and leaned forward, elbows on his knees and hands steepled thoughtfully under his chin. Calculating, considering, until finally: "Is that what you think?" he asked. "You plug that in, and I die?"

"That's the idea," she said, unflinching. She was out of her depth on a lot of things. The violence, the politics, the big pictures. Not this, though. "Unless you tell us everything you know about the Deadworld Code—who designed it, who ordered it made, where it's been used, where it's *going* to be used— everything you know, and everything you *think* you know." A confession. Intel like that would be enough that even the Union couldn't look the other way, and more importantly, it'd give them a chance to get out ahead of it. No more geocides. No more mass graves. "You tell us that, this drive goes back in my pocket, you keep breathing happy, nonmurderous air, and—and I'm sorry, why are we still smiling? Did I miss something?" She glanced back at Drestyn. "Does he think I missed something?"

"I think he does," Drestyn replied, and his expression might not have changed, but something happened in his eyes. Kind of vicious. Kind of satisfying.

Anke spun back around in her chair. "You know, I think I see what's happening here," she said, like *duh*. "See, Otho here— can I call you Otho? Otho thinks we're threatening to infect the *station*. Which, gasp, he's fine with. I mean, yeah. Shit-ton of people would die, but this guy, he gets to ride it out in his cozy little hidey-hole. Can you imagine the corporate kudos when he phones home and tells 'em the good news? Like, wow. Can you say *merit bonus*? Bet they'd even throw in a promotion, get him back home to the fam in the center spiral. You know," she said over her shoulder to Drestyn, "if you can get past the mass ho-micide and the butt-puckering heinousness of it all, it's a pretty sweet gig." The more she talked, the tighter Yarden's smile got. The paler his face. The straighter his back.

"Yeah," she said. "We know about the panic room's life sup-port systems. Whole station could flatline and you'd still be totally hunky-dory. But you know," she added, leaning forward with the drive wiggling between her index finger and thumb. "Works the other way, too, pumpkin. So let me rephrase: you talk, or I bypass all the station's systems and ram this virus straight up your panic room's ass. You die ugly on candid cam-era, and maybe that makes our jobs a little harder trying to pin all this back on your bosses, but"—she shrugged—"it'll be a labor of love."

In the faint reflection on the screen, she saw Drestyn's eyebrows twitch. Yeah, she'd surprised herself, too. A month ago, Anke couldn't even swing a convincing glare; and now, she threatened a man's life like it was nothing, because countless more were on the line.

She'd changed in ways she hadn't even believed she could. She'd met a girl who could take on the universe with a plasma torch and a grin and sipped coffee with a soldier whose only cause was the people he loved. She'd cracked killer code with an AI more human than most people she'd met, and watched a lost man find himself, even if he never got to make it home. Each one taught her something. *Gave* her something.

At the end of it all, she hoped it was worth what it'd cost them.

"So," she said, staring at the man on the screen and all the graves that stood behind him, and wondering how many would stand behind her when all was said and done, "what's it gonna be?"

CHAPTER TWENTY-ONE

NASH

Nash had just about had her fill of elevator shafts. They were kind of cool, sure—the engineer in her got a kick out of the pulleys and counterweights. People had played around with magnets and suction over the years, but some kinds of tech just worked, so there wasn't much reason to mess with it. Between Noether's underground, though, and floors twenty-eight through fifty of the Lewaro Administrative Building, even Nash's inner engineering geek had gotten more than its fill.

They were liminal spaces, elevator shafts. Dusty little pocket dimensions, near identical from one to the next. Hoistways and buffers, cables and rails. Every sound echoing endlessly up and down, and the musty bitterness of old grease and ever-present *damp*.

Also? Her arms were fucking tired.

"Don't know why you bitched about the plan, Saint," she panted over the comms as her boots and gloves *clang, clang, clang*ed on the maintenance ladder rungs. "Pretty sure I'm the one getting shafted on this one."

Saint let out a bark of laughter that, coming from anyone else, probably would've sounded out of place amid the gunfire and shouting. But that was his element: a steady presence in the chaos. It'd only taken him a few shots to get the security officers coming, and after that, the fire fueled itself. Drestyn's people shooting down at the Trust officers, the officers shooting up at

Drestyn's people, and neither hitting the other because the stair angles were a marksman's nightmare.

Meanwhile, somewhere in the middle, Saint methodically picked his way up the stairs, all single-minded focus and a knack for dodging crossfire. "Puns are the lowest form of wit," he said.

"I thought it was funny," Eoan chimed in.

"Thank you." Cap had her back.

"Of course, dear," said Eoan. "Status report?"

"Considering other employment." Saint swore, and Nash couldn't tell if she heard a body dropping, or just Saint ducking for cover. "*Strongly* considering."

"Shooty McBlastinshit complaining about an old-fashioned shoot-out? Say it ain't so." Nash hooked an arm around the ladder vertical and turned, surveying the gap between her and the elevator doors. *I'm just a girl, standing in front of a bone-shattering drop, wishing I'd skipped fewer arm days.* "I'm here," she said. "You got eyes on Drestyn's people?"

A pause, and what sounded like the fizzle of a piezoelectric round dangerously close to Saint's earpiece. "I've got two on the top landing," he said. "No sign of Anke or Drestyn, though, and they've still got all the cameras. Don't take any chances."

"Right, because historically *I'm* the risky one." Nobody doctored the doctor; she preferred to know what she was walking into, and she packed the tech to make it happen. This time, it was a little square of opaque polymer. No bigger than a tab of gum, but Nash pitied any dumbass who made that mistake; a quick squeeze, and eight thin filament legs unspooled around the edges. Same material as her augments—high tensile, full range of sensory feedback. "Okay, Chiclet, show me what we're working with." Off it went, skittering from her palm around the edge of the shaft. An incident ray sensor and light-emitting polymer meant she lost sight of it, camouflaged against the grease- and dust-caked metal, but she could *feel* it. All those sensory inputs, fed directly into her augments, and it wasn't that she could *see* what the microdrone saw when it wriggled between the doors; she just knew it. As if it'd just skipped her eyes completely and encoded itself directly into her brain. A déjà vu sort of feeling—took a while to get used to, but handy.

"Coast is clear," she said, and with a quick shake of each limb to get the blood pumping again, she rocked back and launched herself across the open shaft. It wasn't a very forgiving leap, with barely a half-dec ledge under the door and a thin beam on either side to grab onto, but she made it. *Suck it, gravity.* "Nearly there."

"Hurry," Saint said. "Rent-a-guns're starting to fall back. Don't think they're digging the shooting gallery."

"Yeah, well, some days you're the bottle, some days you're the BB." She reached back and slid her baton from her bag, flicking it to full extension and wedging the tip in the gap of the doors. "Just another minute. Step up your decoy game over there."

Saint snorted down the line. "Sure, why not? Highly decorated sniper playing clay pigeon. Really feel like I'm living up to my full potential here."

"Your mother would be so—" She shoved the baton and managed to pry the doors open far enough to dive through and book it for the stairwell. "—*proud*," she grunted as she slammed the open door shut. Dead bolt, check, but she slapped a charge grenade on the handle for good measure. Door was too light to be solid metal, probably layered fiber and some kind of thermosetting resin. Not conductive. That handle, though, was a different story.

The grenade beeped a warning, but it was a few seconds too late for whoever shouted on the other side. That *thump* sounded awfully person-shaped. "I get one?"

"Sounds like," Saint said. "Forgot to say *clear,* Doc. Hippocratic something something, do no harm."

She snorted, jogging back down the elevator bay toward the

hall. Chiclet mapped out the floor ahead of her, but it felt like she'd mapped it out herself. Knew the hall before she turned the corner, knew the conference room behind the translucent doors before she passed them. "That's patients. I don't *have* patients."

"Don't I know it."

"With a *T*, you dick," she growled.

Eoan didn't have a throat to clear, but as always, they made do. "One down, four security officers and an agitator with the high ground to go." Their voice sounded weird. False-cheery, and yeah, all their tones and timbres were, by definition, artificial, but this one sounded forced. Made Nash wonder if they'd heard something on Jal, or if it was something else. That indescribable *shift* she'd noticed earlier . . . Eoan had never liked putting Saint and Nash in danger, but it'd never tripped them up before.

What the hell happened to you on Noether? she wanted to ask, but no; better to focus. Better to let *Saint* focus, too, on keeping Drestyn's other friend occupied, because as soon as they figured out the rest of the door wasn't zappy, it wouldn't hold them long. "Saint, be ready. As soon as Nash gets cover and a visual on Drestyn, we'll need you up here. I'll disable the charge grenade when you're close."

"Do you have to?" Nash teased, a little breathlessly, and Saint's snort nearly disappeared into the fizzle and pop of gunfire behind the door, echoing louder and louder through his comms. He was gaining ground. Getting ready. *Good,* but maybe not good enough. "Gonna put a rush on that, McBlastinshit," she said. "I found Drestyn. Anke too. Got them in the office, at Yarden's console, but they definitely know I'm here." If by some miracle they hadn't heard the door slam or their person get zapped, they were still bound to see her on the cameras. "Think Drestyn's headed this way." Silent as the grave, and still out of sight around the corner, but her little fly on the wall was hard to fool. He probably figured he'd corner Nash in the lobby. Stairwell was covered, and the elevator shaft was a death sentence. Straight line all the way down—somebody like Dresytn could make that shot with his eyes closed.

"Cover?" Eoan asked. Fretting was usually more Saint's gig, but it sounded like he had his hands full.

"Working on it," she said, crossing to the other side of the lobby. She had the whole floor etched in her head, every corner and cranny imprinted in her mind's eye like something from a dream. Perception without sense. Without sight, sound, feel, just feedback filtered straight through her augments. Wasn't practical for big spaces or quick jobs, but with a bit of a head start and only three rooms to scope, couldn't beat it. "Should be right about . . ." She trailed her fingers along the wall until her fingertips caught the barest trace of a seam in the mock-wood panels. "Here." She pushed, and something clicked soft and satisfying in the wall behind her fingers. Which, as she'd guessed, wasn't a wall at all.

The panel swung open into the conference room beyond, and Nash wasted no time ducking in and toppling the wet bar beside it for a makeshift barricade. "Hospitality entrance." For all the staff comings and goings they didn't want popping up in a vid conference. Aftermarket, so it wasn't on the floor plans, and camouflaged to keep from disrupting the carefully manicured design of the room, but like she said: her augments were a lot harder to fool than her other five senses. Chiclet caught the shifting airflow, and she made an educated guess.

Shiny crystal decanters shattered, slicking the floor with blur, as she scrambled over to the conference table. *No time, no time.* She threw her full weight into it, and after the first lurch from *object at rest* to *object in motion,* it slid across the conference room to wedge neatly against the hallway doors.

Made it.

The way Drestyn moved reminded her of Saint. No trace of Saint's military background, but he had the same efficiency. Fluid, from the heel-toe roll of his boots to the steady sweep of his gunsight over the hall. So completely in control of his body that she'd barely registered his eyes on her through the translucent hologlass before his gun sighted straight at her. Two shots, head and chest—or they would've been, if they hadn't pinged off the hologlass with the rainbow ripple of a layered screen.

"You knew it was bulletproof, right?" Eoan said, though they didn't sound sure.

Nash smiled.

Drestyn's jaw twitched.

The race was on.

The hospitality entrance had a twin on the other side of the conference room, straight into Yarden's office. Coffee, food delivery . . . she tried not to think of the other uses for a secret door into a sleazeball's penthouse office as she shouldered it open. *And the hacker makes two,* she thought, because there she was. Anke had claimed Yarden's desk, hunched over the controls like they belonged to her. Nash wasn't even sure she heard Nash come in; there was something on the screen, someone talking over the speakers. Male, unaccented, unless *private school legacy* counted as an accent. Nash's chest squeezed at the sight of her, but she shook it off hard as the sound of fast-approaching footsteps reached from the other side of the office. Still no time, but she'd come prepared.

"Cap, how about some rain?" Because Anke had the building's security on lock, and much as Nash would've paid to see a cyber smackdown between her and Cap, playtime was over. *Fight the enemy where they aren't.*

She'd patched Cap into the life support systems instead.

With a hiss of pressured pipes, a half-dozen fire suppression sprinklers dropped from the ceiling, spewing cascades of water across the office. Shelves, desk, floors, people—a half second, and everything was drenched.

Drestyn's boots splashed across the threshold. "Stop." Nash didn't need to look at him to know that Drestyn had her in his sights. That was definitely a locked, loaded, and fully pissed-off *stop.* "Drop the weapon."

"Don't think you want me to do that," Nash said. "It's a shock baton, smiley. Society might've moved past the days of water-soluble electronics, but there's enough amps in this thing to short the whole system, and we're standing in a giant conductor." She held her baton out over the shimmering surface of the tile. A threat and a promise. "I drop it, you drop me—either way, you'll have a damn hard time with your hostage situation when all your tech's fried to a—"

"Wait!" Anke stood so fast from her chair that she sent it rolling backward into the bookshelves. Eyes wide behind water-spotted glasses, chest heaving, face pale . . . she looked *stricken.* Scared. "Both of you, wait! Nash." She hissed Nash's name so urgently that Nash had to listen. In spite of everything, in spite of the hurt and the betrayal and the gnarled tangle of briars squeezing between her ribs, she couldn't have possibly done otherwise. "You can't fry the systems."

"All evidence to the contrary."

"No," Anke said, but it sounded like a plea. "You don't understand. We missed something. All of us, we—"

Even Drestyn looked confused, though his aim never wavered. "What are you talking about?"

"Yarden." The sprinklers plastered Anke's hair to her face, rivulets of water streaming like tears down her cheeks. She looked so small, there at that console. So small, but so goddamn *sure.* "He said—you can't fry the computers, all right? If you do . . . Nash, if you do," she said on a shuddering breath, "the whole station's going to die."

ANKE

Nash didn't believe her. Anke could tell, could see the doubt clouding those clear eyes, and she couldn't blame her. *I wouldn't believe me, either.* Not after what she'd done.

She didn't have time for disbelief, though. None of them did.

"I know," she said. "I know, and I'm not asking you to trust me. Just listen." She had Yarden muted, figured he didn't need to be privy to the topside drama, but it was the work of a couple of keystrokes to get his mics live again. "Say it again," she told him, dragging her chair back under her and sliding back up to the console. She had work to do.

"What?"

"What you told me just now. Say it again." *Where they can hear you.* Leave it to Drestyn to be halfway down the hall when shit hit the fan. Nash was a problem, yeah, but this . . . this changed everything. "Now!"

Any other time, she might've enjoyed the way Yarden's composure had slipped. Hair a mess, shirt collar unbuttoned and dark with sweat. Sure, he puffed his chest and kept his chin up high, but fear had a funny way of bleeding through.

If only they weren't as boned as he was.

Yarden cleared his throat. "I said we could help each other. We—"

"No!" Anke snapped. "Cut the shit and tell them what you told me! The fire."

"The what?" Nash said. Skepticism aside, it seemed she at least had Nash's attention. A good start.

"Fire," said Yarden tightly. He had the same ticking clock in his head that Anke did, but the timing wouldn't matter if Anke couldn't get everyone on board. She couldn't do this without them. "Officially, it's a demolition system, in the event the station is ever decommissioned or condemned. Do you have any idea how expensive it is to scrap and ship an entire station to a waste processor? *Prohibitively.* But the Union penalties for abandoning large spacecrafts is absurd. Just a blatant grab for capital, if you ask—"

"We didn't." A faint line drew itself between Drestyn's eyebrows. Nothing else in his expression changed, not his grip on his gun or the set of his jaw, but those eyebrows always gave him away. "You're wasting time. Anke, plug in the drive."

"No, no, wait!" There it was—that fear she'd seen in Yarden, bubbling to the surface. "You do that, you're killing yourselves, too. The demolition device feeds into the station's life support, floods the entire station with a highly combustible gas. One spark, and *poof.* Enough heat and pressure that Lewaro will be nothing but calx and ash. And," he added, "this panic pod. When the demolition protocol triggers, this pod will automatically eject from the station. Separate life support system, enough supplies to sustain a ten-soul crew."

"The Trust is going to detonate the station?" Nash shook her head. "Of course they are. Couldn't let you shitbags have all the fun."

"Have all the—wait." Anke paused to bump her glasses back up her nose. *All the better to gape at you with, my dear.* Because seriously, no way. "You thought we were gonna nuke the whole station?" Something in her shriveled at the thought, repulsed. "We weren't—we were never—" Full sentences would probably help. "We knew Yarden had a panic room. Practically threw rocks at his window and shouted, *Go hide, Mister Rich Evil Dude.* The copy of the Deadworld Code is for him— preprogrammed the console and everything. You plug that drive in, the virus goes straight down to Yarden. Full stop." She could hardly believe she had to ask, but, "You really think I would do something like that?"

"I don't know what you would do," Nash said. "I don't know

you. I don't *want* to know you." And it was fair. Anke deserved so much worse than a few barbed words, but God, that didn't make them hurt any less. Especially coming from *her*.

She took a breath. "I'm not asking you to trust me. Or to trust Yarden," because she wasn't where she ranked against him, but it didn't seem smart to assume. "I've opened up the security network; Eoan's free to check it out themself. But they'll tell you the same thing I'm telling you: the countdown's already started. If we don't stop the demo, this whole station's going to blow."

"Cap?" Nash asked, quieter; meant for her earpiece, Anke thought, and not the room proper. Anke had only been on the *Ambit* a couple of weeks, but she still half-expected to hear Eoan's answer floating from the room's speakers. Instead, silence, until the sprinklers suddenly halted and Nash's shoulders fell. Forced calm and Nash's usual aplomb—getting her game face on. "All right," she said, so Anke assumed that meant it all checked out. For better or for worse, they'd decided she wasn't lying. "So how do we stop it?"

"You can't stop it," Yarden snapped. "You really think the Trust wouldn't build in fail-safes? You kill it at the console, it'll trigger manually at the life support pumps. Even I don't have the key to abort. Your best chance is this pod, which stops *being* a chance the second it becomes nonviable. Do you understand what I'm telling you?"

Anke opened her mouth, but Drestyn spoke first. "How much time do we have?" Even-keel and a level head; if Anke didn't know better, she'd wonder if he even understood what was happening. The Trust was gonna atomize the station with them inside, and the only safe space was the panic room they planned to infect with the Deadworld Code.

But she *did* know better. Drestyn understood perfectly. He knew better than most what the Trust was capable of, the kind of damage they could inflict. They'd already blown up his world once. He just wasn't afraid of the fire anymore.

"It triggered as soon as we picked you up on facial rec. There's a programmed half hour to make arrangements for evac."

"Half an hour for you to get your ass in the clear." Nash shook her head, though Anke had already killed the camera feeds from the office. Somehow Anke didn't think it was for Yarden's benefit. "Just when you think you company pricks can't get any worse."

"Say what you like. This panic room is the only thing that can save you from a no-doubt promising future as star dust, and that virus—"

"The Trust's virus," said Drestyn. "Say it, Yarden. Own it or die with it. I won't tell you which I'd rather."

Clearly, Yarden knew which *he'd* rather. "The Trust's virus," he ground out. His chin quivered as he spoke, as if it took every muscle in his body to say the words, mouth pursed as if the taste of them soured his tongue. He'd held the company line this long and made out like a king. Probably hard to break the habit, even to save his own skin. "The Deadworld Code. Call it whatever the fuck you want. If you sic it on the life support systems of this pod, you're not just killing me; you're killing yourselves. And then what's the point of this whole *intrepid* scheme of yours? No proof. No one left to tell the story. A terrible accident to be sure, reparations to be paid to grieving families, and the Union will get its piece of the payout, of course. But the tide of progress rolls on, as it always has. As it always will."

It was a hell of a speech, Anke would give him that, but Drestyn was unmoved. He was mercury, liquid and cool. "Did you get all that?" he asked Anke.

She managed a stiff, confused nod. "Backed up to my GLASS." For whatever good it would do them. Somehow she suspected her replacement tablet wouldn't survive a thorough immolation any better than she would.

"A confession. *That's* what you're worried about?" Nash started toward the console, but the sharp crack of gunfire stopped her short. A vase on the shelf behind her exploded in a shower of painted clay, but a breath to the right and that bullet would've hit meat. "What the fuck is your problem?" Nash snapped.

Drestyn's finger lay steady on the trigger. "Yarden's right about one thing. We die here without a word to the rest of the spiral, the truth dies with us. Nothing changes. But by my count, we have twelve minutes to ignition."

"Eleven minutes, forty-three seconds," Anke said, uneasily.

He acknowledged her with a nod. "We may not be able to stop the demo, but Anke, if you can crack the signal jammer, we can still get the word out. A comm packet with the Deadworld Code script, Yarden's confession, coordinates for the other planets—whatever you can put together and ship out. If we die, we don't die for nothing."

"Nobody has to die!" Nash said. "Any time she'd spend cracking the jammer is time she could spend hacking the demolition protocol."

"And then what? The fail-safes kick in, and the station burns anyway," Drestyn said, gun still leveled at the center of Nash's chest.

Nash didn't even blink. "So we stop the fail-safes, too."

"You *try*. Maybe you pull it off, but far more likely, you waste the only chance we have to save *millions* just to make yourselves feel better," Drestyn said, not without sympathy. He gestured broadly to the window. "I know those people out there don't deserve to die, Anke. You don't deserve it. Your friends and mine, none of them deserve it." Anke couldn't help noticing he didn't put himself on that list. "Neither did those people on Noether, or the trading depot, or the countless other planets that have or will fall prey to this monster they've created, and I wish it were simpler. I wish we could save everyone, I do." She knew he meant it. The way his eyes shined, the fervor in his voice—he wasn't an evil man, or a cruel man. Just a practical one. "But there's a reason they call it *sacrifice*."

Anke didn't know what to say to that. How could she make that kind of choice? To weigh all the lives on the station with all the lives they could save by taking the Deadworld Code off the board.

Fortunately, Nash found her voice just fine. "Fuck you." Brisk and razor-edged, completely uncaring of Drestyn's gun sighted down her sternum. "You want to let a hundred thousand people burn because you *think* it's for the greater good. That ain't sacrifice, sunshine; that's playing god." The words were sharp, meant to cut; but underneath, Anke felt like Nash was the one bleeding. "We know better. All of us—we've *seen* sacrifice, real sacrifice. It's personal, and it's messy, and it's painful. It's cutting out your own heart to keep someone else's beating. Giving up the one thing that means more to you than anything else, because you can't bear to watch someone else lose what matters to *them*. It's throwing yourself off a goddamn ledge"—her fists clenched, baton trembling faintly with the force of her grip—"not knowing if you'll survive the fall, not knowing if it'll help, not knowing if it'll be *worth it*, and doing it anyway, because it's the right fucking thing to do.

"So if we're talking sacrifice here, Anke," and for a handful of seconds, Anke and Nash were the only ones in the room. The gravity of Nash's stare, the *intensity,* gripped Anke's core and held tight, and she wasn't even sure she breathed as Nash finished, "Then you know what we have to do."

We. Maybe it was just a slip of the tongue, but Nash chose her words with the same brutal precision she did everything else. It meant something to her.

It meant something for Anke, too.

It's not too late to do the right thing. A ferocious oversimplification. The *right* thing was like Schrödinger's cat; you really only knew what was what when the lid came off. Truth was, she didn't know the right thing to do.

But she knew the wrong thing. It lived in that horrible, sinking pit in her stomach when she'd watched Jal disappear over the roof's edge, and she felt it now, with her fingers poised over the keys, ready to either hack the jammers or take a crack at the station's self-destruct.

Right or wrong. Alive or dead. Time to open that box.

"I'm in."

Drestyn already seemed to know the choice she'd make. Perceptive, decisive—good traits in a partner, not so good in a partner-turned-nemesis. Did people even have nemesises anymore? Nemeses? Bloody hell, he was fast. He'd crossed half the distance to the desk by her first keystroke and closed it completely by the second, and she didn't even have time to wonder what he was gonna do before he'd already done it.

The GLASS disappeared from her hands, the Deadworld drive was in the port, and Drestyn—

"Holy shit," she gasped as Drestyn dove through the open doorway behind the bookshelf. The doorway to the panic room shaft. The *plummet to your death* doorway. There he went, leaping through it like he was about to tuck in for the most badass double-somersault cannonball. For a heart-stopping second, Anke was certain she'd hear the meaty, vaguely squishy *thwap* of body meeting floor at terminal velocity. *Again.* She started to brace, but a beat later a *click* echoed up from the shaft, trailed by the friction-y *zrrrrpt* of a zip line clip on a woven cable.

So, not a picketer pancake.

Nash stared at her flatly when she turned back around. "No, you're right," Anke said, though Nash hadn't actually said anything. Hadn't really needed to. Her expression, as the saying went, contained *volumes*. Anke bit her lip, dragging the console keyboard into the space her GLASS used to be and picking up the superspeed scripting right where she'd left off. "Totally see my mistake. Should've been, like, three hundred percent subtler on the double cross. Triple cross? Honestly, I'm having a really hard time keeping up here."

"Whose fault is that?"

Anke glanced up over the rims of her glasses. "Ouch." Nash's very determined, very *drippy* face held no sympathy, though. "I deserve that. I deserve way worse, but at the risk of sounding like I'm trying to avoid the conversation, would now be a good time to point out that Drestyn loosed the Deadworld Code in Yarden's hidey-hole and we have"—a quick glance at the screen—"less than nine minutes now to stop the station from going boom?"

"So un-loose it," Nash said. "Yarden can't die. He knows more about the Trust's movements in the frontier, and he's not allowed to croak 'til we wring every bit of it out of him."

"In that case, you're gonna want to get to him pronto, 'cause the patch is a no-go. Even if you had it preloaded on a drive in that *very* fashionable boiler suit, it'd take me at least five minutes to get it up and running, and that's five minutes I desperately need to be spending keeping the entire station from exploding." Yarden didn't get to jump the line ahead of everyone on that station, and she needed every second she could get.

"No, the only way to get him out of that box is to unlock it," she said, decisively. "Which I wouldn't recommend even if I *could* do it. Pretty sure the only thing that'd kill him faster than some quality time in a locked room with the Deadworld Code is some quality time in an *unlocked* room with Drestyn. Man's serious about his rebel ways, but he's got an itch that only hardcore vengeance can scratch."

"Should we tell Yarden that?" Nash asked.

Anke shook her head. "Can't. I've got cameras in the safe

room, but zero comms." Score one for her *Deadworld kills the comms* theory. "Not sure he needs the warning, though. Yarden's a gelatinous glob of garbage juice, but he's not stupid; keeping a locked door between him and Drestyn for as long as possible seems like pretty solid survival strategy. Long as we can get to him before his clock runs out, I wouldn't worry about it." Pause for gasps: Anneka Ahlstrom, *not* worrying about something.

She just didn't have the bandwidth. Too much to do, no time to do it. "Don't suppose you've got a secret twin somewhere," she said. "'Cause somebody's got to get Yarden before he bites the big one, somebody's got to get the blow-shit-up tanks, and I can't leave this console." Too busy firing off command lines like bullets from a semi-auto assault rifle. The fail-safe wouldn't matter if she couldn't kill the executable code. She hadn't stopped typing the whole time she was talking. "We need to be in at least three places at once, and unless I'm way behind on my technological advances, we're still a few decades shy of spontaneous human cloning!" All said in a single breath, no pauses, and there probably would've been more, if it weren't for the smirk twitching at the corner of Nash's mouth.

"We don't need clones," she said, stowing her shock baton in her bag. Her smirk inched higher, pride and purpose and a dash of pluck. Nash was always something else, but with a fire in her eyes, she was kind of breathtaking. "We've got a crew."

A series of sure-footed splashes, and Nash moved into the space behind Anke's chair to eye the screens. "Patch Eoan the rest of the way in. Full system access." Nash gave orders like they were facts. Foregone conclusions, because only stupid people wouldn't obey, and for all Anke's faults and mistakes, she'd somehow made the short list of *not stupid* people.

By golly, in the time it took the words to register, Anke had already thrown open the proverbial back door for Eoan. "Mi space station administrator access es su space station administrator access, Cap," she said, and got a polite, airless hum over the systemwide comms in response. How long would it take them to map the station's entire infrastructure? A second? Maybe two, just to make Anke feel better about herself. She could hack with the best of them, but her human brain had limitations; Eoan had no such restrictions.

It felt good to be on their side again, even if there'd be hell to pay at the end of it. *Or we'll all die in a fiery explosion. No consequences if we all die in a fiery explosion. Embrace the positive mental attitude.*

"Cap, you in?" Nash said.

"Thoroughly," Eoan replied. "Between the two of us, we should have things sorted here. Anneka will direct you to the life support tanks."

The sound of echoing gunshots cracked across the speakers. "Yeah, great," Saint grunted. Anke guessed there wasn't much point in keeping her out of their comm lines, now that they were all on Team No Go Boom. "I'll just stay here with my thumb up my ass!"

"Think Saint's done playing decoy, Cap," Nash said. "Hey McBlastinshit, Drestyn's making a run for Yarden's panic room. Up for a game of fetch?" *A game,* she said, with such quiet viciousness that it sent a chill up Anke's spine.

Saint's answering growl was worse. Savage, almost subvocal, rumbling across the comms. "I'm on my way."

His comms went quiet, and Anke swore she heard her own throat click as she swallowed. "He's just going to catch him." *Right?*

Nash only leaned forward over the back of Anke's chair, grip white-knuckled on the desk's edge. "There's no neutral ground, here, Ahlstrom," Nash said in her ear, voice as cold as the sprinkler water dripping down Anke's neck. "We've picked our sides. Which one are you on?"

The one that saves lives. She knew it wasn't the answer to the question Nash had asked; maybe it wasn't an answer to anything at all. Just a hope. Just a choice.

"Eight minutes and counting," she said instead, cracking her knuckles and bumping her glasses back up her nose. "Let's do this."

CHAPTER TWENTY-TWO

SAINT

A man like Saint didn't *get* satisfaction. Doing what he'd done for as long as he'd done it, he knew there wasn't a damn thing that could bring him peace for what he'd lost. What he still stood to lose. Taking down Drestyn, that wasn't going to undo what'd happened on Noether. It wouldn't put Jal's broken body back together or wash the memory of his blood, slick and searing, off Saint's hands. All that was wrong, it wasn't gonna right.

But it would square it. Eye for an eye, and folks could philosophize all they wanted, but the world was already blind. Had to be, because the good ones got hurt and the bad ones, the bent ones, the busted-up old broken ones like Saint, got to keep going. A simple man's justice—it wasn't all he wanted, but it was the very least he'd settle for.

Drestyn's man in the stairwell made a decent start.

It didn't take much. He'd seen it before: some men just didn't have the patience for the bird's nest. Got so caught up in shooting that they forgot there might be shots coming the other way, and after what felt like a fistful of eternity playing target practice in the stairwell, that head of his got awfully high over the railing. Squeeze. Bang. Drop.

See, Saint could be patient, when he had to be. From the sounds of things, though, his wait was nearly up.

"Drestyn's man's down," he reported over comms as he jogged his way up the last few flights two, three stairs at a time.

"Down or *down*?" Saint's molars still ground together when

he heard Anke's voice over their comms. She hadn't fired a single shot, but every time he heard her, it set off a whisper in the back of his head. *Her fault. Her fault. Her fault.*

"Riot round." In case he had to deal with any Trust security officers, not because he felt charitable. Drestyn's man was out of the way. That was what mattered.

"What about the other one?" Nash, this time. She hit the elevator lobby right as he came through the door, soaked to the skin and ready to raise some hell.

He glanced back into the stairwell. "The other one?"

"Lady in a Trust security kit," said Nash. "Zapped the shit out of her."

"Marei." Anke again, from down the hall this time. "Hang on, I can find her on the cams."

"Not a priority," said Eoan, crisply. "Nash, the elevator that's just opened—you'll take it down to the subbasement. Anneka will take it from there."

Nash jerked her head in a nod, but Saint caught her arm before she ducked through the elevator doors.

"Careful," he told her, voice low. He knew she could handle her shit; wasn't anybody better than her at keeping themself out of trouble. But she was taking her cues from rosy-haired Judas, and Saint wasn't losing anybody else. "Just watch your six." *Don't trust her to do it for you.* Even the smart crews made mistakes from time to time, but they sure as shit didn't make them *twice.*

Nash's eyes met his. Not a word of acknowledgment, but the swift jab she gave his shoulder was as good as one. *Don't forget,* it said. *I'm the brains of this operation.* With a leveler head on her shoulders than Saint'd ever had.

She'd be fine.

"Into the office," Eoan told him, and he left the lobby as the elevator doors slid closed. Pretty intuitive floor plan—straight down the hall into the office, and his eyes skimmed over Anke only in passing on the way to the hole in the wall behind her.

"Let me guess," he said, crossing over to it. "Drestyn's down there." Through the hole, another goddamn elevator shaft plunged straight down into a coal-smudge dark. Didn't even seem to have a bottom, just a pair of cables dangling an arm's length from his nose. *Taunting* him. "Sure, why not? Starting to like heights."

Nash snorted. "Bullshit."

He clipped his carabiner to the nearest cable with a tight-lipped grin. "Bullshit," he agreed, and down into the dark he went. His carabiner screamed against the braided metal cables, and stale air bit at his clothes, his skin, and everything else it could reach as he plummeted. Wasn't so much a descent as a controlled fall, and not so controlled that his knees and ankles didn't holler when his boots hit bottom. *Too damn old for this.* But his feet were on solid ground again—the roof of an elevator car, from the looks of it—and his stomach only took another second or two to catch up to the rest of him, so he shook it off and lowered himself into the car through the still-open hatch.

"All right?" Eoan asked as he wedged himself against the front panel. Somebody'd already pushed open the doors, and not too long ago judging from the boot prints still shining wetly on the rubberized floors.

"Peachy." No sign of Drestyn outside. *Not yet.* Just . . . filing cabinets. A fuck-ton of filing cabinets, each nearly a full dec taller than Saint and arranged in rows across a room not much bigger than the *Ambit*'s galley. "What am I looking at here, Cap?"

"There's nothing on the building schematics," they replied. "Given the lack of cameras, the single secured entrance, and the archival décor, I expect it's a hard copy record repository."

"Hard copy as in *paper*?" The rapid-fire tap of keystrokes

beat a busy tattoo in the background of Anke's feed. "Who uses paper records anymore?"

"Can't hack a Redweld," Saint said, not all the way through his teeth but close enough that Nash would've hit him with a side-eye, if she'd been standing close enough.

As it was, she had to settle for a whistle. "Gotta be some damn ugly skeletons hiding in that closet. Anybody else wanna fuck around and find out?"

"Busy trying not to *be* one of those skeletons," Saint murmured, darting out across the first aisleway. No security cameras meant Eoan couldn't keep him out of trouble, and with a deadeye like Drestyn lurking somewhere close by, he wasn't too keen to poke his head out around any corners. "Time check?"

"Seven minutes, twenty—"

"For Yarden," Saint clarified. Anke and Nash would handle the self-destruct; nothing he could do about that. *Yarden* was his problem.

Eoan didn't keep him waiting. "The atmo pumps in the panic room are drawing air from the fuel stores," they said. "Hydrogen sulfide, carbon monoxide, water." White damp. He'd never had the pleasure, but he'd heard stories. So many ways a ship could kill a man. Suddenly the *Ambit*'s electrified floors didn't seem so bad. "More variables than your average suffocation, but at the present asphyxiant saturation, I estimate he'll be unconscious in six minutes or less."

Or less. "Not very precise, Cap," Saint said.

"Human physiology isn't very precise." Accusatory, like what they really wanted to say was, *It's you ridiculous man-apes screwing with my math.* "Another minute or two, and you can expect significant brain damage or death." Eoan spoke quickly and clearly, but in their *I'm multitasking* voice. They weren't just running numbers; they were running whole scenarios. Open the door now, what happens? One minute? Five minutes? Weighing the variables, the outcomes. If they didn't open the door eventually, Yarden would choke. If they opened it too early and Drestyn got in, he'd eat a bullet. Either way, Drestyn got something he wanted. Either way, he'd fucking *win*.

Saint couldn't let that fly.

"Fuck it." He dove across the rest of the aisles in a madman's dash, sliding into place against the very last row of cabinets as the first bullets pinged against the other side. Music to his ears. Meant he was close. *There you are.* Drestyn had hunkered down somewhere at the other end of the row. Two crack shots with an open aisle between them. It happened to every sniper at some point—staring out across a valley, a bustling street, a sprawling roofline, and you feel it: that unmistakable prickle between your shoulders that means you're in somebody else's scope. Only one way that ended. *May the best man win.*

He dropped his back against the cabinets and grinned into the dark. "Found Drestyn, Cap," he said. They'd done their job. They'd gotten him where he needed to be. "I'll take it from here."

NASH

Nash's foot bounced impatiently on the mock-wood floor, wildly out of time with the music crooning through the elevator speakers. *What kind of bland-ass bossa nova* bullshit *is this?* Hell wasn't a place; it was fifty stories of relentlessly upbeat elevator music. "You found Drestyn?" *Bang, ba-bang, bang, bang,* right in her earhole. She'd worked with Saint long enough to know he wasn't the one shooting; didn't have the right rhythm. Saint didn't *syncopate.* "Sounds more like he found you."

"That too." Calm, cool, collected. Not adjectives that usually belonged to men under heavy suppressive fire from an ace marksman, but she had her comfort zones and Saint had his.

For the record, waiting in an elevator while shit went down for everybody else? *Not* her comfort zone. "Can't this thing go any faster?"

"Sure, if you want to break it and fall to your death in a glorified shoebox," said Anke, fingers tapping feverishly in the background. The sound made Nash's eye twitch. "You're almost there, just sit tight."

"Should've just rappelled," she muttered.

The line switched again, back to Saint and his gunshots. "Overrated." *Bang, ba-bang, bang, bang.*

First item on her to-do list after all this: *better noise cancellation for the comms.* She was starting to get whiplash.

Starting to get goddamn impatient, too. "Anke—"

"There!" Anke exclaimed.

Nash stood up straighter. "There? You stopped the self-destruct?"

"What? No. There. You're there." *Ding* went the elevator, almost on cue. "Lift should let out in the support systems bay. It's, like, seriously the biggest room I've seen in my entire life, but be not afraid—looks like it's arranged on a grid system. Sections numbered and lettered. Think reference section at a library."

"You balk at paper records, but you frequent library reference sections?"

"Print books are a totally different vibe. Don't judge." As if there weren't a thousand other things she'd judge Anke for before she judged her taste in reading material. "You're looking for section C-Eleven. Should be a pair of tanks. Not very big, compared to some of the others in there, but you know—size isn't everything. Wait."

Nash had a feeling she already knew what Anke was going to say. A dozen decs away, a pair of security officers had apparently noticed her arrival. They started toward her, guns on hips and frowns on faces.

She matched their frowns with one of her own—one that said, *I'm meant to be here, but I'm not fucking happy about it.* Good news was, Anke was right about the layout. Each column

had a painted sign at eye level, A-5, A-6, A-7, and more signs
hung between the many-colored pipes bending and stretching
their way across the high ceiling. Made it a hell of a lot easier
to look like somebody with clearance when she knew where she
was going.

"Fancrapstic," she heard Anke whisper. "Just stall them for
a second and I can gen up an ID for your GLASS—"

"I got it. Keep working on the override." Let Nash handle the
see something, say something boys; Anke had more important
work.

Up ahead, one of the security officers' hands fell to his holster. "You're not supposed to be down here."

Nash made a show of looking around. Gunmetal-gray walls
with splashes of bright yellows and reds for signage. Caution.
Danger. Her personal favorite, DO NOT CLIMB IN THE TANK, on
the nose of a gargantuan rig labeled BIOGAS DIGESTER. Basically,
don't climb in the shit tank. Had to be a story behind a sign like
that. She kinda wanted to know it.

Something told her the S⁴ boys wouldn't be up for story time.
Shame. "I don't know," she told them. "This looks like the right
place. Got a ping about a leaky pipe. Hope it's not that one," she
added, jabbing a thumb at the digester.

She could almost hear the whistle as it soared over their
heads.

"You got ID?" said the officer who'd already spoken. Apparently he was the talker of the duo. She dubbed him Number One.

One out of two ain't bad, big guy. "Sure hope so," she said,
grabbing her GLASS out of her armband holder and holding
it out to them. *Little closer. Little closer.* As soon as Number
One reached out to take it, she had him. Grabbed his wrist and
yanked him into her thrust-up knee, and when the groin shot
doubled him over, she slammed his head sideways into one of
those columns. A-6. With a pivot on her back foot, she rode the

momentum a full 360 and hooked a spin kick into the back of Number Two's head.

The metal of the column rang dully as the officers crumpled at her feet. "C-Eleven, you said?" she asked, stepping over them and jogging on her way. "Status check?"

"Typing my little fingers off and trying not to hyperventilate," Anke replied.

"I meant on the self-destruct."

Anke made a noise that could've been a hiccup or a giggle. "Right, I mean, I'm close to wrapping up here. If you'd asked me a few weeks ago, I'd have said this is some nasty code, but after a week of Deadworld diving, this is basically eight-bit. Gonna Frogger this bitch like it's 1981. I'm the car in this analogy, so we're clear." It was like she didn't even *need* to breathe. Like those hard-core musicians who learned to inhale through their nose at the same time they exhaled through their mouths, so they never had to stop making *noise*. "And hey—you're downstairs and ready to make shit happen, which is great. Only a little over seven minutes 'til blow time, which is less great. Also, *blow time* sounds super weird, so I'm sorry I even said it. Where are you?"

"A-Ten, I think." While the section system was easy enough to follow, each section was about a hundred decs across, so it was gonna take a goddamn second. She ran as fast as her legs would carry her, whipping past tanks and fans and clusters of tubing as big around as she was. The place was a monument to engineering. Under different circumstances, she could've spent whole days nerding out over every section, admiring the clever machinations that kept such a massive station up and running.

Under the *present* circumstances, she barely had time to check she'd hit row eleven before she ducked between a couple of humming hydropumps on her way to the Cs. The floor vibrated with the force of so many moving parts. Steam and smoke made the air heavy, brought to life with the roar of a whole station's insides. Each pump and fan and filter was an organ—heart, lungs, liver, beating and pulsing and sustaining, and the Trust had buried its bomb right at the center of it. Anybody asked, they'd say it was a requirement. *Gotta have it. Rules are rules.* And if it just happened to malfunction, well, whose fault was it really? The Trust was just doing what they were told. Brought a whole new meaning to *malicious compliance.*

"Okay," Nash panted as she slid to a stop in one of the narrow walkways. A sign overhead read C-11, but this machine had no label. No title. It didn't hum or rattle or hiss. It sat there, waiting. *An aneurism.* Biding its time. "I'm here."

"Give me a second," said Anke.

"We don't have a whole lot of those." This was a *wicked* beastie. Dozens of cylindrical tanks feeding into a pair of drums—mixers, to get the right chemicals in the right proportions for the right effect, before it flushed it through the dozens of innocuous gray pipes rising from the machine. Must've fed into every system on the station. Every structure, every room. At the front of it all, a control panel teased a big red SHUTDOWN switch, but when she went to pull it, "Ah, shit."

"Shit what? What shit?"

"There's a fucking key," Nash said. Not a password, not a bio reader. An actual hole for an actual key that she *didn't have.* "Okay." She would make it okay. "Plan B. Control panel's locked down, so I'm gonna have to open her up. Just tell me when I'm good to work," she said, dropping her bag off her shoulder and shimmying in between the gaps in the tanks. "Might have to rearrange some shit in here, don't want to step on your toes."

"Please be careful," said Anke.

"I said I'd wait."

"No, I meant you." *Taptaptaptaptap.* "You're sitting in the middle of a metric ass-load of toxic gas and an igniter. You clip the wrong thing and—okay!"

"Okay as in—?"

"Done! Donezo. The code is my bitch and I am its queen and you're up to bat so *swing, batter, batter.* And do it fast, because you've got incoming. Major incoming."

Nash swore under her breath and kneeled behind the console. "I need a number."

"Five, no. Six. Seven?"

"You asking or telling?"

"I don't know. They're, like, popping out of the ground or something. Do you have any idea how big the subbasement is? Probably been down there the whole time."

Of course they have. If Nash had built a space station, she'd want her life support systems buttoned up tight, too. Definitely practical. Fucking inconvenient, though. "I need you to hold them off."

"Sure." Anke inhaled, exhaled, inhaled again. "Sure, yeah, I can do that. How long?"

"Four minutes and twenty-seven seconds until immolation," Eoan offered helpfully.

Nash rapped a knuckle against the back of the control panel. Low-pitched ring, thick metal. *Hello, plasma torch.* "Less than four minutes and twenty-seven seconds, then," she said. Four and a half minutes to disarm a bomb the size of the *Ambit*'s whole-ass engine with seven—*question mark*—bogeys incoming. The casing of the panel fell out in a neat-cut square, exposing a belly full of wires and switches.

Just not the ones she needed.

"Wrinkle," she said. "I'm seeing some flow control circuits for the drums and maybe the igniter, but I've got fuck-all for the chem tanks. Meaning," she added before Anke could ask, because even her *inhale* sounded confused, "when the clock hits zero, the gas is coming out of those tanks. Period." *Fuck. Fuck. Fuck.*

No.

Don't freak out.

Think, Nash.

Eoan said, "I've got your bodycam feeds, dear. Is there something I can do?"

Was there? Nash closed her eyes, tried to remember the front of the machine. *What did you see?* Gauges. Pipes. No valve handles on the gas tanks, but maybe on the intake for the drum? And if she could manually adjust the flow . . .

She sat up like a bolt and nearly brained herself on a row of pipes. "Cap, I need burn rates on the chems," she said quickly. Eoan could keep up. "And max pressure on those pipes. How low can those valves go before something pops?"

"Oh, I see," said Eoan. *Of course* they did. "Controlled burn?"

"Exactly." Like gas flaring, but with something a whole lot meaner than methane. "Torch it before it torches us." *So buckle up, buttercups.* She had a hell of a lot of work to do.

SAINT

Drestyn was a son of a bitch, but *man*, he could shoot.

He'd turned the filing cabinet into a target at the gun range, dented and shot-through and chewed to hell. Just a few shots at a time, enough to keep Saint pinned down at the end of the row. Low. High. Shallow. Deep. No way to guess exactly where the shots came from, or where the next ones would go, and Saint swore the echoes of one round hardly faded before the next one came. No time to stick so much as a toe out past the cabinet, unless he wanted to lose it.

He kind of liked his toes. Maybe not a top ten body part, if he had to rank 'em, but what could he say? He was still kind of attached.

"Saint?" Unexpected—a voice from the other end of the aisle, instead of another spattering of bullets. *Drestyn.* "You're Saint, right? The one inside the ship. I heard the blond one say your name before—"

"Shouldn't finish that sentence," Saint interrupted gruffly. No good way to end it. *Before I shot him. Before he fell.* Another few rounds nipped the side of the filing cabinet. *Don't get any ideas,* those bullets said, and just for now, Saint listened.

"Understood," Drestyn said through the echo. Not over, but through—he didn't have to raise his voice to make it carry; he just spoke, and every other sound seemed to make room. Hush up now, the preacher's talking. "Just wondering how long you think Yarden has left."

"Not very," Eoan offered helpfully in Saint's ear. "Two minutes at the most, but I'd expect less. He's altered. Agitated. I think he can hear you through the door."

Drestyn probably planned it that way, or he wouldn't have kept talking. Risky move, making noise like that. The bullets might not've given him away, but if Saint listened close enough to the sound of his voice, the shape of it among the dim-lit shelves, he could start to make out whereabouts Drestyn stood. Not on the other end of the filing cabinets, like he'd thought, but closer to the middle of the aisle. A doorway, maybe. Probably some kind of antechamber between the archive and Yarden's safe room.

Hell of a risk, but Drestyn must've thought it was worth it. "I've got it down to seconds." He said it *to* Saint, but *for* Yarden. Dripping poison in his ear. "Can't say it's more than an educated guess, but I've seen what this thing does. How it works. Never the same way twice, but always *fast*. It's the air, isn't it?" he asked. That one might've been aimed at Yarden outright. "Bad way to go, suffocation. Feels like your lungs are peeling themselves from the inside out. Like your eyes are going to burst in their sockets. The panic sets in . . . I've seen men claw their own throats bloody before their hearts finally gave out. So, by all means, stay in there. Stay and fucking *rot*." It hit Saint's ears off-key, the profanity in his crisp, cool tone. His creek-water voice, a baptism of words, hot with brimstone. "My brother was a good man; he'd have wanted it over quick, even for someone like you. But he's not here, and I'm not him. So if you want to make it last, Yarden?" Drestyn called from the end of the aisle. "If you want to make it *hurt*? Well, that'd be just fine."

You didn't hurt a man like Yarden with a gun, or even with the code. *Fear* was the weapon you used against a man like Yarden—a man who'd never met a responsibility he couldn't shirk, a consequence he couldn't avoid. *Fear* was how you got at a man who'd never been brave a day in his life, and Drestyn knew it.

"Saint, you're out of time." Eoan's warning was whip-quick in his ear. "He's going for the door." If Saint was right about Drestyn's roost, no way he'd miss that shot.

Saint couldn't let him take it.

"Just say when," he ground through his teeth, pushing up from his crouch. Getting ready to move. "Don't do it, Drestyn!" he shouted, and it carried not because the air parted or his voice was clear, but because he was a big fucking man with a big fucking mouth, and he wanted to make a big fucking racket. "He'll get his."

"How? Prison?" Drestyn's laugh was airy, full of cordite and bitterness. "You think they send someone like him to the labor crews? Think a man like that *does time*? You're not that naïve."

No, he wasn't. "So you kill him, and he's a victim. A martyr. You think that sends a better message?"

"I'm not here to send a message. That's an idealist's game. You and I, we're something else."

Saint ducked as Drestyn loosed a few more bullets. High this time. The sparks off the cabinets fizzled at the corners of Saint's eyes. "Killers?" he said.

"Pragmatists. Which." Another gun-smoke laugh. "I suppose ends the same way, when you get right down to it. Some people just need killing. Surely we can agree on that much, at least."

"He's at the door," Eoan said. "Hand's on the handle. He's hesitating."

Come on, you spineless shit. Just a little longer. "You think I want to kill you?"

"I think it'd be mightily unwise of me to stick my head out past this doorway." Drestyn sent three more shots into the filing cabinet by Saint's shoulder. Damn near clipped his ear. "I don't want to kill you, Saint, but I'm going to do what I have to do." One more thing they could agree on. They were more mission than man, the two of them, and what mattered was seeing it through. "Yarden's done too much damage. He's hurt too many people, with the Deadworld Code and without it. You're worried about a virus, but that man is a *plague.* So whatever else happens, he has to die."

That was Drestyn's mission. Not the confession, not the code—Yarden cold and rotting. *Tough shit,* Saint thought, curling his fingers in the handle of a drawer. They were well made, those cabinets. Deep and wide, dense metal in layers that didn't always manage to stop Drestyn's bullets, but at least seemed to slow them down. Saint had his own mission; he just needed the word. One word.

Interference fizzled faintly over Eoan's comm line. Waiting. Not yet. Nearly. And as the next burst of bullets struck high against the cabinet's corner, Eoan's voice came crisp and even down the line.

"Now."

Saint came out low, fired one shot. Squeeze. *Bang.* Drop. Just like Drestyn's man in the stairs. He lingered just long enough to see Yarden and his lilac shirt crumple in the doorway of the panic room. Gravity and the force of a well-aimed riot round to the chest took him down fast—fast enough that Drestyn's shots went high, over his head. He'd heard the door open and turned around expecting a running target, not a falling one, and Drestyn's half second of furious confusion gave Saint all the opening he needed.

A hard yank, and he ripped the drawer clean out of the cabinet. Files scattered like playing cards at his moving feet, and an easy, familiar drawl echoed over the ringing in Saint's ears. *How many for poker again?* That drawl, that ready smile, that warm-bright man from that cold-dark world who'd climbed too high and fallen too far, shot and bleeding and trapped out of reach because of *Drestyn*.

Saint hurled himself forward with a roar in his throat and the drawer raised like a shield, and the ping of bullets against metal was the *pop, pop, pop* of palm berries in his ear on a hot rooftop. A graze on the arm, a clean hit in the meat of his thigh, but they were the easy kind of pain. They bled; they healed; they scarred. What the hell was another scar to someone like him, when each step took him closer, and closer, and—

He slammed into Drestyn with a thundercrack of bending metal and rattling bones. No grace, no strategy. Just mass and speed hurled violently, artlessly into a half-braced rail of a man. Just an impact so fierce it carried them both off their feet, as the blinding white of the panic room reached out to swallow them whole.

Just the beginning of an end.

NASH

"Saint?" Nash called over the comms. She'd heard his shout, heard some kind of collision, then deafening silence. "Saint, are you—"

"He's exactly where he needs to be, doing exactly what he needs to be doing," Eoan interrupted quickly, stonily. They'd split the comms, Nash realized. *Eyes on your own papers, dears.* They cared; they did, and Nash never doubted it. They were also the captain, and part of that meant keeping all the parts moving, even if they had to move independently. "And right now, we all need you to do the same. You have ninety seconds before the fail-safe triggers."

Nash gritted her teeth and yanked another wire. Quick and dirty. They didn't have time for anything else. "I know, I know. Got a date with the mother of all hair spray cans and a lit match." And a security officer, from the looks of things. Through the cage of tanks around her, she saw him approaching, dark uniform against the pale gray of the life support bay.

"You're not authorized to be back there!" the officer called.

"No shit," she called back. "FYI, everything in these tanks is hilariously explosive, so for both our sakes, I'd keep that pistol in your pocket, pal." Lower, she said, "Anke, where the hell's my backup?"

"I'm working on it."

"Work faster."

"When people tell you to work faster, does it actually help you work faster?" Anke shot back.

Nash paused with her multitool between her teeth and a pair of wires pinched between her fingers. "Good point." Still, a little bit of double time would be real damn helpful. The officer moved closer, although with a reluctance that said he'd maybe taken the *hilariously explosive* thing to heart.

"Step out from the tanks with your hands raised."

"I'd love to. Really." She still had to get the flow rates into those drum tanks adjusted manually, and that wasn't gonna happen from behind the control panel. "But I get the feeling you're gonna make a run at me, and I'm not feeling a love tap from that Taser of yours."

"Ma'am—"

"Seriously, Terry, I'm doing you a favor!" Spoken around the grip of her multitool, which at present played the role of laser solder on the wires she rearranged. Who needed a third hand when you had a very dexterous mandible? "Cap, I really need those numbers."

"Sending them to your GLASS now." Because it might've taken mere mortals hours to run those kinds of numbers but not Cap. Cap was a *badass*.

Terry—whose real name Nash neither knew nor cared to know—was categorically *not*. "This is your last warning," he said.

Nash had a pithy reply, but she got beat out by a sharp yelp and the sack-of-potatoes thump of a falling body as Terry dropped abruptly out of sight. Confused, she wriggled out from behind the tanks with her GLASS in hand. "What was that?"

"You said Terry had a Taser," Anke said simply. "Now *I* have a Taser. Several Tasers, actually."

"Seven?" Nash guessed.

Anke hummed. "Seven." Begrudgingly, Nash thought she was a little bit badass, too.

"And *you* have forty-one seconds," Eoan said. "You should get on with that plan of yours."

"Aye aye." Nash squatted by the drum tanks' intake valves, turning a few handles until the gauges dipped and settled at the right levels. Manual solutions to complex problems—Nash's very own take on the law of parsimony. One last item on the to-do list: couldn't have a furnace without a flue.

"Is that a good idea?" Anke asked as Nash switched on the plasma torch and took it to the cluster of outflow pipes.

"Meh." It was the only idea she had, though, so she carried on lopping the pipes off a couple hand heights above the tanks, until they jutted up like chimneys. "If it doesn't work, let's just say I don't expect complaints."

"Twenty-five. Twenty-four. Twenty-three."

"Just need a pilot light," Nash said, rooting around in her bag until she found what she was looking for.

"Unless that's some really special tape, I don't think it's going to—oh." Anke fell quiet as Nash lashed her plasma torch to the side of the pipes, burner tube aimed over the hole. Might not hold for long, but it didn't have to. Once the fire started, the gas would keep it alive.

Unfortunately, her torch wouldn't survive the encounter.

You've been good, girl. She didn't stop taping until the roll ran out. All told, it was a hack job: the wires, the valves, the makeshift pilot light. Dozens of ways it could all go wrong, only one way it'd go right.

"Nash," Eoan said softly, "are you sure?"

Sure. Yeah, she was sure. Sure that if Eoan's math was off by even half a psi, the pipes would explode when the gasses started flowing. Sure that if she'd pulled the wrong wires, the valves would fly wide open when the count hit zero and flood the station with a raging inferno.

Sure that if she didn't try, they were dead anyway.

"Trust me," Nash said, willing her hands steady as she switched on the torch and stepped back. *Like you always have.* Cap and Saint both—they'd found a stowaway, a thief with a smart mouth and smarter hands, and they'd let her stay. Let her help. Let her into their weird little family on their ramshackle little ship, and she'd gladly keep reminding them they'd made the right choice. "I've got this."

Ten seconds.

"Damn right." Saint's gruff agreement crackled over the comms, and it was such a relief to hear his voice, even with the clamor of pained grunts and brutality behind it. Fist fight? Knife fight? No way of knowing, but he hadn't doubted her, so she wasn't about to start doubting him.

Eight.

"I'm not sorry!" Anke said in a choked-off rush. "I mean— for lying to you, I am. And for hurting you, and—but I'm not sorry it was you guys that found me. I'm not sorry I'm here with you. You guys are the first crew I've ever been part of, and

I know it was a trainwreck, but it was an *epic* trainwreck. You guys are an epic, *epic* trainwreck."

Three.

"Showtime, dears." Nash pictured Eoan's soft, brilliant smile so clearly they could've been right there beside her. Surrounded by the makings of death, with all their lives in her hands. Alone, but feeling for all the world like she wasn't, because from the moment she'd stepped aboard that beat-up old gyreskimmer, she'd never *really* felt alone.

Two.

She grinned in the flickering light of her plasma torch. "One."

CHAPTER TWENTY-THREE

SAINT

Nothing happened.

A fuck-ton was *happening*—Yarden still sprawled in the safe room doorway, out cold, and Drestyn was well on his way to proving he was just as deadly *without* a gun—but nothing *happened*. The countdown went three, two, one, and no amount of faith in Nash's ability to unfuck a situation could stop Saint's gut from clenching in anticipation of . . . something. Anything.

Nothing.

Even Drestyn looked sort of gobsmacked, like he'd been keeping track of the countdown and knew it'd passed. Probably so. Sharp little bastard. Breathing hard in the thin air of the safe room, blood on his mouth and a slant to his side that said *yeah, that rib's broken.* He was still standing, though, floating back a step or two with that knife of his glinting at his side. Tactical, full tang fixed with a skull-cracker pommel, but slim and simple; the kind of blade meant to be felt before it was seen. Could've fit inside Saint's tac knife with room to spare, but Drestyn moved quick enough to cover the difference in reach. Saint had the bleeding arm to prove it.

"We're not dead," he said, voice low. "Nash, you dead?"

After a long, speculative silence that didn't do a damn thing to loosen the knot his insides had tangled themselves into, he heard Nash's voice. "Unless hell is a big blue birthday candle," she said, "I'm gonna go with *not dead.* RIP Torchie, though. She will be missed."

And that was that. Nash and Eoan were safe, up in that penthouse office. The people of Lewaro were safe. Somewhere in a hospital operating theater, *Jal* was safe.

It didn't ease the furious, swirling redness in his head, but it focused it. One mission done. One mission to go.

He flipped his knife. Reverse grip, edge out, meant for close and nasty as he prowled at the edge of Drestyn's reach. Man was smart, kept clear of the corners where Saint could jam him up. Light on his feet, always dodging out to the middle of the room, trying to get close enough to Yarden to pick up where that riot round left off. He tracked Saint's movements with shrewd, dark eyes.

"All this, for *him*," Drestyn spat, winded. Seemed he felt it, too, the effects of all that exertion in bad atmo. Knife fights were a sprint, not a marathon, anyway; but a minute or two trading blows in that box, even with the door open, felt like an *hour*. Blood, his and Drestyn's, dripped red and stark onto the light gray carpet. "Yarden's not a man you die for."

No, he wasn't.

Saint didn't care.

He took a swing, backhanded with his empty fist, but Drestyn knocked it away easily. Didn't manage the same with the knife that followed it through, though, blade angled to swipe across Drestyn's stomach. Fabric tore, flesh parted, but it wasn't a solid hit. Too shallow, and Drestyn twisted out of the way and cracked an elbow into Saint's cheek.

For a slight man, he packed a hell of a punch. Saint's head jerked sideways, and the taste of metal coated his tongue as he stumbled a step or two. Better to stumble and keep his feet under him than hold his ground and fall. All Drestyn needed was a second or two. A clear line of sight and a good throw, and his knife would kill Yarden as surely as any bullet.

He didn't waste any openings, either. By the time Saint had his bearings, Drestyn had already moved two paces closer to the door and lined up a throw. Just before he loosed the knife, though, Saint managed to get a fistful of his shirttail and *yanked*. No fair play in a fight like that; a second too slow, too late, too cautious, and somebody died.

Not this time. Drestyn lost the shot, but he kept hold of his knife, pivoting on his heel to take a stab at Saint's arm. Fucking fast little scarecrow—up there with some of the fastest Saint had seen, and he'd crossed knives with mutants and augmenteds on the regular. The blade barely missed the hinge of Saint's wrist as he pulled his arm back, throwing out a boot to catch Drestyn while his balance was off.

"Saint, dear, your heart rate is abnormally high. It's not safe to be in that room."

No shit, Cap. White damp, knives, pissed-off agitators with an axe to grind—it was a party in there. Even if he could get himself and Yarden out in one piece, though, that'd still leave Drestyn with an impenetrable door and a manual lock. Maybe he'd die, maybe he'd find a way to break the pod loose and slip away; anybody with scars like that was a survivor. Saint wasn't leaving it to chance.

His boot caught Drestyn's instep, his arm caught Drestyn around the middle, and Saint had lifted produce crates heavier than that man. A lift and a twist, and he flung Drestyn back toward the middle of the room into the cluster of expensive, anonymous furniture that turned out not to be that sturdy. He heard the crack of the sofa frame buckling under the impact as Drestyn pitched ass over kettle over the top of it. The coffee table didn't stand a chance against the landing, legs buckling outward and shiny mock-wood top shattering to bits.

"Get out *now*," ordered Eoan. A command smoothed over the brittle edges of concern, crisply authoritative, stern, impossible to ignore. Felt like their voice arced straight across his jawbone. Vibrating through cartilage and the blood pooling beneath the skin of his split cheek. "It's been too long. Blood loss, hypoxia, elevated heart rate—if you pass out, Nash may not be able to get to you in time."

All very good points, and all probably true. Saint's mission hadn't changed, though, and Drestyn was relentless. Before the pieces of the table had finished scattering, he'd gotten back to his feet. One smooth roll to get his head up and his soles down, and he sprang forward like a startled hare. Cleared the back of the couch in a leap, and Saint braced to meet all that momentum with a hard slug in the face, but Drestyn went low at the last second. His knife swept an arc toward Saint's side, a kidney shot, and the angle it took for Saint to grab his wrist left him wide open for the one, two, three quick jabs from Drestyn's empty fist to the soft part of his gut.

Saint choked on spit, blood, stomach acid. Sputtered on noxious air. He took a swing with his knife hand, but it was too wild. Too imprecise. Drestyn knocked it aside—deflected the blade and drove his knuckles into Saint's wrist, into that damn bundle of nerves that made his hand flash numb and his grip go loose, and the clatter of Saint's knife hitting the floor was bad, but the knee that snapped into the gunshot wound on Saint's thigh was worse.

Pain seared blinding white across Saint's nerves, and in the wake of it, his mind went blank. Not a single clear thought; just instinct. Simple, brutal instinct, and the kind of strength that only came from being *so goddamn angry*. He hooked his forearm under Drestyn's knee, and with an animal howl, flipped the bastard clear over his shoulder. Oh, he'd pay for it later—every bit of scar tissue and badly healed bone hissed with the promise of it—but Saint didn't care.

Drestyn hit the ground back first, wrist still pinned in the vise of Saint's grip, knife still clutched in his white-knuckled grasp. A Saint-sized fall straight onto his spine and even a hard-ass like Drestyn saw stars. For a stunned second, he didn't move, and that stunned second gave Saint all he needed to turn around, trapping Drestyn's arm between his knees and twisting that bird-boned wrist until something popped.

Drestyn didn't cry out. Wouldn't have mattered, wouldn't have changed anything if he had. What mattered was that he dropped the knife, and more, that Saint caught it.

Saint saw the moment Drestyn realized his . . . not a mistake, really. Wasn't a whole hell of a lot a man could do to keep his grip when his bones were in more pieces than they were meant to be. When he realized what'd happened, more like, and when he realized what was *about* to happen—stunned or not, uncaring of the shattered wrist still seized in Saint's grip, he surged up with a snarl.

And sagged right back down when Saint slammed that skull-cracker pommel against his temple. In an instant, everything about the man changed. Taut limbs went loose. Keen eyes went glassy and rolled back. Blood beaded against a pale, pock-marked cheek, and that sharpshooting, quick-thinking rene-gade politico was just like any other sack of meat Saint had ever seen when all the lights went out.

It was just luck, Saint decided as he drew the knife away, that he'd caught it blade side back. Good luck or bad, he couldn't say. Supposed it depended who you asked, and though Drestyn was still breathing, Saint didn't think he'd be answering questions anytime soon.

"Saint?" Eoan was quiet this time. Deliberately so; everything they did was deliberate. Didn't have a brawl to talk over, or maybe they sensed the silence, the stillness, that had settled into the panic room like a dense, stewing fog. "Saint, are you all right?"

"I'm—" *Fine* was what he meant to say, but as he stood, the world skewed sideways and darkened at the corners. He staggered. Kept his feet only by virtue of knowing where they were in relation to the rest of him, if not in relation to the floor. *Not fine,* he observed for himself. *Dizzy. Nauseous.* His head

pounded like a beaten drum, and a chill had settled in his fingers and toes that seemed to be spreading inward. "On my way
out," he finished aloud, and that was true. His legs had trouble
grasping *forward* as a concept, though how much was the slow-
burn suffocation and how much was the bullet wound was anybody's guess. The swoop to pick up his knife felt dangerous; the
swoop to pick up *Yarden* felt damn near impossible, but with
a sweat-slicked grip on both of Yarden's wrists, he managed to
drag his dead weight out of the doorway and down the aisle of
filing cabinets.

"Get him to the elevator," Eoan instructed. "The air is clearer."

He complied, because compliance was easier than thinking.
Easier than dragging a full-grown man across a room full of
secrets, the likes of which he was probably better off not knowing. Bit of light reading, and Saint might start wishing he'd let
Drestyn have Yarden. Or he might start thinking about taking
a turn himself.

As it was, he didn't take any great pains with him. Dropped
Yarden on the floor of the elevator like heavy luggage and steadied himself on the pried-open doors for a beat. The metal felt
cool against his flushed brow; solid, where the rest of the world
felt soft and ill-defined.

"Feeling better?" Nash, this time. "Slow, deep breaths. Won't
help the headache, but you might manage not to pass the fuck
out."

Passing the fuck out sounded great, actually. Yarden was in
the clear. Drestyn was the kind of unconscious that probably
needed a brain scan, shallow-breathing in poisoned atmo; he
wasn't gonna make much trouble for anybody. All Saint had to
do was get that damned safe room door closed, stop the bad air
flooding the basement.

He took one of those slow, deep breaths Nash suggested and
raised his head from the cool metal of the elevator door. *One
foot in front of the other, soldier.* Wouldn't do him any good to

get this far if the whole basement went toxic before Eoan could get the elevator working again.

"What about Drestyn?" Chalk it up to oxygen deprivation, but Saint's jaw didn't even clench at the sound of Anke's voice.

"What about him?" His mouth was dry and metallic, a little sour. *What about Jal?* That was what they should've been asking, but he was too chickenshit to say so. Wasn't sure he'd believe a good answer; wasn't sure he could take a bad one.

Anke seemed to have her heart set on the agitator anyway. "You can't just leave him in there. Please. I know what he did to Jal, and I can't imagine how you're feeling right now, but he's saved so many people. From the Deadworld Code, from the Trust, from smugglers and scavs and starving to death because this system just takes and takes and doesn't give anything back. I don't know where that all lands on the karmic scales of justice or whatever, but." Her voice broke, wet and desperate. "But the good things he's done have helped a lot of people, and the bad things he's done, he did for good reasons. How is any of that *any* different from what the rest of you have done?"

I didn't shoot Jal. Grimacing, Saint made his way along the filing cabinets with heavy, limping steps, blood sticking his pants to his leg and drying, itchy, in his beard. "I was gonna kill him before." Would've shot him dead in the antechamber if he'd had the angle; would've put a knife someplace permanent if he'd dropped his guard when they were fighting. Anke knew that. Had to know that. He hadn't heard a peep out of her about it, then.

"It's not the same thing," she said. "He's *helpless.*" Which was a hard word to pair with the man who'd put a bullet in his leg and a knife in his arm, but as Saint turned the corner to the antechamber and caught sight of him lying there, he couldn't deny it. "You can save him."

Of course he could. Yarden outweighed Drestyn by a good ten, fifteen kilos. A few steps farther into the room, but even in the shape he was in, Saint could probably drag him out before he shut the door. But that wasn't what she was saying.

She was saying, *You* should *save him.*

"Think about what you're asking," Nash said, biting off each word like she didn't trust them not to build into something sharper. Sounded like she was on the move again, but sitreps were Eoan's problem; Saint had to focus on keeping himself upright. *Shoulders over hips over knees over ankles, soldier.* "Good reason or not, Drestyn's killed a fuck-ton of people. Your buddy's best-case is a labor colony in the frontier 'til he's old or dead, and I don't know him from Adam, but you do. You think that's what he'd want?"

Man like Drestyn, probably not. Like this, he could just slip away. Wouldn't even wake up, wouldn't even *feel it*. There were worse ways to go.

Gasping and bleeding in the mud half a universe from home, Saint thought, but it just made his chest ache. He was usually better at this. Had a locked door in his head where the bad things went when he didn't have time to fuck with them, but the lock had broken, and the door had gotten stuck, and it was just bad, bad, bad slithering out of the dark. A fucking snake pit in his skull, as Anke and Nash debated the moral nuances of saving Drestyn's life or not.

"Isn't that a point in favor of saving him?" Anke argued. "Penance, or whatever."

Or whatever, he thought, wryly. Fuck, Drestyn was farther inside than Saint thought, and Saint's legs were heavier than they had any right to be. The lights of the panic room crystallized in their pretty prismatic halos, shifting, drifting, swirling. He could feel himself slipping with every breath, but he needed—

"It's not about penance." That. He needed *direction,* clarity, and Eoan had always had a knack for giving it to him. Christ, he appreciated Nash—he loved her like a sister, would've died for her—but she saw everything as a system full of broken pieces. Machines. People. Politics. To her, it was all the same, and she did her best to fix what she could and do the least harm along the way.

Saint had lost that game a long time ago. Too many broken things, too many ways to do harm, and it'd stopped being about fixing things and started being about *finishing* them. Completing the mission.

Nash was a good person.

Saint was a good soldier.

And Eoan . . . Eoan was a good captain. They understood Nash, and they understood him. Understood the choice on offer: leave Drestyn to die and give the bastard the kind of easy, *go in his sleep* death a jarhead like Saint could only dream about; or drag Drestyn out to face the consequences of what he'd done, knowing it meant saving the man responsible for one of the worst fucking moments of Saint's life.

He'd known there was no peace waiting at the end of this. No satisfaction. But he realized now that there wasn't any balance, either. Whether Drestyn lived or died, it wouldn't square the loss of that easy-grinned kid and his cheap deck of cards who'd found the angriest, most beaten-down soldier on the shuttle and said, *Still, I think he's worth a damn.*

As he stared into the panic room through the gray creeping in at the corners of his eyes, it was Eoan's voice he heard. "It's not about consequences," they said. "Or being angry, or being hurt. It's not about deciding what he should do, because he knows. Don't you, Saint?" And he did. For better or for worse, indecisiveness was not his cross to bear. He just had a door, and a lock, and a pit full of vipers, and every day the same question: *How much more can you take?* And of course Eoan knew that, too. "He just has to figure out if he can stand to do it."

Could he?

"You can," Eoan said, and they knew, because it was their

job to know, even when he didn't. Especially when he didn't. When he thought the door was stronger than it was. When he thought he knew what it would take, what *he* could take, but he was wrong. "You can, so you will, because you're you."

Because he was a good soldier, and in the end, he did what good soldiers did.

He did what he had to do.

EOAN

After everything, it seemed only right they'd found their way back here. To the galley of the *Ambit,* counters littered with remnants from breakfast, from dinner the night before. Eoan had never had much use for hyperbole, but it felt like a lifetime since they'd gathered around that table. Since they'd watched Anke coding furiously on her tablet while Saint, without a word, kept her coffee mug full and her water glass fuller. Since they'd watched Jal sneak spoonful after spoonful from the pan simmering on the burner while Bodie wove around his feet and Nash played lookout in the hallway. Since there had been music and laughter and dancing in that reckless, beautiful way humans had when their smiles were true and their hearts were light.

There were no light hearts in the galley now.

Saint sat at the table, an untouched mug of coffee losing steam by his elbow and a medkit balanced on his lap. Blood puddled a drop at a time on the floor beneath him; stained the fresh bandage tied neatly around his leg; painted the deft fingers mending the knife wound on his arm.

Nash said nothing of it, or anything else for that matter. She'd been the first one in, only a few minutes ago. Fixed herself a cup of tea and, unlike Saint, stubbornly drank it down like it was just another day—or like it would be, might be, if she only forced it back into the routine.

The dregs sat abandoned on the table with Saint's coffee. She'd set it down when he stumbled in and hadn't picked it up since, and Eoan couldn't help wondering if this wasn't part of the routine, too. Patching Saint's wounds while he passed her tools . . . it wasn't every mission, but it was enough of them to feel familiar.

The silence, though—that was alien to them.

Saint finally broke it, scrubbing a hand down his face and sighing like a gale from his tortured lungs. "I'm sorry about your plasma torch."

Nash, who'd settled herself cross-legged on the table with Saint's arm pulled across her lap, finished sealing the wound with dermapoxy and hummed. "I'm sorry about your face." And Eoan was sorry about it, too. The cut along his cheekbone was shallow, but the skin around it had already started to swell and color. He'd be a riot of bruises and bandages in the morning. Nevertheless, knowing him, he'd be up making breakfast by 0600 sharp. "I'd say you've still got your personality, but." She shrugged.

"Nice."

"Feel free to fill out a comment card," she replied. "But I meant what I said about the cryopack." She'd managed to balance one on his shoulder, but it had already fallen once when he tried to pet the cat. *Next time I'll staple it on,* she'd threatened. Since it was hard to know when Nash was joking, Saint had kept very still since.

A square of gauze, a roll of bandages around his forearm, and though there remained—clearly—some work to be done to get their XO back in fighting form, Nash seemed satisfied he'd live for now.

As she wiped her hands on a wet towel, her eyes drifted forlornly to her teacup. *Too empty.* To her cabinet. *Too far.* To her own two legs. *Too tired.* And last, to Saint's mug, as he slid it closer to her with a split-knuckled hand.

They weren't really *thank you* people, but Eoan saw one hiding in the way Nash hugged the mug between her hands.

"What about you, Cap?" Saint asked, dropping his head back with a flat, skyward stare—a signal that their quiet observation was at an end. They never could go unnoticed very long with Nash and Saint around; always just a matter of time before one of them reached out, before one of them drew Eoan into whatever argument or banter or idle conversation they'd drummed up.

Suddenly, it seemed strange to think they'd ever felt *excluded*. Strange to think they'd held themself apart, so caught up in a difference they'd thought insurmountable, when Nash and Saint had only ever treated them as equal. *You're my goddamn family.* It was like a shroud had been lifted from the world—a new brush of color, more vibrant and more beautiful than any new star, new world, new *mystery*. They'd chosen these people, and these people had chosen them, and for the very first time in their impossibly long life, they knew what it meant to be *fulfilled*.

"Cap?" Nash prompted, gently. "You hanging in there?"

Ah. Eoan realized they hadn't answered Saint's question. "Frankly, dear," they said as they settled their projection into the chair opposite Saint's, edges fuzzy and colors plain. They didn't adjust for the light or give much thought to the way their clothing fell. They didn't try to feed any more energy or life into the projection than they absolutely had to, because they didn't have it to spare. "I'm *exhausted*."

It had been hours since the countdown—hours spreading themself thin across multiple systems; hours of juggling dozens of tasks and comm lines and questions, from Trust and Guild and Union alike; hours of worrying about the people they cared so dearly for, who had been through so much and still had to carry on a while longer. Their limits were exceptional, and they had reached them anyway.

A pair of weary smiles said they weren't the only one.

Yes, they thought, *we're really not so different at all, are we?* "I'm sorry I couldn't join you sooner," they offered, and perhaps they meant the last hour or so they'd been distracted, or perhaps they meant the past few years. Either way, Eoan was with them now. *That's what matters.* "And I'm sorry for your plasma torch," to Nash. "And for your face," to Saint, and their own smile seemed worth the effort. "As you might expect, the Guild had . . . inquiries." *And the Union had demands, and the Trust had excuses.* And Eoan had work for themself and for their crew that was more important than any of it. "But at least they should be able to take things from here."

"Things." Nash weighed the word and wrinkled her nose. Could've been the coffee, too; every time she took a sip, she cringed a little. She kept going back, though, because as far as Eoan could tell, she needed the warmth more than she hated the taste. "Does that mean we know where wonder girl's going?"

Nash hadn't stayed with her, after she got back upstairs from the life support bay. Someone had to, as much to protect Anke as to watch her, and given that the Trust wasn't known for their fondness of whistle-blowers, they could hardly hand her off to the security officers. Since Nash hadn't seemed especially interested in her company, and *Saint* hadn't seemed especially interested in spending more time in Yarden's archive, they'd made a trade. Saint upstairs, watching Anke and—Nash had stressed this bit—staying the *candy-coated fuck* off his leg; and Nash downstairs, quick-scanning all the files in the cabinets for Eoan's personal archives. They were, as ever, a curious being.

"It does," they said. "Despite what happened, she *is* still under the Guild's jurisdiction. Citizen to a sovereign state, for all intents and purposes. So, in the short term, she'll be taken back to the center spiral for martialing before the Captains' Council."

"And long term?" Nash pressed.

"Pretty sure that'd be up to the Captains' Council," Saint

muttered, and got an audible flick to the ear for his trouble. "Ah, fuck, Nash. Ow."

"Big baby."

"I'm injured."

"Not there," she replied, utterly unrepentant. "Not yet." With just a touch of menace that struck an odd contrast to the careful way she leaned over to adjust his ice pack, but then, Nash always marched to the beat of her own drum. "Just wish we could call dibs on that fucker Yarden, too. Give me ten minutes, a locked door, and a vegetable peeler, and I'd get him singing for those Union regulators like a tuned-up engine."

Vegetable peeler? Saint mouthed, then shook his head as if to say, *Never mind, I don't want to know.*

That made one of them, but Eoan regrettably didn't ask. "Yes, well. While I'm sure they could benefit from your expertise, I don't think they're having much trouble getting Mister Yarden to talk. Now that the regulators have his little private library downstairs—"

"Not that little," Nash muttered, prodding bitterly at a paper cut on the side of her thumb. With the help of her Chiclet and a half dozen of its siblings, she'd managed to scan nearly every page in nearly every filing cabinet before the first Union ships touched down, but Eoan suspected it would be a while before she didn't cringe at the sight of paper products.

"—of his not-that-little private library," Eoan amended, and smoothly carried on, "he's got to know the Trust won't back him. They won't be very happy with his *recordkeeping.*"

Saint snorted. "No honor among assholes."

"Would've made a hell of an insurance policy," Nash said. "Or a bargaining chip. The kinds of dirt he had in those filing cabinets . . . I'm betting the Trust had no idea he was stashing those records." Probably a sound bet. Eoan had taken a few peeks at the scans, in between the other dozens of tasks they had to juggle, and if Yarden's superiors had an inkling of what he'd been doing, Eoan suspected there wouldn't have been anything left of the library—or Yarden, for that matter—for them to find. "Kind of makes you wish you could be there, huh? See the C-suiters' faces when they realize what Yarden did. All that dirty laundry, and a boardroom full of Union regulators just itching to dive in, and there's fuck-all they can do about it."

Saint didn't seem quite so enthusiastic. "You think a scrap of that's gonna see the light of day? Union'll use it, sure, make the Trust pay out the nose for all the shit they've been sweeping under the rug. But if it's as nasty as y'all make it sound, the Trust won't pay one damn cap 'til the Union agrees to burn after reading; and the Union'll do it, because they can't risk the Trust walking away from the table. That's the goddamn problem— got the left hand swatting the right. They need each other too much to do any real damage."

"I see Drestyn made an impression." To be fair, Eoan probably deserved the acidic look Saint leveled their way. "Right. I'm sorry, but you're quite correct. Odds are the Trust will demand the records be sealed, the Union will concede to get their way and keep the peace, and those papers will never make it to the public eye. But there's something you're missing, dear." Their projection leaned forward, head tilting with a dark smile. "It isn't up to them."

There was something to be said for the instant dawning on Saint's face. As if he knew them so well, he didn't even have to think about it. "The scans," he said.

"The scans," they agreed. "It may take me a day or two to parse through them all, but after that, I see no reason why they shouldn't find their way to a much, *much* wider audience." Because Saint was right—they couldn't rely on the system to fix the system. The Union needed the Trust, and the Trust needed the Union, and if they were being honest with themselves, perhaps the Guild needed them both.

The people, though, didn't need any of them. They could tear it all down and rebuild, as they had before and as they would again. What they needed was a chance to choose their own fate, as Eoan had, and to *know* what they were choosing. Choices changed everything; if Eoan had learned anything since the start of all this, that was it. Choices changed lives. They changed people. They could change the entire universe, for better or for worse, and Eoan had chosen *better*.

They only hoped it would empower others to do the same.

"It's settled, then," said Nash in that decisive way of hers. The deed was good as done. "Gotta say, Cap, rebel's a good look on you. And on the subject of rebels"—which they supposed was as good a segue as any for the inevitable question that followed—"what about Drestyn?"

"He's alive," they said, hating all the while the fresh wince that crossed Saint's face. That discomfort had nothing to do with the bullet wounds or bruises, but he'd made a choice of his own. Not an easy one, but the right one, and Eoan loved him all the more for it. "He's being treated here in hospital, for the moment. Head trauma, various lacerations and contusions—I expect you don't need the laundry list."

Nash set the mug aside, half-full and still steaming. She'd evidently reached the limit of what she was willing to endure for the caffeine. A pity. Eoan would've liked to know how she'd handle the whole mug. An experiment for another day, perhaps.

"You never did say," Nash began, leaning back on her hands and looking over at Saint. "Which one was it? The one you weren't sure you could stand—was it leaving him, or helping him?"

Saint's throat bobbed, and when he spoke his voice was a scrape against the quiet of the galley. "Does it matter?"

It would've been easy for Nash to bristle, but she huffed a laugh and shook her head instead. "Guess not. Don't worry,

McBlastinshit," she added, earnestly, "you're a hard-core mother-fucker either way."

Which was, in Eoan's estimation, one of the highest compliments Nash knew how to pay.

They cleared their throat. "Yes, well, you can imagine he's a very popular man. Probably a small army of Trust and Union reps fighting for first crack at him as we speak, but they'll have to wait their turn."

"Guild's got dibs?" Nash asked.

"More like Guild's got guardianship," Eoan replied. "Trust might not be, well, *trusted* with his care and safekeeping, but they don't want the Union to speak to him first. So until they sort it all out, it looks like he'll be staying in Guild custody. For the best, I'd say. The Guild isn't terribly eager to get involved in a full-scale Union investigation, but there are plenty of questions we could ask a man like that while the children are busy squabbling for the first turn. Not the least of which being where his accomplices ran off to."

"The lady from the stairwell."

"Correct. And the man in the rockhopper," they added. "Seems they made their getaway while we were otherwise occupied. Anneka believes Drestyn warned them somehow."

Saint scoffed. "You sure it wasn't her?"

"Maybe it was, maybe it wasn't." Eoan wouldn't opine, not because they lacked an opinion, but because Saint clearly lacked an interest in hearing it. Humans were, as a species, beautifully irrational. *Angry* humans even more so. "It's beside the point. The point is, they're out there, and we're not sure where."

"You think they'll try to break Drestyn and his guy out?" That seemed to perk Nash up more than the coffee had. Her feet hung over the edge of the table, swinging idly in the electric-blue and magenta socks she'd knitted herself—a creature comfort, like the tea and the galley. She didn't wear her wounds so close to the skin, but she'd taken just as many hits as Saint, in her own way. "Kind of hope they do. Is that weird? Hate to leave a set unfinished."

"We ought to keep a close eye on them," Saint said. "Just in case."

Eoan's projection tipped its head, *no.* "I've already coordinated their transport back to the center spiral with one of the relief crews en route. I know you'd prefer to handle it personally, but it seemed . . . prudent, to make other arrangements. Given the word on Ranger Jalsen."

It was like a bolt of lightning. *Now* that's *hyperbole.* At the very least, though, a firm tap from Nash's shock baton. Saint flinched upright, head jerking toward Eoan's projection. "You got word on Jal?"

"Of course," they said. "I've been checking periodically."

"And when the fuck were you gonna share with the class, Cap?" Incredulity. That was better than some of the alternatives. Saint did have *exquisite* range.

They offered what they hoped was a suitably apologetic smile. "I didn't want to distract you," they said. "And yes, before you say it, I know you would've done your jobs. Of that I have no doubt. But this has been hard enough on the both of you." Hard for Eoan, too, to see them suffer. To know that they had to keep asking more of their crew, when they'd both already lost and given and taken so much. It had seemed crueler to tell them when they couldn't *do anything* about it. "That's why I didn't tell you earlier. If I may, though." And perhaps it was the wrong time for the question, but they couldn't help asking. They still had their programming, after all. "Why didn't you ask?" They'd wanted to know about Anke, about Yarden, about Drestyn—but they hadn't asked about Jal.

Saint opened his mouth, but Nash beat him to it. "'Cause

he's a chicken," she said matter-of-factly. Affection and admonition in equal parts.

He shot her a glacial look. "Didn't hear you askin' after him, either, Doc."

"Yeah, well." She seemed to run out of steam after that. "Whatever. You want to keep jawing at me, or you want to know how miner boy's doing?"

He did, and Eoan knew it, but they wouldn't have guessed it from looking at him. He paled a shade, and a stillness spread through him. "Tell us what you know," he said. "Don't pull your punches."

An idiom, but he and Nash both looked braced for a physical blow. Poor dears. They didn't regret waiting, but they certainly wouldn't do it any longer. "He's out of surgery," they said, which . . . didn't seem to compute. Nash's shoulders might have relaxed, incrementally, but the lines between Saint's brows sank even deeper than before. "It's good news. *Good.* He's not stable, but as of the last check-in, his vitals are trending in the right direction."

Silence, again. It really didn't belong in the galley.

Again, Saint broke it. "He's gonna make it?" His voice sounded rougher than usual, and they'd never heard it so small and uncertain.

"All signs point to it." It was the best they could offer, and it was better than they'd dared hope for when Saint and Nash first carried him back aboard.

Quieter, Saint repeated, "He's gonna make it."

"You said that, dear."

Before they could offer to repeat themselves, Saint sprang to his feet. "He's gonna make it!" With his broadest, brightest grin, he swept Nash off the table in a hug. His wounds seemed a distant memory; his ice pack, a casualty forgotten on the floor. He hugged Nash so fiercely, her feet never touched the ground, and all the while he smiled so wide his eyes disappeared above the dimple of his cheeks. He had *dimples*. They weren't even sure they knew that about him. *Dimples*. And laugh lines, and a smile that flashed teeth despite the smacks Nash struck against his back.

"Shoulder!" she yelped. "Your shoulder, you stupid caveman!" But she smiled, too, and that *I'm not tense, you're tense* tension eased out of her frame as her socks finally found the ground again. "Yeah, now look what you did."

He'd braced his hands on the edge of the table, bent forward like he thought he might pass out, and Eoan wasn't sure if it was the sudden rush of relief or the sudden rush of blood—of which he had a couple pints less than he should—leaving his brain. Either way, they'd never seen a man happier to ride the wave of a vasovagal syncope, and Nash had never looked happier to scold him.

They'd been waiting for this, Eoan realized. The silence in the galley hadn't been exhaustion, but a bated breath. The one unanswered question they couldn't bring themselves to ask, and now they knew. *Now* they were done.

Eoan couldn't cry, but for a single overwhelming moment they wished they could. They *wanted* to. Good tears, happy tears, tears like the ones shining in Saint's and Nash's eyes as Nash clapped Saint on the side, surreptitiously swiping her sleeve across her face.

Unworried, un*burdened*, Saint dropped into his chair with that crinkling grin, and Eoan grinned along with him. "All right, then," he said, nodding to himself. Relaxing, for the first time in a long time. "What do we do now, Cap?"

Saint seemed entirely different now. Nash too. Maybe their hearts still weighed a little heavy, still a little broken, but Eoan knew their crew. Saint could shoulder the weight. Nash could mend the breaks. Although Eoan could take no credit for their strengths alone, they were so very proud of what they'd built together—their beautiful crew of impossible souls, and the promise of an uncharted future *together*.

"Now, my dears," they said, "we all get to go home."

EPILOGUE

JAL

Sometimes Jal still felt like he was falling.

Docs said he was healing up decent, for being a couple weeks off a near-death experience. *Better than anticipated,* they kept telling him, except for Nash, who mostly just slugged him on the shoulder with some variation on *good job not dying, dumbass.* Maybe his spiffed-up genes had a thing or two to do with it, but the docs seemed pretty happy to take the credit and he was pretty happy to let them. Compared to the scavs and their duct tape medicine, the folks at the Guild's outer station were a goddamn dream. They'd unscrambled his egg, patched all the holes he wasn't born with. Knee was still a work in progress, but the bone scans stopped looking like when he dropped his mama's nice porcelain, so he'd call it progress.

That feeling, though . . . it stuck with him. Crept up when he dozed off, jolted him awake with his heart in his throat. It came when the room got too small or the noise got too big or the stink of antiseptic brought him back to that ammonia-soaked scav sick bay.

He had it now, that feeling like the ground beneath his feet wasn't really there. Like one of Bitsie's cartoons—the second he looked down and saw the great big nothing underneath him, he'd drop all over again.

"If you're gonna be sick again, you wanna warn a guy?" Of course, Jal couldn't be falling, because Saint stood right there in front of him. Had an eyebrow ticked up toward his hairline and a teasing quirk to one side of his mouth, and a scrutinizing stare that said he kind of meant it, though. "These're my nice boots."

These're my only boots. Jal looked down at himself awkwardly. Somebody'd shined them up pretty and stitched the tears in his coat, and he could still smell the packaging on his new shirt and pants. He still felt like folks could *tell,* though. Not just by the brace on his knee or the bruises still yellowing around his eyes—it was him. He was scuffed-up and threadbare, and they could stitch up his clothes and put a shine back on his boots, but they couldn't do the same for the rest of him. Hadn't mattered so much when he was on the run, but now . . . it'd just take some getting used to, was all.

"Chin up," Saint said.

Jal rolled his eyes. Every chance Saint couldn't see it with the lights down low, but it felt good to do it. "Relax, old man. I'm fine."

"No." Saint snorted and tugged his collar. "Lift up your chin, kid. I can't see this last button." When he'd walked in and realized Jal had done his shirt up wrong, he'd kindly offered to redo it. Which for him meant huffing and hawing and charging up like he was gonna take a swing, but that shirt wasn't gonna fix itself, and Jal's hands were shakier'n shit on a good day.

He angled up his chin. "When'd you say the Guild ship was supposed to get here?" Trying to sound casual, but yeah, all right, it did sound kind of queasy.

"Ship's already here," Saint said, straightening Jal's coat and stepping back. He'd had a bit of a limp himself there for a while, but there was barely a trace of it anymore. "They're on their way up."

Oh. He swallowed and hoped it was nowhere near as loud as he thought it was. Never thought he'd miss the beep and trill of all those damn monitors. "So, this is it, then." He'd played it out in his head for days now. Rehearsed what he'd say, how he'd say it. But if he'd learned anything stumbling onto the *Ambit,* it was that practice didn't mean shit when the show went live. *You got need of an extra hand?* Poor dumb bastard hadn't had a clue what he'd gotten himself into.

"This is it," Saint agreed. "Sure you're not gonna be sick? You're looking kind of—"

"Shit-scared?"

"I was gonna say *peaked*." The corner of Saint's mouth quirked again. "But yours works, too. Hey." He put a hand on Jal's shoulder, dipping his head to catch Jal's eyes. "The hard part's done. The Council's seen the footage. They're out for blood, but it ain't gonna be yours. Still trying to get a lead on whoever else was involved; half the crew's gone private sector, so they're harder to track down. We'll find them, though. And I hear Fenton's already on a shuttle back to the center spiral. They won't tell me when he's getting in."

"Probably smart," Jal said.

"Probably so. Still, I wouldn't mind a chance to introduce myself."

With the business end of a balled-up fist, most likely. Or something a little more permanent. Jal shook his head. "He ain't worth it."

"But you are," Saint said, with a weight in the words that dared him to do anything but believe it. *I said it, and I meant it,* said the jut of his jaw, *so you'd best just accept it.* And then he cleared his throat and carried on like he hadn't said anything at all. "Listen, you just take a deep breath, stop fussing with your hair"—Jal dropped his hand from the fuzzy patch they'd shaved behind his ear; couldn't seem to stop prodding the seam of fresh-healed skin in the middle of it—"and quit worrying so much. All you have to do now is stand there, look pretty, and keep your head on straight. Nobody's gonna expect any answers you're not ready to give."

Jal started to snort, but his ribs had some strong opinions about it. Negative ones. Real negative. "You sure about that?"

Saint's heavy brows bunched, drawing those lines across his forehead that Jal wished he could just reach up and smudge smooth again. "You want me to talk to them first?"

"Nah, I think you've spoken for me enough, old man." Smile to take the edge off; it was supposed to be a friendly jab, not a dig. There were nuances to conversations that he hadn't gotten back yet. "You remember it? *Jalsen Red will either be the reason you die, or the reason you live.*" Even after all these years, he'd never forgotten a word. "Folks used to ask me about that, you know. Every time I got shipped off somewhere new, captain or XO or somebody'd always say, *What's that about, anyway?* Never really knew how to answer them."

Saint's mouth did something that wasn't quite a smile, but wasn't a frown, either. A little soft around the edges, and his hand stayed a warm, steady weight on Jal's shoulder. "I was right, though," he said, and it was such a Saint thing to say that Jal couldn't help but snort, opinionated ribs be damned. "I'm alive right now because of you."

"So you were only *half* right, you smug bastard," he corrected with a crooked, stupid grin. He had more to add, but the door panel pinged—place that fancy, folks couldn't just knock—and all that easy humor they'd had going died like one of Regan's houseplants. Took the air in his lungs with it, too. "Guess that's them." He tried not to let the nerves show, but his voice went raspy.

Saint gave a stiff nod. "Guess so."

"You're heading out then?"

"Tonight," Saint said, and it could've been Jal projecting, but he swore Saint's voice sounded a little rough around the edges. "Drestyn's on a Union station not too far from here, but we're carting him back to Guild HQ as soon as he's cleared to make the trip. Cap got *voluntold* to lend a hand on his protection detail. Gotta say, it's good to be back on our side of no man's-land, but I think I'd take another stint in the frontier over babysitting duty." Said with the air of a man who'd rather take another *bullet,* if it meant ducking that detail. "Anyway, Nash knows some people in the scrapyards back on base, so she's good with it. *Ambit* could use some TLC."

"Would you thank her for me? For the coat, I mean." No way in hell that was Saint. The man couldn't darn worth a damn. *Hah.* "And, uh. The whole *not letting me die* thing. Eoan too. I wasn't always the most gracious guest, but I appreciate them letting me tag along." Not that they'd given him much choice, at first.

Saint gave another nod, stiffer than the last. Like overcooled metal, Jal thought. He looked all strong and tempered, but a few more knocks and he'd shatter. "Fuck," he breathed, grip tightening on Jal's shoulder. In the dark of the room, his eyes still seemed to shine. "I don't know how many more times I can say goodbye to you, kid."

Except he hadn't said it last time. He'd left without a word, and Jal used to hate him for that. Used to think it was just another choice he'd taken away, or, on his more forgiving days, a way to spare them both the pain of saying it aloud.

Standing there, though, seeing that brittle look on Saint's face . . . he wondered if he hadn't been wrong. If maybe Saint hadn't said it, because despite what he'd done, he hadn't wanted it to be true. *Goodbye* was a closing door.

What if he'd just wanted to keep it open?

Jal's eyes stung, but he smiled. "So let's don't say it," he said, mirroring Saint's grip on his shoulder and pulling him in. Not a hug, just the touch of their heads. A deep breath. An important stillness. A soft laugh. "Clearly our paths're meant to cross." They always had, in one way or another. On a crowded shuttle. In a bustling outpost. Years and scars and a universe apart, in spite of the odds, they'd found each other again. Luck like that never gave out, his mama used to say, because it wasn't luck at all. "I'll see you around, old man."

It was there when they parted—a *real* Toussaint smile, rare as a diamond-studded moon and tucked into the corners of those every-color eyes of his. "Don't be a stranger," he said, with one last squeeze to Jal's shoulder, and then he pulled away. Step by step, until Jal had to let go, too; but unlike before, it didn't feel like such a loss. "Just maybe call ahead next time."

"Aye aye, McBlastinshit." A lofty salute, and as Saint went to get the door, Jal finally felt ready. He wasn't shiny, and he wasn't the same starry-eyed miner boy who'd set out to the frontier all those years ago; he was tired and worn down and full of broken pieces he hadn't even begun to put back together again. But against the odds, by the skin of his goddamn teeth, he'd made it here. He'd made it back to—

"Uncle Jal!"

Christ, that voice was *everything*. It was every dream he'd had since he'd lost his way, every smile he'd savored as he fought to find it again. It was all of that, and it was more, because it was finally fucking real, and the sound of it nearly brought him to his knees as the door slid open and Regan and Bitsie came pouring in. *There you are.* It was more a feeling than a thought, like a compass finally finding its north. A return to right, and the pieces might've changed shape a bit—Regan's face was softer, touched with unfamiliar lines, and Bitsie'd shot up like a sprout and traded her last baby teeth for her mama's sunny grace—but they still fit just right in that hollow, raw-edged space he'd been carrying.

No hesitation. Big, teary grins all around, and it was gravity—the same gravity that'd kept him going, kept him moving toward home when he thought he had nothing left to carry him. They crossed three years in the span of three seconds, crashing into him with open arms and blotchy cheeks, and Jal choked on a sob and a laugh and all those words he'd practiced saying to get himself through the day. The words didn't matter, not when he could wrap his arms around them. When he could kiss Regan's hair and hold Bitsie to his chest. When they were there, right there, finally.

When he was *home.*

He didn't see Saint turning to leave. Couldn't possibly have heard it—not with Regan's airy, happy laughter and Bitsie's hiccupping-firm *I told them, I knew it, I missed you,* and the sound of his own heart coming back together again.

So maybe he just felt it, that open door and Saint with one foot already through it. He raised his head from Bitsie's wild, tear-damp curls and felt his mending heart give a sad but determined squeeze. "Hey, old man," he said, and when Saint turned . . . for a second, Jal was fresh off the mines again. No idea where he was going, no idea what he'd do when he got there, but somehow sure that with that surly stranger with the kind-sad eyes, he'd make it out all right.

No, he decided, it wasn't goodbye at all. And he knew exactly what to say.

"Good fucking luck."

ACKNOWLEDGMENTS

At its heart, this is a book about an extraordinary crew, and it took an extraordinary crew to bring it to life. All my love and gratitude to each one of them—to Mom and Dad, for instilling in me the curiosity to seek my own stars and the courage to reach for them. To Meagan, for being the best sister, pastry purveyor, and trusted coconspirator I could ever ask for, and to Andee, Lara, and the indomitable Remy Rose. To my Aunt Sandi, whose memory remains an inspiration in everything I do. To Claire, for enduring countless late-night (and early-morning—yay, time zones) rough-draft reads and rambles, and for generally being all the best kinds of awesome. To Courtney, for your friendship, book recs, and absolutely legendary GIF game. To Jessica and Laura, for all the good times in the bookish trenches, and all the better times to come. To Hannah, whose mad editorial skills have changed my storytelling so much for the better, and to Sara, my agent, for your enthusiasm, savvy, and sage wisdom. And finally, to my brilliant, meme-slinging editor, Jen, and the rest of the team at Tor, for helping me share this chaotic space fam with the world. The *Ambit* crew wouldn't exist without all of you.

ABOUT THE AUTHOR

L. M. SAGAS is an author of rowdy, adventurous science fiction and fantasy stories full of characters who live hard and fight harder. She writes to give folks a few good laughs, but has been known, on occasion, to tug a few heartstrings along the way. When she isn't writing, Sagas daylights as an intellectual property attorney in Nashville and moonlights as a dirt-smudged gardener, breakfast food enthusiast, and professional pillow to the world's snuggliest shelter pup. *Cascade Failure* is her debut novel.